GW00992300

Broken Paths

SUHEL AHMED

RΞTHINK PRESS

First published in Great Britain 2013
by Rethink Press (www.rethinkpress.com)

Cover images © Andrey Kuzmin (istockphoto.com/andrey_kuzmin)

Supported using public funding by ARTS COUNCIL ENGLAND

Winner of 2009 Muslim Writers' Awards (Unpublished Novel)

"Don't limit your child to your own learning,
for he was born in another time."
Rabindranath Tagore

"The heart of a mother is a deep abyss at the bottom
of which you will always find forgiveness."
Honore de Balzac

For Syed Israil Ahmed, my father.

"I read the book for, and with, pleasure, and was often delighted by the switches in narration and tone. I found it constantly gripping. I liked the double POV and the interweaving of timescapes and of landscape, of quasi-theatrical set pieces and long passages of interior monologue. Congratulations on a fine first work."

Aamer Hussein, Author of *Another Gulmohar Tree*
and *The Cloud Messenger*

"*Broken Paths* is a courageous and accomplished first novel. Set in the Bangladeshi community it is a story of disenchantment, deceit, betrayal, unfulfilled desires and obsessive love. Suhel offers us a wonderfully evocative and nuanced portrayal of Amina – the mother – and Samir – the son – in a novel whose graphic and convincing evocations of place is outstanding."

Jacob Ross, Author of *Pynter Bender*

"*Broken Paths* is a brilliant first novel, a compelling story about faith and love written with energy and great style. It includes an exquisitely nuanced portrait of a mother-son dynamic. The clashing cultural and religious values that test this relationship are handled with great insight and in an entirely fresh way. Characters are rich and believable throughout, and the urban environment is itself shown as a rich and believable character."

Robin Yassin-Kassab, Author of *The Road from Damascus*

A pregnant promise

The heat of the *grisma* season subdued everything in the village. The sun was a livid thing that bore down, leaving the earth cracked and the river low. A crow perching under a jackfruit tree waited for the noonday sun to pass as it pecked at the ripe yellow fruit which had fallen and burst open. Bulls bound for the bazaar moved on lazy legs, their bodies barely flinching each time the herdsman's crop cracked their hides. The trees flanking the roadside were as soundless as mountains; not a branch stirred, or a leaf rustled. Amidst this torpor the farmers were confined indoors, a few hopeful faces staring out of their grill-barred windows, waiting for the monsoon to break and revive their dusty fields.

There was only a faint trace of activity outside the tea stall. Under its grubby awning idle men were shooting chips on a carrom board while listening to Runa Laila songs on a battered old tape deck. A man perching on a stool peered over his broadsheet and glanced at the small earthen house in the distance. He nudged his friend sitting on the stool beside him.

'Is Azad dead yet?'

The friend lowered his newspaper and flicked a glance in the same direction.

'I don't know,' he replied.

'Isn't his wife pregnant? Has she had the baby yet?'

'I don't think so,' the man said.

'Doesn't bode well for the child when it finally arrives,' the other added, shaking his head as he looked up to the heavens.

'Fatherless before birth, it's tragic.'

And with that brief tête-à-tête the men slid back behind their newspapers and resumed reading about more worldly affairs.

The focus of their fleeting interest lay beyond a stretch of fallow paddy fields where an earthen house stood alone rippling in the heat haze. Its door was closed and window shutters were drawn. Inside one of the rooms, a light bulb jutting out of a wooden beam wore a dust skullcap. Deprived of fresh air, the room gave off a dank odour – an odour of illness. A hurricane lantern hung from a hook on the wall. The flame burned serenely and attached a shivery shadow to every object in the room.

And in one corner under a mosquito net, a human figure lay curled up in bed. His eyes were three-quarters closed and his chest barely rose with each inward breath. Every time he coughed his body bucked from the effort. A closer look through the muslin gauze and it was clear that Azad was on his deathbed.

Four years earlier he had played his part in the country's civil war. He had travelled to the capital Dhaka and joined the *Mukti Bahini*, declaring himself a freedom fighter after being inspired by one of Tagore's poems. He was trained up by the Indian Army and was then conscripted to serve East Pakistan's fight against the hegemony of the western wing.

But four years on, after the euphoria and the aspirations that follow a nation's birth, life for Azad had deteriorated. His youth had been devoured by cancer of the liver and what remained of his his life was now reliant upon regular shots of morphine.

After the war had ended, Azad returned with a spirit that had been slaughtered on the battlefield. Upon seeing his wife his first instinct was to break into a guilty smile.

'Kemon acho?' he had asked, tense and timid, the strength battered out of his voice.

His wife had barely recognised him at first. The weight had fallen off his cheeks, his hair was matted to his scalp, his lips were cracked and a jagged chip had halved his front tooth. But, most horrifying of all, he was propped up on crutches, his right leg reduced to a stump below the knee. Saufina's hand had slammed against her jaw in shock.

'Don't worry, it'll be fine,' was all he had managed to say at the time.

But that optimism was a mask hiding the capacity for self-destruction simmering beneath. Within a matter of weeks the trauma of his experiences began to haunt him. The shootings, the bombings, the sight of lacerated limbs, the charred skin, the wailing families, the smell of congealed blood and flesh rotting in the streets. There was the harrowing incident when a Pakistani division pulled up in a military vehicle, and accosted him and his close friend as they tried to sneak back to their cantonment in the middle of the night. Both were ordered to lift up their lungis. Seconds later, his friend was shot in the chest for being uncircumcised. For being a Hindu.

It was naïve to think that Azad could return to his small clerical job in the village as if none of this had ever happened. His wife and in-laws could do nothing to salve the psychological wounds inflicted upon him. Eventually his employer was forced to let him go, noticing that Azad kept staring at the amputated stump of his leg instead of filling in the ledger pages, which remained empty at the end of each day. Thereafter, Azad stayed at home, only venturing out on his wooden crutches to Malik Enterprises whenever he needed money and had to pawn something. Beginning with bits of furniture, crockery and other knick-knacks around the house, he took it upon himself to secretly pawn his wife's wedding jewellery and, as the financial burdens grew, he eventually hired a bullock cart to transport their rosewood *almari* to Malik Shaab's yard where it was sold for a *very* reasonable price. It was a purchase that the local entrepreneur, Malik Shaab, revelled in, rubbing his hands and whispering into the ear of an employee as they watched Azad hobble away, 'A desperate man is a man worth bargaining with.'

Azad soon developed a reputation among the local children for being cantankerous and a bit loopy. While doddering along on his crutches, he imagined the kids behind him hopping en masse, with cruel smiles on their faces:

'Hai, dekho jarr lenghra Miah!' he heard them utter in a high-pitched chorus.

During waking hours phantom pains began attacking the leg that wasn't there, causing those dearest to him to begin questioning his sanity. Under-resourced doctors could only prescribe placebos in the hope that Azad would soon snap out of his behaviour. Seeking Allah's grace, the family gave offerings to the local mosques and mukkams. The news about his growing madness spread from village to village. One day, a shady Mullah knocked on their door. His beard was dyed with henna to a fiery red colour. After revealing his credentials to Saufina, he invited himself into the house. The man took one look at the ailing Azad and turned to his wife with a prophetic glare.

'Your husband is possessed by a demon and needs an immediate exorcism.'

The next day he arrived with an entourage. The men ranged around Azad like surgeons and spent two hours uttering prayers in their fluid a-cappella voices, the mullah's hands quaking with an operatic flamboyance as he pressed Azad's temples hard and blew holy breath after each incantation. Afterwards he tied a *tabeez* around Azad's neck and piously accepted the gratuity, which he wordlessly slipped into the breast pocket of his *panjabi*. Thereafter, he sent over a *tabeez* each week for the next two months, claiming that he was slowly beating the evil out of Azad, though no one else saw this happening.

Azad found his exorcism not in prayer, but in drink. It began with a few sips of arrack in some seedy part of town, thanks in part to the oily-nosed bartender who, noticing the war veteran perched glumly at the counter one afternoon, slid a bottle in his direction and promised that it would ease the burden:

'Bhai, this is bottled happiness. It will wash away your pains.'

It wasn't long before those first mouthfuls graduated to a bottle a day and then slowly to an irreversible dependency. For days on end, Azad lay in bed all day and drank at night, not entirely oblivious to the effect this behaviour was having on his wife. Sometimes she became so angry she threatened to leave him.

'I can't take any more of this!' she would scream at the top of her voice and then stomp to the almari, wrench the metal door open and begin gathering up her belongings. Almost immediately, her husband's crutch would clatter to the floor, Azad's body collapsing with it, and then he would drag himself towards her using his arms, wrap them around her legs and begin blubbering like a child, begging her to stop.

At other times the mere sight of her enraged him so much that he would order her to leave. Even then he would later rouse from an inebriated sleep and frantically grope her side of the bed hoping she had not acted on his drunken threats. Throughout the ordeal, Azad never experienced what alcoholics refer to as a moment of clarity. It was as if that moment had passed when he first decided to drink himself to death. Long before he had become an alcoholic. In fact, long before before any alcohol had touched his lips. It was with sober intent that Azad had flung open this window from which to throw himself. Now, years later, with the cancer spreading to his bones, it was his wife's duty to play the nurse, ensuring that her husband's slide towards death was as painless as possible.

Saufina was sitting on the charpoy in the next room, her eyes fixed on the framed photograph hanging on the wall. Her hands rested on the magnificent cupola of her pregnant stomach. Her feet dangled over the bed (the legs of which were set on bricks as a precaution against the rising floodwaters of the monsoon rains).

She peered closer and tried to summon the memory captured by the picture, to quell the sadness she felt. Lately, whenever the emotion hijacked her thoughts it led to the morbid realisation that she would have to raise a fatherless child by herself. But she refused to brood on the matter. Over the last few months she had tried to perceive her husband as an empty shell with its person sucked out. It wasn't hard since in Azad there was little trace of the man she had known before the war. The sparkle of youth, the bounce and brio were all consigned to a time long gone. She knew that the remainder of his existence was nothing but a body kept numb with morphine.

With this in mind, she was quick to fend off people's concerns with trite platitudes. It was important to face the truth with temperance as a way to get through this dark passage in her life, to look to the future for the sake of her unborn child.

As Saufina gazed at the photograph, past joys shone in her eyes and memory spread its colour over the sepia image. The picture had been taken five years ago, on the day her younger sister, Amina, was leaving for England with her new husband, Jamaal. Azad looked handsome in his shirt and trousers. She was draped in her blue sari which shimmered with sequins. The pair flanked Amina like proud parents, a trio gazing squarely at the camera, hands pinned to their sides as if it was a military pose. It was a sweltering day. Saufina was concerned about the heavy *Benarasi* sari Amina had been made to wear by her in-laws. Underneath the bridal decorations, her top lip was peppered in beads of sweat. When Saufina used the end of her sari to dab her sister's face, she recalled Amina brushing her hand away. Even as a child she had considered Amina the more headstrong, the stubborn one with the impulsive streak. She had also been their father's favourite. *His little white princess*, he used to say, because she was the most fair-skinned in the family.

The sound of a pained cough came from Azad's room and jolted Saufina from her reverie. Nostalgia scurried off with its palette and the sepia tone returned to the picture. So much had changed since that day. Her sister was now living alone. Just two years into the marriage, Amina's husband had filed for divorce because she was unable to bear him a child. Amidst the war, news from England had travelled in fits and starts, and been put together like the torn pages of a book. Once Amina had stopped writing to her, Saufina only knew what her father had told her, and whatever he knew amounted to the facts he had cobbled together from Amina's letters. Letters that had arrived through accident rather than design, and in no particular order after drifting for months in the fractured postal system of a country ravaged by war. Of course, back then the news had come as a shock because nobody had ever doubted that Amina was being whisked off by her Prince Charming to a wonderful life in a rich country of the West, away from the poverty of the village. When her father had learned about the divorce, it had left him bitter and heartbroken. He had called her husband a 'son of a pig' and wanted to wring his neck. After that he had not spoken to anyone for days, not until he had gone to see Amina's in-laws where he had demanded immediate redress while waving the document of her *khabin* in his hand.

Amina was back from England now. She had returned two days ago to their father's house. Her brother Kamal had cycled three miles from their village to announce the news. When Saufina opened the door he was leaning against the wobbling handlebars, trying to catch his breath, the sweat glistening on his forehead:

'*Appa, Appa*, guess who's come back home, guess, guess!'

Naturally Saufina longed to see her sister. And if circumstances were different she would have immediately taken a rickshaw to welcome back the sister she had proudly escorted to the airport all those years ago. But she couldn't. Unable to leave her husband, Saufina could do nothing but wait for her sister to come to visit her in their crumbling mud hut.

During the previous night she had cooked the welcome feast. Kamal had bought and slaughtered a chicken for her. She had cooked the meat with chickpeas and some dall. She had fried silver tilapia fish in a paste of golden mustard. Just before midday she had cooked the rice in rosewater. The foods were now waiting in saucepans under an unlit stove. A yogurt dessert lay settled in a red earthen pot. A jug filled with homemade lemon *shorbot* was sitting on the table, a clutch of pips settled at the bottom.

Saufina kept clock-watching while surrounding herself with bits of housework. She straightened the furniture and re-straightened it. She swept the floors of each room and swept them again. She spent the afternoon sitting on the high bed, picking out stones and dead weevils from the rice drum. She patted her stomach every time she felt the wonderful force of a foetal kick. And whenever a passing rickshaw rang its bell, she gathered up her bulk and leaned over to peer through the window bars. Between the wait she attended to her husband's needs as a matter of routine. In this manner the day turned to dusk and the muezzin's call drifted from the minaret of the village mosque.

Finally, with the crickets beginning their nightly trill under a growling sky, a distant rickshaw sounded its bell. The tinkle sent a ripple of intrigue through the tea stall; idle men stopped shooting carrom to gawp at the passenger.

The breeze had picked up and the banana trees in the front yard flapped their leaves wildly. The taller date palms behind the house swayed with a more supple grace. A loose shutter clapped noisily against the window grille. The rickshaw pulled up outside the small house. The neighbourhood kids immediately gathered around the vehicle.

'Look!'

'Who is that?'

'She must be an actress!'

'Why is she here?'

'Let's ask her.'

'Go on then.'

'You ask her.'

'No, you do it.'

Upon hearing their shrill cries, Saufina rushed out of the house. All eyes watched as Amina dismounted the carriage and paid the fare. The children

7

kept nudging each other, gasping at the sounds of her clinking bangles and the silky hiss of her red sari. Saufina took a few steps towards her sister whom she immediately noticed had grown into a beautiful woman. The English air had been good to her. She came closer and held Amina at arm's length, taking in the sight of her, then hugged her as close as her pregnant belly would allow. When her nose brushed the nape of Amina's neck, she breathed in the sweet, foreign perfume. She stepped back and gently cupped her sister's face.

'You look beautiful, like a *rajkumari*,' she said.

Amina wished she could return the compliment, but Saufina, in contrast, looked wan and weary. There were dark crescents beneath her eyes. Her lank hair, parted in the centre, fell over her ears like a pair of ragged curtains. Amina kissed her sister's hands and did all she could to hold back the tears.

'I can't believe I'm finally seeing you with my own eyes.'

Saufina smiled. She took Amina by the hand and ushered her indoors. The village kids followed the women all the way to the door, their eyes locked on Amina in absolute awe. Saufina looked back over her shoulder.

'*Jao, jao!*' she ordered the kids, shooing them away.

Once inside, she closed the door. She pulled the window shutters, then guided Amina to the charpoy and asked her to sit down. She poured the lemonade slowly into a glass making sure the pips did not stray past the lip of the pitcher. Amina watched the shine of concentration in her sister's eyes. Saufina returned the gaze with an affectionate smile.

'After so many years away in a cold country this heat must seem unbearable. Have some *shorbot*. It's very refreshing in this stifling heat. The rain must begin soon.'

Amina took a sip of the drink. Over the curved rim of the glass she saw for the first time the reality of her sister's plight. There were empty spaces where pieces of furniture used to sit. Tucked under the table was a single chair when she distinctly remembered four. The wall against which the steel almirah once stood was a lighter shade – a testament to its years closeted behind the furniture. Azad's bookcase was nowhere to be seen. Homeless hardbacks sat in unruly piles and filled a corner of the room, like debris. The kitchen door was propped up against the wall beside the doorway, deprived of its handle or hinges. The space looked like the salvaged aftermath after a dacoit raid. Amina finished the drink and handed the glass back.

'Would you like some more?'

'No, thank you. I have something for you,' Amina said.

She unzipped her handbag and rooted through it. She pulled out a neatly folded cashmere shawl. It was a deep green colour.

'You shouldn't have,' Saufina said, her eyes pouring admiration over the soft cashmere fabric. Amina unfolded the gift and draped it over her sister's shoulders.

'It really suits you, *Appa*.'

A groan came from the other room. The sisters looked at each other like a pair of startled gazelles.

'How is *Dula-Bhai*?' Amina asked, a little embarrassed that the question had got buried under the thrill of reunion.

'*Abbu*'s told you, then,' Saufina said.

'Yes,' Amina replied.

'He's very weak now, drifts in and out of consciousness. It's the medication to ease the pain. He needs to rest as much as possible.'

There was a pause.

'And how are you?' Amina asked.

'I'm well.'

Amina's first instinct was to raise objection, but she thought better of it, bit her tongue and swallowed the thought.

'Can I see him?' she asked.

Saufina led her sister through the doorway and into her husband's room. It was dark inside. A few seconds elapsed before Amina's eyes adjusted to the wan glow of the lantern flame. But even then the musty smell of decay and the sound of laboured breathing hinted the worst. As Amina strained to look, outlines slowly began to emerge from the blackness. There was a chair, a table and a bed under the opaque hang of a mosquito net. She saw a radio, a calendar and a row of medicine bottles lining the shelf. A cloud of midges whirred over the bedside table and fed on the grapes in a plastic bowl. As her pupils widened, she saw behind the mosquito net a frail figure lying in bed.

His ribcage barely rose with each inward breath. She stared at his green, encrusted eyelids. A clear plastic tube emerged from under the linen that was concealing his frailty. It led to a pouch that sat indecently under the table. She was shocked at the way his flesh had shrivelled so savagely, from the robust figure packed with the energy of youth to something so immobile, so decrepit, so useless. Then she saw the space where his leg had once been – a grisly reminder of where the rot had begun. She pawed back the mosquito net and sat on the edge of the bed. She tried waking him:

'*Dula Bhai...*'

She glanced up to enlist her sister's help.

'Look who's here, it's Amina,' Saufina said. 'She's flown all the way from England to see you. Doesn't she look pretty?'

For a while Azad didn't move. He then opened his eyes, revealing life at its lamest. He looked through the wet slits and dozed off. Seconds later he opened them again, became more alert and tried to speak, mumbling something that neither woman could understand. He looked as if he wanted to smile but was being let down by the muscles of his face. Saufina mopped his head with the flannel.

'He does recognise you,' she reassured Amina.

'Is he in pain?'

'He can't feel much because of the medication.'

'We mustn't put him under any strain.'

Saufina lit a mosquito coil and placed it on the stool by his bed. The smell – a mixture of incense and camphor – rose in a delicate plume.

'Mosquitoes seem to double at this time of year. I'm not even sure if these coils actually work any more,' Saufina said.

'Have any of his own family come to see him?' Amina asked, glancing at the single plastic slipper by her feet, the rubber bearing the indentation of his five remaining toes.

Saufina's eyes widened in surprise.

'You know he hasn't seen them in years.'

'Has anyone been to tell them, at least?'

'His father has banned anyone from coming to see him.'

Azad had been the most troubled of five children, born to a family who lived in a small village outside the city of Mymensingh. Much to his father's chagrin, Azad had never shown much enthusiasm for working in the fields. In years gone by, he had often regaled them with stories of how he preferred to sit on the banks of the Brahmaputra under an old mango tree reading Tagore's poetry while the silver braid of the river flowed swiftly through the reeds. He had told Amina that, growing up, he hated working in the fields and what farm work he did was under familial duress, driven by a father who had stood like a snarling dog in the way of his bookish aspirations, often beating him for wanting an alternative future for himself. Under the constant whine of his father's disapproval, Azad grew tense and rebellious. He felt a plastic bag had been thrown over the dreams blossoming inside his head and he looked for a way of tearing himself out of it, if only to let his aspirations breathe.

One day, under his supervision, a young goat had got separated from the herd, fell into the rushing river and drowned. The carcass was washed up in the backwaters a mile downstream. When Azad hauled it up he found that its legs were twisted around the branch of a *neem* tree and its dead eye was glaring up at the sky. At home, Azad wasn't sure how to break the news and feared the consequences of his neglect. After dinner he hung around his father waiting to be noticed. Once his father's suspicions were aroused, Azad cleared his throat but the words weren't forthcoming:

'Erm, erm, *Baba*...'

'What?'

'I, I, I...'

'Stop stuttering, boy, what's wrong with you?'

'The young goat, it's dead.'

'How?!'

'It slipped into the river...'

His father banged his fist down hard on the table. The force of it travelled up through Azad's toes to the tips of his hair.

'*Haraamkur,* you probably had your head buried in that stupid book of poems!'

'No, I –'

His father didn't hear another word. Instead, he pulled Azad by the ear through the house, threatening to tear him limb from limb. He tied him to a clothes rack and flogged him with a bamboo cane.

'You can stop this reading nonsense at once. We are farmers! Who do you think you are, indulging in these idle fantasies?' he raged, with a pique that started with a kink in his brow and ended with a silky thwack on the boy's trembling flesh. The next morning, Azad found his books tossed in the front yard where the chickens were curiously pecking at the pages. Funnily enough, the dead animal wasn't mentioned once.

The beating became the push Azad needed. He knew he had to follow his heart. Two days later he took off. He travelled light, with four *parathas* tied in a shawl, his favourite poetry anthology stowed away in his pocket, and a head crammed with dreams.

The sisters sat with the dying man. Amina put her arm around Saufina; she leant in and rested her head on her sister's shoulder. Saufina tilted her head and kissed Amina's brow.

'I'm sorry, *Appa*,' was all Amina could say.

'I'm sorry, too.'

After a few minutes they slunk out of the room. The light was brighter in the next room. Saufina forced herself to smile. This was a reunion after all.

'I've been slaving over the stove since yesterday,' she said, brightly. 'I was beginning to wonder whether you would turn up. You must be hungry.' She pulled out the chair and ushered Amina into it. 'I'm afraid I can't offer any *vilhayetti* foods. You'll have to struggle through the tough meat. Be careful with the rice. It's the cheaper variety. I've sifted it so many times, but you can never take out all the stones. It's impossible.'

'Don't be silly, *Appa*. You're the better cook. *Abbu* always complained about the tea I made and thought the rice I cooked was too stodgy. Anyway, this is my home as much as it is yours. Why should I have any complaints?'

'We've all missed you so much.'

'I've missed you all, too.'

'You must have found it hard living on your own in England?' Saufina asked.

'I've been lucky. An Indian family helped me out. They were very kind to me when… *he* left. They employed me as a nanny to look after their children.'

'*Al'hamdulillah!*' Saufina exclaimed.

'Not that I had any experience with children.'

Saufina looked up at Amina. The faint lines around her eyes deepened. She felt a sense of pride at the way her younger sister had negotiated her bad fortune alone in a foreign country.

'All of it was Allah's decision. Who knows what the future holds? There's every chance Allah might still bless your womb,' Saufina said. 'And when that time comes all the experience you now have will stand you in good stead. I have no doubt you would make the perfect mother.'

'*Insha'Allah*,' Amina muttered to herself, momentarily attuned only to the memory of the doctor's cold prognosis ringing in her ear.

'Thank you for the money you sent after the war. It arrived when we most needed it. With your brother-in-law stranded in Dhaka I had very few people to turn to.'

'You would have done the same for me,' Amina replied.

Amina wondered whether to use this opportunity to steer the conversation to discuss things that mattered. Soon Saufina would be bringing a child into the world but without a father to do the providing. She looked too brittle to take care of herself, never mind a newborn baby. Saufina had been so evasive up to now that Amina could not determine how her sister was likely to respond if pressed. She studied her sister's face and tried to gauge her thoughts. She tried to make sense of the steely detachment in her voice, and imagine what her sister was going through nursing a man who had one foot in the grave. She wondered why her sister acted so distant, as if she were keeping up appearances to assuage the suspicions of a nosy neighbour. Why was Saufina shutting her out?

Saufina attended to the food. She poured the curries and *bhajis* from the saucepans into plastic serving dishes. She sunk a spoon into each and brought it to the table, attentive only to the task itself.

'When's the baby due?' Amina asked.

Saufina arranged her sari so that it fully covered her distended belly. It wasn't any kind of embarrassment that made her respond in this coy manner, but deference. She wanted to appear modest to the Almighty and not seen to be parading this blessing, because when she looked at how her fortune had changed she couldn't help thinking that *good* fortune was fragile. It was important to wrap it up in humility and carry it with discretion to keep the Almighty appeased and the evil djinns at bay.

In the last few months of her pregnancy, her troubled mind had latched on to the belief that the baby was Allah's way of squaring the books with her. It was simple: a son exchanged for her husband. Not so much a gift as a transaction. She felt safe having reached this understanding with Allah because it provided the security of sound arithmetic.

But for now, something wonderful stirred inside her when conversation turned to her unborn child. She blushed and withdrew at first but then decided to afford herself some excitement.

'In another three months,' she said happily. 'It will be a boy!'

'How do you know?' Amina asked.

Saufina passed a pewter bowl filled with water and Amina washed her right hand.

'Nazrine Chachi told me.'

Amina narrowed her eyes in doubt.

'Don't you remember her?' Saufina asked, a little disappointed. 'She's the palmist we used to go to see when we were kids. She now lives in a small mud hut on the banks of the Surma.'

Amina remembered Nazrine Chachi as the medium, which the elderly cursed, many grown-ups avoided and the children mocked. Years ago the rumours ran that she controlled her husband with mind spells and other devilish devices. Just before Amina had left for Britain, there was a great hoo-hah over an incident in which the middle-aged Nazrine had torn off her clothes and run naked around her small patch of land because the government had reclaimed it to erect a power mast. The village was divided in its opinion of her demonstration. Some regarded it as an act of desperation while the less sympathetic saw it as proof of her insanity. Saufina held out the flat of her palm and ran a finger along a faint stroke.

'Can you see that line? It's perfectly clear.'

Amina peered at the hand. She narrowed her eyes and homed in on an indistinct mark.

'Are you certain of this? I mean, you shouldn't go by what that woman has said.'

Saufina clicked her tongue.

'*Ishh* Amina, surely living in England hasn't made you so judgmental. You know Nazrine Chachi only tells the truth, for which she never demands money. She's looked at my palm three different times and has no doubt that this line here symbolises a baby boy.'

Amina didn't doubt Nazrine Chachi's faith as much as her sister's association with a woman who held pagan views. Inwardly she was adamant that Nazrine Chachi was best kept away from expectant mothers because of her involvement with the spirit world. But realising her sister's unswerving faith in the woman, she did not express her concerns. Instead she congratulated her sister:

'*Maash' Allah!*'

Saufina set the table. She put a plate in front of Amina, piled it with rice, picked the best chicken pieces and spooned them out onto one side.

'What about you, *Appa*, will you not eat with me?'

'I'll eat later.'

'Remember, you're eating for two.'

Amina glanced up from her plate to see whether her sister had taken offence at a younger sibling's light chastisement.

'There's no need to fret. This baby means everything to me,' Saufina said. 'I won't let anything happen to him.' She patted her stomach and gazed at the bump with a doting smile. It exacted from Amina the slightest wisp of envy.

Saufina fanned the humid air with her pakkah while Amina ate, but was unable to prevent the tiny beads of sweat from breaking out on her sister's forehead. She watched Amina take another morsel of food, then pour some more dhal over her rice. Saufina stopped swivelling the pakkah.

'I even have a name for the baby,' she said.

'Really?'

'Well, he...' Saufina pointed in the direction of Azad's room, '...he chose it.'

'What is it?'

'Samir,' Saufina said, joy sparkling in her eyes.

Amina looked a little uncertain.

'What's the matter?' Saufina asked. 'You don't like the name?'

'Isn't it a Hindu name?'

'The name can be found in both Sanskrit and Arabic.'

'Wouldn't it be better to give the baby a proper Muslim name?'

'It was the name of his friend who was killed during the war.'

There was an awkward pause as the pair wondered whether the association was a suitable homage, or a bad omen.

'He insisted I name the baby Samir if it's a boy, which it will be,' Saufina said.

'It's important, then.'

Saufina instantly perked up.

'Even Nazrine Chachi liked the name,' she declared.

'You seem to have everything planned.'

Saufina picked up her shoulders as if braced for whatever life was planning to throw at her.

'There's only the baby to think of now,' she said.

She noticed Amina looking around the room, her demeanour seeming reluctant to share the same optimism.

'I know what you're thinking, Amina, and I know it must be a shock for you to come back to this, but please try to believe me, the door without the hinges, the missing almirah, the books on the floor, none of it really matters.'

'But –'

'And neither do I care about the hushed mutterings I hear day after day of my husband's illness and the damning judgments that sneak from house to house like a bad toilet odour! Do you know the kind of things they say behind my back?'

Amina shook her head. Saufina narrowed her eyes. She turned down the corners of her mouth and then spoke with a boorish rustic accent:

'Ooh, that Azad! He's possessed by the devil, seduced by his brew, and now he's paying the price. The man is being pulled towards the gates of Hell.'

'That's horrible!'

'It no longer bothers me.'

'Really?'

'Would I lie to you?'

'I'm not saying – '

'Look, Amina, my life hasn't quite slammed into a dead-end. I've just been forced to turn a corner and start afresh on a new route. My kismet is giving me a second chance, and that chance is beating inside me. I'm determined to give my son everything I can. I promise to bring him up to be a doctor, or an engineer, someone people will respect. He won't go down the same route as his father by studying Hindu poets or the like, and delude himself with false aspirations. I'll make sure he stays close to Allah and understands his grace.'

A flash of lightning lit up the night outside and speared in through the wooden slats of the window shutters. A second later the skies clacked and rumbled. Azad suffered another coughing fit. Saufina quickly got up and rummaged through a small drawer. She picked out a vial of morphine and went to him quietly, leaving Amina gazing up at the framed photograph on the wall. She looked deeply into the smiling face of Azad. Her brother-in-law who had been so handsome back then, consigned now to his deathbed. Amina dropped her head and looked away.

A rose in a razed garden

Sitting at his work desk while waiting for the phone to ring, Samir flicked through the college prospectus for a third time. He read paragraphs at random, pausing every so often to gaze at the photographs of students whose youth and beauty cast the establishment in an otherworldly light. Their clear eyes and bright smiles filled Samir with fresh optimism. He had been engrossed in the brochure for some time, hunched over its glossy covers, his lips curved gently in deep concentration. And as he turned the pages, he saw an exciting future beginning to flower for him. He imagined walking through the glass doors of the building and into one of the classrooms, eager to learn – to become more than he thought he ever would. The pique of an adolescent excitement made him giddy, knowing that fate had given him a second chance to salvage a dream he'd consigned to an early grave the day he left school.

The phone on his desk started to bleep. Samir's pulse quickened from the sudden surge of adrenaline. He put the book down. He cleared his throat and took a deep breath. He picked up the handset and brought it to his ear. The plastic felt cool against his febrile lobe.

'Samir?'

'Yes.'

'It's Douglas.'

'Hello, Professor.'

'Are we still on for that drink?'

'Yes, sir.'

'Jolly good.'

18

'I'll bring the application form for you to look at,' Samir said, pitching his words halfway between a question and a statement of intent.

'If you so wish, though there is no need.'

'Really?'

'Why, is there a problem?'

'I'm worried about the entry requirements. In the prospectus it says —'

The man chuckled.

'Don't concern yourself with that, young man,' he assured Samir with a pompous air. 'Tell me where would you like to meet?'

'The Old Oak pub?' Samir suggested.

'Where's that?'

'It's on the same road as the library.'

'Oh yes, fine.'

'It can be anywhere you want,' Samir said.

'No, no – The Oak sounds perfect.'

'What time would suit you?'

'Half-eight?'

'Yes, sure, absolutely.' Samir replied.

'Splendid.'

'Thank you, sir.'

'Glad to be of help,' the professor said. 'It's time to channel the passion. See you shortly.'

Samir set the phone down gently back onto its cradle. He could feel the pulse throbbing in his palm. Over the last few weeks it had become equally a source of joy and trepidation that, even now, in his twenties, it was possible to enrol on an art history course in college and alter the trajectory of his life – a trajectory his mother had always steered him away from, claiming that the study of art was against their religious beliefs. She was convinced that such teachings would turn him into the worst kind of heathen, a *kaffir*, and this would break her heart.

With his hand still on the phone, Samir muttered the professor's words several times to himself. *It's time to channel the passion, it's time to channel the passion, it's time to channel the passion...* He grabbed the small notepad on his desk, pulled it towards him, opened a fresh page and wrote down the sentence: *Its taim too chanell the pashion.* He underlined it hard with his ballpoint pen, receptive only to the sound of the nib scrawling the paper. He read the words back out loud and felt each syllable bolster his newfound belief.

The fortuitous encounter with Professor Baines, a retired university lecturer, at the local library had sparked a small-voiced ambition to rise up from within and fill the vacuum of disenchantment. Up until that point Samir had accepted that his life would never amount to much – devoid of aspiration, direction, focus or a single qualification. But, now, he imagined himself as the future owner of a small art gallery, taking it upon himself to climb a ladder and paint those very words above the regal archway entrance which he could proudly call his own. He would have the same quote printed on flyers and posters. He would give interviews to local reporters and tell them how it all blossomed into a verdant garden of artistic achievements after the early setbacks. If any of his own sketches were good enough, he would hang them up under a made-up name, and eavesdrop on the remarks made by visitors. In homage to his mother's faith, he would devote a room to Islamic art. He would take his mother by the hand and usher her blindfolded to the room, then remove her blindfold so she could see for herself that art was all-inclusive, not evil – as she claimed it to be – and could celebrate the Islamic faith as much as anything else. He would prove to her that despite their differences he was a good, respectful son.

Samir put the pen down and glanced at the time. It was already half-past six. All the other employees were gone for the day, leaving a ghostly array of empty chairs, neatened desks and banks of computers humming on standby. In its emptiness, the office appeared a more soulless place than usual. Samir picked up his rucksack and slipped the prospectus inside one of the pouches. He hoisted the bag onto his shoulder and strode out, his head fizzing with excitement.

Outside, a pale half-moon hung in the evening sky and beside it a star twinkled, which Samir guessed was either Mars or Venus. The elegant rooftops were silent silhouettes overlooking the hubbub at street level where the lights and colour adorning the shop fronts attested to the libido of commerce. Christmas was still several weeks away, but fairylights, tinsel and snappy slogans already draped a few shop fronts which sought to steal a greedy march before the festive mayhem began in earnest. Samir paused for a moment on the doorstep. He rolled up a cigarette whilst surveying the commuters who were streaming out of the office blocks – the capital's workforce hurrying towards the tube station in a single mobile mass, their bodies unshapely in thick coats, the chill turning their breaths into tiny puffs of steam.

Samir lit the cigarette and took a few quick drags before stepping into the throng, head bent low, his gaunt frame hunched against the sudden blast of icy air. En route, he cast an oblique glance at the window of a wine bar and saw shiny media professionals clustered around the counter. A group of office girls were sprawled on the plump leather seats, enjoying their happy-hour cocktails with a relish that was reserved especially for Fridays. Next door, a Thai waitress was serving the customer sitting nearest to the window. Steam lifted off the dome of the rice which she placed on the table. Samir felt a pang of hunger. It evoked the memory of the way his mother cooked rice on special occasions like his birthday or during the *Eid* festival, lightly frying the raw grains in ghee before boiling them, then adding cloves and cardamom to give them that mouth-watering fragrance. The thought led to a rush of other equally tantalising memories: a dribble of dall on his tongue, a bite of fresh *bindhi bhaji* garnished with fresh tomatoes, the press of curried mutton against the rugged roof of his mouth. The memory of mother's cooking made his mouth water and stomach growl. Samir pulled the hood over his head and tugged the drawstring. The material devoured his floppy fringe making him resemble a tortoise that had retreated into its shell.

He stopped at a cash machine and withdrew some money for his mother. He counted the notes and slipped them into his wallet. He'd been handing his mother housekeeping money ever since he got his first job stacking shelves at the local supermarket. As an only son raised by a single parent, he was determined to support her financially, even if she didn't need the money and the offering was little more than a symbolic gesture. A dutiful gesture. A gesture of love. Every pay day he queued up at the cash machine outside his workplace, withdrew a portion of his salary and slipped it into an envelope to place in her palm.

A disorderly queue was building up around the subway entrance. The tube sign above it was lit hard and brilliant. A yellow cordon had been slung across the archway barring access to the public. Ever since the attacks in

New York, security alerts on public transport were a constant threat to people's punctuality. The uniformed guard announced that delays were inevitable. Samir stood in the throng with the cigarette dangling from the corner of his mouth. Dread twanged inside him. What if he arrived late, would he find Professor Baines still waiting patiently for him? What if he was really late? Would the professor write him off as a timewaster? Samir pulled out his mobile phone. He scrolled down the contacts list, tapping the button repeatedly, furiously trying to reach the professor's number. But before he could punch the quick-dial button, the handset began to vibrate in his hand. The buttons lit up. *Amma* flashed on the screen.

'Damn it!' Samir cursed, remembering that he was meant to see his mother this evening. He scrunched his eyes closed and rubbed the back of his neck, scratching the taut flesh with his fingernails. He tried to think of a gentle way of letting her down, sifting through the flimsy excuses flashing up in his mind, but knowing that whichever one he used would not make the slightest difference. He took a deep, icy breath, pressed the green button, put the phone to his ear and braced himself for the verbal bomblast.

'*Assalumu alaikum.*'

'Samir?'

'Yes, *Amma?*'

'Where are you?'

'I've just left work.'

'What's all that noise?'

'It's the traffic.'

'I can't hear you.'

'I've just left work. It's the traffic,' Samir shouted down the phone.

'When will you get here?'

Samir put the phone to his other ear.

'I won't be coming tonight,' he replied.

There was a pause on the line.

'Why?'

'I have to see someone.'

'Who?'

'Someone who's promised to help me.'

'With what?'

A police van raced by, its siren bleating and its lights flashing blue as it carved a parting through the dense traffic. Samir stuck a finger in his ear.

'What was that?' his mother asked.

'A police car.'

'What's happened?'

'It's just driving past.'

'You promised me you would come home tonight.'

'I know, but something's come up.'

'What?'

'I've already told you, I need to see someone. I'll tell you about it later.'

'Who's going to eat all the *somosas* I've cooked?'

'Put them in the fridge, they'll keep. I've got some housekeeping money for you.'

There was the sound of a harsh breath on the line.

'I don't need your money.'

Samir took a deep draw of his cigarette, spat it out and dropped it on the ground.

'*Amma*, please try to understand. It's important that I see him.'

'Who is this *someone*?'

'He will help me get back into college.'

His mother's tone softened.

'When will you come round then?'

'Next week.'

'Which day?'

'I'm not sure.'

'Can't you come tomorrow?'

A couple of carrier bags swiped his legs. Samir looked up. The guard stationed at the subway entrance had lifted the cordon, allowing a small party to charge down the steps. The impatient crowd around him shuffled forward, a few tutting and snarling as they slid past him.

'*Amma*, I have to go now,' he said.

After a brief pause his mother replied, '*Acha!*' which was followed by an abrupt click and the flat drone of a dead line.

'Damn it!' Samir uttered under his breath. 'Damn it, damn it, damn it!' He knocked the handset against the side of his temple before he slipped it back into his trouser pocket.

Samir's mother had good reason to slam the phone down on her son. Samir had lived all his life with his mother in their council house. But that had changed six weeks ago when he committed the profane act of leaving home. The intention had been simmering inside him for several years, but when it happened, it happened very suddenly. In an innocuous argument with his mother, when Samir remarked how it might be considered blasphemous to be both a Muslim and to believe in ghosts and black magic (because his mother had suggested that someone from his father's side had cast a spell on him, which had floated all the way from Bangladesh to turn him against her), he had felt the burning flash of his mother's palm on his cheek. It left a red welt across his face.

'How dare you question my faith!' she screamed, fixing him with stern eyes, her face framed by her headscarf. 'Have you no idea about the *djinns* Allah has created from fire and which roam the earth? Living in this country has made you ignorant. I don't know what I've done to deserve an infidel for a son.'

Samir was reduced to a sinner just because he had expressed a perfectly rational thought. It wasn't the first time either. Nevertheless, he refused to rise to her rant and simply walked out of the room. But this time he felt more determined than ever to assert his independence. With that slap still seething on his skin, he sat in his bedroom that night with his mind made up. The next morning he began trawling through the local paper, searching the classifieds section for a place to rent.

That same evening he stood under the living room doorway with a packed bag at his feet. His mother was sitting on her rocking chair watching the news on television. In the dark room the light from the screen lit up her face. Sprightly shadows danced like ghosts on the wall behind her. Eventually, out of the corner of her eye, she noticed the rucksack wedged between her son's legs. She switched on the table lamp, muted the television and turned around, the yellow light on her face.

'I'm moving out for a while,' Samir said.

'You're leaving me?'

'It's temporary.'

He said this quickly, as though it was the one assurance he had decided to give her; the one thing he thought would soften the blow. His mother cast her attention back on the television screen, her face now ashen.

'It's only until I sort out my head,' he continued, peering down and toying with the cord of his hooded top. She looked at him once again, turning her head in that same slow manner. The conviction of the rightness of his decision threatened to evaporate under her seething scrutiny.

'What's wrong with your head?' she asked.

'You wouldn't understand.'

She furrowed her brow and rubbed the wet corner of her eye with her knuckle.

'No, I wouldn't.'

She glared at him long enough to deliver her disappointment, then threw her attention back on the television. She left the mute button on.

'I need to do this,' Samir said.

But this time she refused to be drawn in, trying to hide the crack in her heart, the sudden dryness in her throat, the tear that threatened to spill out of her eye. A part of him had wanted an angry reaction and expected his mother to act on that fractious impulse of hers. He had wanted the opportunity to explain that he felt his place was no longer under her roof, that it was making him bitter at heart, and that the distance would do them both good because it would give him an opportunity to grow up. With hindsight he wished she had leapt off the chair. If only she had run up to him and landed another slap on his face, then at least in this parting exchange he would have taken away a scrap of moral vindication, something to cool the heat of guilt. But he got nothing. So he picked up his bag and left the house, bristling in silence.

The anger soon abated and the dust settled. Since that day he had made a decision to visit his mother a couple times a week in an effort to smooth over this difficult transition period. He always found it uncomfortable stepping back into the house, shuffling quietly into the living room, frequently finding her sitting in that same rocking chair, the crooning of its bow filling the otherwise silent house. On each occasion he would have to think of the most delicate way to begin a conversation, their relationship now lopsided with distrust.

'*Assalumu alaikum, Amma.*'

'Why are you here?' she would say, her eyes gleaming with hurt.

'I've come to see you.'

'What for?'

'To see you.'

'Am I supposed to be grateful for your small mercies?'

On these occasions he would draw a deep breath and sometimes look away, trying to distance himself from the confrontation she wanted, but which he felt was no longer necessary. He would then turn back, shuffle closer and gently place his hand on her shoulder.

'Please don't be like this, *Amma.*'

'What do you expect?'

'Do you want me to go?'

His mother would turn sharply to face him.

'No.'

Her voice would then soften, the love she tried so hard to keep frozen melting through the angry carapace.

'Are you hungry, *beta?*'

'Yes.'

A part of Samir couldn't bear the guilt of knowing that, unless he paid her a visit, she spent the whole week by herself. The last thing he wanted her to think was that he had abandoned her completely; these visits were a way to keep that fear at bay.

He was aware that his mother had started cooking special treats like *sondesh* and *somosas* for him. Of course he knew it was bait she put down to lure him back home. She would fill the air with his childhood fragrances and, upon entering, he would breathe in the familiar food aromas. He would watch her lay the table and then obey her demand to sit down and eat before he 'wasted away'. And as he took each mouthful, he would be all too aware of her eyes locked in on him, her lips pursed and her breaths deep, the sound filling the pensive atmosphere. He would be silently poised knowing that this was merely a hiatus before she addressed his 'thoughtless' behaviour, keeping her tone soft to begin with so that it didn't sound like she was censuring him with a lecture.

'You're an intelligent boy. Just explain to me why you're doing this?'

Trapped by the array of delicious foods, and sensing his mother's expectations curling around him like tendrils, Samir would say nothing. This would be met with a mild vexation at first, then give rise to frustration and set her mouth aquiver:

'What you are doing is wrong, absolutely wrong. You must have a heart of stone to be doing this to me. I am your mother!'

'I know.'

'You're still a boy. You don't know what you're doing.'

'I'm no longer a kid.'

'But the world isn't what you think it might be.'

'*Amma*, even if that is true, it's something I need to find out for myself.'

'By running away from home, from me, that's what white children do!'

'You don't know any white children.'

'Can't you see what's happening?'

'What?'

'There's a war against Muslims that's raging in Afghanistan. It will spread. It's the white man's crusade against our people, and now you're living amongst them. You are playing into *Shaitaan's* hands.'

'*Amma*, you're being paranoid.'

'Open your eyes, *beta*. The age-old prophecies, which the imams have translated from the scriptures, are finally coming true. We've arrived at that final age when Muslims around the world will face persecution from all the non-believers. On that same day people like us living in foreign lands will be at the greatest risk. We have to guard ourselves against the efforts made by non-believers to lead us astray.'

'*Amma*! You're watching too much news on television.'

'You're not listening. It's all preordained: war will be the world's ultimate fate which will end with the complete destruction of civilisation before every mortal being is summoned into Allah's courtroom to be judged individually.'

'Stop being so melodramatic.'

'Don't you realise that you'll end up in *Jahannum* where your skin, flesh and bones will burn. And once you are reduced to cinders, Allah will order your body to reform so that it can burn all over again! You'll be pleading for water but your cries of thirst will be answered with showers of hot molten brass. Just remember, Allah will hammer iron pins into the white man's tongue for lying to the world and killing to serve his avarice.'

'Please, *Amma*, stop this.'

'Allah has an unmentionable punishment planned for those Muslims who allow themselves to be blinkered by the white man's lies, and especially those who relinquish their faith.'

Samir knew that she scored these crude boundaries along racial lines in a desperate effort to keep him rooted to his culture. The last time she had served him food, her stare had flitted between him and the steaming plate of rice before she remarked that she'd only come to Britain to escape the poverty that plagued their own country:

'Try to understand, *beta*,' she had said in a caring voice. 'We'll always be second-class citizens here, like the toilet-cleaning *Metthors* or the tea-picking *Coolies* in Bangladesh. My decision to settle in Britain was always to give you a future. Here we are Bengalis living in a foreign land and with no claim to its decadent culture.'

On the train platform Samir rose on tiptoes and craned his neck only to see a whole sea of other heads bobbing for a better view of the dot matrix information board. To everyone's despair it hung mutely black. As time went by more people were gathering on the platform, their bodies bunching up and pushing behind his elbows. Mindful of the pickpockets, Samir kept palming his pockets and seeking the reassurance of the bulge of his wallet.

A train had just departed. Those promoted to the platform edge inched forward and turned their heads in the direction from which the next train promised to arrive. Samir managed to thread his slim figure up to the front, and stood behind the yellow safety line. He looked in the same direction, only to see the tunnel caulked in impenetrable darkness. Then came the realisation

28

that he'd forgotten to call Professor Baines. Samir glanced over his shoulder at the entrance leading to the concourse, now crammed with commuters. He considered turning around and swimming against the forceful tide of people back up to street level to make the phone call, but knew it would be futile and simply add to the delay. Samir rubbed his palms, which were now slick with perspiration.

Several commuters were reading the evening tabloids. On the front page a grainy photograph taken from a Stealth Bomber captured the blast of a missile striking a mound which looked no different to the other mounds surrounding it. Other than the violence of the explosion it was difficult to make anything out of the black-and-white picture, especially since it had been snapped from a two-mile altitude. The headline made the jubilant claim: *Osama on the run!*

Samir turned to gaze at the poster pageant sweeping the platform wall and could not dismiss his mother's feelings of estrangement. A whisky brand asked everyone to 'think big'. A ruby-red lipstick was wrapped around the perfect smile, its slogan promising a 'smudge free kiss'. The blue-gloved hand of the National Lottery pointed out to the crowd, the motto underneath read: 'It could be you'. Life in those posters was sequined with superlatives, brazenly feeding the miserable platform folk the secret to happiness. Even the lowly cleaner walking through the concourse, dragging away the day's litter, couldn't stop her eyes from stealing a glance at the billboard that offered 'the taste of paradise' in a chocolate bar.

Samir felt a tap on his shoulder. It had behind it an insistent force. He tore his hood down and swung his head round sharply. Two police officers hovered over him, looking stout in their stab-proof vests.

'Good evening, sir.'

'Yes?'

They fixed Samir with a funereal stare, devoid of humour. Their faces were clean-shaven and their skin looked obscenely pale as if the job kept them permanently working in the tunnels. They looked Samir up and down.

'Sir, we're carrying out random stop-and-searches.'

Samir didn't say anything. His mother's warning about their kind being second-class citizens echoed inside him.

'What's your name?' one of the officers asked.

'Samir.'

'Where are you going?'

'Nowhere.'

'What's that supposed to mean?'

Samir shrugged.

'Well?'

'There's no train at the moment.'

'We would appreciate it, sir, if you were a little more co-operative.'

'What do you want?'

'Do you mind if we check your bag?'

Samir handed over his rucksack.

'Are there any uncapped needles inside?'

Samir shook his head. He watched one of the officers tear wildly at the zip. His hands were sheathed in a pair of thin rubber gloves. The man shone a black Maglite torch inside the bag and then plundered it in search of anything nefarious. After running his hands through it, poking his fingers into each lint-ridden corner, he found only the college prospectus and a sketchbook. Even those items seemed to arouse his suspicion as he took them out and turned them over in his hands, flicking through their pages several times as if certain something incriminating would fall out. The other officer asked Samir for his full name and address and jotted the details down on a pink notepad. He demanded to see some form of identification. While Samir rooted through his pockets he tried to avoid any eye contact, mindful of the officer's inimical stare roving over him, from his slightly dishevelled hair, his patchy stubble, his Adam's apple to his tatty footwear. Samir handed him a debit card, which the man scrutinised by the light of his own torch. Satisfied that Samir posed no threat to national security, he tore off a carbon copy of the pink chit and handed it to Samir.

'Have a safe journey.'

The rucksack was then returned and the pair went off. Samir felt the crowd's eyes burning into his skin, although the majority weren't looking or even cared, too busy staring at the tunnel and willing the next train to pull in so they could escape the horrible crush. He shuffled his feet self-consciously and yanked his hood back over his head belligerently, as if he were showing them the thick finger. He studied the chit. The handwriting was a messy scrawl. The only legible bit was his surname, written in block capitals.

The surname which had come down from the paterfamilias and, in the absence of a single memory, was the only link other than an inherited copy of Tagore's book that he could claim to his father. In fact, if he stared at the moniker for long enough, the name became as meaningless as the image he held of his father. His friend, Ali, had once told him that if the Oedipus complex was anything to go by then a son could never inherit his father's characteristics because he was destined to rebel against them. He sometimes wondered whether that applied to a son who had never known his father. Perhaps. Perhaps not. He thought about his mother and recalled the melancholy that occasionally afflicted her even now; a sadness he always assumed was a symptom of his father's death, and which he could not share in since the man had exhaled his last breath before he had drawn his first. He had to admit that life in Britain had been lonely for his mother, and what he was doing now was adding to that loneliness. But he felt cheated by his mother too. Over the years she had built a wall between him and any real knowledge of his father. She hardly spoke about him. It was as if the man had betrayed her by dying, even though the truth was that he had died in the fight to liberate his country, and she felt justified in consigning his memories to a vault that she kept eternally locked. Samir screwed up the bit of paper and flicked it into the tracks. It lay there like a pink rose in a razed garden. He took the prospectus out of his rucksack and began flicking through it once more.

'Sam, Sam, hey, Sam!'

A man with beaded braids had pushed his way through, using the bulk of the guitar case to shunt people out of the way. He stopped in front of Samir. He was gnawing a matchstick in his mouth, which he skilfully rolled under his tongue.

'Hey, bro!'

'Ali?'

The two young men hugged, not in the traditional sense but in a modern hip-hop manner, clasping hands, yanking one forcefully towards the other and merely knocking chests as if testing the strength of each other's ribcages.

'What's up?' Samir asked.

The man thrust out his chin and scratched the stubble. His long fingernails created a rasping sound. Samir noticed Ali's pupils were dilated; they were the size of marbles.

'You stacking?'

'No.'

'What's with the faraway look?'

'Long day at work.'

'You don't work!'

'Don't suppose you want to buy an eighth?' Ali asked.

'You what?'

'Herb.'

'Sorry, not tonight.'

'Any blues or betas?'

Samir glanced over both shoulders. He looked back at Ali. Samir's pupils in contrast were darker, smaller, focused and serious.

'I'm giving up this shit, dude. I'm getting my act together.'

'Serious, bro?'

'I'll be going to college soon.'

'Come on, dude. We both know what you're like. And anyway, students are my most profitable clients.'

'Why are you so intent on pushing this stuff on to me?'

'I got needs.'

'You're off-key,' Samir said.

'Why you being so serious, bro?'

Samir cocked his head back and gave Ali a reproachful glare. He wasn't deliberately being mean, only trying to protect himself from temptation. He leant over Ali's shoulder and whispered in his ear:

'You wanna get yourself busted?'

Ali glanced sideways and saw the two burly police officers making their way through the crowd. He tugged the strap of his guitar case on his back so that it rolled to its side and shielded his face.

'Have ta split, bro!' he said with an easiness that seemed a hallmark of criminal cool and with a couple of side steps slipped deftly into the throng.

Guided by stars

Everywhere Amina looked all she could see was the spectre of her son's absence. It hung from the empty hangers in the wardrobe. It lay tucked inside a bed that hadn't been slept in for weeks. It sat on the emptied shelves like undesirable vermin. The vase of fresh carnations on the table was the only sign of residence in the room: a refusal on Amina's part to believe that her son's absence was permanent and his decision to leave was no more than a child abandoning his toys. She was convinced that given time he would see the error of his ways and, once that realisation blossomed into maturity, he would come home. Latching onto this belief, she had been replacing the vase with fresh carnations every week.

Amina had been sitting in his room since late afternoon, partly bathed in the winter sun which had been slanting in through the bay window as she mended his green-hued summer shirt. When Samir had told her earlier that he wouldn't be calling in tonight, anger had got the better of her and she put the phone down on him.

As the evening wore on a temperature had crept up on her. A stubborn cough still worried her throat. Amina tried to retch up a hunk of phlegm into a tissue, but it refused to budge. Her forehead glistened from the effort.

A gust of wind made a rude incursion through the small window she had left open and it sent a wild ripple through the net curtain. Amina got up to pull the window shut. She poked her head out and lifted up her spectacles. She saw the familiar tumble of her neighbour's hair as the woman strode up to her front gate with an envelope in her hand. A wide-hipped, curvaceous woman, her body seemed blessed by nature to birth a dozen children. Amina used to bump into her regularly taking her twin boys to the crèche in a double buggy; even then

Amina thought the woman looked a picture of good health. Always smiling, the whites of her eyes clean as a summer cloud, her thick, lustrous hair forecasting a fertile future, a future realised already with the birth of two beautiful children. Sometimes Amina knocked on her door and offered the family Indian sweets. *Rashmalis* and *russgullahs* and *jilhabis*. The kids loved them. Last week while Amina was hanging out the washing, over the garden fence she caught a glimpse of mother and father encouraging the boys to cycle across the lawn, both children reluctant to lift their feet onto the pedals now that the tin stabilisers had been removed. Their efforts made her smile.

Amina picked up the needle and shirt. She returned to the room where the light was brightest and peered closely at the garment as she slowly fed the thread into the fabric. And she began sewing. And sewing she looked up. And looking up she continued to sew. In the lull, Friday night stretched out before her like an empty highway, each stitch no more than a road marking. Amina took off her spectacles and rubbed her eyes. She only stopped when an envelope slid in through the letterbox and the flap snapped back on its spring hinge. The quiet thud of her neighbour's departing footsteps took on the significance of an opportunity lost.

Amina leapt up. She put the shirt, needle and thread on the chair, along with her specs, and padded down the staircase. She scooped the envelope off the doormat, unhooked the chain, turned the key, twisted the latch and pulled the door. It juddered as it came away from the frame.

'Hello,' Amina said, in a hoarse croak. The neighbour turned around to find Amina silhouetted in the hallway light – a slim figure in a white sari.

'I thought you weren't in,' she said, caught by surprise.

'No, I am in house.'

'Your letter was delivered to our house by mistake.'

'Aah,' Amina said. 'Postman is no good.'

'Yes, he's utterly useless.'

'*Ut-ter-ly,*' Amina whispered to herself. She liked the sound of the word and was able to pronounce it perfectly. She couldn't be sure what it meant.

'He won't be getting his Christmas box this year,' the neighbour added, with her hand poised on the iron gate.

Amina hadn't the faintest clue what a Christmas box was either. *A box where Christmas was kept?* But she liked the dimples on her neighbour's face. They were deep and friendly dimples.

'Hope it's not too important.'

'What?' Amina asked.

'The letter...'

Amina glanced at the envelope but couldn't focus on the words. The image of the *Shahid Minar* on the four stamps, though blurry, was enough to suggest that the letter was from Bangladesh.

'Is it important?' the neighbour asked.

'No,' Amina assured her. 'My mother write letter. She in Bangladesh. My home.' Amina stuffed the envelope into the pocket of the woollen cardigan she wore over the sari. The neighbour turned to leave.

'How are you?' Amina asked, quickly.

The answer *busy* immediately sprung to the neighbour's mind and what she wanted to say, but she sensed the faint plea in Amina's voice. When she turned back she saw Amina's eyebrows rearing up with an eagerness she couldn't ignore. So she lifted her hand off the gate. The hinge, laden with rust, yielded with a lazy moan.

'I'm fine, how are you?' the woman asked, her dimples deepening once again.

From the tone of her voice it wasn't hard for Amina to draw the distinction between courtesy and care. Over the years she had come to realise that English people could be friendly in a polite and distant kind of way. Neighbours, in particular, moved and made gestures like the living, their smiles having an unfeeling quality about them, as if they were marionettes.

'I am fine too,' Amina replied. Over the woman's shoulder she glanced at the derelict house a few doors away with its windows boarded up. A cat padded past a skip outside filled with a sagging mattress and an old television lying face down with its large bottom in the air. The cat clasped a dead chick in its mouth; the eggshell of a skull dangled from the death-trap of its jaw.

'I am safe as house. Everything tip-top,' she said.

The neighbour noticed the phlegmy raspiness in Amina's voice.

'I hope you're taking something for that,' she said, tapping her own throat.

'Only little cough.'

'Irritating, I bet,' the neighbour said. She leaned in closer and tapped her nose. 'I'll let you in on a secret. Whenever the kids have a slight tickle, Peter insists on dropping a smidgeon of whiskey into their fruit juice.'

Amina sucked her mouth in disgust.

'Children all right?' she asked.

'A handful, as ever.'

'Hard work, children.'

The woman rolled her eyes.

'Tell me about it. The last time I left them alone they managed to blow the main fuse by overloading the socket in the living room.'

'Boys naughty.'

'Mine are a couple of monsters. They're screaming for chips tonight.'

An idea popped into Amina's head.

'You come inside?' she asked.

The woman looked down at her purple slippers.

'I do have to get back to them.'

'For one minute,' Amina said.

'Some other time, perhaps.'

'Please come. I give something.'

The woman resisted.

'Please.'

The neighbour stepped into the house and stood in the hallway. Amina rushed off into the kitchen to fetch this *something*. The woman could smell the spices in the hallway, an aromatic mix of turmeric, curry powder and fried onions that the house had acquired from all the curries Amina had cooked over the years.

Her attention was caught by the framed Qur'anic verses up on the wall, the beauty of the letters, the way they were arranged like pieces of artwork. She stopped to stare at the cork noticeboard which had a few bills pinned to it. Minutes later Amina returned holding in front of her a plate of *somosas* covered in clingfilm.

'For you and children,' she said.

'No, no please – '

'You like?' Amina asked.

'Well...'

'Something different from chips,'

In her sudden gaiety Amina forced them on to the woman who had no choice but to extend her arms and accept the offering.

'Thank you.'

'Taste,' Amina said.

'Really, I'm not that hungry.'

'Please taste,'

'Erm – '

'I cook fresh today.'

The woman tore a hole in the clingfilm. She picked out the smallest and handled it with the ends of her fingers as though it posed a physical threat.

'It isn't hot, is it?'

'You want hot in microwave?'

'No, no, I mean it's not spicy hot, is it?' the woman said fanning her tongue.

Amina shook her head.

'Please try.'

Amina watched her neighbour eat, who began gnawing at the food with her two front teeth in the manner of a squirrel unsure what it had unearthed. Usually she stuck to her Atkins regime of baked and boiled foods, seafood and green salads. For the past two years she'd been doing all sorts to retrieve her tight tummy, thickened from carrying the twins.

'You like?' pursued Amina. Her eyebrows fluttered with all the eagerness of a child seeking approval from an adult.

'Yes, it's tasty.'

She nibbled a bit more. A colourful array of diced onions, potatoes, peas and carrots spilled into her mouth and the flavours fanned across her tongue.

'Mmmm... it's very nice,' she murmured.

'Homemade *somosas* better always than shop *somosas*,' Amina said, in singsong.

'Thank you.'

'I cook for my son, but too many in fridge.'

'How is your son?' the neighbour asked. 'I haven't seen him in a while.'

'Samir is living away.'

'Oh?'

'Temporary. He come back every weekend,' Amina added. 'Today he have too much work.'

'I suppose they have to fly the nest sooner or later,' the neighbour said, finishing the last of the *somosa* and licking the tip of her fingers. 'You must teach me how to make this. My husband would love it, especially – '

'Fly the nest?' Amina interrupted.

'Excuse me?'

'Fly the nest. What you mean?'

'Oh, well, yes... like young birds once they grow their wings, they have to fly away. I'm sure it breaks every mother's heart to see their child step into the big wide world, but it is only natural to let children go once they are old enough.'

'Temporary,' Amina repeated, more forcefully.

'I see' the neighbour said.

'Only temporary!'

There was an awkward pause.

'Yes, commuting can be a nightmare... I mean the *trav-el-ling*.'

'Yes, the trav-el-ling,' Amina said. The lines around her eyes and lips relaxed as she wrapped all conviction around that very reason for Samir choosing to live away.

'Well I must be off,' the neighbour said.

'Please give to your children. *Somosas* is not hot. Lots of fresh flavour.'

'I will. Thank you so much. You're very kind.'

'My pleasure,' Amina said, a little embarrassed for sounding curt.

The neighbour showed herself out. Amina watched her go, clutching the plate in both hands. The streetlights flowed like liquid over the clingfilm as the woman slipped back into her house.

Amina came down a few steps and waited for a moment, staring at the line of Victorian terraces standing in serried ranks. The sloping street seemed to stretch out endlessly as if viewed through the wrong end of a telescope. She could just about make out its mouth forking in the distance. The depth of it oppressed her. She rubbed her eyes and stared at it with greater intensity, at its endlessness, at the monotony of its severe line. She stepped back into the house and shut the door. She flicked the latch, slid the bolt, turned the key and fastened the chain.

Amina climbed the stairs holding on to the banister. The ageing wood of the top three steps creaked underfoot. She went back into Samir's room and closed the door. She sat down and draped the shirt across her lap. Head down. Knees together. The spectacles were once more resting on the slender bridge of her nose.

She slid the needle into the fabric, drew it through the cotton and tugged the loop into another tight stitch. She did the same once more. But on the third loop her enthusiasm waned. Her fingers slowed, lost their dexterity. Her eyes smarted. It was all because of her neighbour's blunt remark: *They have to fly the nest sometime... it's only natural.* The words echoed inside her head, the unease and tension they created made her hands tremble.

She stopped in mid-weave. Her attention fell on Samir's desk – its surface bearing the scars and pen marks from his childhood under the peeling varnish. She leant forward and ran her fingertips over the notched surface, behaving like a blind woman trying to decipher braille, but finding nothing legible within the scores, dips and notches.

In the few weeks since Samir had left she had acquired a bottle of holy water and written prayers sheathed in cheap metal casings in a mission to get him back. Each time he came round she badgered him to wear a *tabeez* around his neck without success. She had visited a Muslim cleric three weeks ago and had rock salt blessed with Qur'anic verses, which she secretly added to his food for whole fortnight until Samir started complaining about the bouts of diarrhoea. She felt powerless. She couldn't bear to see her only child turn foreign before her eyes.

Amina looked around but could not shake off the neighbour's words taunting her like a schoolyard bully: *It's only natural... only natural... to fly the nest. Only natural, natural, natural...*

'What do you know?' Amina hissed. She pulled the needle towards her and fed it into the buttonhole. Back and forth. Needle jab, loop, taut thread, tight stitch. And again, with greater speed. *Jab, loop, taut thread, tight stitch, jablooptauththreadtightstitch, jablooptauththreadtightstitch.* She repeated the motion over and over until it became a way to jettison her pent up frustration. Then the thread snapped and the needle jabbed the air. The shirt slipped off her lap and fell on the floor, as if a ghost had fled from inside it.

Amina looked at the darkness pressed up against the window. She reached out and wiped the dampness from the pane and peered out. She looked up at the sky. The glass became foggy from her breath. She remembered her final night in Bangladesh when she was sitting on the cool verandah steps. That night she also happened to be looking up at the sky and feeling sad.

It was the month of December, in the year 1968. The crickets were crooning under the stillness while the call to the *Isha* prayers, the last of the night, drifted angelically from the village minaret. Amina was filled with anxiety, oblivious to its soothing sound. She was only eighteen, barely a woman but already a wife and a man's possession, soon to be leaving home forever. A tear trembled in her eye. Her father came outside and put his arm around her and tilted her head to the sky. Taking recourse in an old saying to comfort his youngest daughter, he whispered:

'Look at the stars – it's the celestial magic that binds us forever. You know, my child, no one's ever alone – even the ships lost at sea are guided by stars.'

He drew closer to her. She could smell the familiar musk of his body.

'Do not believe that you'll ever be alone in this world.'

Amina took comfort in his words and pressed her face into his warm palm, allowing him to smother the tear that had rolled down her cheek.

'*Arre Beti*, I hope these are happy tears,' her father said. 'You are going away to a fairytale land. Your husband's taking you away from this poverty. Don't you realise that you are the envy of the village.'

'I know *Abbu*, but I'm scared.'

'Scared of what?'

'I'll never see you again.'

'Don't be silly.'

'I'm going to be all alone in England.'

'You'll meet new people. And then you'll come back to visit us, and we'll be waiting to hear all your good news, details about your fairytale life. Don't you worry, we'll always be here.'

Still trembling with emotion, Amina held her father, held on to him, bound by his words, reassured by the stars in the sky, the celestial magic that he promised would act as her guardian and guide her through the perfect storm.

Amina made the journey to England to start her new life. Despite a long voyage that took her up into the skies, above the clouds and over the seven seas and thirteen rivers, the fairytale did not end with a glorious sunset but with Amina staring up at a rundown estate in Oldham during a bleak winter month. There was no castle for her to cross the threshold of but a doorway to a rickety lift that took her up to the fifth floor of a high-rise flat and into a musty hallway which led into the living room.

'*Hai Allah!*' she exclaimed, staring up at the dusty curtains draping the window. The walls were pockmarked and covered in torn paper. She looked down to see cigarette butts trodden into the carpet. The frilly pages of an old calendar left abandoned on the wall flapped a sinister welcome when a draft funnelled in through a fist-sized hole in the window. Cobwebs draped the light fixtures like ghostly necklaces. Everything was smeared with the grievous stains of gloom and neglect. Through the window of the taxi, she had seen that the English trees were naked, angular and arthritic. An impenetrable grey stretched from the sky to the very deck of the earth. She saw a white man in a thick tan coat walking a dog, defying the cold with his shoulders hunched up to his ears. It was hardly the fairytale scenario her father had envisaged for her. Nevertheless, that evening she composed her first letter to her parents, preserving in their minds the belief that she had reached her castle. She imagined them reading each word, their eyes sparkling with tears of pride.

On the second day her husband took her on a tour through the estate to show her the shops and the post office. To the white people she was a rare exotic sight draped in a burqua. Her husband, Jamaal, introduced her to the local shops, and a couple of the South Asian shopkeepers. He started with the greengrocer – a small man who had a peculiarly soft voice and a humility matching that of Mahatma Gandhi, whose picture he kept behind the counter presiding over the mini mountains of tomatoes, potatoes and radishes rising from their hessian sacks.

'*Bondhu!*' he said, spreading his small arms into a large welcoming gesture. 'Come, come. I haven't seen you in months. And who is this?'

'My wife.'

'*Adhab, adhab.*'

Amina smiled behind her burqua. The grocer turned to Jamaal in mock sadness.

'Jamaal, not even an invitation to the wedding? I'm very disappointed in you.'

'My mother was keen for me to get married in Bangladesh. She wouldn't let me leave a single man.'

'And she was right to do that!' the grocer joked. 'You'd better keep an eye on him,' he advised Amina with a wink.

'No more late-night poker in the cafeteria for your *janaab* then.'

Amina swung her head round to face her husband. The rashness of it seemed to discomfort him immediately. It was as if she had embarrassed him in front of his friend.

'We'd better go,' Jamaal said to Amina, and took her by the arm.

'You do realise that cards are a pathway to *Shaitaan*'s playground,' she whispered as he gently dragged her away.

'The man's only teasing.'

He took her to meet the Bengali butcher. They passed a church en route, which Amina's eyes had dwelled upon, struck by the icon of Christ perishing on the cross above its arched doorway; she was unable to see beyond the macabre. Her husband marched ahead, Amina following a few paces behind. He greeted the butcher with an easy familiarity.

'*Assalumu alaikum, bhai.*'

'*Walaikum-assalum.* You're back,' the fat-cheeked man exclaimed, his white coat stained in halal blood. He looked over Jamaal's shoulder and clapped his eyes on the beautiful form of a young woman gazing demurely at the ground.

'So you weren't joking. You really meant it.'

'Yes, I'm no longer a single man. This is your *bhabi.*'

'*Arre Bhabi,* welcome, welcome. How are you finding life in England?'

Amina looked at her husband, who nodded, giving her permission to speak.

'There's a lot to get used to,' she said, diplomatically. 'It's only my first day out of the house. It's very different from what I was expecting.'

'It's a land of few wives. But don't you worry, I'll be bringing my wife over soon.'

'This is where we will buy our meat,' her husband interrupted. 'Will you remember the way? It's pretty straightforward.'

Amina nodded.

'Shall we buy a pound of *keema*?' Jamaal asked.

'Whatever you wish,' Amina said.

The weeks went by. Amina tried her best to adhere to normality by leaning upon ingrained rules. She built her life according to the advice her mother had imparted on how to be a good wife. So, even in England, other than permitting herself the occasional extra hour in bed, she led a disciplined life – cooking the foods her mother had taught her to make, setting the table just before her husband returned from work, running his bath, seeing to it that a freshly ironed shirt was waiting on a hanger upon his return.

The longing to go back home was always sharp, aggravated by the cold season, and the fact that she spent most of her day stuck indoors. During the first few months she poured her feelings of homesickness into letters she wrote to Saufina. While her husband was at work she would sit at his desk under the soft glare of a lamplight, tear a sheet out of his notepad and begin spilling her thoughts, the handwriting blocky and childlike.

> *… Appa, I think about you and Abbu and Ammu all the time. I miss so many things. I miss the sunshine, I miss our house, I miss the boroi chutney. I even miss the travelling sari-wala who comes to our village with the huge basket on his head…*

After asking her husband to post the letter, a week would pass and then Amina would begin to listen out for the postman at the same hour each morning. Eventually a letter would fall through the letterbox and Amina would rush to pick it up. She would tear it open, wanting desperately to get to her sister's words. Saufina's reply was always curt, an older sister's mature response:

> *My dearest Amina, time moves on, we all have to grow up, take charge of our lives. You are now the izzet of your husband and a simple guest in our parents' village, as much as I now belong to my husband's village. England is your home…you are lucky to be a wife of a Londoni man.*

43

Amina was four months into her new life when Gladys O'Connell – a retired schoolteacher from Dublin – moved to Oldham and set up the local Women's Advancement Society. She rented a room at the church hall and conducted a tailoring workshop for the local mothers, holding them for two hours a week. It was the young Punjabi woman who lived three floors below who knocked on Amina's door one morning to tell her about Gladys' arrival:

'Amina, did you not get the leaflet?' she said, her English fluent.

Amina didn't understand a word and looked blankly at the woman whose wide eyes attested to some wondrous event. She flapped the leaflet in Amina's face as if the action would explain everything.

'Don't worry, I'll call round to collect you on Monday morning,' she finally said.

So on Monday she knocked once again and they went together. And they enjoyed the class. They returned the following week, and the week after that, until the classes became a regular fixture in their lives. Every Monday, while her husband slept after returning from his nightshift, Amina walked to the church hall with her Punjabi neighbour. For two hours they learnt about different cuts, weaves and stitching. Amina watched carefully with all the keenness of a ballerina trying to commit intricate steps to memory. Gladys, an eccentric septuagenarian who wore a blond wig meant for someone several decades younger and clothes that paid homage to the likes of Gardner and Garbo, was impressed by Amina's application, even more so because she couldn't speak a word of English and yet managed to understand all the instructions from simply watching the old woman's demonstrations. Gladys would sometimes hover over her protégé, her thickly painted lipstick stretching in delight as Amina's nimble hands did exactly what was asked of them.

Within six months Amina had completed the course and was an accomplished seamstress. Encouraged by the teacher, she invested in a set of sewing accessories. She knitted her husband a jersey with the sleeves in mohair and a scarf with boat patterns on it using a purl stitch. As her confidence grew, for Gladys' newborn grandchild she crocheted a pair of baby boots, which included snap buttons so their size could be altered as the baby grew. When the *halal* butcher complained that his business was losing money, it was Amina who humoured him and turned up one day with a drawstring purse made from a gauzy fabric.

Meanwhile, her husband, working six days a week, pivoting between afternoon shifts in a copper factory and nightshifts in a restaurant, was eager to build two homes, one for himself in Britain and a house for his parents back home. As the eldest son, he had been sent to Britain as the avatar that would kick-start their drive for upward mobility, enabling them to become rich-folk in their remote village. Azure-coloured aerograms would regularly arrive from his father, frequently making fresh demands for money. Jamaal would rub his forehead pensively while reading these letters.

'What's wrong?' Amina would ask. 'Is everyone ok?'

'*Babu* needs another 20,000 *taka* to build the roof of the house before the start of the next monsoon.'

'Can't it wait?'

'You expect my family to live under a roofless house?'

'They could make do with a thatched roof until the money becomes available.'

'What kind of son do you take me for?'

In these letters there would often be a couple of lines written on behalf of Amina's mother-in-law; a note meant for Amina:

> *My most beautiful daughter-in-law, I hope you are happy. Do let me know how your health is…*

Her husband would read this out loud and immediately search Amina's eyes for an answer, for he was equally eager for the same news.

'They're waiting, it's completely natural of course,' he would say, smiling.

Little did she know that the glimmer of his teeth presaged the first glimpse of danger, because a year later news of the patter of tiny feet still eluded them. While floral wallpaper and pieces of furniture began turning Amina's flat into a home, it remained incomplete, merely an empty set waiting to stage the arrival of new life. And the letters kept coming. Even on the eve of the second year, the couple had nothing to report to the family. The pressure began to gnaw away at her husband.

'Amina, I think we should go to see the doctor. Something might be wrong.'

'Allah is just waiting for the right time.'

'Still, there's no harm in finding out.'

'Of course not,' Amina said, the smile tight on her face.

In the middle of the night Amina slipped out of bed and wrote another letter to her sister, desperate for advice.

Appa, please you must help me. It's coming up to twenty months, and there's nothing. Absolutely nothing. He's beginning to treat me differently...

While doctors conducted their tests and prepared their report, Amina began praying intensely, prostrating herself on the prayer mat and begging for her womb to be blessed with one of life's seedlings. Her religious efforts were supplemented with lotions, potions, amulets and mystic rituals, all propped on top of what conventional medicine had to offer. But for all the effort no seedling blossomed inside her womb.

As the weeks turned to months, her husband's face began to darken. His mood grew dour and his personality began to change. He became easily irritated by Amina and saw red at the slightest thing.

'Why do you make so much noise when you wake up in the mornings? Don't you realise how tired I am from my nightshifts? You can be really thoughtless at times!'

'I didn't make any noise.'

'Are you accusing me of making it up?'

'No.'

'Or is it that I'm imagining sounds now?'

'I didn't say that.'

'Just stay out of my way!'

Soon he began to raise his voice without provocation, smash glasses in blind frustration. His outbursts turned increasingly vicious, crushing the honeycomb of happiness that was supposed to define their first years of marriage. He began to nitpick, criticising the way she kept house, maligning, amongst other things, her cooking and ironing because they were easy targets. Amina despised his behaviour but refused to react, biting her tongue each time. Despite her maturity, his behaviour became even more flagrant, exacerbated by yet more letters from Bangladesh. His mother soon began to levy blunt warnings to him:

You do realise that infertile women are considered worthless in our community. The rest of the family keeps asking and I have no answer to give them.

The couple's lovemaking became loveless, strained more by his refusal to express anything tender. Now his hands would grip her naked shoulders in the dark, bearing down with the weight of expectation, making the single demand as he emptied inside her his end of the bargain. He would then roll off her, light a cigarette and lie there trying to get his breath back.

'Are you all right?' Amina asked one time, tentatively, staring blindly at the ceiling.

She could only hear his heavy breaths.

'Would you like a cup of tea?' she suggested.

Her husband struck a match. He brought the flame to the cigarette in his mouth.

'Say something.'

He let out a grunt, took a drag; his eyes were surly and serious. He exhaled through puffed cheeks and the acrid smell filled the air.

'You can't treat me like this. I'm your wife.'

'Can't I smoke my cigarette in peace?'

Amina stroked his arm.

'Have faith in Allah. It will happen,' she said.

'When?'

'It takes two to have a child.'

'What are you trying to say?'

There was an uncertain pause.

'The problem could lie with either of us.'

Her husband let out a fractured laugh.

'The problem has nothing to do with me.'

'How can you be so sure?'

Her husband took a deep drag of his cigarette.

'I've already fathered a child,' he said.

Amina turned to look at him, speechless.

'It was a long, long time ago, when I first came to this country. I needed companionship. I met someone.'

'A white woman?' Amina asked.

'Yes.'

'What happened?'

'It didn't work out.'

'What about the child?'

'Didn't take a single breath.'

'What?'

'He was stillborn.'

That night Amina dreamt of a black bird that visited her in sleep and presided over her like some evil Djinn, siphoning the very alluvium from inside her. She woke, clutching her stomach, and lay there staring up at the ceiling, cursing the horrible vision while her husband continued snoring beside her. The next day she dispatched another letter to her sister and had to endure a month's wait before the reply came, the advice curt, bullet pointed:

- *Introduce ghee into your diet*
- *Stay indoors between 12 and 3 in the afternoon*
- *Do not bath for three days after consorting with your husband*

A piece of paper folded to the size of a coin was also wedged inside the envelope, carrying a verse from the Qur'an. Amina put it into a tin casing, sealed it with wax, put a thread through it and wore the amulet on her arm. But no matter what she tried, how many prayers she uttered, each effort perished under her unwavering monthly cycle which arrived with clockwork precision to wash away like silt the faith that had built up in the preceding days.

Matters came to a head in the spring of 1971. Amina's husband was sitting in the dark at the kitchen table after returning from a nightshift. Bewildered to find his side of the bed cold and empty, Amina lifted the covers off and came out of the bedroom. She switched on the kitchen light. Its sudden assault made her eyes sting. And there she found him. Her husband didn't even flinch. She rubbed her eyes with the heels of her hands and edged closer. He didn't look at her, but calmly asked her to sit down. He pressed a letter into her lap.

'What's this?' Amina asked.

'Your test results.'

'You went to the doctors?'

'Yes.'

'Why didn't you tell me?'

'I'm telling you now.'

'What do the results say?'

Her husband sniggered.

'Of course, you can't read English.'

Amina ignored his condescending tone, desperate to know what her future entailed – her future inscribed on the piece of paper that was now in her grasp, yet the English words making it unreachable.

'You suffer from a rare problem. You'll never have children,' her husband said.

Instinctively Amina touched her belly.

'The doctor suggested adoption,' he added.

'What are we going to do now?' Amina asked.

'We?'

'Yes.'

'There is no "we".'

'How can you say that?'

Amina's husband threw another letter at her.

'You should be able to read this. It's a letter from home.'

The aerogram frightened Amina. She scrambled for the piece of sky blue paper and unfolded it. Her eyes skimmed the sentences, jumped the routine salutations and ignored the requests for more funds. Her eyes froze and glazed over the moment they met her mother-in-law's words:

> *Listen to what your mother is telling you, Jamaal: women who cannot bear children are not honourable and are unfit to be called women. They are a curse to the good name of any family and a poison to its continuing legacy. We call them banjis. Any family that harbours such a poison will see the family tree wither to a stump. You are a vilhayetti. You can marry anyone. I cannot bear to see my eldest remain childless for the rest of his life.*

The letter fell away from Amina's grip. The mother-in-law, who had heaped a thousand blessings upon her right up to the time that they had said their goodbyes in the village, had turned into a snake. Amina looked back at her husband, seeking solidarity, expecting it.

'We live in England. There are other doctors we can see.'

'Are you stupid?'

'But we must try.'

'Are you a complete country bumpkin – don't you get it? You're a *banji*, a fucking *banji*. You're a barren valley that has wasted all my seeds.'

He stabbed the door keys into the wooden table, leaving ugly gouges on the surface. Like an evil magician he then pulled out their marriage certificate.

'What are you doing with that?' Amina asked.

'It's meaningless. I didn't plan this. Do you really expect me to wade through life with you, no more than a dead weight shackled to my ankle?'

Amina lunged forwards and tried to rescue the document from his grip. He slapped her hand away. She lunged at him a second time. This time she missed the piece of paper altogether, but scratched his face.

'You're mad,' she said. 'You have no idea what you're doing. Your mother has filled your ears. You're a grown man, why are you even listening to the old woman?'

'How dare you call my mother an old woman!' he yelled, his face knotted like a fist, a hairline of blood appearing on his cheek – the only part of him still human in Amina's eyes. He seized her wrist and pushed Amina away. She rocked back, fell on the floor and lay there in a heap. Her hair came loose. Her strength had abandoned her. She saw her husband holding the paper in the air.

'This is a joke,' he said.

He began scoring the document with the keys until he perforated it, eventually tearing it down the middle. He screwed the pieces up into a ball and tossed it across the room. He pinned her with a face furrowed in malice and invoked the triple *talaq* law:

I divorce you,
I divorce you,
I divorce you.

They had nothing more to say to each other.

For the next few weeks Jamaal came and went as he pleased while she lived like a mouse in her own home, hiding her raw nerves, only coming out whenever she heard the front door shut. She never asked for any reconciliation. She didn't want one. During their fight she had merely left a graze on him, but he had cut her so deep that any love she had ever felt had bled away. Even if she was fertile she no longer wanted to bear his child.

Separation soon followed. The arrangements were made according to his wishes. Both parties signed the divorce papers, and the finances were settled. He volunteered to move out. He offered to pay for her flight back home as if she were a consignment of damaged goods that he could simply return to her father's house. She refused, not prepared to sully her father's good name by returning to the village to spend the rest of her days as a spinster. She had learned a skill and was ready to put it to use. Her friendship with the Punjabi neighbour became an outlet; a place Amina could spend many of her lonely hours. With her young face freshly made up, her eyes thickly lined with kohl, Amina would smile graciously at her neighbour's show of concern, hiding the agony of feeling so fragile in a foreign country.

'I happy. I work, my money,' she kept reminding her neighbour.

On the final night, Amina stayed in the kitchen while Jamaal packed his belongings and carried them into the taxi waiting downstairs. A week earlier he had told her that he was returning to East Pakistan at his mother's request, and had apologised to her and asked for forgiveness. She now waited behind the door, her ears sensitive to his every movement: the clink of coat hangers – coat hangers that she had arranged carefully in their wardrobe; the crackle of plastic bags – plastic bags that she'd amassed through hauling groceries back from the Co-op; the slam of drawers – drawers that she'd hitherto been the custodian of. Each time he returned, she heard him dismantle another one of her wifely duties and carry it out of their home. Finally, the echoes of his footsteps receded; out in the corridor the steel doors of the lift clanged shut.

Once he had disappeared, she emerged out of the kitchen. Silence surrounded her. The home had turned into a husk. She went into their bedroom and saw that he had left a wad of cash on the bedside table, with a single fold in the middle, the sides splaying open. Guilt money. She hugged herself, placing a hand on each elbow, and soothed the wild beating of her heart. She told herself that this was a new beginning.

Who let the dogs out?

Very little was original about The Old Oak pub. The wooden plaque above the entrance doors used an archaic script to brand the establishment as *the only original Irish pub in North London,* despite the fact that in the last three years it had undergone several refurbishments and changed management twice. Currently, the wooden pillars flanking the doors were carved into the shape of tree trunks, which ascended to the signboard where the name flashed across it in neon lights, combining the truly inspired with the downright insipid.

Samir slipped in through the revolving doors behind a group of girls in matching skirts and stilettos who were out celebrating a hen party. He stopped and pulled his hood down, allowing the swell of people into his field of vision. Around him the Friday night crowd was mostly young, and dressed up. The girls were adorned in plunging necklines, slinky skirts and fancy shoes while the boys looked equally fetching in their designer shirts and slick haircuts, coolly clutching their beer glasses as they checked out the girls.

Samir spotted Professor Baines sitting in one of the alcoves at the back, holding an empty wine glass loosely by the stalk, looking bored. He strode towards him as quickly as possible.

'So sorry I'm late,' Samir said, as soon as their eyes met.

Professor Baines stood up from his chair, stooping a little to allow for the difference in height.

'That's fine, Samir,' he replied, smiling.

'How long have you been here?'

'Not long.'

Samir pointed at the empty wine glass.

'Would you like a drink, sir?'

Professor Baines looked around him.

'Don't you think it's a little loud in here?'

Samir peered over his shoulder and surveyed the environment, his eyes homing in on the snatches of debauchery that suddenly seemed to litter the place. Three lads in chequered-shirts had tequila shots lined up at the bar. In unison they sprinkled salt on the back of their hands, ran their tongues along them like a pack of slobbering dogs and slammed back the squat glasses before shoving a wedge of lemon into their mouths. Behind them a young lad was made to endure brutal initiations by his rugby club teammates, gulping down a potent concoction of ale and spirits from the club trophy. After drinking the last drop he placed the trophy over his head to a round of applause followed by boisterous chants of: *Smithie, Smithie, Smithie.* Samir turned back to the professor, his expression sheepish.

'It's not the type of place I had in mind for our discussion,' the professor said.

Samir wasn't sure what to say. He had only suggested the venue as a rendezvous point because it was close to the local library where he had first met the professor and he assumed was easy for both to get to. But now, as his gaze flitted between the eminent figure of Professor Baines and the rest of the pub patrons, the *faux pas* of inviting the man to such a decadent den dawned on him. Dressed in a smart jacket over an open-collared shirt, Professor Baines had about him a distinction that was suited to classrooms and the corridors of academia. The heat rose in Samir's cheeks.

'Would you prefer to go elsewhere?' he said.

'No, it's fine,' the professor said, waving his empty wine glass by the stalk. 'I may be something of a dinosaur, but I do prefer to be surrounded by the energy of youth than the soul-sucking cynicism of some my contemporaries.'

'Are you sure?'

Professor Baines chuckled.

'I wasn't always a grey-haired academic. At one time I worked as a talent scout for a record label. The type of crowd that used to come to see bands like the Sex Pistols and The Clash would make this lot look like choir kids.'

Professor Baines pulled out a crisp twenty-pound note from his black leather wallet and flicked it between his thumb and forefinger.

'I'll have a glass of merlot.'

Samir raised his palm to decline the money.

'I'll buy this round,' he said.

Professor Baines slammed the note into Samir's palm.

'No, take it. I insist. After all, it was my idea that we meet for a drink. I thought it would make a nice change from the library, which is awfully restricting.'

Samir took the money and slunk off towards the bar. He returned minutes later with a glass of wine and a double vodka for himself. He removed the bag from his shoulder, laid it at his feet and sat on the stool opposite Professor Baines. He took a large gulp of his drink. Nerves were playing havoc with his grip on the glass.

'How have you been?' Professor Baines asked.

'Fine, thank you. And you, sir?'

Professor Baines raised his finger in gentle protest.

'Please. My friends call me Doug.'

The professor supped from the broad bowl of his glass. He set it down on the table and rubbed his hands.

'So, we're here to do our best to get you enrolled in college.'

'Only if I'm good enough,' Samir said.

The man grunted in disbelief.

'Of course you are. Don't you worry about that!'

Samir unzipped his hooded top and fished out a brown envelope from the pouch lining the inside. The envelope contained his application form. He pinched the corners to make sure none of them had curled up, and then drew out its contents. He unfolded the form and smoothed it open with the palm of his hand delicately, as though he was handling a valuable parchment. He examined his handwriting one last time, each letter a block capital of excessive neatness. For the umpteenth time he skim-read what he had written, making sure every single letter was legible, assured and competent, suggesting a confidence completely at odds with the uncertainty with which he had committed them to paper. Over the last fortnight he had written several drafts and had asked a work colleague to correct the spelling mistakes. The sheets came back obliterated with red marks. He accepted the fact that spelling would never be his strongest suit.

'I've filled in the form,' he said.

'Well, let's take a look.'

Professor Baines took the form into his thick-fingered hands, and unfolded it with a snap of his wrist. He put on his tortoiseshell reading glasses and scanned the pages. He peered up every now and then to smile at Samir, his eyes kindled with a raffish charm, the lines around them deepening each time he approved of a thoughtful answer or an elegant turn of phrase.

'Hmmm, very good.'

Samir rocked in his seat, the hind legs of the stool lifting off the ground. He hadn't expected the professor to read every word of his statement right now. The ice cubes clattered against Samir's teeth as he took another sip of his drink, his eyes locked on the professor's face in anticipation of a sudden lifting of a brow or a pursing of the lips, something that would connote a shadow of doubt. When Professor Baines had finished, he took off his glasses, put them back in his pocket and scratched his nose.

'All fine.'

Samir's brow lifted in surprise.

'Really?'

'It will get you an interview, I'll make sure of that.'

'And you will write me a reference?'

Professor Baines took a fountain pen from the inside pocket of his jacket and grabbed a paper napkin from a metal holder which was sitting next to the condiments. He wrote something down in spidery handwriting and slid the napkin across the table towards Samir, who picked it up and tried to read the inscription, but could only gawp at the words: *Aut viam inveniam aut faciam!*

'Short and to the point,' Professor Baines declared. 'Do you know what it means?'

'No.'

'*I will either find a way or make one!* It's Latin.'

'Really?'

'And I stand by every word. Would you like to know why?'

'Yes.'

'Because you have passion for the subject.'

'That's very kind of you, sir.'

Professor Baines raised an eyebrow.

'Though I may renege on the offer if you keep calling me *sir*.'

Samir smiled stiffly at the man's quip. He took another sip of his drink. The ice cubes clattered against his teeth once more.

'You seem a little tense?' Professor Baines asked.

'Do you mind if I smoke?'

'Go right ahead.'

Samir rolled up a cigarette. He sparked the end with his Zippo lighter. He took several lungfuls. He looked around, searching for a topic of conversation. A city slicker at the next table caught his attention. *There's profit to be made in war,'* the man bragged loudly to a friend, sharing his inebriated wisdom with all the showmanship of a celebrity psychic. *The ticket's in oil and gas, my friend, oil and gas!* In another corner a man was slamming the buttons of the fruit machine, seduced by the early clatter of coins, and feeding all his loose change into the slot. Samir stole a glance at the clock on his mobile phone. He wondered whether there was time to check in on his mother, give her the housekeeping money, get a plate of wholesome rice and curry into his belly and assure her that things would work out. But propriety kept his bottom nailed to the seat.

'I should have suggested a better place than this,' he reiterated to Professor Baines.

'Really, it's no bother.'

Professor Baines leant forward. He made a little church steeple of his hands, put them to his lips and tapped them in contemplation.

'I was wondering…'

'What?'

'Why you didn't finish school?'

Samir didn't want to admit that he was no good at school. He thought for several seconds before he spoke.

'I'm the only child of a single mother and at the time I couldn't expect her to carry on paying for my upkeep, especially when she was against what I wanted to do with my life. It didn't seem right.'

Samir tilted his head to one side and scratched his temple.

'But I've always wanted to study art and get myself a job in something art-related. And now that I have this opportunity I want to grab it with both hands. I won't let you down. I want to prove my mother wrong.'

The professor shook his head in disappointment.

'So you want to get back into education merely to prove a point to your mother?'

'No.' Samir said.'

'What then?'

Samir touched his face as if to shield himself from the question. A thread of smoke spiralled from his cigarette. The professor's gaze refused to let go, demanding from Samir a more erudite answer. Samir perched the cigarette on the edge of the ashtray.

'When I was fourteen, I went on a school trip to an art gallery in London. The other kids thought it was boring and pointless, but I loved being there. I saw these amazing worlds captured in canvasses of different sizes. Each picture said something different and interesting and honest about the human soul. And the best thing about these paintings was that they weren't trying to force-feed me an idea, they were giving me the space to think for myself, to, you know, what's the word, be more active. I didn't want to leave the place. Being there made me feel restful. I decided then that I wanted to work in a gallery when I grew up.'

Admiration shone in Professor Baines' eyes. He was refreshed by the fact that it was an emotional reponse, not an intellectual one.

'You know that trying to lead a life of flourishing and achievement, of learning and of good relationships, is what's going to yield happiness in the end. You are lucky to have found something that touches your soul.'

'Do you think so?'

'Absolutely.'

Samir considered taking out his sketchbook and showing Professor Baines some of his drawings, but his confidence failed him at the final moment; he drew his hand away from his rucksack and instead held the edge of the table, drumming his fingers because he was frustrated by this familiar flood of doubt.

'I really appreciate your help.'

Professor Baines placed his palm over Samir's hand. His fat-fingered hand patted it several times suggesting that he was completely receptive to Samir's misgivings. His eyes were like bright windows shining an almost overbearing light onto Samir. Samir blinked and then looked down.

'It's been a long time since I've crossed paths with a pure, unaffected soul. You know Samir, it was partly all the pride, pettiness and pretentiousness I was surrounded by that forced me to leave the academic profession, as well as the bleeding bureaucracy. The goddamn bureaucracy!' Professor Baines chuckled to himself. 'One day I woke up, went to work and was in the middle of giving a lecture on Hopper when I realised how lonely and unhappy I was. I felt like a subject of an Edward Hopper painting: you know, outwardly calm, fitting perfectly into the conventions of my setting, but beset by a silent desperation. Most of the students I taught seemed ambivalent about the subject. They had no fire in their belly. That's when I decided to take early retirement. After leaving the academic circle, I spent a year travelling around the world before returning to England and finding myself the job at the library. But now it all makes sense because this new road has brought me to you.'

Samir shuffled in his seat.

'What do you mean, sir?'

'Well, spotting you one afternoon, snuggled up in a chair at the back of the arts and culture section, browsing through a compendium of René Magritte's work, seemed to have stoked anew that passion I've always had for mentoring. You know, after that I noticed you coming in most evenings, padding upstairs as quietly as a church mouse, picking up a book and sitting in the same seat. In this manner I saw you devour the shelf of books on Cezanne, Chagall, Da Vinci, Degas, Gauguin, Kahlo, Matisse and Van Gogh.'

'I enjoy looking at their work,' Samir clarified.

'In you, I began to see a person who was brimming with enthusiasm, but who simply needed help channeling it in the right direction.'

Samir smiled a nervous smile.

'And I'm grateful for the company,' the professor said. 'It's not often in my life that I've come across such a focused young man. Passion is something that is impossible to inculcate in one. I see a lot of myself in you. It gives me an enormous sense of joy that our paths have crossed.'

Still refusing to break eye contact, Professor Baines picked up Samir's hand and brushed the arc of his long fingernails.

'I'll make sure you get a place on the course,' he said.

Samir snatched his hand back as though he was pulling it out of a flame.

'What's wrong?' Professor Baines asked.

'Nothing!'

For a moment there was a murky silence between them. Professor Baines then leant forwards and reached out to place a concerned hand on Samir's arm.

'What's the matter?'

Samir stared back coldly. The man's eyes were dilated. They did not shy away.

'I want to help you. Consider me your benefactor.'

'What?'

Professor Baines' height allowed him to lean even closer to Samir in an effort to calm him.

'My word to you is as good as gold.'

Samir caught the tart odour of wine on the man's breath. He recoiled from its proximity, kicked his stool back so that it hit the wall of the alcove. He stood up. The expression on his face changed from that of boy who was deferential and enthusiastic to that of a man smouldering with hostility. Professor Baines noticed the shine of sweat that was beginning to gather on Samir's brow.

'Please sit down,' he requested softly.

Samir's eyes were as still as death.

'One more drink?' Professor Baines asked, his face reddening a little, though the tone of his voice remained steady.

'No.'

There was a pause.

'What do you say to us going for a bite to eat?'

'I'm not hungry.'

The man smiled.

'Fine, but please sit down.'

'Why?'

'Because you're behaving impulsively.'

'How?'

'Like some kind of frightened child.'

'Screw you!'

'Let's talk about this.'

The atmosphere around the pair was full of merriment, all eyes awash with the euphoria of alcohol. The music was getting louder. A few people were taking to the small dance floor at the back of the pub.

'Just sit down,' Professor Baines demanded in a more serious tone.

Samir crouched back down. The man supped his drink. Samir saw that the professor's teeth were stained and ugly. The shadows under his eyes now looked like those painted on pantomime villains.

'You told me you left school without any qualifications,' Professor Baines said. 'And you need to show something to enrol on this conversion course. I can tell you that for a fact. A levels are usually a prerequisite. Of course, you could do GCSEs, then study A levels. But how long will that take? And how will you fund it? And can you still work full-time and support your mother?'

The man tilted his head and furrowed his brow in sympathy. His voice softened.

'I have a sound reputation in the field. If I push hard enough I may even land you a scholarship. Imagine how helpful that would be. On top of that I can get you some work experience in one of the top galleries in the capital. I'm sure you know the Tate Modern. I have a good contact there.'

The professor dropped his gaze and inspected his fingernails, using the brief lull to let the facts sink in. He cleared his throat and looked up.

'What you must realise is that I really want what's best for you.'

Samir picked up his cigarette. He took a deep drag, his eyes protruding as he sucked in as much nicotine as he could. He stubbed the butt into the ashtray, twisting it with a hint of violence, and stepped out of the alcove.

'Where are you going?' Professor Baines asked.

'For a piss.'

The men's toilet was down a narrow staircase with dirty steps that led to a door with a porthole and a 'Gents' sign, and then to another door – identical but without the sign. A brown carpet stretched down the steps, stained and threadbare. It was bulleted in chewing gum and harboured a residual stench of vomit, stale beer and pork scratchings. Handprint marks smeared either side of the narrow passageway, from drunken men staggering nightly up and down the steps while holding on to the sides. When Samir went through the second set of doors he was greeted by a black African man in an immaculately ironed white shirt. The man's skin was so uniformly dark that under the halogen spotlights it gave off an exquisitely violet sheen.

'Evenin', sir,' he said with a gravelly voice, thick with boredom. His drooping eyes, like crushed sultanas, looked in dire need of sleep. He was perched on a stool beside the ceramic washbasins, ready to offer tissues once people had washed their hands. Behind him was a colourful line-up of aftershaves, and beside it a silver salver ready to receive drunken donations from those who helped themselves to a squirt.

Samir nodded an awkward hello and slipped quickly into a cubicle. He threw the plastic seat cover down and slumped on it with his head in his hands. He tried to lock the door but the bolt had been ripped out, so he was forced to lean against it to stop it from swinging back in.

He suddenly felt like a child who, in the face of a fright, had resorted to estrangement and sought the darkest corner to hide away in. Sweat beads stippled his upper lip. His hair was damp and his scalp had developed a terrible itch. Samir raked his head with both hands, leaving a dishevelled thatch of wavy, black hair. Finally a harsh sigh escaped his lips, and with it the belief that he might have been introduced to something brighter than the purposeless life that he was desperate to escape. For a moment he questioned whether he had misread Professor Baines' intentions. A part of him hoped that a childish fear had foisted something untrue and imagined upon what was supposed to be a fated encounter. But Samir could not shake off the shock coursing through him. He tugged at the toilet roll and tore off several sheets. He piled them into a wad and mopped the panic off his brow. He then let his shoulders drop and buried his chin into his chest. The ambition to better his life had culminated in a false dawn.

Samir was ready to give himself over to the attack of emotion when the sound of heavy footsteps made him flinch. A group of men shot their way into the toilet, whipping up a clatter of doors closing behind them. A pair of them darted straight into the adjacent cubicle. The other two were left standing out-side. Their bodies fractured the light and their shadows slid under the door and into Samir's cubicle. He heard their whispers, voices that were frothing with impatience. *Hurry up, I don't have all night, where is it? Get it out. Be careful!* The slam of the toilet seat and the rustle of cellophane let slip their intention.

The pair waiting outside nudged Samir's door, but he held it tight by lean-ing against it. They stepped away and banged the other cubicle with their fists. *Hurry up!* Finally, after some more shuffling, Samir heard the snorting highs followed by a snowball of expletives – *fuck, shit, fuck, fuck, this is a fuckin' stinger! It's been cut with Vim or fucking Daz!* The pair took several more snorts and after each hit made snarling sounds of satisfaction.

The door lock clicked open and the two emerged from the cubicle while the other two bundled in for their fix. Samir opened his door a fraction and peered through the gap. He saw the two men rubbing their noses and swag-gering up to the bathroom attendant. Their backs were turned to Samir.

'Awrright, my man,' one said.

'Evenin', sir,' the attendant replied.

'Fancy some tart juice?' one asked the other.

'How about a Chupa-chup first?'

'Yeah.'

Samir saw the pair help themselves to a lollipop each, tearing the packag-ing with their teeth. They each picked up a bottle and began to spray the contents into the air as though they were cans of cheap air-freshener. The attendant's expression turned dour as he watched his nightshift paying for someone else's cheap thrill.

'Can you please not do that,' he asked.

'Hey dude, chill,' replied one of the men.

'Give the bottles back please,' the attendant commanded.

The men hurled the bottles at his chest and he managed to juggle both and grasp them at the second attempt.

'Ooh, great work! Where'd you learn that?'

They noticed the scarring on his upper cheeks. One of them waved his fin-gers mockingly at the attendant's face. 'What's that?' he said. 'Are they tribal markings?'

Samir watched through the tiny gap in the door, his insides now filling up with quick-dry fear. Unable to do anything, he picked up the straw from a glass left abandoned in one corner and screwed it inside his fist. He then scraped the sharp edge hard across the back of his neck trying to force some bravery into himself. He wanted to stand up for the man. Help him. He opened the door fractionally, readying a protest, but at the last moment his courage failed him.

'I will have to inform management,' the attendant warned the men. One of the men stepped forward and clamped the black face between his pale hands.

'I suggest you stack up on some tester bottles, mate.' He planted a kiss on the attendant's forehead. The attendant looked startled and pawed his forehead in disbelief. The man stepped back to dust down his shoulders as though he was a boy being smartened up by his mother. The other two burst out of the cubicle.

'What's the problem?' they demanded, waltzing over quickly. They spoke so fast that their words piled into each other.

'Nothing, lads,' said the ringleader, holding the attendant in his wild gaze. He flicked his wrist and flung a five-pound note into the attendant's salver. One of the younger lads ran his tongue over his front teeth and distended his tightly pursed lips into a simian pout, sucking out whatever cocaine was lodged up there. Another began chanting: *Who let the dogs out: Who, who, who, who?* The others joined in: *Who let the dogs out: Who, who, who, who? Who let the dogs out: Who, who, who, who?*

They stormed up the staircase, up the dirty, threadbare carpet and back onto the busy pub floor.

It was suddenly quiet in the toilets, the lull punctuated by the bass from the dance floor upstairs rhythmically ringing the mirrored walls. The attendant had forgotten about Samir and was surprised to see him come out of the cubicle, but pretended otherwise. He kept reorganising his bottles into various combinations of neat lines. Samir walked up to the basin and ran his hands under the cold tap. He kept his attention fixed on the stream of water trickling onto his palms, and then pressed them to his face to conceal his shame. Once Samir had finished he wrung his hands hard and shook them over the basin. The attendant offered him a paper towel.

'Thanks,' Samir said. He looked up for the first time. 'I'm sorry,' he added in the smallest voice he could find.

'It's all right,' the attendant said. 'Never known respect in their miserable lives.'

'Yes, I suppose.'

'They probably speak to their parents in the same way. It's all in the up-bringing.'

'Probably,' Samir said.

'I'm Geoffrey.'

The man held out his hand and when Samir offered his, he took it and pumped it with genuine enthusiasm, like a priest standing at the doorway of his church, welcoming a new member into his congregation.

'Christian?' the man asked.

'No.'

'I'm a qualified accountant,' he quickly added.

'Really?'

'Yes, but they won't recognise my papers in this country.' He was a proud and hardworking man. 'I'm sorting it out.' The man stood to attention and thrust his chest out slightly. *Thou shall decree a thing and it shall be established unto thee and a light shall shine upon thy ways.* That's from the Bible, Job 22:28.'

'I see.'

'The Lord's word sure means a lot in times of attrition.'

Samir nodded and walked towards the door.

'Excuse me.'

Samir turned back.

'You have blood on your collar,' the man said.

'Huh?'

'You've grazed your neck.'

Samir pawed his neck and it felt sticky. For the second time the man offered Samir a tissue. Samir rolled it into a ball and dabbed it under the collar, suddenly aware that the skin was stinging a little. His immediate instinct was to offer the attendant money, but on seeing the five-pound insult lying on the tray, reached for his cigarette packet instead.

'I don't smoke,' said the attendant.

Samir nodded approvingly. Rounding his shoulders, he then ambled back up the stairs, contemplating what he might do if the Professor was still waiting for him.

The pub floor was packed. People were vying for space, snaking this way and that amidst a single roaring noise. Samir took a circuitous route back towards the alcove, hoping that his long absence had exhausted Professor Baines' patience and the man had taken leave. To his relief, as he made his furtive approach, he saw no part of a tweed arm resting on the table. A young couple now occupied the seats. A raven-haired girl was reading the application form which he had left on the table. Samir snatched the piece of paper off her dainty hands and tore it into quarters. He deposited the pieces in the ashtray and walked away. He went to the bar next to the dance floor, ordered another double vodka and finished it in a single slug. The barmaid, who had just deposited the money in the till, was surprised he wanted another so soon.

'Are you sure?' she whispered.

'Yes.'

Samir slammed back the second in similar fashion. And at once a lovely snap went off in the back of his head. Through glassy eyes he studied her for a moment and smiled. He had appreciated her show of concern. Samir turned back to face the crowd, the pullulating cacophony of merriment. The dance floor had become a playground of libidinous liaisons where the Friday night bump'n'grind was reaching fever pitch. A glitter ball dangled from the ceiling, splicing the light into shards that revolved slowly over the people like confetti. The hen party dressed in school uniform outfits were twirling their pigtails and gyrating their pleated bottoms, creating a stir that saw men sliding onto the floor like crocs moving in for the kill. Samir spotted the cocaine crew sidling over with beer bottles in hand, attempting to dance their way closer to the girls. A few men standing on the fringes were forced to absorb the frustration of both lacking the confidence to engage with the girls, and the despair of seeing others freely participating in this wholesale mating ritual.

Samir lit another cigarette, suddenly conscious of being in a place completely alien to him. He was no more than a scab on this limb of the Friday night merriment. He didn't belong here. Samir finished the cigarette. He pulled the hood over his head and, looking like a hoodlum, went back to the table and picked up his rucksack. He elbowed his way through the crowd and headed for the exit.

After a short bus journey, the lonesome walk back to the flat was cold. From afar Samir looked a ghostly figure, hands in pockets, his footsteps silent, his mouth trailed by misty breath. The wind had picked up. And in the forecourt where it swirled, the cold brushed across his face. He could feel the chill on his teeth. When he stuck his tongue out to wet his lips, his saliva immediately turned icy. The deadness of the path made him feel odd. Only hours ago the walk from the station to the pub had seemed like a route to an exciting adventure, which gave his soles a healthy spring. But now each step felt flat and hard and arduous, as if his mobility had suffered a puncture. He tried to forget everything and wondered how his mother was feeling and how he could make up for letting her down. He feared she had gone to bed still angry with him. The thought was shunted aside when his phone bleeped. It was Professor Baines. Samir deleted the number and switched his phone off. He then spotted a stone on the pavement. He skipped up to it and booted it hard. The stone flew through the air and clattered against the side of a car. It packed enough fury to set off the alarm. The car began to wail and the flashing headlamps showed him up clearly as the offender. A scratch on the door gleamed in the light, like gunmetal. The car belonged to his landlord. The sight sobered him up in an instant.

Samir's instinct was to throw his hood down and look up even though he knew his landlord would be out on a Friday night. But the young woman who lived on the second floor was standing out on her balcony leaning against the grille. A child was there beside her, holding carelessly under her chubby arm what looked like a teddy bear from a distance. The woman stared at him. The shape of her was cool, stolid, and she looked as alert as a night owl. The pale white light from inside the flat gave her outline a halo. Although Samir could not see her eyes, her silhouette frightened and fascinated him in equal measure. He immediately looked away and slipped into the building as quietly as a cat.

A twisted apology

The clock was about to strike midnight. Amina had finished sewing the buttons back on Samir's shirt. She spread the garment over the bed to check the alignment. The buttons were green and a fraction elliptical. Staring at it she thought about the lilypads in her parents' pond in Bangladesh, which were used by the toads that lived on the banks. As a young girl, often she used to hear the toads croaking away after a heavy deluge in the night, while her arthritic grandmother gathered the children in the candlelit darkness to recount scary *kitchaa-kahinis*, turning those guttural sounds into the burps of a mythical giant in these stories strewn with magic and mayhem. The frightened siblings would always tussle for space under the safety of her soft, leathery arms: *Once upon a time, there lived a naughty girl called Amina...*

Why me, Nannijee?

OK, Saufina then...

Why me, Nannijee?

Let's start again. Once upon a time, there lived a naughty boy called Kamal...

No, no, no, he's too young to be eaten by a rakkash!

Outside a group of young men walked through the street with their arms locked in a chain. They had just been turned out of a pub and were going home chanting a football song. On every third beat they kicked their legs up in the air like dancers in a musical show. In her own country, during a balmy night, Amina had been accustomed to sitting on the verandah steps and being serenaded by the sounds of the busy undergrowth while inhaling the smell of damp bark, the waxy leaves of the mango trees, and listening to the muezzin's call to prayer coming through the tannoy from the height of the mosque's minaret. In contrast, for the last six weeks in Britain her ears had been clogged by the hum of living alone.

Lately, Amina would find herself wide awake in the middle of the night, her eyes pushing against the dark lid of the ceiling trying to find some light in it. But the world sought to keep her in darkness, and no matter how hard she looked she could not find a solution to her dilemma. Eventually she would have to get up and busy herself with something: perhaps sew a hemline, continue a knitting project, patch up a pillow, or stitch a button back on one of her son's abandoned shirts.

Amina put the shirt on a hanger and into Samir's wardrobe. She pulled the curtain back a little and looked out of the window. A trickle of water from the cracked roof guttering of the house opposite had slid across the edge of the bay window and resolved itself into a tiny icicle in one corner, like a frozen tear. She pressed her face into the wet glass and watched the men high step along the pavement.

'Here we go, here we go,' they sung, far too inebriated to consider lowering their voices for the sleeping community. They turned the corner and the voices disappeared into a chorus of laughter. Amina pulled the curtains and fumbled slightly when a hook caught the rail. The letter she had earlier stuffed into her cardigan pocket fell out. She had completely forgotten about it. Perhaps forgetfulness was one of the effects of the pills that her GP, Doctor Godwin, had prescribed on her last visit. It made sense. To be unable to remember the reason for your sadness meant that there was no reason to be sad. She picked up the letter and went to her own room. She sat on the bed, tore the envelope open and unfolded the letter.

Amina,

Firstly, I deliver to you my prayers. I hope this letter finds you in good health. With Allah's blessing, I am fine, living here with your brother and his wife and my grandchildren.

Thank you for your letter and the money. Rashid collected it from the bank last week. He is doing very well with the taxi business. He is so grateful to you. Whenever he does his namaaz, he always remembers to pray for you. Kamal is looking for a bride for Rashid now that Rashid is an earning man, but Rashid insists he wants to go abroad to earn money. Kamal is against the idea of sending him abroad as Majid is already in Bahrain, and he can't bear to lose both sons to foreign lands. How is my grandson, Samir? I pray everyday that he is a good son to you. I realise how difficult it must be for you, but he will see the light of good. I am sure of it. What he needs is to be around family. Try to convince him to come to Bangladesh, or ask him to take a holiday with you. Surrounded by our love and affection, he will never wish to return to England.

Your brother, Rashid's mother, Rashid and Fareed send you their salaams. Majid is well in Bahrain. I am thinking of you everyday, and even now, after so many years, I still worry that you are so far away from us. When your father was alive, he used to say that you were living seven seas away in a fairytale land. I sometimes worry that you are trapped in England. How long do you plan to stay there? Yesterday, I dreamt that you had come back to us, just the way you suddenly turned up all those years ago. Your father was so surprised and happy to have you back. And so was I.

I am now getting old, but I long to see the face of my daughter and eldest grandson before Allah calls me into his Kingdom. I prayed today that the same impulsive streak, which brought you back twenty-six years ago, brings you back to us again. I hope Allah answers my prayer.

Do take care of yourself.

Allah haffez,

Ammu.

Amina peered up from her mother's words. She wondered whether she should read the letter to Samir on his next visit. She rubbed her face in contemplation, uncertain as to whether her son would even bother to listen. She decided to raise the idea with him at least – mother and son going on holiday to Bangladesh, like they did in the summer of 1984. Yes, that's what she would do. She made a stern face, as if she were locking the plan of action inside her head. Where had she lost that bold spirit of youth? She looked back at the letter, at her mother's final words, intensely, as if to retrieve that lost part of her.

...I prayed today that the same impulsive streak, which brought you back twenty-six years ago, brings you back to us again...

Yes, Amina, once the young woman with an impulsive streak, who twenty-six years ago had rushed home to pack her bags after her ex-husband (flanked by a fertile new wife who was standing behind a pram), had tapped her on the shoulder in a crowded marketplace in Oldham. 'Amina, is that you?' he had asked.

Back then, Amina was so shaken to have clapped eyes on a man she thought she'd never see again that she dropped the carton of eggs in her hand, breaking most of them. She could only splutter a pathetic excuse before scampering off as fast as she could, trying to lose herself in the throng of shoppers.

A panic-stricken Amina, fearing her ex-husband had returned with his new wife to set up home in Oldham, quickly booked a plane ticket and, a fortnight later, found herself back in Bangladesh, amidst the *grisma* heat of 1975, under the livid sun which was bearing down and subduing everything in the village.

On that day she was standing on her parents' verandah waiting to surprise her father as he pulled up to the house on a rickshaw. He was making his way back from the fish bazaar. A silver-scaled *Elisha* lay curled by his feet.

'Just stand there and do nothing,' Amina's mother instructed, hiding behind the door, still pinching herself in disbelief.

Amina watched her father step off the rickshaw clutching his *lungi* with one hand. The other searched the ground with a walking stick. A silver lock of hair fell over his forehead when he stepped out of the rickshaw's canopy. In that instant he had about him a quality so ethereal that in Amina's eyes he could have been a mirage, a preminatory vision, a dream. Amina's homecoming dream – for he was the personification of the family homestead she had carried inside her during her exile.

When her father saw her he put his hand to his mouth, then dropped it immediately and changed his expression to something more befitting his stoic character. They looked at each other. In the distance a stake was being hammered into the ground to tether a grazing cow. Each stroke emitted a wholesome echo.

'Has your mother not taught you any manners? Are you just going to stand there or are you going to say salaam to your father?'

Amina came down the steps and knelt down to touch her father's feet.

'*Assalumu Alaikum, Abbu.*'

'*Waalaikum Assalam, beti.*'

He drew her up by her shoulders and rubbed his nose with hers. And it might have been six years ago, he thought, on that very day he waved goodbye to her at the airport and asked her husband to take care of her, for in that moment the intervening years of guilt and self-admonishment seemed to disappear. The years of beating himself up for making a mess of his daughter's life no longer mattered. His angel had returned to him. 'Can you believe it?' her mother rejoiced as she leapt out from behind the doors. Her eyes were glazed in happy tears too.

The next day Amina walked out onto the verandah holding a cup of tea for her father who was sitting cross-legged on his charpoy, taking great lugs from his bronze hookah pipe. Water burbled inside the canister and each time he exhaled the smoke billowed from his mouth and became an extension of his greying beard. The fragrance drifted through the still, thick air. Amina closed her eyes and inhaled deeply; the familiarity of its smoky, spicy aroma flung Amina back to those long afternoons when Azad would come to visit with a rolled-up newspaper tucked under his armpit. Sitting under the shade of the verandah, he would discuss politics with her father. The kettle on the stove would be on constant boil and it would be Amina's duty to rush cups of tea to the two men occupying their chairs like thrones. Azad's voice would rise and fall with a politician's fervour as he read aloud the newspaper articles, dispensing his own opinions about the state of the country at regular intervals. Sometimes her father would call her for a head massage and Amina would have to sit amongst the two men, kneading her father's temples, and grow weary listening to the pair dissect every political debate and local and national wrangle they heard on the streets. It would make her eyelids weigh down with boredom:

'*Dula-bhai*, how about reciting some poetry instead?'

71

Never one to shy away from performance, Azad would sit up and clear his throat and recite Tagore:

...the sleep that flits on a baby's eyes
does anybody know from where it comes?
Yes, there is a rumour that it has its dwelling where... where... where...

Azad would take out his crumpled copy of *Gitanjali* from his back pocket, find the page, recover his poise and carry on:

...where in the fairy village
among shadows of the forest dimly lit with glow-worms,
there hang two timid buds of enchantment.
From there it comes to kiss baby's eyes...

Amina looked out in the courtyard. The leaf of every shrub, tree and weed lay still under the humidity and the ground appeared baked in the white glare. Red ants skirted the cracks in single file. Seeing her father in the familiar lotus position, Amina questioned whether she had left time suspended in the village. Only a few years ago her eyes had been frozen livid on the black and white BBC pictures, watching her birthplace being ground by war's brutal jaw. There were tanks rolling through dusty streets, bombed out buildings, refugees fleeing into the forests over the Indian border, khaki uniforms crawling over the land wielding their muddy rifles fronted with bayonets, their marauding numbers making them as pernicious as a plague of locusts. Things in the news had moved at a thousand miles an hour. Daily reports had carried her from towns to villages, from schools to hospitals, from smoking towers to capsized boats, and shook her mind as if someone had taken a whisk to it. On board the aeroplane she had brooded over the imminent reunion with her birth land – now with a new name, its own sovereignty and its own flag – and considered how she would feel. Would she meet it with celebration, delighted to have a country to call her own, or instead begin hankering over the loss of an essence that had coloured her past life? A cynical part of her expected war to have swept across the landscape of her childhood like a twister and to have ripped out everything familiar. But now, everything appeared exactly as she had left it, untouched, almost as if it had been awaiting her return.

Her father waved the nozzle of his pipe to catch Amina's attention. She blinked and her eyes pulled back from the middle distance. She came and sat down beside him. She placed the cup of tea next to the hookah canister. He rested his palm lightly on her cheek and smiled at her.

'No letter, no telegram, nothing?'

'I wanted to surprise you, *Abbu*.'

'A surprise…' her father mused.

'Yes.'

'You know I've been expecting you to return ever since you left us.'

He brushed his chin with the pipe in a troubled manner.

'Did you come back alone?' he asked.

'Yes.'

'Are you thinking about moving back here for good?'

'I don't know.'

'You should be here with your family.'

Her father tried to keep smiling but could not stop the slight tremor in his lip.

'I am sorry, Amina,' he said, softly. 'All I ever wanted was the best for you. I never thought it would turn out this way.'

He turned away to stare at the horizon, still and forlorn. Amina took the end of her sari and dabbed the sweat off his brow.

'It's not your fault,' she assured him. 'It was my kismet. It was my body that failed me. I cannot blame you for trying to do the right thing by me.'

Her father turned back to look at her. He saw a new fullness in his daughter's face. She had left as a teenager and now, at twenty-three, returned a grown woman. The time abroad had lightened her complexion and given her a foreign look. Her maturity took him by surprise.

'Why, my little girl has bloomed into a beautiful adult!'

Amina reached for the small *punkah* on the table and began fanning the space between them. The air was heavy, laden with moisture. The first of the monsoon rains seemed imminent.

'Have you seen him since he left you?'

Amina shook her head, weakly at first, but then with a greater conviction, worried that a father would otherwise see through the lie.

'Do you know that he returned several years ago and remarried?' her father asked.

'No.'

'I went to see him and took your *Khabin* with me.'

'You didn't have to do that.'

'I was desperate. I wanted to make things better for you. After all, I was responsible for arranging the marriage.'

'It's not important. It's all in the past now.'

'He bought back the land apportioned to you by the document. He gave me the money, which I've deposited into a bank account for you. The bankbook is locked in the almirah. Would you like it now?' The words came out in a rush as if he had been carrying them for a long time, lugging the small recompense like a millstone around his neck which he was desperate to relieve himself of it at the first opportunity.

'I'll look at it later,' Amina replied.

'Please don't forget,' he said, hard-mouthed. He stared back at the horizon.

'What's the matter, *Abbu*?'

'Nothing.'

'Are you sure?'

The robustness in her father's mouth suddenly collapsed and he began rubbing his face to cover the grief which was beginning to overwhelm him.

'I have made so many mistakes. I have failed to do the right things by you and your sister. It's all a complete mess.'

'I don't understand.'

Amina knew Saufina was pregnant but it did not explain why her brother-in-law hadn't called by to see her. It wasn't as if they lived miles away. She had expected to see Azad's face by now. He was usually so enthusiastic and it was unlike him to miss out on a reunion.

'Why hasn't *Dula-bhai* come to see me?' Amina asked.

Her father hooked the pipe back in its cradle and reached into his pocket to pull out a Capstan tin, inside which were rich green betel leaves folded into triangular shapes, each packed with flakes of betel nut. He took one out and put it into his mouth.

74

'Your brother-in-law isn't the same man he was before the war. He wasn't prepared for the sacrifices he ended up making for the country. When he left to join the *Mukhti Bahini* he went with a romantic notion of martyrdom, but returned a disabled war victim. That was the beginning of the end.'

Amina's brow creased with confusion.

'What's happened to him?' she asked.

'He's ill.'

'Why wasn't I told?'

Her father sighed and dropped his head.

'I should go to see them,' Amina said.

'No point.'

'Why?'

'He's an ailing man, a shadow of what he used to be. It will only upset you to see him.'

'But I must go.'

'Why don't you stop skirting around the edges and tell her the full story?' her mother heckled from indoors.

'What does *Ammu* mean?'

'Things have been very hard for him,' her father said.

'What's happened?' Amina pleaded. 'What is it that I haven't been told?'

Amina watched her father's mouth move as it formed words. Then her eyes dropped in dismay. She felt disgusted. It wasn't a word she ever expected her father to utter.

'*Modh!*' she repeated, in a harsh whisper.

'I couldn't bring myself to put it in a letter.'

Amina sat stunned. Her brother-in-law an alcoholic? Impossible!

'*Ishtakfirullah!*' she uttered. The morally upstanding man, the diehard educationalist, the freedom fighter, reduced to a drunkard. Amina's concern shifted to her sister.

'What about *Appa*?'

'I visit her as often as I can, but it upsets her to be seen like that.'

'But she's expecting a child. How are they coping?'

Her father didn't say anything at first. He spat out the scarlet betel juice into the spittoon by his side.

'Not well. The man has squandered everything on drink. He's pawned off the furniture bit by bit. He's even sold off all her wedding jewellery. He's very ill now.'

Speechless, Amina stared at her father. A bluebottle hovered around her and tried to land on her face. She swiped her hand across her face.

'What do you mean, how ill?' Amina asked.

'The last time I saw him was at the hospital. He looked skeletal. He is barely forty but looks a man twice the age. The hospital has sent him back home.'

'I must go to see them.'

'I'll take you tomorrow.'

'I'll travel by rickshaw this afternoon. It might be easier for *Appa* to see me alone. She knows I'm back. Yesterday, Kamal went to give her the news.'

Amina rose to her feet. As she turned to leave she took his hand and gave it a reassuring squeeze.

'*Abbu*, don't worry. Everything will be fine.'

That night Amina returned home late from her visit. After paying the rickshaw wallah, Amina had to rush for shelter under the verandah as the sky finally broke into an unrelenting rainstorm. She hadn't seen rain like this in a long time. The drops lanced down and drummed against the tin roof of the house. Runnels raced down the corrugated ridges and snapped against the concrete steps. Puddles were forming in the dips on the forecourt.

With the image of her decaying brother-in-law now burned onto her mind's eye, Amina felt she was being mocked while coming back on the rickshaw, as it threaded through the bustle of the city centre. The outside world appeared sprightlier, almost cartoonish. She saw people scurrying to get under tree canopies and shop awnings, looking at the heavens as forks of lightning stabbed down on the earth. She heard the market cows bellowing after each clack of thunder. Pye-dogs, curled up into dirty balls, lifting their heads with frightened yelps. The *dhobis* at Zindabazaar's public pond were slamming clothes on the *ghat* with a worried frenzy. There was something ludicrous and indulgent about how life seemed more panic-ridden after her encounter with the slow, silent demise of her brother-in-law.

She sank down on the *charpoy*, a deadweight against the wall, drained and dejected. She had not been prepared for the images that had travelled back with her:

A bed-ridden Azad, his face drawn, the yellow skin stretched tight over his skull. His eyes sunken like two dried-up wells. The limbs bony, sallow and blotchy. Then there was the leg amputated at the knee, the site from where the rot began.

For the short while that Amina had sat with him, she wasn't sure whether Azad had even realised that she was there. Saufina had whispered into his ear, 'Look who's here, open your eyes, *chouk kulo, deko, deko, deko,*' but even when a sliver of life had managed to peer through those slits, the eyes had never hinted at anything close to recognition. The mouth had murmured nothing coherent. The hand had barely squeezed back. When her mother came out of the house, Amina threw her arms over her and cried on her shoulder.

For the next two months Amina spent all her time at Saufina's house, providing the support her sister needed but was too proud to ask for. Amina was adamant about helping her brave, older sister, who had developed shadows under the eyes from sitting forever at the back of her husband's bed, applying wet flannels to his forehead, talking to him, administering the morphine injections at the right time, and in doing so ignoring her own body, exhausted and brittle from the task of carrying the baby inside her womb.

On that fateful day in the middle of August, Azad finally slipped into a deep coma and before twilight the shallow breaths stopped altogether. By an ill-fated coincidence, on the same day the nation's leader – Azad's one-time hero – was also gunned down by assassins. The shock news of Sheikh Mujib's murder spread through the village and into Saufina's house when the high-pitched voice of a neighbour was heard crying: '*Bangobondu's* been killed, *Bangobondu's* been killed!' He ran from one village house to another, shaking his head, waving his arms and yelling at the top of his voice. Amina switched on the small transistor radio on the shelf above Azad's bed. Her trembling hands turned the dial furiously, sweeping past the crackling static until it found the national radio station. The newsreader made the formal announcement: *The Father of the Nation, Sheikh Mujibur Rahman and twenty-three members of his family were shot dead in their home in Dhaka during the early hours of the morning: Innaa Lillaahi Wa Innaa Ilayhi Raaji'oon...* The news had brought the whole country to a standstill: supporters were falling into each other's arms and crying in the streets; government ministers were struggling to put together a coherent statement in the effort to maintain a semblance of authority. Less than two hours after the newsflash, Azad quietly passed away.

While the mosque was still being informed, Saufina's waters broke and she doubled over into labour. Amina called for help, drawing the village wives and mothers who came running with their towels and hot water. The women found compassion in themselves despite having shunned the couple and labelled the house *Satan's Den.* They ushered Saufina into the next room and propped the hingeless door over the doorway. An hour later they called for the village doctor. As if fate was intent on having the final laugh, the family found itself yielding to a bizarre irony. While the men attended silently to the death rituals in one room, the other room was filled with the scarlet screams of childbirth.

Amina's father took charge of the post-mortem arrangements and called the local mosque official who helped wash the body under its bedclothes. And all the while he kept an eye on the door leaning against the doorway, behind which he could hear the wailing of his daughter in labour. Amina and Kamal stayed close to him and the triumvirate drew strength from each other, praying for the two lives in the other room, now locked in a duel to survive each other.

Two hours later they heard the cry of a newborn. Amina ran to the door and shunted it enough to squeeze by. Meanwhile, her father and brother sat by Azad's body. A vague smile lifted the downward curve of her father's lips, sensing that the death had been ameliorated by a divine silver lining. It would be some kind of sacred rebirth that redeemed the passing of a tortured soul. A new grandfather and a new uncle sat poised, ready to welcome the youngest member into the family.

Five long minutes passed. Nothing moved. Their eyes bore anxious holes into the hingeless door leaning awkwardly against its frame. Amina eventually slid out, her face drawn and impassive.

'What's happened?' her father asked. 'How's the baby?'

'The baby's fine.'

'Is it a boy or a girl?' Kamal asked.

'A boy.'

'And how is Saufina?' her father asked.

There was another silence. Amina's shoulders fell. Her head dropped. She didn't answer. She could not speak the words.

'Amina?' her father shouted.

'*Appa?*' Kamal shouted.

'Amina?'

But her depthless gaze said it all. The cut made to get the baby out. The fierce, bright-red left between the thighs, a darker colour staining the bed sheets, the bloody towels, the doctor's helpless hands. Her sister's face drained to a dead white, sleeping that cold and exhausted final sleep. And lying beside her was a slick, warm, bawling baby, being massaged into the world by one of the women.

And so in a hot and overcast August month, the family conducted the twin burial just before the midday *Zuhr* prayers, putting to rest the young mother and father who were denied the opportunity to take their baby into their arms to check for deformities, to count his fingers and toes, or even to kiss his beautiful forehead and dream a perfect future for their perfect child.

The men carried the shrouded bodies outside, leaving a house without a household, but still filled with smells of the living. With food on the stove, washing on the line, a framed picture on the wall. The funeral took place under a sky honeycombed with chinks of watery blue. The small congregation of mourners stood with umbrellas by their sides like sheathed swords, as the cortege ushered husband and wife to the burial ground at the back of the mosque. They were still shaking their heads and muttering their disbelief, their nerves inflamed by these deaths as well as the feeling that they were now an orphaned nation.

Amina stayed indoors, crying quietly to herself. She went back into the birthing room and looked at the small baby lying in the bassinet, its scalp still matted in its mother's birth juices. She listened to its breathing as it slept after its long battle. She coaxed her finger inside its limp fist and felt the baby-grip coil upon her nail. She recalled Saufina's words in recent weeks. The promises she made. The future she saw. She loved her sister – her beautiful sister who had recoiled from pity, who had blinked away any suggestion of tears, who whooped with delight whenever the baby had kicked inside her.

In that moment the answer came to her. The tiny life was nature's twisted apology. She could make possible all her sister's dreams, all the promises she had made to her unborn child, by taking the child away from its orphaned beginnings to raise it as her own. She could be the mother that nature told her she couldn't and bring the child up to be the perfect son. Amina reached into the cradle and gathered the child into her arms. She checked for deformities, counted its fingers and toes, kissed its forehead. She remembered her sister's words, called him Samir, took him to her breast and claimed him as her own.

Twenty-six years on, with creases in her face and a dark *sajdah* mark on her brow, Amina folded the letter back inside its envelope and then peered up at the clock-hand ticking towards midnight. The clock struck the hour. Its twelve chimes travelled the depths of the house, marking a new day on the calendar. Amina feared it was the beginning of another sleepless night.

She went into her own room, slipped her mother's letter into the dresser drawer, made her way to the bathroom and clicked the lock on the door. She pulled the light cord. The flash from the fluorescent tube stung her eyes. The tiled floor felt wonderfully cold beneath her feet. She turned on the taps and performed her ritual ablutions.

Once in bed, Amina pulled the cold duvet over the night and lay there staring up at the ceiling. She told herself that she would act on her mother's suggestion. The next time Samir called in she would try to convince him to take a trip with her to Bangladesh. The boy needed to be shown how much his family loved him. With these thoughts racing in her head, Amina tossed and turned, disposed her body in all manner of positions in an effort to summon sleep, but no matter what she did it eluded her. Frustrated, she turned the radio (which she had borrowed from Samir's room) on beside her pillow hoping that some sound, some kind of human talk, something akin to her grandmother's *kitcha-kahini* voice would arrest her thoughts, carry her off to another place and lullaby her to sleep. She spun the dial, hopping from station to station, but only raucous music blasted out from everywhere: snatches of pop, rock, R&B and hip-hop. After a while Amina switched off the radio and tore the duvet off her body. In a burst of purposefulness she went into Samir's room armed with a pen and her letterpad. She sat at his desk in her dressing gown, flicked on the desk lamp, put on her reading glasses and began composing a reply to her mother.

November bees

Three market research companies and two business directories operated on the floor where Samir worked as a telemarketer selling advertorial space for one of the directories. The newly built reception fascia at the entrance was screened off by a panel of frosted glass and lent a cheap, schmaltzy glamour to the place. Raised on a wooden plinth, the deck was stamped with the parent company's logo and furnished with a couch and coffee table. Select marketing material was left fanned out over its glass top. Such was the neat, ostentatious display that waiting guests who happened to pick up a brouchure felt inclined to replace it exactly as they had found it.

Behind the façade, however, the glamour surrendered to a carpet the colour of oatmeal which stretched over the remaining office floor. The work desks were arranged in clusters to demarcate the publications. Grey filing cabinets lined the back adding to the sense of officialdom and order. There were stacks of old magazines in one corner, leaning against the ageing photocopier which droned all day from overuse. Despite the cardboard charisma up front, it was just another typical office.

On this Monday morning Samir had arrived to work a quarter of an hour late to find his workstation oddly empty. He looked around and spotted his manager Jill through the glass doors of the meeting room. His colleagues were packed in there. Picking up a pen and pad he rushed to join them, swinging the door open and bursting in, bringing with him an outdoorsy odour.

By the time Samir had entered, the meeting was over. His three colleagues were getting up, tucking their chairs in and filing out of the room. Jill gave Samir a stern glance, noticing that the ankles of his jeans were sodden and streaked in mud.

'Samir, a word please.'

With the last of his collegues gone, the door closed with a click, divorcing the space from the melodic din of phone rings and the soothing clack of keyboards.

'Sit down.'

Samir lowered his bottom into the nearest seat, nervously chewing the inside of his bottom lip. The manager continued scribbling notes. Her silver pen scratched the paper harshly. Once she finished, she pressed the top of the pen and the nib retracted. She put the instrument down, pulled the sleeves of her mohair sweater up to the elbows and ran her fingers through her neatly shorn bob. She looked up at Samir and pursed her lips in annoyance.

'What is it with your timekeeping?'

'I'm sorry.'

'Sorry simply isn't good enough. I can't do anything with sorry. Sorry doesn't get the work done. It's not as if it's the first time either. Also, next time I suggest you knock first instead of barging in like that!'

Samir nodded.

'What's your reason for being late this time?' Jill demanded to know.

Samir saw his image reflected in the severe expression on Jill's face. He could see his foibles. He knew that his face needed a shave and his hair a comb. His thick fleece hung off him like tarpaulin. He looked a complete mess. In a vain effort to restore some respectability to his appearance he raked the damp fringe back from his forehead. He rubbed his face, and was ashamed by the rasp of his stubble.

'Well?' Jill asked.

Samir tried to think, but his mind hummed as if a nest of bees were beating their papery wings under his skull. With his plans left abandoned in a cubicle on Friday night and with no prospect of improvement, a dark cloud had assailed him late last night, and had him reaching for the vodka bottle he kept in his room. As he sat drinking in the dark, he could only see the wrongness of things, of being in the wrong place, of having made wrong choices, of having wronged his mother, which seemed a barefaced transgression now that Douglas Baines had revealed his true nature and his offer had proven too good to be true.

'You have nothing to say?' Jill pressed.

Over the last few weeks everyone, not least his manager, had seen Samir's commitment to work fall away to such a degree that at times it seemed as if his attitude had crossed over into disregard.

'I'm really sorry,' Samir said with greater emphasis.

'You do realise you're not setting a good example?' Jill warned.

Samir dropped his gaze. A dignified silence was best, most earnest, he thought.

'We're at a critical stage and I need a team I can rely upon,' Jill explained.

'Yes,' Samir replied.

Jill studied him with suspicion, watched closely for the slightest sign that could connote some kind of defiance, but only saw a dazed exhaustion as he childishly sucked on his sore, mottled lips.

'Until deadlines are met, you do realise that all temporary contracts are subject to review?' she asked.

'Of course.'

'Are you sure about that?'

'Yes.'

She eyed him sceptically.

'You do want to be here?'

Faced with the oblique threat, Samir felt his cheeks heating up.

'Yes, I do.'

'Good.'

Jill picked up her folder and strode out of the room leaving Samir to follow a few paces behind her.

At his desk, Samir drank a pint of water to ease his hangover. His colleagues were oddly conscientious with everyone dialling numbers from their lists and speaking into their headsets, repeating the same patter with the same forced intonations. When Jill vacated her seat to attend another meeting, Neville, who was sitting next to Samir, cast his attention on him.

'You OK?' he whispered.

Samir smiled and then scrunched his eyelids close before opening them again. 'I'm fine.'

'You don't look too good.'

Samir put his hands together in the posture of a prayer and pressed the balls of his eyes with his thumbs. For a brief moment the thumping ceased. But when he took his thumbs away, it started up again.

'I'm just tired.'

Neville could smell the nicotine that clung to Samir's fleece.

'Sam,' he whispered, 'you can't carry on turning up late to work.'

As Samir leafed through his contact list, staring at the columns of phone numbers, all he could think of was the professor's advances and how he might have misread them and overreacted. Samir shook the thought away and stared blankly at his computer screen. Neville touched Samir's arm.

'Is it something to do with that personal statement you asked me to look through?'

'Forget about it.'

During his lunch hour Samir left the office for a cigarette. Outside he leant against the cold brick wall of the building and blew smoke rings into the sky, his cheek caressed by the white, wintery sun which gave off a pallid glow, its warmth diffused by a chiffon cloud. Amidst the traffic of pedestrians he watched the same group of students from the nearby City University who had made it their weekly ritual to go into a quaint falafel store to buy their lunch and sit around the same bench having – he imagined – learned conversations. But as he watched them this time, his bitterness piqued at the thought of how fertile their futures seemed because his own, in contrast, had reverted to a barren wasteland. Averting his gaze he rubbed his face and felt the pores of his skin tighten, as if they were offended by the touch of his own fingers.

After stubbing the cigarette out on the wall, Samir went into Woolworth's and raided the pick'n'mix shelf with hungry hands. He bought a bag of his favourite sweets. He came outside and, in schoolboy fashion, emptied the assortment of liquorice, jellybeans, winegums and cola bottles into the baggy pocket of his fleece. He discarded the paper bag and watched the wind sweep it away, making it perform ragged cartwheels along the pavement.

The sugar rush had lifted his mood and boosted his productivity during the afternoon, even galvanising his phone voice with a kindly tone that led to a rare sale of an ad slot. Before finishing for the day, he slipped into the toilets and tore at his trouser pockets for his mobile phone. There was one thing that he had been hankering for all weekend.

'It's Samir, bro. I need some herb.'

'College boy, is that you?'

'Do you have some?'

'I thought you'd turned into some born-again teetotaller?'

'I can always take my business elsewhere.'

'Camden Lock,' came the quick reply.

Samir stepped out of the tube station into the melée of Camden High Street. He pulled up his hood and burrowed through the press of people, moving hastily towards the lock to reach his supplier. He knew that Ali, like most dope dealers, wasn't the type to wait around for long.

Samir crossed at the traffic lights to avoid the queue forming outside the Palace nightclub – a visual cacophony of people dressed as goths, waiting for the doors to open so they could stomp down the sticky stairs to a night of dark revelry. Mostly he was keen to escape the noise: the urgent patter of pedestrian footsteps; the clatter of shutters that came down over the shop windows like corrugated eyelids; the vexed man raining blows on an overcrowded bus because the driver refused to open its doors; the man cooking the burgers in his van, the fat hissing, spitting, spewing.

Samir turned the corner into a side road. Gradually the din of Camden dissolved into a profound quietness. Several streets later he arrived at the metal steps that led down to the canal embankment. He felt his heart beating from the exertion, his excitement pulsating at the prospect of a smoke. He kept moving briskly to get to the rendezvous point, holding on to the rail which was stippled in raindrops. The water collected in his fingers and slid off his palm in frantic droplets. He wiped his hand on the back of his trousers then wiped his wet nose with the back of his hand. He walked up and down the embankment to make sure Ali wasn't tucked away in any of the crevices and, once certain of this, came to sit down on one of the damp wooden benches. He tore open a packet of cigarettes and pressed one between his chapped lips. He tried to light it, but no matter how fast he turned the thumbwheel of his Zippo lighter it emitted an impotent spark. After a dozen attempts he tossed it into the water.

A movement on the bench about twenty feet away caught his attention. Samir narrowed his eyes and saw a teenage couple locked in a kiss, their bodies entangled in new love. He tried to ignore them, but found his stare drawn back in their direction. When the girl used her thumb to feather the boy's lips, he met the touch with a feathery kiss. For them love was a fresh, shiny thing. Their tactile world evoked in Samir a vague feeling of wantonness. Samir felt the slight pinch of envy and momentarily considered what it was he envied. The simple physical contact or the tableau of young love made watertight by the power of innocence, that ephemeral strength of sweet sixteen. He himself didn't have the right credentials to share his life with anyone. Love and romance were not colours he had ever dipped into. Marijuana provided a good, airy substitute. As for physical contact, only a year ago, he had visited a brothel near Paddington, paid a whore, sweated and snorted on her body for twenty minutes and then come out into the abrasive daylight, his pocket relieved by sixty pounds but his soul more pent up than before he went into the squalid room. He couldn't ejaculate. Just couldn't. It hadn't felt right because the whole craving had about it a whiff of tragedy.

Samir reached into his rucksack and pulled out a pencil and his sketchpad. He opened it to a fresh page and began drawing the couple, emphasising the shadows to create a chiaroscuro effect, a style at which he was particularly adept. As he worked away, the cigarette butt in his mouth became moist with spit.

A few minutes elapsed before the couple heard a page flapping in the breeze and turned their heads like a pair of startled deer. They noticed the strange man hidden under his hood, a hunched and clenched figure stooped over a book – cutting an odd and creepy silhouette against the dusk. They instantly unclasped their bodies, got up and walked away hand in hand in search of another place where they could make out without being disrupted by any peeping Toms.

Samir closed the sketchpad, but continued to follow them with his eyes. Their wholesome devotion to each other induced in him a certain fascination. It wasn't envy he was feeling but something different. Something more tender. More kindly. He felt touched by the passing heat of another's love.

'Wassup, Bro!'

Ali's hard voice swooped down like an eagle's claw, tearing Samir out of his romantic chrysalis. A familiar herbal smell wafted from his clothes, his beaded tresses and from the short tassels that swung wildly on his guitar casing. The men touched fists.

'You gonna smoke that stick or just keep sucking it?'

Samir took the cigarette out of his mouth.

'You got a light?'

Ali sat down beside Samir and rested the guitar between his legs. He reached inside his khaki jacket, which was covered in small hashrock burns fallen from slack joints, and pulled out a matchbox and a lump of marijuana. It was packed tightly in a cellophane skin. He flung both into Samir's lap. Samir slipped the sketchpad back into his bag before he struck a match and cupped the flare to his face. The heat licked his eyelids.

'You look like shit,' Ali said.

Samir gave him a wry smile.

'What was up with you the other day, acting so serious?'

Samir ignored the question.

'What is this?' he asked, picking up the bag and smelling it. 'You got no weed?'

'This is a new grade, try it.'

Samir flicked the match, took several swift drags of his cigarette and sighed. He emptied the contents of his wallet onto his palm and held it out under Ali's nose. Ali picked out the twenty-pound note and the pound coins and stuffed the money into his pocket. He wasn't the type to own a wallet.

'The rest on credit?'

'I owe you another fiver,' replied Samir.

Ali thrust out his bristly chin and regarded Samir with shrewd eyes.

'Nine pounds, actually,' he said, jabbing his palm with all the emphasis of an exclamation mark.

'You sure?'

Ali ignored him and began humming to himself, drumming the guitar case as he paused to think. From the pensive expression on his face it seemed that he was ruminating on a profound matter.

'Bro, have you ever wondered how much the KFC Colonel looks like Rolf Harris?'

'What?'

'They're one and the same person.'

'No they're not.'

'Yes they are?'

'Obviously, they're two different people,' Samir said.

'Obviously, you're blind.'

'How can you be so sure?'

'I'll bet you a bargain bucket.'

'I hate fried chicken.'

'Too bad.'

'OK, for a bargain bucket,' Samir agreed.

'But you hate fried chicken.'

'Joker!'

A look of irony gleamed in Ali's eyes as he engaged in this light banter. Part English and part Moroccan, he was a light-skinned man with oily eyes and a hard, limber body – a perfect casing for the precarious lifestyle he had fallen prey to since hitchhiking to London with only a guitar on his back. Six years on, he was now privy to the street wisdom, the hook and crook, the back alleys, the ghettos, the street patois, the squat houses, the muggings, the fist-fights and the shankings. Over time, the sharp cut of his ethnic features had become marked with the battle scars of the homeless. But he was liberated, too, by the strange security of uncertainty, of having no fixed abode, of chance meetings and the frivolous banter with regular punters like Samir.

'Hey, on a serious note, were you threatening to turn me over to the scum last Friday?'

'Don't be an idiot!'

Ali held his gaze.

'I had stuff on my mind,' Samir conceded.

'Yeah, well, I'll let it go this time.'

Ali looked away and gazed abstractedly at the arm of the bench, at the damp wood gouged with people's names, and magic-marked with declarations of love, crude phallic impressions and a multitude of swearwords.

'I saw a big fat bee today,' he said, pulling a joint out from behind his ear. He rolled it between his fingers to iron out the creases and made sure the roach was still securely in place. Samir threw the box of matches back to Ali.

'There are no bees in November.'

'My point precisely.'

Ali lit up the joint and smoked it. He took it out of his mouth and studied the burning amber end with a look of intense glee.

'I was smoking a shisha on the Edgware Road when it came out. I think it must've crawled out of the cellar. Could've hitched a lift with some foodstuff. Well, it couldn't fly. I tell you, it couldn't lift a wing. It crawled along the floor like it was moving through treacle. I tell you, it was massive. A bunch of kids gathered around and kept prodding it.'

'So what?' Samir said.

'I had to get out my chair and stamp on the poor thing.'

Samir searched Ali's face for an explanation.

'Is this some sort of riddle?'

Ali smiled.

'It posed, whachyacall, a moral dilemma,' Ali said, shaking his head. 'Check this: if you were a bee in autumn with no flower in sight, not even a petal, wouldn't you ask to be put out your misery? I mean, your life's a bit of a nonsense.'

After several more lusty tokes Ali took his guitar out from its soft case. He traced his fingers along its neck and flipped its smooth hourglass figure onto his lap.

'I've been practising this piece for years,' Ali said. 'Still can't get it right.'

'You gonna serenade me?'

Ali smirked and braced the instrument under his chin. The tips of his fingers were calloused from the years of playing, the fingernails long, hard and stained in nicotine. When he rocked forwards to settle into his performance, he tilted his head and his beaded braids toppled over one side of his face. He looked like a male Medusa with a mane of rattlesnakes.

He played 'Twelve Etudes' – a piece by Brazilian composer Heitor Villa-Lobos. The chords were tight, shrill, crisp and muscular. The joint jutted from his mouth and, under the curl of his top lip, the edge of his gold tooth twinkled in the glow of a streetlamp. His long fingers glided over the strings like a spider spinning an intricate web. Behind closed eyes, Ali imagined a beautiful brunette dancing to his rendition in a red Flamenco dress.

As he played, a crumpled news sheet blew into the embankment and got caught up against the leg of the bench. The page splayed open to reveal a picture of a mighty aerial bombardment. Great plumes stretched like napalm over a mountainous region. The spectacle of war filled the spread.

Ali raised the tempo of his play. The notes climbed to a crescendo, but at the most difficult part his fingers tripped on a chord. His mastery collapsed and a deluge of bum notes followed.

'Bro, that was pretty impressive,' Samir said.

'Fucked up the ending.'

Ali swung the guitar back between his legs. He opened his eyes and picked up the newsprint. He turned it over in his hands.

'I saw on CNN, bro. They have this Mark 83 bomb, 2000lb of TNT. Drop that and you take out a whole village.'

'That's precision bombing for you,' Samir said.

'You wanna hear a joke?'

'Sure.'

'Why does no one watch TV in Afghanistan?'

Samir shrugged.

'Because of the *Tele-ban*.'

'Ba-boom.'

A thread of thick smoke curled from Ali's joint. Samir pursued it with his eyes and nostrils.

'You wanna blaze?' Ali asked.

'Since you've sparked.'

Ali passed the joint to Samir.

'What is it?' Samir asked.

'New batch.'

Raising the splif, Samir put it to his lips and held it for a few seconds. He sucked hard, drawing its magic into his lungs. Almost immediately a tingle started up in the back of his neck. The weight drained from his fingertips, his limbs and then his torso. He tilted his head back and closed his eyes. He let the feeling of weightlessness course through him, delighting in how it turned his body into something diaphanous, almost ethereal.

'Hear this,' Ali trilled. 'Soon any of you Muslim folk even go out and talk about your shit, see how long it takes before you hear the shriek of tyres and you're bundled into an unmarked van. And then there's the torture. Those fuckers yanking your toe nails out with pliers and shit like that!'

Samir opened his eyes and looked at Ali.

'What are you talking about?'

'I end up vexed when I hear this ignorance, man,' Ali said. 'I'm like whachya call part of the peace-marching brigade.'

'Peace-marching?'

'You get to know some decent folk on these marches. Some of them have IQ scores that go into the double hundreds. You know, the big uni types. The other week I met an ace couple, Julian and Alma. They invited me back to their yard for a smoke. They're squatting in this gutted building somewhere south of the river. We toked for hours. They told me about all the shit that's going down.'

'Oh yeah?'

'It hurts me, bro, that you're so blind to it.'

Ali embarked on a long, looping elaboration, studded with mini anecdotes, which dragged Samir into several tangents before returning him to the point. The more Samir heard, the more his face twisted in suspicion until finally he was forced to raise issue:

'Look, since when did you become interested in world affairs?'

'Eh?'

'Have the pigs been scoping you because of the thick Arabic stubble?'

'What's wrong widdya man? This spliff's mashed up your brain!' Ali said, snatching the joint back. 'Ain't you supposed to be a Muslim?'

"I'm no Muslim. I don't pray. I don't go to Friday prayers. I don't fast during Ramadan. I don't do any of that.'

'You were born a Muslim.'

'Come on, religion is a lifestyle choice, it's not something you absorb through the umbilical cord.'

Ali regarded Samir with a carping stare as he exhaled smoke from the side of his mouth. Briefly, he wondered what Julian and Alma would make of Samir's refusal to engage. They'd probably call him *obtuse*.

'So what are ya then?'

'Nothing. Certainly not a Muslim.'

'But your mum's a Muslim.'

'Yeah, sure, she's a proper believer,' Samir said. 'And she also thinks the devil and all its forms have found a home in me.'

'Sounds like you need an exorcism,' Ali said, passing back the joint. He pulled out another from behind his ear and lit it for himself. Samir was only too happy to find the joint in his hand again, now for him to keep.

'It's what my mother tells me,' Samir said.

'Harsh,' Ali replied.

'Hear this: According to her, on the Day of Judgment, under the Almighty's celestial glare, my ribs will open up and my heart will reveal itself for what it is: empty, cruel and loveless. I will then be cast aside, thrown into the pit of hellfire with all the white infidels where I will spend all eternity frying.'

'Sounds more like a snuff movie to me.'

The pair collapsed back and laughed and laughed, their laughter haunted by a melancholic madness.

'Oh, it's so tragic.' Ali suddenly said.

'What?'

'This hatred of your roots.' Ali snapped his fingers. 'That's it!'

'What?'

'You hate your own kind. They've got a name for you.'

'What's that?'

'A coconut! Brown on the outside, a honky underneath.'

Samir gave Ali a wry look.

'I get this kind of talk from my mother all the time.'

'You should listen to your mum more.'

'I'll be sure to give you the job when she dies.'

'Show a little respect, bro!'

'Speaks the model son!'

Ali sat back and inhaled the splif quietly, his cool rudely interrupted. Clearly, family was one thing he didn't want to be reminded of. He shifted uncomfortably in his seat.

'I told you this is really good shit, really,' he reiterated. 'And I'm giving it to you for a bargain price. Mates' rates.'

Samir manoeuvred a flake of tobacco to his lips and spat it out before putting the joint back in his mouth. He stopped and lowered the stick again, staring at the dry gash on Ali's lower lip, surprised by the ease with which he had pierced Ali's veneer of cool. Surprised by how thin the fictional garb was, like stretched chiffon, made up of smoky eyes and amusing anecdotes. He wondered what Ali might have become if fate had only dealt him a better hand.

'Hey, bro,' Samir said. 'I didn't mean to diss' you.'

Ali instantly perked up.

'Whatchya chattin' about? We're cool, bro. Anyway, my old dear's a loser.'

Ali used his thumb and forefinger to make an 'L' sign on his forehead. At that moment a skateboarder sped past and clipped him. Sparks flew from the joint in Ali's hand.

'Hey, watch it Tony Hawks,' Ali shouted, craning his neck so that the sinews tightened. The skateboarder twisted his head round and he retorted with the finger, brazen in the knowledge that his board was carting him to a safe distance – although, in truth, a couple of potheads posed an unlikely threat.

'You need a tough skin and know when to keep your mouth shut to survive in this game,' Ali said.

The pair sat back and watched the skateboarder leave a winding trail of dog shit as he disappeared into the night. They smiled at each other, delighted that the curl of crap had delivered the karmic retribution.

'I'm pretty lean,' Ali said.

Samir was high as well. His eyes were bloodshot and kind, his thoughts shapeless, liberated from worldly concerns. He regarded the joint with deep reverence as if all existence had coalesced into that tiny spot of amber – the sun around which his soul currently orbited.

'I do see the resemblance between Rolf and the Colonel,' Samir admitted.

The black sky was beginning to shift and warp under his gaze. 'But you're right. It isn't fun having people look at you like you're the Grim Reaper every time you board a bus or the tube.'

He grabbed the errant sheet of newspaper and began folding it into a paper aeroplane. He felt a sudden fascination with flight.

'What with this war and stuff my mum thinks it's the end of the world,' Samir said, scoring another fold. 'She thinks it's the final coming, and that somehow I've defected just because I don't buy into her vision of the truth.'

'That's heavy,' Ali said.

Samir thought for a while.

'I miss being at home.'

'What?'

'I've left home.'

There was a pause.

'Why don't you just go back?'

'I can't.'

'Why?'

'Because it would be like admitting defeat.'

Samir closed his eyes. He was hunched and quietly annoyed with himself.

'But the world's this big messed up place…' Lost for words, Samir looped a big fat zero around his ear with his index finger. 'It's a pretty messed up place,' he repeated.

Ali began drumming his guitar. He stopped and regarded Samir with a gummy stare.

'Brothers in arms, eh…'

Samir flung the paper aeroplane over his head. It looped up into the air and spiralled serenely to the ground.

'I do believe in God,' Ali announced. 'Sometimes he speaks to me in my sleep.'

'Does he speak to you out of a burning bush?'

'Ha, ha.'

'And what does he say to you?' Samir asked.

'That Ali ain't gonna be dealing forever. Ali's got places to get to. Got plans, plans so fly they got wings.'

'I'll blaze to that,' Samir said.

'What about your plans?' Ali asked. 'College is a good thing.'

'That ain't happening.'

'Tragic.'

'You've found God. Perhaps one day I'll get that message from someplace and everything will fall into place.'

'I'll blaze to that.'

Both men looked away. They stared at a boat bobbing in the canal. They listened to its deck creaking arthritically under the feet of its maverick dwellers. Above the naked branches of the dripping trees, the gibbous moon hung deathly white. Suddenly a firecracker exploded and mushroomed over the trees. It lit up the film of liquid red in their eyes.

'Just imagine if you were a rocket!' Ali mused. 'Blasting into the stars.'

Samir's face sagged into a sleepy smile.

'That would be magic,' he replied, at once considering the exciting and ephemeral life of a firecracker, taking to the skies and shooting off in all directions in a blaze of glory, as majestic as a bolt of lightning, or a star exploding in space – a single act alone encompassing life and death, cutting out all the ennui in between.

'It's better than being a bee in November, I suppose,' Samir added.

'Hell, yeah!'

'Don't suppose you got any uppers?' drawled Samir.

'You hate that stuff.'

'Work's been breathing down my neck. I need something to keep my head in fifth gear, or else I think I might get the boot.'

'Sure,' Ali replied. 'But they're really buzzy. They'll keep you awake all night.'

After leaving Ali in Camden, Samir made his way to Hampstead and walked through the heath for most of the evening, smoking and getting stoned. For a while he sat leaning against the barnacled trunk of an elm tree.

He took the block of marijuana out of the cellophane and rolled the entire stash into joints and put them neatly into his cigarette packet. He then took the college prospectus out of his rucksack, struck a match, set it alight and watched the glossy pages burn, the flame growing in strength, corkscrewing around the book and leaving it black and withered. The light that had soaked into his eyes changed his pupils to tiny pinpricks; they summed up the size of his passion now.

Doctor's orders

In the morning Amina phoned her boss to tell him she would be late getting into work. She posted the reply to her mother in the red pillar-box at the end of her street, then walked straight to the doctor's surgery to see Doctor Godwin. Morning visits didn't require an appointment.

The waiting room was filled with people sitting on a line of chairs that snaked all the way to a corridor and led eventually to the doctors' offices. Each time the buzzer sounded, the patient sitting closest to the corridor stood up and went through, leaving the rest to move up a place.

After registering her name with the secretary, Amina sat down on the seat at the back of the queue. From time to time she glanced at her fellow patients, scanning different parts of the room. A young man whose leg was in a plaster cast had a tabloid paper open on page three. Three seats away from the corridor, an elderly lady was staring stonily at the ceiling, rocking furiously and grunting at regular intervals, which everyone tried their best to ignore. Meanwhile, a couple of pre-schoolers were fighting in the toy corner. The boy refused to give up a truck he had found in the box while the other tugged at it with all his might and let out an ear-splitting screech, forcing both mothers to leap off their seats and settle the dispute by putting the truck back in the box, then dragging their respective children away, smiling sheepishly at their counterpart.

'Ah sister, I haven't seen you in a long time.'

Amina looked up sharply to see Mohan Das's mother looming over her. She was about the same age as Amina, but taller, rounder, more handsome. The woman was originally from Jessore in Bangladesh and had been living in the north London suburb for almost as long as Amina. Samir and Mohan had gone to the same primary school, though Mohan was four years older and, in contrast to Samir, had since realised every immigrant's aspiration for their offspring. Over the years all the mothers in the neighbourhood had been audience to his double degree, city job, the house in Hadley, the Dubai properties, the promotion, the educated bride – he epitomised the rags-to-riches story. The only snag was the rumour that the family had descended from the Dalits class – the untouchables – and because of this the few Bengali families in the locality frowned upon them. Even centuries on, Muslim Bengalis found it a struggle to shake off the prejudices of the caste system.

Mohan's mother was holding a prescription in her hand. Amina's attention darted from the woman's face to the slip of paper.

'What are you doing here?' Amina asked.

'I was just picking this up for my mother-in-law,' the woman said waving the piece of paper. 'She has awful pain in her knees. You know, old age and arthritis. She can't get about like she used to. How are you, sister?'

Amina held her throat and made a deliberate croaky noise.

'Stubborn *khashi*. Can't seem to shake it off.'

Mohan's mother looked at Amina sympathetically.

'Don't worry, a course of antibiotics will fix it *fottaafott*!'

Amina smiled. Her eyes stung of failed sleep.

'How is your son?'

'He's fine.'

'What is he doing now?' Amina asked, knowing how much Mohan's mother enjoyed waxing lyrical about Mohan's achievements.

'He's trying to do so many things at the moment. The boy never stops. Even his father, who has always encouraged him, is now telling him to take it easy.'

'It's the vigour of youth,' Amina said. 'Channelled properly it's a good thing.'

'Everything in moderation – isn't that true of life as well?'

'I hear you're expecting your first grandchild?'

'Yes, that's right. Mohan has called in the decorators to turn the spare room into a nursery, but he's hardly around to tell them what to do.'

'Where is he?' Amina asked.

'Moving around, setting up a new business, he says.'

'That's very impressive.'

Mohan's mother put a palm to her cheek in a show of distress.

'*Hai Allah*, he was in New York when the attacks took place. We were so worried for him. By Allah's grace he was returned to us safe and sound. Mohan told us how the government has set about rounding up young brown-skinned men who have Muslim names to interrogate them. He thinks they will use this opportunity to try to detain and deport as many as they can.'

'That's terrible,' Amina said.

'I know. Things aren't much better here,' Mohan's mother warned.

'They're not?'

'I was speaking to Mrs Shah, the woman who works in Asda. She told me that her cousin who lives up north was a victim of a racist attack last week. Some teenagers threw a brick through her window with a note tied to it that branded them "Terrorists"!'

A morbid pause settled between them.

'We're prisoners here,' Amina said. Her voice then found a more pensive tone.

'Our hopes have been perverted. We don't belong here. Our lives in Britain will never be important enough to matter.'

'It goes to show that you shouldn't bury your roots too deep in foreign soil. It's very important to keep that essential part of you rooted in the motherland. I think the experience in New York helped my Mohan understand what we've been trying to explain to him for years.'

A gallon of the greenest envy suddenly flooded Amina's chest. The double degree, the city job, the house in Hadley, the Dubai properties, the promotion, and the bride about to give birth to a beautiful baby did nothing to rouse that feeling, but hearing about a son who understood his mother made her heart covet for the same thing.

'*Subhan'Allah!*' she intoned.

Meanwhile, the pre-schoolers who'd been fighting earlier had wriggled themselves off their mother's laps and returned to the toy corner, both greedily eyeing up the truck, though this time they were willing to give sharing a go. Watching, Amina had a sudden flashback to the time she had brought Samir for his vaccinations. She remembered sitting him down in the same corner, his bottom bulging in a nappy, giving him some Lego bricks to play with. She had to keep scolding him for putting the bricks in his mouth. Amina nibbled her lip at the memory.

'You're very fortunate to have such a wise son.'

'How is your boy?' Mohan's mother asked.

'Good,' Amina replied.

Mohan's mother looked at Amina with tender eyes. She could see Amina had lost weight. But she hadn't coughed once. Intuition told her that Amina was suffering from something else, something perhaps more serious that she wasn't willing to admit. The skin beneath her eyes was puffy and her words had a heavy inflection, as if speaking was an effort.

'Are you sure everything's all right, sister?'

'Yes, *Appa*.' Amina said, smiling with wet eyes.

'Once you feel better you'll have to visit our house.'

'I will,' Amina said.

'I must be off.'

'*Khoda haffez*,' Amina said

'*Adhab*,' the woman replied, and Amina watched her leave the surgery.

When Amina stepped into the office, Doctor Godwin smiled and nodded an official but polite greeting. As always, his hair was neatly parted in the centre and his shirt beautifully ironed. Amina nodded back, a little embarrassed, a little apprehensive. She wondered what he might be thinking seeing her back so soon after her last visit. She cleared her throat and pawed her face self-consciously.

'Only five minutes, Doctor,' she said, softly.

'Please take a seat.'

Amina perched down on the patient's chair. The felt upholstery was worn thin, still warm from the previous occupant.

'How are you finding the medication?' he asked, his tone delicate and warm and courteous. The eyes behind his glasses were jade green, and bright with intelligence.

Amina's shook her head to indicate that the pills weren't having the desired effect.

'I see.'

'Everything the same.'

The doctor nodded and the corner of his mouth twitched, a familiar expression that meant: I have parried this complaint far too many times in my career.

'Well, it is far too early for you to notice any significant changes, but I'm sure you will begin to feel better soon. Is there any other problem?'

'No sleep, doctor.'

'I see.'

'Tired every time,' Amina added.

Although Doctor Godwin was fully aware of what he had recently prescribed for Amina, he called up her medical records on the computer screen as a matter of procedure and read the name and strength of the drug.

'One of the most common symptoms of depression is insomnia, as well as fatigue and a general malaise.'

'I not understanding, doctor.'

Doctor Godwin leant back in his chair in the manner of someone for whom experience had instilled in them a self-assured detachment.

'To anyone who comes here with sleeping problems I tell them the same thing: sleeping tablets are not the answer. They are no good for you. They can lead to greater problems further down the road, addiction even.'

'No sleep, no good.'

The doctor slipped his index finger behind his glasses and rubbed his eye. His specs moved up and down, appearing to nod, as if they were the only part of him that understood Amina's predicament. Amina flicked a glance at the doctor's table behind a half-drawn screen, the wall behind it a clinical white. The sight intensified the fatigue in her eyes.

'Have you given any thought to the counselling I suggested?' he asked.

Amina wasn't sure what the doctor was asking. She looked at him quizzically.

'Speaking to someone who is trained to listen to you, a person who will help you make sense of the circumstances that are making you unhappy?' he clarified as simply as he could.

'Talking?' Amina asked.

'Yes.'

'Little bit,' Amina replied.

'I think it will be good for you. I've sent a letter to the local authority enquiring about the availability of a Bengali-speaking counsellor. I'll have the secretary call you as soon as I hear back from them.'

Amina smiled. She liked the idea. She had the Bengali words to describe how Samir's absence was a wound in her heart, but no Bengali ears that would understand her feelings without passing any kind of obtuse judgment.

'Thank you,' she said.

'As far as this current problem is concerned, I'm really not that keen on the idea. No sleeping pills, I'm sorry.'

'Now I want tablet for sleep, doctor,' she pleaded. 'For two weeks, maximum, three weeks. I will be better. My work no good. The boss unhappy. I lose job.'

The doctor leant forward from his leather chair and calmed her by laying his finger on her hands, which were threaded together in supplication.

'It really is bothering you.'

'Big, big problem.'

The doctor put his index finger to his lips in deep thought. He drew a long breath, and then another. Amina sensed that he was on the point of concession.

'Please, doctor,' she said, almost wanting to clutch his hand and shake it to show her desperation.

'In two weeks I feel better from other tablet then I stop taking sleeping tablet. I promise, doctor.'

She felt like a little child imploring her father for sweets. She wanted to tell him that she was tired of the country, grateful to it for having given her a chance, but not at the expense of the price she now appeared to be paying. Doctor Godwin reached for his prescription pad and began scribbling his instructions to the pharmacist. His manner was statesmanlike.

'I'll prescribe you a 10-day course. You take one before bedtime. And while you're on them I advise that you find other ways to deal with the problem. There are many herbal alternatives. Perhaps take up some exercise. A change of attitude will improve your situation a lot. Doctor's orders, OK?'

Amina nodded compliantly and took possession of the valuable piece of paper, a little less dispirited. In spite of all the advice the doctor had given, she knew that none of those things would make an iota of a difference unless Samir returned to her.

A wraith in the night

Samir counted the housekeeping money for his mother and put the notes into a manila envelope. He folded the envelope in half and slipped it into his back pocket. He left the flat and darted down the stairwell but pulled up on the second-floor landing. He suddenly recalled the woman who'd been the sole witness to the unfortunate incident of car vandalism a few nights ago. Samir went up to the door and knocked on the frosted glass with three clean raps. He stood back and waited, staring down at his feet. Moments later the door yawned open and the woman with the owl-like countenance was standing in front of him.

'Yes?' she asked.

She appeared more striking up close than when he had seen her silhouette from a distance. Her brows and lips were lightly etched, but her bone structure was scalpel sharp so the face suffered no deficiency of expression. The v-neck top exposed a neck so sensuous that it appeared indecent in its paleness. She wore a beret and the dark curly locks, which stole from the sides, fell over her nape and intensified the whiteness of her skin. For several seconds he stood gawping at her, drawn in by her green eyes that glittered wetly.

'I live on the floor above,' he eventually said.

The woman narrowed her eyes.

'What do you want?'

Samir brushed back his fringe, searching for a suitable opening to broach the subject.

'Is there a problem?' the woman asked.

'What you may have seen last Friday night –'

Samir's face became flushed with anxiety.

'I didn't kick that stone deliberately at the car,' he spluttered.

'What are you talking about?'

There was a pause as they looked into each other's eyes.

'Sorry to have bothered you,' Samir said and then turned to leave.

'Hey, wait.'

Samir turned back around.

'I do remember you.'

'You do?'

'I recognise your fleece. I've seen you several times from the balcony but never up-close like this. So it took me a while –'

'The car belongs to my landlord,' he whispered.

'Your landlord?'

'Yes. I was just walking back from the pub and I saw a stone on the path and I kicked it. It was a stupid thing to do. I didn't mean to hit the car. It just happened. If my landlord finds out it's me, he'll probably throw me out.'

'You haven't fessed up to it?'

Samir shook his head.

The woman's mouth formed a small 'o' of comprehension.

'You'd better come inside,' she said.

'What for?'

The woman rocked forwards.

'It'll be just for a minute.'

Samir caught the tart smell of wine on her breath and although he said nothing, the tiniest quiver in his nostrils betrayed the thought. The woman rocked back and stumbled in a moment of drunken dizziness.

'Come on then,' she said, flailing her arms to restore her balance.

Samir went inside and she pushed the door shut behind him. She disappeared into one of the rooms leaving him standing in the hallway. Looking around, he sensed the place had a sullen quality about it, quite unlike the blithe manner of its resident. The narrow hallway was decorated in deep scarlet wallpaper above the dado rail. A gilt-edged mirror hung on the wall. In the corner was a cardboard box piled with personal items, including several vinyl records, a portable CD player and a silver-framed picture, still wearing the felt of dust of its previous home. He leant over to take a closer look, but quickly returned to the spot where the woman had left him. She reappeared with a lit cigarette in her hand.

'You don't mind if I smoke?'

'Go right ahead.'

'Shhh. My daughter's asleep. I moved in here recently.'

The woman took a draw of her cigarette. She tilted her head and considered Samir.

'What's your name?' she asked.

'Samir.'

'I'm Amber.'

There was a pause.

'Did you leave a big scratch on the car?' she asked.

'There is a scratch.'

Amber carefully set the glass down on the top of an empty bookcase.

'I moved in here recently,' she repeated. 'And I was wondering whether you could help me.'

'With what?'

Amber wrapped a finger around a stray curl that had slipped out of the beret and tugged it coquettishly.

'Can you get me some green?'

Samir frowned at the request.

'I smelt it on you as soon as I opened the door.'

Samir reached into his cigarette packet and pulled out four sticks. He held them out in the flat of his palm.

'Are you sure?' Amber asked.

'Take them.'

Samir suddenly froze when he noticed over Amber's shoulder a little girl in pyjamas, standing at the doorway of one of the rooms, holding a teddy bear and staring at him with her mother's eyes. Hard and incurious, they were fixed on him like poisoned arrows. A shadow of doubt instantly passed across his face. The little girl pursed her lips as if angered by his presence. Guilt shook into him a sense of responsibility. He remembered he had to see his mother and give her the housekeeping money.

'How much for them?' Amber asked, corralling the offering.

'What?'

'How much do you want?'

'Nothing,' Samir said, distractedly.

He turned and opened the door and, without saying another word, disappeared down the stairs like a wraith in the night.

Armour of faith

Amina returned home after the late shift at work. She left the small packet of sleeping pills on the kitchen table and dropped a carrier bag filled with bedcovers in the lounge under the sewing machine. The bedcovers required mending. The job was for Shiny Seams – the dry cleaners on the High Street that employed her to provide its customers with "clothing alterations, adjustments and repairs at competitive rates".

Amina unbuttoned her coat. She untied the knot beneath her chin and took off the green cashmere headscarf. She hung her coat in the small cloak-room under the stairs and left the scarf draped over the arm of the couch in the living room. She drew the curtains, closing the room off from the moon-light falling in the window.

She switched the television on and crashed into the familiar seat of her rocking chair, resting her elbows on the worn upholstery of the arms. She flung her head back and gave herself over to exhaustion, the muscles of her face relaxing into a serene and sleepy expression. Amina lifted her head a little and regarded the ceiling through the slits of her eyes. The ident of The Nine O'clock News danced as an opaque flash of lights on its bobbled surface. She fell back and closed her eyes again. The chair crooned as the bow rolled back and forth over the flattened carpet, her body succumbing to the spell of its movement. She listened to the newscast.

It was a bulletin on the War in Afghanistan. A news reporter was on board the USS Theodore Roosevelt somewhere off the coast of the Arabian Sea where he was speaking to a fighter pilot; he described it as an honour to de-fend the values of the Civilised World. Asked about his sortie, First Lieuten-ant Woodstock expressed relief at finally putting the years of training into a combat situation. The tone of his voice neither suggested a passion for his job nor contempt for his enemies. He simply confirmed to the reporter that his mission had 'come together like a finely oiled machine'. The only concession he made was a smile as he looked directly into the camera and saluted the viewers with the regulation 'V' sign. The news report then cut to an offshore army base where a battalion prepared for the ground offensive.

Amina rocked forwards and opened her eyes to see a fresh-faced Private Ramirez with a young man's nascent stubble. He was dressed in sand-coloured khaki, kissing a Polaroid picture of his girlfriend. In the picture she was cradling their swaddled newborn in the crook of her arm. He held the picture up to the camera and promised to come home soon, but emphasised that until that time the boys had a job to do:

'I love my country. And, as a soldier, it is my duty to fight for the freedom of my motherland to make sure we protect it for the future of our children.'

Amina pressed her big toe into the carpet to stop the rocking motion; the crooning stopped too. She lifted her head and sat up. The light of the television screen fell across her face and illuminated the worry lines at the corner of her mouth. Private Ramirez looked about as old as Samir: an olive-skinned boy about to fight a war so that he could feed and clothe his family.

A terrible thought came to her. With Samir now estranged from her, in years to come would her son's children or their children's children be lured into fighting a white man's war like Private Ramirez? Supposing they were to be swallowed up by its ethnology, its mores, its neon seductions, its divorce-rates and disco-lives; could they so easily slough off their brown skin and turn their back on every value that had passed through bloodlines? Lately, when she lay awake at night, she feared that on the Day of *Qayyamat*, Saufina would rise from the grave and point the finger accusingly at her, screaming at the top of her voice: *he went against his own kind because of you!* These were treacherous times and with Samir living elsewhere, anything was possible. Amina drew a hard breath and switched the television off. A black cloak of darkness left her momentarily sightless, and in that sightlessness all she could see was Saufina's angry face blaming her for everything.

The doorbell rang. Amina re-tied her headscarf and went to answer the ring. On the doorstep a toddler was holding up a plate using both hands. He was dressed in pyjamas but wore a thick toggle jacket over it. His mother stood behind him with her hands on his shoulders. She was eager-eyed; her heart was brimming with pride.

'Go on, Jake, just like Daddy told you.'

'Thank you very, very, very much for the... the...' Unable to remember the word, he turned to look at his mother.

'So-mo-sas, Jake,' his mother said, pausing after each syllable and then glancing at Amina for confirmation.

'So-mo-sas,' Jake repeated.

Amina knelt down, took the plate from the child and ruffled his soft, chestnut-coloured hair.

'Thank you.'

'They were delicious,' his mother added. 'The boys loved them and so did my husband. He said that they were a lot better than the ones they serve at our local Indian. He loves spicy food.'

'Very good,' Amina said, tickling the toddler's cheek, who was suddenly struck by a bout of shyness and turned away to bury his face in the pleats of his mother's skirt.

'Your voice sounds much better,' the neighbour said, gathering Jake and lifting him into her arms. The boy began twirling a lock of her dark hair around his forefinger.

Amina smiled.

'I now much better.'

'I'm sorry if I offended you the other evening,' the woman said.

Amina gave her a confused look.

'I might have spoken out of turn.'

'What you mean, out of turn?'

'About your son.'

'Not problem.'

'Well, if these *somosas* are anything to go by then I'm positive he'll keep coming back for his mother's delicious food.'

'He good boy. Only little bit bad. We argue. Then he go.'

The young woman smiled.

'I understand,' she said looking lovingly at her own child. 'It's difficult to stay mad at them for too long. He does come to see you?'

'Yes. He coming tonight.'

'See. Just be patient with him.'

Amina stood still for a moment, smiling at the thought, surprised by the white woman's empathy, what's more buoyed by her vote of confidence.

'*Insha'Allah*,' she said in a tender tone, glancing up lovingly at the night sky.

'Excuse me?' the woman enquired.

'God willing. Everything he knows.'

'Bless you,' the woman said.

'You very friendly,' Amina said.

'And you're very generous,' the woman replied. 'I'm Josie, by the way.'

'My name is Amina'.

'Ooh, it's getting colder by the day,' the woman said. 'I better get Jake back indoors before he catches a cold. Do come round if you ever feel like a cup of tea or a chat.'

Amina smiled at the offer, although she had no intention of stepping into a house where there was alcohol.

'Say goodbye, Jake,'

'Good-bye, good-bye, good-bye,' Jake repeated, this time without any help, his shyness a distant memory. He didn't wish to be carried back indoors, so wriggled out of his mother's grasp, and the pair walked back to the house hand in hand. Jake swivelled round to wave goodbye to Amina. Amina waved back and, watching, she thought that there was an absurd beauty in bringing up children that immediately absolved them of any wrong they could do as adults. She closed the door once the pair had gone inside, went to the kitchen and washed the plate thoroughly with washing-up liquid before leaving it to dry off on the rack. When she heard the *salaat* clock go off in her bedroom announcing the hour of prayer, she collected her new medication and whispered, '*Insha'Allah, Insha'Allah, Insha'Allah.*'

The key turned in the lock of the front door and Samir stepped into his mother's house. Unlit and deserted, the hallway seemed to look at him accusingly, as if holding him responsible for its beleaguered gloom.

In the lounge he saw his mother sitting on the prayer mat, lit dimly by the lamp on the coffee table. She looked ghostly in her white sari. A waterlily in a pool of darkness. She was reciting her Qur'an, which lay open on its lacquered wooden stand.

أَوْ كَظُلُمَٰتٍ فِى بَحْرٍ لُّجِّيٍّ يَغْشَىٰهُ مَوْجٌ مِّن فَوْقِهِۦ مَوْجٌ مِّن فَوْقِهِۦ سَحَابٌ ظُلُمَٰتٌ بَعْضُهَا فَوْقَ بَعْضٍ إِذَآ أَخْرَجَ يَدَهُۥ لَمْ يَكَدْ يَرَىٰهَا وَمَن لَّمْ يَجْعَلِ ٱللَّهُ لَهُۥ نُورًا فَمَا لَهُۥ مِن نُّورٍ ﴿٤٠﴾

Respectfully he waited, not wanting to distract or interrupt her, as he knew it would be sinful to do so. He listened to the recitation, her voice swelling in song. And, as he listened, he felt awed by the strength of her faith. Her eternal source of guidance. He waited for her to finish reading the passage, then before she turned the page he tried to draw her attention.

'*Amma.*'

His call was awkward. His lips quivered.

'*Amma.*' he repeated.

Amina glanced up, but carried on reading the next passage. She didn't reply at first but finished the *sura,* marked her page with the ribbon, closed the book and touched it gently to her forehead to draw its blessings.

'You're back!' she finally said, her voice sunny from worship. Samir sensed the hope in her words but said nothing. His silence was enough to imply that he would soon be off again.

'Are you hungry?' Amina asked.

Samir pulled his hood down. The hunger on her son's face was stark naked.

'There's fish curry left over from yesterday,' Amina said. 'And I've saved some *somosas* for you.'

'Fish curry's fine.'

'Do you want any chicken? I've cooked some *chana bhaji*, too.'

Samir's mouth watered.

'Anything will do.'

Samir sat at the table, peeled. His hooded top hung on the backrest. He washed his hand and dipped his fingers into the food and began eating with a wolfish frenzy, chewing open-mouthed, his lips smacking – the gratitude pure in the graceless, animal display. Amina, meanwhile, sat at the sewing machine mending the torn valances. Every so often her attention broke away from the task and fell on Samir, her eyes momentarily awash with vindication at the sight of her son reduced to a ravenous chick, hoping that the abrasiveness of the outside world had finally rubbed off that juvenile fantasy he had of 'finding himself' – whatever that meant.

She turned the wheel of the machine with a firm stroke and pressed down on the pedal. The burst from the jabbing needle filled the distance between them and perforated the tension. She looked up and noticed the haste with which her son was gobbling up the food.

'Watch out for the fish bones,' Amina warned.

'I'm fine,' he snapped without meaning to.

He was anything but OK, she thought. Wan and waiflike, it was hard to imagine how her son had been surviving alone. Away for only six weeks and the world had reduced him to this! It was as though a neglected animal had turned up on her doorstep – scruffy, shivering and gnawing at its limbs.

'Your *Nannijee* sent a letter,' Amina said.

'How is she?' Samir asked.

'She's good.'

A pause.

'She would like to see you again.'

Samir busied himself picking out fish bones. The one time he peered up he saw the needle flashing between her skilled fingers and the treadle see-sawing under her feet, but averted his stare the instant she looked up.

'Your cousin Rashid has set up his own taxi business now,' she said brightly.

'*Bala.*'

'Yes, he's doing well for himself. Your Uncle Kamal is looking for a bride for him.'

'*Bala.*'

'You boys are about the same age. He still remembers you.'

'*Bala.*'

There was a pause. Amina steeled herself.

'I was thinking, maybe we should fly back for a holiday this year. See your cousins, your uncle and aunt. Your *Nannijee* wants to see you too. Shall I read out her letter?'

'No, it's fine.'

'You do realise you're her first grandchild and that carries certain responsibilities. She isn't getting any younger.'

There was an insensitive lack of response, which seemed to imply that her son didn't care.

'Do you remember your *Nannijee?*'

'There are a lot of fish bones to pick out,' Samir said.

'You better be careful.'

Amina was used to the door slamming in her face. She tugged hard on the valance in her hand, wishing she could prise his mind open, step into his confused world and reorganise things with the zeal of a military coup.

'How about your Uncle Kamal?'

'What about him?'

'Do you have any memories of him?'

Samir shrugged. Sometimes her son's attitude was intolerable. Amina remembered the book Uncle Kamal had posted to her after a phone conversation several weeks ago in which he suggested that a more instructive approach might fare better than constantly berating him.

'Uncle Kamal's sent you something.'

Samir looked up in surprise.

'What?'

'It's a book. I have it here.'

Samir was secretly pleased and excited, hoping it was another gift from his father's bookshelf – anything that would bring him closer to learning something new about him. Amina picked up the small paperback. She got up and handed it to her son. He glanced at the orange-coloured cover: *The Bible, the Qur'an and Science.*

'Make sure you read it,' Amina said.

'I'll try,' he replied, noncommittally.

She continued to study her son, wondering why he was being so difficult.

'You need a haircut,' she said.

'I haven't had the time.'

'It's indecent to have hair hanging over your earlobes. You look like a ruffian.'

Samir applied a concentration to his eating that excluded his mother's voice altogether.

'When was the last time you prayed?'

'I don't know.'

'What about the six months we spent in Bangladesh? You were such a good boy back then. The *Maulana* taught you all the suras for praying five times a day. When was the last time you stepped inside a mosque? Don't you remember all the things the *Maulana* taught you?'

Samir said nothing.

'How's the curry?' she finally asked.

Samir murmured his appreciation.

'You are Bengali. You have a Bengali stomach – the traditional rice and curry appetite. I don't know what kind of food you are eating but you've lost a lot of weight. Look at your eyes. They're sinking into your skull.'

'Stop exaggerating, *Amma!*'

Amina gazed thoughtfully at her son.

'I made the mistake of raising you outside a Bengali community,' she said.

'Well I'm raised now, and there's no turning back time.'

'Did you know that when you were eleven, the Mithanis sold their shop to the current owner and moved away?'

'So?'

'The new owner took me aside and said he would understand if I wanted to leave, offering a small redundancy package, but was equally happy to keep me on.'

'Why are you telling me all this?'

'That's when I made the mistake,' Amina exclaimed. 'I should have taken the money and moved to a Bengali community, somewhere in Tower Hamlets, Coventry, Luton or Leicester. It's much friendlier in those neighbourhoods. You would have had a better schooling in your own culture.'

'Why didn't you do it, then!' Samir snapped.

'I didn't want to unsettle you.'

Amina turned away and pressed her foot down on the treadle once again. The truth was that she *had* been tempted to make the move, but also considered it a minefield for a young, single mother. For a mother who had no desire to be pressured into a second marriage and be exposed once more to the *banji* stigma. At the time she feared any proximity to the mealy-mouthed matriarchs in these Bengali communities. She knew how those know-it-all village wives would have eyed her as a golden ticket for some poor nephew back home – *hmmm, a husbandless young woman with a British Passport, the bridge between the continents!* They would have begun circling her like sharks, courting her with kindly words: *Poor beti, you can't be expected to bring up a child on your own. I have a nephew back home.* In fact, Amina counted herself fortunate to have avoided such predicaments by living in a white town. Up until the last few weeks she had been quite happy to tend to her small life as if it were a window box, watering her dreams – her son a lone plant growing all the while to provide the shade during the winter of her life.

'It's a bit hot,' Samir said, blowing his tongue.

Amina got up and went to the kitchen. She returned with a glass of water and put it on the table in front of him. A cough tickled her throat and she hacked, shielding her mouth with her forearm.

'What's wrong?' Samir asked.

'What do you care?'

'Are you taking anything for it?'

She refused to reply.

'I'll get you some cough syrup,' he said.

Samir went on with his food. In the silence the tension frosted around them until Amina could no longer ignore it.

'What do you intend to do with your future?' she asked.

'What?'

'Your future?'

'I don't know.'

'Meaning?'

'Meaning, I don't know.'

'You've got no direction. You're wasting your life. These are precious years. They will never return to you.'

'I'm thinking about becoming an art teacher,' Samir said.

'Out of all the things in the world, you keep coming back to that. How many times do I have to tell you that drawing images of beings created by the Almighty is *haraam* and forbidden to Muslim eyes as swine is to our mouths. Art has always been a vehicle to idolatry. Why can't you be a bit more like Mohan? '

'Who?'

'Mohan Das. I saw his mother today. Do you remember Mohan? He was a few years older than you at school.'

'What about him?'

'He's now opening his own business. He is also married and his wife is expecting their first child.'

'Good for him.'

'He was raised in this country too, but respects his parents' wishes. He's made a success of his life.'

'Not everyone is blessed with his planet-sized brain, *Amma*.'

'But you're clever too. Why do you have to be such an *awara?*'

Samir felt himself bridle.

'I have some money for you,' he said. He pulled out the manila-coloured envelope, extracted the sheaf of notes and placed them on the table.

'This should cover some of the rent.'

He did not stop to think how humiliating it appeared to her. But for Amina, the act cut much deeper. A scene flashed before her. It sent a chill through her as if history had sneaked in through the backdoor.

'Why are you doing this, *beta*?'

'Doing what?'

'All this!'

Samir slackened his grip on the folded notes and left them on the table. The fold splayed open revealing the Queen's royal smirk.

'Why don't you answer me?' his mother demanded.

Samir's face remained still, utterly composed.

'What's going through your head?' Amina asked.

'Nothing.'

Amina found her voice blistered by anger.

'I have brought you up since your birth on my own! With so much love. And this is how you repay me. Soon I'll turn old and what will you do, throw me into a hospice? Allah is my sole witness. He will see to it that you suffer by your own children.'

Samir clenched his jaw, knowing that the best way to calm his mother was to say nothing.

'It's not right what you are doing, leaving me the way that you have. You're living with a bunch of *kaffirs*, sharing in their sins, eating from the same plates that have touched the flesh of swine, drinking from cups that have held alcohol. These people are guiding you into darkness. You're not stupid, can't you see what's happening? We should never have come to this deplorable country. This is a nest of devilry from where Allah has been denied and forgotten, and where you've been brainwashed. I don't know what you're doing with your life. You're probably wandering the streets in stray groups, gangs and other troublemakers.'

In the ensuing lull, her breath heaved with rage and anguish.

'It's so stuffy in here. The room needs some fresh air,' Samir finally said.

He quickly left the table and pushed open one of the smaller windows, releasing the dry air. He breathed in the fresh consignment and gazed at the world outside his mother's emotional fortress. He wanted to return to his rented space; it appealed to him because it was remote, indifferent and far away from his mother and her oppressive regime of probity and emotional suffocation.

He sped to the kitchen, washed his hand at the sink and returned with the glow of renewed intention pumping through his body. He quietly slunk into his hooded top, but the rip of the zipper betrayed his intention to leave. His mother peered over her glasses.

'Where are you going?' she asked.

'I have to go.'

'Why do you *have* to go?'

'I have work tomorrow.'

Samir pulled his hood up.

'I really have to go,' he repeated.

Amina sneered in disgust.

'You don't know what you're doing and you don't know what you have become. When you look at a mirror you will never see a white face, don't you forget that!' She got up and shuffled about the drab room, collecting the empty glass and cupping up the stray grains of rice off the table. The money lay untouched. Stacked notes, the sides splaying open. Worthless.

'I'll be back in a few days. I'll even stay over,' Samir said. Guilt told the white lie. So as not to offend his mother, he picked up the book and stuffed it into the pocket of his fleece and left the house.

When Samir stepped outside the house and the rusty front gate refused to give, he gave it an angry kick, causing it to fly open. A shower of paint cascaded down exposing the rust underneath as the gate knocked uselessly against the bent catch, whining and wobbling. He was furious with himself. For while he had walked out of his mother's house, he could not walk out of her life, now stuck in a pathetic arrangement, rejecting her plea to return, but frequently sniffing his way back to her house for food and a dose of her suffocating love. Why couldn't he find the courage to completely tear down the Bengali dream his mother had tacked in front of his eyes instead of making these feeble perforations?

It took Samir several minutes to twist the metal catch back to something resembling its original shape. Afterwards he stood there for a moment. He looked up and saw the last light shining out of the window of his mother's bedroom. He dropped his head and skulked off down the dark band that was the street, only glancing back once to see that the light had gone out, his

119

mother now lying asleep in bed. She was safe. Little did he know that behind that brick and mortar his mother held on to his parting words as she slipped underneath the bed cover. The promise that he would return. A sign that Allah would help to guide her son back. She felt protected by her armour of faith. In the dark she recited a quick prayer – *Ayatul Kursi* – and afterwards, as the pills plied the sleep, briefly considered what devil could have got inside her son to suck his heart dry and leave it gnarled and pitted like the stone of a *boroi* fruit. For a while she sifted through his childhood to see where she might have gone wrong in raising him.

A hand span on the atlas

Things might have started to go wrong in the summer of 1984 – the year Samir went on holiday to Bangladesh for the first time in his life.

The excitement began on the final day of school term when the bell rang to announce the start of the summer holidays. Children spilled out of the classrooms, itching from the sweat and dust and playground grazes. They ran to their parents holding their paintings mounted on sugar paper and their end-of-year report. Amidst the pigtails, freckles, shrieks and squeals, there was Samir running towards his mother while squinting up at the bright summer sky. His satchel hung low off his shoulder and kept knocking against his rushing knees.

'*Amma*, look!' he said, pointing at the small speck of an aeroplane that was flying high over their heads. 'Tomorrow, we'll be on a plane!'

'Look where you're going!' Amina said, worried he would trip on the trailing shoelace leaping under the frenzy of his strides.

Blinded by the light, Samir furiously rubbed his eyes. Behind his eyelids he could only see an orange darkness in which the silhouette of the aeroplane floated by. For the last three weeks Samir had been counting down the days to his first holiday abroad, crossing off the dates on his bedroom calendar with a thick marker that he always held in his small palm like a javelin.

He knew everything about the country because his mother had been feeding him stories about their birthplace like morsels of an exotic treat. For the last six months she had got into the habit of sitting by his bed at night-time and recalling the memory of her beloved birthplace while pulling him close to her and running her hand through his hair.

'Our land is one of the most fertile in the whole world. Everything wholesome grows on it. During the rainy season the waters come down from the Himalayas and feed the soil its goodness. Afterwards, the farmers plough the fields and sow the seeds. The land is then bathed in sunshine and turns into lush green paddy fields. There are also the banana palms, bamboo orchards and mango trees that people plant around their houses. You actually see how the food grows. You don't just buy it from a supermarket. You get to witness Allah's bounty.'

Samir loved being taken on an imaginary safari through the mangrove swamps in the *Sundarban* region – home to the elusive Royal Bengal Tiger, a creature steeped in mystery and the shadowy figure in so many tales and fables. In these stories his mother talked about the intricate tapestry of coves along the coastline and mentioned the tigers that lived within that gnarled and secretive habitat, away from any human invasion. Samir was so enthralled by the tigers that he asked his teacher to help him look up the creature in the school library's copy of the *Encyclopaedia Britannica*. He drew a picture of it and earned a gold star for his impressive effort.

Once the tickets had been booked, his mother went to see Samir's teacher, Mrs Cunningham, and explained to her that she wished to remove Samir from school for six months so she could take him on his maiden trip to their homeland:

'Important teach my culture to my son', she stressed to the teacher.

Mrs Cunningham was unsure what the protocol was in this situation. She ushered mother and son into the headmaster's office where the adults resumed the discussion. Samir's eyes darted from face to face as the godlike adults decided his immediate future. Amina repeated her plea to the man sitting behind the desk. The headmaster scratched his balding head, careful that he did not disrupt the few strands that were combed long across his scalp. He tapped his index finger on his lips in deep thought.

'Of course,' he said with a solicitous air. 'I do understand how you feel, but I'm sure you realise that it will disrupt Samir's schooling here. Six months in a young boy's life is a long time. It will put pressure on him to catch up when he returns.'

'Eight years in England, eight years! Only six months in Bangladesh,' Amina countered. 'Bengali culture important education too.'

The headmaster drew a breath and ruminated on her case, stopping every so often to ask Amina questions and then nodding at the answers she gave, his stolid expression neither suggesting concession or disagreement. After consulting with Mrs Cunningham outside the office, he came back and asked Samir what he wanted.

'I want to go, I want to go, I want to go!' Samir repeated, jumping up and down on his toes.

The headmaster smiled at the boy. He granted his permission by signing the release form. When the dispensation finally came, Samir waltzed out of the office whooping and rejoicing, Amina following behind him with a gracious smile on her lips. That night he drew a picture of himself and his mother sitting on the nose of a jumbo jet. He gave it a face with eyes and a mouth. He also made up a short poem in his head and sang it to himself over and over again:

Mr Aeroplane high in the sky
flying to countries far and wide.
Over the green and over the blue,
Mr Aeroplane, I am flying with you.

At school he asked Mrs Cunningham to work out the distance from the small atlas he had pulled out of a shelf in the school library. He watched her trace the route by running her finger across the page. Her fingertip raced through Europe, Iran, Afghanistan, Pakistan, India, and finally stopped over Bangladesh, burying the country's breadth under the nail. She looked at the scale. About 5000 miles, she calculated in her head.

'That's really, really far,' Samir said.

'It's only a hand span on the atlas,' the teacher replied.

The flags of the world were listed at the back in alphabetical order. The Bangladeshi flag was a red disk on a deep green field. At home, when Samir shared this new morsel of knowledge with his mother, her face lit up with pride as she explained to him its symbolic meaning:

'The red disc represents the sun rising over our lush and fertile Bengal and also the blood of those who died fighting for the country's independence.'

'Like my *Abbu?*' Samir asked.

'Yes.'

Samir leapt off the chair and began marching around the room, swinging his arms.

'Hup two, three, four, hup two, three, four,' he chanted, kicking his knees up in soldierly fashion.

The next morning began serenely, with a clear sky that awaited the sun's rising. But for Samir the wait was over. As soon as dawn's first light slipped into his room through the gap in the curtain, his eyes popped open and he whipped off the warm duvet. He leapt out of bed like a cub. The first thing he did was mark off the final date on the calendar, leaving a row of crosses on the page. He pulled back the curtains and the white light of a new day flooded in.

His travel clothes were neatly folded on the chair: corduroy trousers, a stripy shirt and pair of black shoes made by Clarks. A red tie hung over the backrest. Samir put on the shirt and trousers and went into his mother's room, loosely holding the tie, its broad end trailing along the carpet.

'Aren't you dressed yet?' she asked, as she adjusted the pleats of her new silk sari. She looked pretty. Her lips were rouged and her eyes lined with kohl. She wore her jet-black hair in a chignon with a stone-studded hairclip. Samir held up the necktie and made a horrible face.

'What's wrong?'

'I don't want to wear this.'

Amina knelt down and took the tie from his hand. She slid it under her son's collar and tied it with a huge knot. She grabbed the silver hairbrush from the dresser table, clamped Samir's cheeks with the other hand and combed his hair to a side parting. She put the brush down and kissed him on the forehead.

'You look very handsome.'

Samir twisted his head from side to side, annoyed that the necktie he desperately wanted to leave behind had now become a permanent fixture for the journey.

'It's too tight around my neck,' he protested.

Amina held him by the shoulders and smiled.

'You're seeing your grandmother for the first time. You don't want her to think that her eldest grandson's a scruffy boy now, do you?'

'But I look like a bank worker,' Samir complained.

Amina laughed and ruffled his hair.

'What's wrong with looking like a bank worker?'

'I don't want to,' Samir whined.

'Aren't you excited about seeing your *Nannijee?*'

Samir nodded.

'When your Uncle comes to collect us from the airport, remember to pay your *salaam*,' she instructed. 'It's important to show respect.'

'But do I have to wear a – '

'You must make the best impression possible, *beta*.'

Samir relented. It was beyond him to figure out how wearing a tie made a good impression, other than making him look like a boring bank worker.

At the airport they checked in their luggage and went to the departure lounge. Walking through the wide aisle, Samir glanced at the passing mirrors and noticed that he was up to his mother's midriff in height. His gaze quickly shifted to the window display of the gift shop in the duty free section. Several Battle Beast action figures were arranged in war formation, the goodies and baddies facing off, just like in the cartoon. Samir stopped and tugged on his mother's forearm.

'*Amma*, look! They sell them here.'

Amina didn't look. She continued walking. Up ahead she saw a family draped in hand luggage and carrying their gifts in carrier bags, making their way to the departure gate: mother, father, son and daughter. They epitomised the 'nuclear' definition.

The sight pricked a thorn of doubt into their trip because, up until now, Amina hadn't paid much attention to a specific detail of their homecoming; that she would be returning as Samir's mother while her family knew her to be the aunt, and Samir her accidental inheritance. The thought that her mother and brother would remind her that she was lying to her son (as if she wasn't already aware) began to needle her. The thought that they might insist that Samir was old enough to be told the truth horrified her.

'*Amma?*' Samir called out.

'What?'

'Can I buy it for my birthday?'

'What?

'The Battle Beast figure.'

'Not now,' Amina replied.

'Pleeeaaase.'

'I said no.'

'But it's for my birthday.'

Amina threw Samir a shotgun look, dismayed to see him scraping his new shoes along the dusty carpet. He was doing his best to scuff up first impressions.

'Stop this *Shaitani* at once.'

'But I'm not – '

Amina tugged hard at her son's arm.

'I said just stop it!'

Samir dropped his shoulders and refused to move. He crossed his arms and stared stubbornly at the floor.

'What's the matter with you?' she asked. 'Why are you being so disobedient?'

'Why do you have to shout?'

'Because you're behaving like a spoilt little brat!'

'I only want a present for my birthday.'

By this point Amina had stopped listening. She grabbed her son by the wrist and dragged him to the departure lounge.

The departure lounge was crammed with passengers waiting to be called to the gate. Since moving to North London, Amina had never seen so many Bengali people packed into one room. But there they were: the Bengalis-cum-*Vilhayettis*, exiled by poverty, now returning with wealth and prestige, with extra meat on their torsos, fuller faces and fairer skin. The children who were going to their parents' homeland for the first time were squealing with excitement at the prospect of taking to the sky. Mesmerised by the flock of steel Boeings

126

parked outside, four little boys scampered towards the large windows and pressed their faces against the cold glass, leaving greasy smears on the surface.

Amina and Samir threaded themselves through the concourse and sat down opposite a set of identical triplets. The trio were dressed in matching *Jamawer* suits, their necklines draped in twenty-two carat jewellery which had earlier sent the metal detectors at security into a bleeping frenzy. Their portly mother stood by them like a sentinel, puckering and unpuckering her lips in the manner of a blowfish, extremely anxious that with all these Bengali eyes in the vicinity, someone might cast an evil one over her precious daughters.

'I expect they have bridegrooms waiting for them in Bangladesh,' Amina whispered to her son as she swept back his floppy fringe, feeling a little remorseful for snapping at him only moments ago. '*Insha'Allah*, one day we will return to Bangladesh to find a beautiful wife for you.'

Samir yanked his head away and sat glumly in the plastic seat. Both waited in silence for their flight to be announced. A proud mother and her sulking son.

The plane landed on the sunbaked runway of Sylhet Osmani Airport and Samir stepped out of the cabin door holding his mother's hand; the heat of the monsoon season hit him like a wall. The light was unnaturally bright, unlike anything Samir had ever seen in England. The air smelt of freshly tilled soil, damp and heavy in his nostrils. He noticed that the armpit of his mother's blouse was already stained from a sweat patch. His hand was clammy inside her grip, easy to slip out of. The pair followed the queue into the arrivals building, their best clothes now crimped and creased, their knees and ankles stiff from the ten-hour haul.

'Are you OK?' Amina asked.

Samir nodded. Amina took deep, revivifying breaths. The musk of the earth, the glow of the sun and the lushness of the trees were all familiar to her. She closed her eyes and delighted in the scent of home, thrilled by the spirit of intimacy it had evoked. As she stepped closer to the building, the thrill softened into an irrepressible joy, of warmth and wellbeing, the comfort of being able to nestle back into the bosom of her birthplace without the fear that the passing of time had taken it away from her.

'Come on, *beta,* let's collect our bags,' she said to Samir.

Chaos reigned inside the airport building. A curdled mixture of eagerness, fatigue, stress and urgency spun the male passengers into caricature: some, worried about the safety of their luggage – *sure, we love our homeland but let's not forget what a den of thieves it is!* – rushed to the baggage carousel; others set off on a palm-greasing mission and initiated furtive dialogues with airport officials to avoid paying duty on the electronic mod-cons packed into their obese suitcases. The women held on to their flustered little kids, a few of whom were beginning to sob, 'It's so hot!' 'I hate this place,' and 'I want to go home.'

Once Amina managed to extract her luggage from the surrounding bustle and bribery, she handed Samir one of the suitcases to wheel along the ground and took charge of the larger one. They made their way towards the exit. Amina saw the myriad faces waiting behind the dirty glass panel: the families who had come to collect their *Vilhayetti* relatives, all poised behind the barricades, high on tiptoes, ready to welcome their kin. And, as soon as the first group wheeled its trolley through the exit doors, they charged against the railing: *Can you see them? No, not yet. There they are. Where? Look there. Where? There!*

Amina made sure her son stayed close to her as they went through to the other side. The noise and clamour suddenly intensified, as families threw their arms around each other; the years of living apart became a springboard to a new level of love, with people cupping each other's faces, dabbing their eyes, and demonstrating their affection in all its raw and raucous splendour. Samir was a little unnerved by the effusive display and sidled closer to his mother.

He was a little disappointed, too, to find that the reality compared poorly to the amazing things his mother had told him about the place. The distempered walls of the building were scratchy, blistered and in heavy disrepair. The stench of urine drifting from the public toilet hit his nostrils hard and was acrid enough to put an instant knot in his bladder. From the seat of the aeroplane things had been so different. When Bangladesh first emerged through the clouds Samir had pressed his face against the porthole and watched through the lens of his mother's romantic stories. He saw a lush green, just like the backdrop of its flag.

Flat squares of land slid past underneath the wing of the aircraft. Sheets of water glistened over the paddy fields, the green introducing itself as the first sprigs of foliage, flourishing quickly into tropical forests; within them the many dots and scratches found the shape of civilisation, growing into tiny huts, modest buildings, arterial roads and smaller lanes.

Samir shuffled behind his mother, holding the straps of his rucksack as if it was a parachute or a safety harness. From somewhere, a dark-skinned coolie hustled his way through the lax security and snuck up to Amina.

'Sister, sister, sister,' he implored. 'Let me help you with your luggage.'

'Actually my brother's waiting outside.'

'I'll help you get to him.'

'Really, there's no need.'

'Please, let me, *didi.*'

The coolie wasn't to be denied. He possessed a desperate obstinacy – an obstinacy mastered by those condemned to poverty and afflicted by a hungry stomach. His dark arms were lithe from physical labour and his ribs were visible behind the half-buttoned shirt which hung off him like a rag. He grabbed the suitcases, one in each hand. Amina drew Samir closer to her.

'Come on *beta,* keep up.'

'Where are we going?'

'We're following the kind man. He'll take us to your uncle.'

Outside, the sun pierced through a cloud after a downpour had cleansed the air. It glowered at Samir with a light and heat that he'd never seen in England. Before Samir's eyes could take in the new landscape, though, a crowd of beggars rushed forward and shocked him with a naked display of poverty. Decaying lepers, their wounds weeping, held out coconut shells and rusty cans, pleading for money. Amputees edged closer on their crutches and reached out with dirty, cupped hands, offering up their stump for inspection. An old woman tugged at Samir's trousers with her bony fingers and repeated *Allah-r vasté.* Her pupils were fogged by cataracts and flies were feeding on the fringes of her eyelids. She mimed hunger by putting fingers to her mouth and rubbing her stomach.

'O *baba, Allah-r vasté, doya koro Allah-r vasté, Allah-r vasté,*' she pleaded again and again, lunging forward and stretching out her withering palm.

'*Amma!*' Samir yelped and nestled into his mother's sari. Eventually, Uncle Kamal muscled his way through the human detritus. He took the visitors under his arms and ushered them into the hired minibus that was parked several feet away. Meanwhile, the driver snatched the suitcases off the coolie who looked on helplessly at Amina. Amina searched her handbag for some loose change.

'Don't give him any money, *Appa!*' Uncle Kamal warned.

'Please,' the coolie begged. 'Show mercy in Allah's name.'

'Beat it!' Uncle Kamal snapped. '*Jao, jao,* there's nothing here for you.'

But the coolie stood his ground, hands threaded into a plea. Uncle Kamal rolled his eyes and tossed a fifty-*anna* piece at him. He ushered sister and nephew into the vehicle and pulled the metal door shut with a brutish clang. Safely inside, he let his anger spill over:

'What an actor! We are besieged by these filthy people,' he said as he took his seat. 'They snatch bags from you, walk four paces, drop everything and then demand to be paid in *pound* coins. As for the beggars, what an irritating lot they are! *Baap-re-baap,* they put their self-pity to your throat like a knife and more or less try to mug you!'

After he finished his rant, Kamal wiped his face with a handkerchief. It seemed to wipe away his anger because with avuncular joie-de-vivre he turned to Samir.

'How are you my dear nephew? Wow, the last time I held you, you were a tiny thing,' he said with a beaming smile on his face. 'I think you might have peed on me the first time I held you in my arms.'

'Go on,' Amina encouraged. 'It's your uncle, my brother.'

'*Assalamu-Alaikum,*' Samir said.

'For heaven's sake, *Appa,* take the boy's tie off,' Uncle Kamal said. 'He must be boiling underneath all that clobber.'

Samir needed no second invitation. He yanked the tie off and stuffed it into his trouser pocket before his mother could say anything.

The journey through the city crush was a bumpy affair. At each pothole Samir's bottom popped off the hot leather seat as the bus rattled its way through the dense and lawless traffic, lurching and braking, the gears grinding painfully up and down. When he peered out of the window he saw the swarm of rickshaws, the bullock carts, the street hawkers, the hundreds piled upon a battered old coach and hanging off the sides like ants on a biscuit crumb. At Keane Bridge, a corrosive black smoke billowed out of the exhaust pipe of a truck carrying a load of pots, pans and pitchers which were shackled together by thick twists of jute ropes. There were more beggars and lepers in various states of ruin, including a legless amputee lying on a skateboard, his bare back burning under the sun like a slab of meat left out to dry.

Past the town centre the traffic lessened. Several miles eastwards, the minibus turned down a dirt road and into the village, the vehicle lurching violently as the chassis navigated an axle-snapping ditch. A boy in shorts who was herding his goats watched from a distance.

When the minibus pulled up to the house, its people were already standing in the courtyard ready to ambush them with love. *Nannijee*, Uncle Kamal's wife, their two boys Rashid and Majid, and Shilpi – the young maidservant – made up the welcoming party. It was Amina who jumped out first and lost herself in the folds of family. Samir stepped out and watched from afar, clutching his rucksack, fearing that the huddle would be closing in on him next.

'Let me see my grandson,' *Nannijee* said.

Uncle Kamal placed a hand on the back of Samir's neck and steered him towards *Nannijee*. She pulled Samir towards her and hugged him, then held him at arms' length. She looked, blinked back the tears and roamed the young boy's face in search of Saufina. Whether the resemblance was there or not hardly mattered, for her vision was clouded by emotion, by nostalgia, by the knowledge that the cause of Saufina's final pain had really grown into a perfectly formed life. Staring into his heart-shaped face, all she could see was her eldest daughter's eyes staring back at her.

'So much like Saufina,' *Nannijee* said, tilting her head to the heavens.

Inwardly, Amina bristled at the baldness of the comment. She flexed her lips and addressed Samir immediately.

'Would you like something to drink, my son?'

Samir didn't say anything.

'How about some coconut water?' *Nannijee* asked.

Samir shook his head.

'Why not? Don't be shy in your own home.'

Samir wasn't shy. He just didn't want any coconut water. He wanted Coca-Cola.

'Fetch some *jilebbis* and *shingaras* for my grandson,' *Nannijee* said, looking over her shoulder.

'Where's that Shilpi gone, she's such a lazy *khamchor?*'

Young Rashid ventured to put a hand out. He tugged Samir's arm and offered a chequerboard grin. Majid, the three-year-old boy who was wedged between Rashid's legs, inspected Samir with shy, curious eyes. He was a skinny kid swallowed up by a t-shirt far too big for him and accursed with a perennially runny nose. Samir looked at Amina who smiled back as if to say, *it's OK, go with them.*

The boys took Samir by the hand and led him into a junk room at the far end of the house. They wanted him to themselves. The disused furniture piled to one side emitted a dark and musty odour. Rashid struggled to open the window which was swollen from humidity, but when it eventually rattled away from the frame, a rich blade of sunlight fell across the slats of a broken high bed. Dust motes tumbled inside the beam. An excited Rashid asked Samir to sit down.

'What's that?' Samir asked, pointing at the built-up enclosure in one corner.

'It's the rice godown,' Rashid replied, almost dismissively. He was eager to ask his own set of questions.

'What does being in an aeroplane feel like?'

'What?'

'Flying.'

'Flying?'

'Don't you understand Bengali?' Rashid asked, a little annoyed.

'I do,'

Rashid chuckled.

'What's wrong?'

'You sound funny.'

Majid, too young to join in but no less eager for the spotlight, crawled under the bed. He writhed through the bundles of jute and pulled out a birdcage. He held it up and wiped his snub nose with a quick swipe of his hand.

'*Mynah Pahki, Mynah Pahki, Allah koh, Allah koh,*' he squealed at the little black bird cowering inside, trying to make it say something. Rashid clipped the back of Majid's head.

'Go away and collect some crickets for the bird to eat.'

Majid bolted outside with the cage, his bare bum bouncing towards the task. When it was quiet again Rashid summoned to his lips the bit of English he'd been repeating all morning to himself:

'M-y nem ij Rashid end I em eeorr cuu-jon,' he said, pleased with his effort. 'My mum said we have to look after you because you're our special guest. Don't be shy. Whatever you want, anything you need, just ask me.'

'Can we go to the tea garden?' Samir asked.

'Not during the *barisha* season.'

'Why not?'

'It's muddy and full of leeches.'

'What are leeches?'

'They're ugly things that crawl up your leg, stick to your skin and become fat sucking on your blood.'

Above them a gecko cackled and moved swiftly across the godown wall, trying to escape the claw of a ginger tomcat perched on the ladder which was propped up against the wall. The gecko's tail fell to the floor where it thrashed about like a miniature bullwhip.

'Do you want to hold it?' Rashid asked, picking up the piece of flesh. It was still wriggling on his palm. Samir leapt back in fright. 'It's only a *tiktiki*'s tail. They fall away all the time if you touch them.'

'Noooooo!'

From the verandah, Samir heard his mother's call.

'Where are you, *beta*? I have some *shorbot* for you. It's homemade lemonade.'

'I have to go,' Samir said, and rushed to find his mother.

At night Samir lay sweltering in bed, staring up at the soft white mosquito net curving and swaying under the languorous whirr of the ceiling fan. The low voltage made the light bulb as weak as a candle flame and allowed him to gaze at the strange insects orbiting it incessantly, as if the world was a prison and freedom lay inside the glass shell. He was suspicious of the dark space outside the netting, convinced that this alien land was infested with the strangest creatures.

The magical world of Bangladesh as rendered by his mother had long since dropped off his imagination as completely as the tail of a *tiktiki*. Samir began to think of himself as an English boy and nothing of this foreign country made any sense to him. He yearned for England, his *home*, and knew how happy he would be to return to all the things he recognised, all the things he loved. His own room. His own bed. The after-school trips to the local sweetshop. Even Mrs Cunningham's spelling tests, which he hated because he was so bad at them. Samir pressed his head down on the sweat-sodden pillow and tried to think of home, ransacking his memory for the familiar sights and smells until jetlag freed him from the anxious longing and he fell asleep.

In the next room Amina was catching up on the lost years with her family. Mindful of her sleeping son, she spoke in a hushed voice and eventually broached her fear (which had caused her to snap at Samir in the airport).

'Please don't say anything to him about *Appa* and *Dula-bhai*.'

'But he has a right to know,' *Nannijee* insisted.

'Not now *Ammu*,' Amina pleaded.

'When, then?'

'Not now.'

'But it's not right.'

'Please, please!'

Amina extracted the agreement from her family not to say a word, threatening never to forgive them if they mentioned anything.

During the first couple of weeks Samir found himself tagging along with Rashid on many of his exploits. Rashid regularly played truant from school. He began sneaking back home to spend time with his cousin as soon as his father left for the fields. On the first day he stood outside Samir's bedroom door just after eight in the morning, scratching the wood like a cat wanting to be let in.

A nervous Samir put his ear to the door. The scratching stopped but was followed by wild banging.

'*Bhai*, are you in there?'

Samir opened the door.

'Aren't you supposed to be at school?'

Rashid's head was wrapped in a bandana, its corners knotted around the ears. He looked like a boy auditioning for the part of a pirate in *Peter Pan*.

'School-schmool,' Rashid replied, and snuck into the room holding a wooden box.

An earthen pot was tucked under his armpit with a muslin cloth covering its mouth.

'Won't you get into trouble?'

'You *vilhayetti* boys have no sense of adventure.'

'What will your teacher think?'

'The teacher won't even notice. There are a hundred of us packed in the classroom chanting the alphabet with a slate tablet on our laps.'

'What's that?' Samir asked pointing at the box.

Rashid flashed a look over his shoulder.

'Where's *Amma?*'

'She's gone to the bazaar.'

'Did she take Aunt Amina with her?'

Samir nodded.

'Why didn't you go?'

Samir shrugged. Rashid kicked the door shut with a backheeler. He set the box down on Samir's bed and opened it. He took out a wooden instrument. It was carved into a shape that resembled a capital 'Y'. A spike jutted out between the splayed arms. The arms were covered in something that resembled putty, but a lot stickier, with the consistency of a tree sap that could fossilise insects. It didn't look like an object a nine-year-old boy should be in possession of.

'What is that?' Samir asked.

'It's a *duang* trap.'

'What's it for?'

'Bird hunting. It belongs to *Abbu* so I have to be very careful.'

135

Rashid lifted a tiny corner of the cloth from the earthen pot and allowed Samir to steal a peek. Inside were hundreds of disorientated moths clambering over one another, fluttering their frail grey wings.

'That's the bait to lure the birds to land on the sticky *duang*. The feathers get caught, and then you pounce. Come, I'll show you.'

'Where are we going?'

Rashid pointed at the grilled window beyond which stood the lush, sleeping hill in the distance. Samir wasn't sure. He rubbed the back of his neck where the humidity had licked the skin.

'What about the leeches?' he asked.

Rashid looked around and saw the pair of wellies his Aunt Amina had unpacked the previous night.

'You can wear those.'

The pair climbed the hill armed with their trap and pot of moths. The most verdant foliage carpeted the incline, its hue so rich that were it not for the fact that Samir could reach out to touch each leaf and smell the fertile odours, he would have believed that the balls of his eyes had been swept by an artist's brush.

They spent the whole morning on the hill. Rashid set the trap while Samir watched, desperate to appropriate something of the task for himself. After setting the trap, the pair hid behind the foliage and watched the impaled moth batting its wings. hoping that its death throes would catch the eye of a passing bulbul, a coucal or a small buttonquail.

A few days later, Rashid made Samir a catapult using wood whittled from a branch, and a sling made from a piece of rubber he cut from a discarded bike tyre. Together they moulded hundreds of clay pellets, concentrating intensely, even to the exclusion of each other. Samir watched Rashid bake the pellets rock hard over the stove. They gathered their arsenal into a leather pouch, then used it to knock cans off the mossy wall that fenced off the old, dried-up well.

'Won't your dad hit you if he finds out you were skipping school?' Samir asked.

Rashid missed a can by a hair's breadth.

'*Sala!*' he cursed. 'Yeah, he'll beat me black and blue with his *chappal*. We have to be careful.'

He slung another pellet at the row of cans. The can took a glancing blow, began to rock but somehow won the battle against gravity and remained upright.

'You're lucky,' he said to Samir. 'You have no dad to hit you.'

There was a silence, an uncertainty about what had been said.

'What's the matter?' Rashid asked.

'I miss chocolate.'

'What's chocolate?'

'Chocolate tastes amazing. It's brown and comes in bars. It's sweet and melts in your mouth. You don't have anything like that here.'

Rashid's sympathy turned into annoyance.

'We do.'

'Where?'

'In town.'

'But not here in the village.'

'We have something much better.'

'Really?'

'Tamarind *Achar*. It's sweet and delicious and would beat the taste of your chocolate any day.'

Rashid dropped his catapult and grabbed his cousin's hand.

'Let's go.'

Led by Rashid, the pair took the muddy track through the undergrowth, clumped all the way to the next village and crept up to Rashid's uncle's house, where the chickens were clucking in the yard. His aunt's singing voice floated out from the backyard. She was busy rending rattan palm with slow, judicious tugs. The pair sneaked into the house to raid her heavy jar of *achar*. Despite her best efforts to keep it hidden Rashid always managed to find it. This time it was stowed inside her wooden cabinet. As an added precaution, she had slipped a padlock through the ringed handles. Rashid prised the lock open with a pair of scissors he had brought with him, anticipating his aunt's additional security measure.

'Are you sure about this?' Samir whispered.

'Yeah, relax.'

Rashid slowly yanked the cabinet door and took out the heavy jar. He unscrewed the lid and plunged his hand inside it. He was about to scoop out a pulp and reward Samir's outstretched palm when his aunt walked in and caught him literally red-handed. Her mouth popped open in shock.

'Why, you thieving little brat! Wait till I tell your father what sort of example you're setting your cousin!'

Rashid dropped the jar in fright. He made a grab for Samir's wrist and the pair bolted out of the door leaving it crashing against the wall. They laughed, high-fiving each other as they scuttled back down the muddy path with the sun's heat striking their bare arms and the backs of their legs.

It didn't take long for the boys to become comfortable in each other's company. In Samir, Rashid found a cousin to whom he could show off his madcap schemes. Samir, on the other hand, realised that beneath Rashid's mask of courtesy and good manners lived a devilish spirit that was forever drawn to mischief, and he positively revelled in the catalogue of capers he was made privy to. That evening Samir told his mother how happy he was to be in Bangladesh and to have a cousin like Rashid to play with.

'That's a lovely thing to say,' his mother said. 'He's like a brother to you, so it is in his blood to love and care about you.'

'*Amma*, he's so much fun. He's the best.'

Samir meant every word. Playing the silent accomplice to Rashid made him feel as though he had cut loose from the confines of his mother's strict upbringing in Britain, made easier by the fact that in Bangladesh his mother's eyes were not as stern or watchful. His enthusiasm was so ardent that it made Amina's heart feel warm and her eyes well up. She knelt down, held her son in a mother's embrace and kissed him on the brow.

'What else do you like about Bangladesh, *beta?*' she asked indulgently.

'Uncle Kamal lets me feed the chickens.

His mother smiled, wiping the glee from her eyes.

'And he gave me the seed of a *Boht* tree. We planted it by the pond so that when it grows big and tall, it'll shelter everyone who bathes in the water. Rashid said that he would teach me how to climb trees.'

Amina pursed her lips.

'Now you stay away from the *peepal* tree. Have you seen the hornet's nest in its bough? I've asked your Uncle Kamal to destroy it.'

Samir nodded.

'And is everyone nice to you?' she asked, almost as if she couldn't hear enough of her son's joyful experiences.

'Yes.'

'Do you see how much everyone loves you here?'

'Yes, *Amma.*'

Amina hugged her son once more.

'I am so happy that you are happy, *beta.*'

At supper she watched him eating with his right hand like a Bengali kid who had never stepped outside his homeland, and wondered whether she had denied him something intrinsic by choosing to raise him in Britain. The thought, though, ushered in a feeling of reassurance: the fact that he'd become comfortable with his surroundings so quickly gave rise to the wonderful belief that his Bengaliness was innate, and that it would stay with him forever.

One evening, when the family were around the dinner table, Amina told Samir that he would start having lessons in Islam.

'Maulana Shaab will arrive tomorrow morning to teach you and Rashid, so make sure you are washed clean. Uncle Kamal has bought you both prayer caps from the bazaar. He'll teach you how to purify your body according to the rules of the *wudu.*'

Samir was oblivious to the man who had earlier paid Amina a visit to offer his services as a private tutor, or that during the hard-sell he had invoked every punishment at Allah's disposal if Amina were to continue neglecting her son's spiritual education:

'It is the obligation of every Muslim parent to guide their children towards the light of Islam. Sister, this applies more so to your son since a Western upbringing has left him in spiritual darkness. Over there, you are living amongst the *kaffirs*, for whom material wealth is their religion. I do not need to tell you that Allah will punish you first, throw *you* in hellfire for keeping him on this path of ignorance.'

'And your fee?' Amina asked. 'Masud's father told me that it's five-hundred *taka* per month?'

The *Maulana* cleared his throat as if irked by the mention of money.

'Unfortunately, to make ourselves worthy enough to walk Allah's garden in the afterlife, we all have to live out this mortal life according to the established laws. Money isn't something I feel comfortable talking about, so I will only say that it's a small price for enlightenment.'

The next morning, Samir and Rashid were waiting at the table in the study, each wearing a prayer *topi* and a new *lungi*. The room, a building annexed to the main house, was surrounded on all four sides by a tall bamboo orchard, which gave it a natural canopy and a summerhouse charm. Their grandfather had had the quarters built a few years before his death which had served as his retreat once he had bequeathed the rice fields to Kamal.

Samir peered through the window grille and saw that the green culms outside were outstretched like talons against the summer sky. The rising sun slipped through their lithe grasp and into the room, falling on the row of books on the shelf, those homeless hardbacks *Nannajee* had salvaged nine years ago from the corner of a house robbed of its household. The bindings were frayed and creased, the pages inside an archive to Azad's markings and thumbprints.

Rashid took his *topi* off and spun it around his finger. He was loathe to remain passively seated. He was the sort of boy who could not sit still other than while out fishing or hunting for birds, and even then the energy was packed like a pressed spring, ready to leap at the slightest stir in the branches or tug on the line. He couldn't quell the worry that had been bothering him for some time.

'Bashir from school told me that he's really strict.'

Samir's eyes grew wide with worry.

'He hits too,' Rashid added.

Samir's eyes grew even wider.

'You'll be fine, though,' Rashid said as an afterthought.

'How?'

'You're a *vilhayetti* kid. You'll be treated differently, like a guest. Teachers generally use me as the whipping boy.'

'It's only because you don't go to your classes and fall behind,' Samir said.

'Studying isn't my thing,' Rashid explained. 'I'm more of an entertainer or a traveller. You never know, I might join the circus.'

'Same,' Samir said. 'Words on a page confuse me. I think I might be stupid.'

'Nah, a bit slow maybe, but not stupid.'

'Shut up!'

'Look at this.'

'What?'

Rashid spun the hat faster on his finger, launched it into the air and tried to catch it on his head. Samir copied him. Soon their hat-hurling turned into a competition, taking turns to see who managed to catch it the most times on their head, but frequently forced to leave their seats and retrieve the holy headgear from all parts of the room.

Completely absorbed, the pair didn't realise that their new teacher was standing at the doorway – a tall, stringy figure blocking the light, scratching his nose, waiting to be noticed. He scratched and waited, waited and scratched. Finally he spoke. His voice boomed thick with reproof.

'*Topis* are meant to be worn on the head and not to be made into the object of a silly game. This behaviour will make Allah unhappy, and the angel on your left side will be marking it down.'

The two boys slammed the hats over their heads and raised their hands in-to rigid *salaams*, like corporals greeting their sergeant major.

'*Assalamu Alaikum*,' they spluttered.

'*Wa-alaikum assalum arahmatullahi wa barrakatahu*,' the *Maulana* replied, using his liquid pronunciation to make a glorious announcement of his cre-dentials. He smelt the air like a stag; from his *kameez* he took out a small bottle of Attar and dabbed a drop behind each ear. A sweet, oily scent assailed Samir's nostrils.

'First lesson!' the *Maulana* said. 'Every time you *salaam* your elders you raise the right palm up to the chest, no higher.'

The *Maulana* sat down and slipped his feet out of his sandals. They dropped to the polished floor with a faint slap. Samir noticed the curly hairs on the knuckles of his toes as he picked up a foot and crossed it over the other knee.

'Now, tell me who's who,' the *Maulana* asked, tugging his goatee beard. The henna on his thumbnail was a deep scarlet, as if it had been dipped in blood. Rashid was the first to introduce himself.

'Of course, Kamal Bhai's son,' the *Maulana* said. He turned to Samir, holding his head at an intrigued tilt. 'And you are Samir, our guest from England, no?'

Samir nodded. The *Maulana*'s face spread into a grin so wide that Samir imagined a coat hanger had splayed open inside his mouth.

'You do speak Bengali?'

'Yes.'

'Can you recite any of the prayers?'

Samir shook his head.

'Well, in that case, we will begin at the beginning.'

The *Maulana* laid down the first pillar of Islam by reciting the declaration of faith, the *Shahadah*. The two boys repeated their *Maulana*'s fluid a cappella chant. *Bismillah ir Rahmanir rahim: Kalima Tayyib, La Ilaha illallahu Muhammad u rassulullah...*

From the start he harried them with demands for perfection.

'It's *Kalima Tayy-ib*, the emphasis is on the *yy*. Now, repeat again after me!' They repeated. He recited again. And they repeated. It only took two weeks for his tone to harden and his attitude to their mistakes to become less forgiving.

'No, no, no! Now listen carefully to how I pronounce the words...'

With daily lessons, by the end of the fourth week he expected the pair to have memorised the first twenty *suras* and to be able to recite any of them on demand. He expected flawless pronunciation and met the slightest stutter with a fish-eyed glare. The first sign of aggression came after six weeks. When he noticed some kind of infringement he reached for Rashid's ear and tweaked it hard.

'Ooooof!' Rashid hollered.

'Why are you staring out of the window?' the *Maulana* asked. 'Is the view so wonderful that it has tempted you away from learning Allah's *suras*?'

Rashid shook his head.

'Well?' the *Maulana* asked.

'It's nothing.'

'If that's the case then why aren't you concentrating on Allah's word?'

'I don't know.'

'Don't let me catch you staring out of the window again!'

After consulting the respective parents, to whom the *Maulana* advocated a more heavy-handed approach, he appeared one day with a cane by his side, convinced that stoking fear in his two pupils would inspire better learning.

'The boys know some of their *salaat* prayers. They have achieved *taqwa*, the first stage of communion with Allah, but not the second strand to proper understanding: the feeling and fearing of Allah's words.'

Later, when his glowering eyes could no longer emit the kind of threat the boys had earlier cowered to, the *Maulana*'s fingers automatically coiled around the stick; he picked it up and brought it to thwacking life, initially through the air, but then on the boys:

'Rashid, you've already forgotten what I taught you last week!'

'Um... um, mmm...'

'Hold out your hand!'

A quaking palm presented itself, though slightly cupped, the flesh of the palm ready to cushion the swat.

'Not like that. Open your fingers out properly.

Rashid uncurled his fingers. He looked away and scrunched his face.

On Samir's birthday the family showered him with attention to make up for the all the birthdays they had missed. They cooked him every kind of food they could think of: *aloo dum, shingara, akhni pulao*. They bought him a set of new clothes; they asked one of the neighbours who owned an autorickshaw to take him for a ride into town. Later in the afternoon, once the celebrations were over, Uncle Kamal snuck into Samir's room holding in his hand a frayed book, its cover stained and its pages dog-eared and moist from the humidity.

'My dear nephew, this is a present from your father,' he whispered.

Samir took the book and flicked through it, his eyes astonished not so much by the present but to whom it once belonged. Uncle Kamal felt a rush of warmth course through him as he watched his nephew eagerly turn the pages.

'It's in English,' Samir said in excitement.

'Yes, it is. It's a translation of Tagore's most famous work. Rabindranath Tagore is Bengal's most famous poet and painter. Your father loved Tagore. There are some photographs of his paintings at the back, too. You could say that Bengal's most famous export was something of an all-rounder.'

Samir quickly flicked to the back pages. There were pictures of rural land-scapes, but also roughly drawn human forms; some of the pictures were dark and haunting.

'Do you like it?' Uncle Kamal asked.

Samir nodded. He looked up.

'I'll take really good care of it.'

'I know you will.'

Uncle Kamal observed the boy turning the book in his hands, running his little fingers over the cover, realising for the first time that Azad was no more than an enigma in his nephew's life, at most a godly presence kept alive in his heart by a faith. He watched Samir raise the book to his nose and try to smell a fragment of history, somehow possess it. Uncle Kamal interrupted him.

'What are you doing, *beta?*'

Samir looked up from the gift in his hands.

'What was my father like?' he asked.

'He was a good man. He fought in the Independence War.'

'*Amma* said he was a soldier.'

'What else has your mother told you about him?'

Samir squinted in thought, tilted his head and touched his temple with the forefinger, as children who are asked a question often do.

'She doesn't say much. She goes quiet if I ask her too many questions.'

'Well, I hope you enjoy the stories.'

Uncle Kamal turned to leave. Samir summoned up the courage, reached out and tugged on his uncle's sleeve.

'Can you take me to my father's grave?' he asked.

Uncle Kamal hesitated at first. He knelt down and ruffled his nephew's hair.

'As long as you promise to keep it a secret.'

'I swear I will never ever tell anyone,' Samir said, pulling an imaginary zipper across his mouth.

Uncle Kamal took Samir on the back of his bike to show him the burial site on the holy grounds of *Shah'faraan* Mosque. Sitting on his haunches, Samir picked at the weeds on the grassy knoll and whispered secrets into the sun-braised soil. He asked his father to become his guardian angel and then sneaked a handful of earth into his pocket before they left.

By the end of November the rains had cleared and the sweaty air had dried to a cooler, lighter breeze. The sunshine no longer shone down with the same ferocious heat, the air had stopped sticking to the skin and fewer mosquitoes prowled the air during night time. The paddy fields, slushy green expanses during *Barisha* months, were now a golden colour and stippled with the scythed stubble of harvested grain. The gullies between the fields were visible once more, providing boundary markers for the village kids who gathered with bat and ball for a game of after-school cricket. The courtyard in front of the house was now dusty and cracked, with a section taken up by a huge truss of hay – winter feed gathered for the livestock. In the backyard the garden fruits were ripening: tomatoes, marrows and pumpkins basked in the sun and slowly acquired their adult colours.

Samir had climbed on the roof of the house and was gazing at the brightly coloured kites looping in the sky. The children on the foothills were battling for air supremacy using string they had coated in an abrasive lacquer called *manja*, and with which they tried to cut each other's threads in an act of sporting cruelty. He watched the kites gliding and looping, bearing right and then left; one would suddenly careen out of control and nose-dive to the ground, sending the pilot speeding off like a little terrier to retrieve the paper wreckage.

Samir spent more time alone now, mostly sitting on the flat portion of the roof that jutted out directly above the scullery. Other times he could be found sitting on the *ghat* of the pond, staring at its green water which on a cloudless day would gleam with a sequin of sunshine, the sky reflecting on its surface occasionally disrupted by the silver twist of a tail. He seemed mesmerised by the tiny *phutti* fish making their skittish advances on the morsels of food that lay on the mossy steps where Shilpi scrubbed the dirty dishes with ash. Usually he sat with the copy of Tagore's short stories, reading them as best he could, then turning to the pictures. He sometimes tried to copy one, after which he would stare thoughtfully at the sky and the pages would flutter in the breeze. The pet mynah bird, shunned by Majid after the novelty had worn off, had become his loyal companion.

On the roof, the bird pecked at the line of red ants hauling a dead spider back to their nest. It hopped and chirped, creating mayhem in the military operation under its claws. Samir was reading to himself. He paused when he heard grown-up voices come out of the scullery door below; they were the voices of his mother and aunt. Samir put the book down, picked up the bird and perched it on his shoulder. He crawled along the flat roof on his hands and knees and, when he reached the edge, lay on his stomach so that his head jutted over the edge. Below, he saw his mother bent over a wicker tray, basting tender pieces of jackfruit in mustard oil and leaving them to dry in the sun. The food was for Rashid's mother who had developed a taste for the pickled fruit early on in her pregnancy and was watching from the doorway, hands splayed over her pregnant belly. She regarded her sister-in-law with admiration.

'It must be tough for a woman to bring up a child in a foreign country.'

Amina smiled.

'Britain is a country where people of all races can generally get along because we can get by without mixing, because they don't mind what we do, as long as we don't bother them with it.'

'Really?'

'Yes.'

'So, it's just you and him?'

'Yes, I suppose so,' Amina said, glancing at her watch.

'Shilpi!' she called out to the maidservant. 'Where is that boy of mine? It's almost time for his lesson. The *Maulana* will be here soon.'

A bolt of dread shot through Samir's body. He stood up and propped the mynah bird back on his shoulder. He sidled along the roof's ledge and straddled over the pigeon coop, dodging the smatterings of bird dropping dotted around the wooden battery. On the other side he had a perfect view of the path leading up to the house. There was no one there yet. He prayed that the man wouldn't turn up.

But moments later, the mynah bird leapt off his shoulder and began flapping, excitedly: *Ashche, ashche, ashche*, it squawked, repeating an isolated human word it had recently picked up. Samir looked back to see that the *Maulana* had turned into the path and the sight made his flesh crawl. Samir ducked to keep his head out of view and crab-walked over the ledge to the back of the house again. He picked up a rusty nail and carved a very bad word on the tin roof and threw the nail as far as he could. He sat down cross-legged, his shoulders cast down in sadness.

'Samir,' his mother called to the space around her. 'Where are you?'

Samir wished he could crawl into the dove coop and stay there among the callow chicks until the *Maulana* went away. But he couldn't. To make matters worse, Rashid had stopped coming to lessons after the *Maulana* rescheduled tutorials to late mornings so that he could fit in his training to become a *Muezzin*. Rashid had hoodwinked Uncle Kamal into believing he had a newfound love for school. He claimed that he was no longer a backbencher but a top division student, always raising his hand to answer the teacher's questions, handing his homework in on time, scoring well in tests. He even left for school half an hour earlier, a turnaround that made him seem a model of punctuality. This sudden change in attitude and application pleased Uncle Kamal greatly:

'He can learn Islam at the local mosque with the other kids,' he had reassured his wife. 'He's a smart boy. Who knows, he might grow up to be a lawyer!'

Samir, however, had no such luck with his mother. She wanted him to absorb as much Islamic teaching as he could during their stay. She treated the *Maulana* with a cloying sycophancy and had labelled him a 'pillar of the community'. She was always keen to remind Samir that he was a man worthy of respect because he was one of Allah's servants.

'What are you doing up there?' Amina said, looking up and scowling from the sun shining in her eyes. 'Get down from there at once. *Maulana Shaab* is waiting for you in the annex. You know he doesn't like to be kept waiting.'

Samir hugged his knees and buried his head in his lap.

147

'What's the matter?'

'I don't want to go,' came the muffled reply.

'What?'

'It's too hard! I'm no good.'

'What kind of attitude is that? If you don't apply yourself, how can you expect to improve?'

'But he doesn't teach right. It's all wrong,' Samir said.

'Get down at once, Samir!' his mother ordered.

Samir climbed down. As soon as his feet touched the ground his mother raced up to him and grabbed him by the arm. She wrenched it in anger.

'Look at the state of you. You're so grubby. You'll need to wash yourself properly before you present yourself to *Maulana Shaab*.'

'*Amma*, please, I don't want to go. Don't make me,' he pleaded. '*Maulana Shaab*'s not nice to me. When I get things wrong – '

'Of course he'll punish you if you don't do as he says. Now stop being such a baby, wash yourself and get to your lesson. You do realise that I'm paying for them?'

'But he's bad man. He – '

Amina shook him in frustration. She could not understand why her son was being so obstinate.

'I don't want to hear another word. Now go!'

Samir dropped his head and headed into the house. He did the necessary ablutions and reported for duty. The *Maulana* occupied his usual chair. He was cracking his knuckles. The mynah bird tottered behind Samir and flew up on to its perch. Samir offered a hurried greeting as soon as he walked in with the Arabic alphabet book held tightly to his chest.

'*Wa-alaikum assalam*,' the *Maulana* replied. 'You can put the *Khai'da* back. Today, I want you to recite all the *Suras* for *Salaat*.'

Samir was a little relieved. He found learning Arabic the most difficult thing ever. It was even more difficult than learning English. The letters were so squiggly, with tiny dots that differentiated them. The fact that he wasn't taught the meaning of any of the words made it even more difficult. With English, once he came across a new word he memorised it by attaching an image to it. The other kids in his class never seemed to have the same problem he did. He loved listening to his teacher reading storybooks, but never put his hand up to read himself. But Arabic was a different thing altogether. It seemed to go through one ear and come out the other. When Samir returned empty-handed he sat on the seat furthest away from the *Maulana*.

'How am I supposed to hear anything from there?' the *Maulana* said.

Samir flicked a glance at the bamboo cane leaning against the wall. He shuffled his chair nearer and sandwiched his hands between his thighs, his eyes fixed on a spot on the table. Sweat was already beginning to gather between his palms. He began reciting the *Suras* immediately. He rocked back and forth to the rhythm of his chant; a hard film fell over his eyes and his voice turned robotic as though he had ordered his soul to temporarily shut down – fearful on some subconscious level that it would otherwise liquefy and collect in a shaming puddle by his feet.

He sang from memory, contained in a bubble of deep-set concentration. His eyes strayed every so often to the clock, to the leaden passage of time that always moved by degrees during these lessons. After he finished, the *Maulana* introduced Samir to a new, much longer *sura*. He went over it several times, reciting each verse for Samir and asking him to repeat it; he wanted Samir to memorise it. He warned Samir that he would be tested in a week's time, and expected no more than three mistakes otherwise there would be punishment.

And so the lesson ended. No mistakes. No telling off. No caning. Dread's shadow lifted off Samir's chest. He rose from his chair and re-knotted his *lungi*. He pushed his chair back and its legs growled against the floor. Just as he turned to leave, the *Maulana* called him back.

'Let me see your fingernails, Samir.'

Samir flashed his hands at the *Maulana* then crossed his arms tight over his chest.

'How am I supposed to see anything from there?' the *Maulana* said. 'Now come here please.'

Samir wanted to disobey, but he couldn't. The man's stare was too knowing, his authority too strong, the threat too big, the ritual well worn. His mother's words haunted him: *Never disobey the Maulana. You will make me look bad. Remember, the man is pillar of the community!*

Samir had no choice but to edge forward to receive the cane. He kept his arms crossed as he shuffled closer. Every cell of his body was pulling him back, but the consequences of disobeying moved him closer towards the man. The *Maulana* said nothing. He didn't comment on the nails. He didn't even look at them. They were of no interest to him. Instead, he grabbed Samir by the waist and pulled him onto his lap. Samir felt the breath leave his body.

'You're doing well. Granted, you might not have the most agile of minds, but if we keep going I'm sure we can get you graduated to the Qur'an eventually. And if we keep pushing, who knows, by Allah's grace, maybe one day you'll become a *hafeez*.'

The man smoothed his goatee. He leant back in his chair and flicked a furtive glance outside the window, where the sound of the fluttering bamboo leaves and birdsong emphasised the space in which they were the only two people present. Into the boy's hand he thrust a stick of sugarcane which he had taken out of his *kurta* pocket.

'Chew this. It's the nectar of the earth.'

As Samir put the stick in his mouth, he felt the *Maulana* lift his *lungi*, slide a hand underneath and begin squeezing his trembling flesh. He felt the strength of the man and tried to resist, but the man tugged at his armpit with a restrained aggression. Samir was too scared so he clenched his fists instead. He scrunched his eyes closed and gritted his teeth, knowing what to follow. He couldn't stop his legs shivering; his fingertips were as cold as ice and his forehead feverishly hot. And then began the pain between his tense thighs.

Samir's feet were suspended in mid-air, his toes curled into a series of question marks, groping the thin air which offered no help. He forced his living spirit out through his eyes, which turned to stone, flew through the air and rested on the framed picture on the wall. The residue of his boyish spirit waited for the *Maulana* to let go so that it could creep back and reconnect itself to his body. What was left in him recited a long forgotten poem.

Mr-Aero-plane-high-in-the-sky,
Fly-ing-to-coun-tries-far-and-wide.
Over-the-green-and-over-the-blue
Mr-Aero-plane-take-me-with-you.

The *Maulana* squashed his nose against the cold, goose-bumped nape of the boy's neck. Samir felt the man's rough face press against his skin. He heard the man muttering: *Ashche, ashche, ashche, ashche…* grunting, snarling, breathing heavily over his neck. His grip tightened on Samir, his breath quickened and his body shuddered. Then all at once his muscles slackened and he let go. He lifted the boy off his lap. There was a brief silence before the man spoke.

'Why do you always make me do that?' he said. For a split second he looked genuinely sorry. 'Now run along. And remember our chat. *Maulana Shaab* knows best. It's our little secret, right?'

Samir nodded compliantly; it wasn't difficult to gag a nine-year-old.

'If your penis hardens, it means you like it too,' the man had explained the first time, leaving the thought dangling hypnotically over Samir's eyes, knowing the boy's tongue would shrivel from the acrid taste of shared responsibility. Like many times before, Samir shuffled off to clean himself, hurting, feeling the sticky wetness running down his thigh, subdued by shame.

Out on the verandah on a cool January morning, Amina was teaching Shilpi how to loop a blanket stitch, just like Gladys had taught her all those years ago. Everyone else was at the clinic visiting Uncle Kamal's wife and her newborn. It was yet another boy. They had taken Samir along with them too.

The women were sitting on low stools with the morning sun kissing their necks. Shilpi was bent over the needlework, concentrating so hard that her eyes had disappeared behind the squint.

'This is very fiddly,' she said to Amina.

'Just keep practising. It will get easier,' Amina replied.

Shilpi stopped and looked up.

'*Nannijee* said that you earn money from doing this. Where do you work?'

'I work in a shop. A tailoring shop.'

'How did you get your job?'

'It's a long story.'

'Please tell me.'

151

Amina's eyes jolted back to the past.

'When I left with Samir eight years ago, I met a couple from the Gujarat in the airport lounge in India while waiting for my connecting flight. They were getting the same flight back to Britain.'

'Did they help you?'

Amina nodded.

'They were a gregarious couple – the Mithanis. During that flight they nattered incessantly in a mishmash of Gujarati and English, cooing over Samir and delighting at the way his legs thrashed whenever they tickled his little dome of a stomach. They wanted to know everything about me.'

'Why were they so interested?'

'I guess they were curious.'

Amina remembered asking herself the same question. How she had misconstrued their innocent curiosity as some kind of inquisition. How she had begun to wonder what they were thinking, sitting next to a woman with a baby, without a husband and no wedding ring on her finger. At that time, the last thing Amina had wanted was to invite their judgment, so she hastily began to manufacture the past, cutting and pasting the details to win over the couple. She posed as Azad's widow (the war martyr, not the alcoholic), and proclaimed Samir to be the remaining vestige of their marriage, her own flesh and blood.

'It was Allah's blessing that I met them,' Amina told Shilpi.

'Did they give you a job?'

'Yes, they were a generous couple. They were opening up a new business in North London and when I told them I was a trained seamstress, Mr Mithani's eyes lit up and he said that fate had brought us together. And that was it. I never went back to my first home in the north of England.'

'*Subhan'Allah!*' Shilpi exclaimed. 'And now you're permanently settled in England and you are independent.'

Amina nodded.

'You will come back to visit us again?' Shilpi asked.

'*Insha'Allah*, once Samir grows up Bangladesh will really be home for us and not just a holiday destination.' And she meant it. During the past six months Amina had felt her shoulders drop and her entire being sigh and sit down. It was a far cry from those routine-filled, mechanical and often isolating days in England where she would rise from bed at seven in the morning, take her son to school, go to work, collect Samir, cook in the evening, perform her five prayers, slip into bed at midnight, and then wake up the next morning to do it all again. England was no more than a means to an end. The provider of a council house and a job. A platform for mother and son to earn their pot of gold and return to Bangladesh, where her son could start a medical practice, an engineering firm or any other business; buy a tract of land, build a double-storey house, marry a beautiful bride (no shortage of girls for an eligible bachelor with wealth) and give her grandchildren she could play with.

Moreover, in Bangladesh, her son had learnt to speak better Bengali. He could pray in Arabic and his pronunciation was better than even the native Bengali kids who had been learning for years. He knew how to speak to elders, how to pay due respect to the white-bearded folk of the village. There was the family support too – of being attended to hand and foot by Shilpi, of having them always watch over Samir. *Nannijee* was there to offer guidance, Uncle Kamal played the male role model and his children had taken the place of siblings. The last six months had seen her mood soften and her smile broaden. It was utterly true, she thought: if a Bengali had money then there was no better place to live than in Bangladesh itself.

She was lost in thought when a man zoomed up to the courtyard on a motorbike. He parked it by the verandah under the overhang of the roof and removed his dark sunshades. The two women looked at each other. Neither knew who he was, and assumed he was one of Kamal's friends. Amina stood up and pulled the end of her sari over her head.

'Kamal isn't here right now.'

'I'm actually looking for Amina.'

'Yes? That's me,' Amina replied, confused.

'My name is Amjad. The sun above his head hid behind a passing cloud and the shade brought out the features of his face. Amina saw an uncanny familiarity that she wasn't willing to admit to herself.

'Amjad?' Amina queried.

'I am Azad's brother.'

The sun reappeared. Its glare lit up the troubled expression on Amina's face. Her first instinct was to turn, irritated, to Shilpi.

'What are you still doing sitting here staring at my face? Go and make some tea!'

Shilpi scurried off, a little aggrieved to be relegated to her maidservant status again.

Amina turned back to Amjad.

'Azad's brother?'

'Azad… your one-time brother-in-law,' Amjad said, a little offended.

'What can I do for you?' Amina asked. The question wasn't meant to be rude but came out icily. The man cleared his throat.

'I've come to see my nephew and take him to meet the family he's never seen.'

'My son is not here,' Amina replied, crossing her arms tight across her stomach.

'Of course, you're more than welcome to come with him,' Amjad said. 'Actually I insist that you do. You are part of the family.'

'My son is not here!'

'Your son?'

'Yes, *my son.*'

'*Acha?*' Amjad snapped, sarcastically.

'Legally he is my son and has been for the last nine years.'

There was an uncertain pause before Amjad spoke.

'What any law court might say still doesn't change the fact that he is not your son. You're his aunt, just like I am his uncle.'

'What are you trying to say?'

Amjad briefly broke eye contact. He slipped the shades into his breast pocket and then pressed his eyelids with his thumb and little finger.

'Please try to understand, sister. I'm his uncle. We're blood-related.'

'There is no relation!' Amina snapped back.

Amjad's mouth fell open, dumbstruck. He took a moment to compose himself before he spoke.

'I have a right to see my nephew and he has a right to see the family on his father's side, as well as his other cousins and his *Dadu-ma* – my mother. She's been desperate to see him ever since the news reached us.'

'He has no one else in this world apart from me.'

'Is that what you've told him?'

'Yes.'

'Then you've done him wrong.' Amjad took a deep breath and pressed his square-tipped fingers to the bridge of his nose. 'Look, it is common law that a son inherits his roots from his father. It doesn't matter which country you live in. What you are doing is wrong.'

'Wrong?' Amina spat the word out.

'It's wrong in every way.'

Amina fixed him with a clinical detachment.

'Aside from my family, your brother never had anyone else to turn to. He had severed all ties with you lot long before the war. I don't even know why you're here.'

Try as he might, Amjad had no words to refute this. For a moment he just stood on the spot with his finger raised. Eventually he spoke:

'It's so frustrating that you're not prepared to listen to a word I'm saying.'

He was right. Amina had stopped listening. All she could hear in her mind was the word 'wrong' which had taken on the violence of a bulldozer and threatened to destroy the very foundation on which she had rebuilt her life.

Old feelings welled up inside her. It turned to fright and fright took the form of fury when it emerged from her mouth: part muffle, part spit, part fear, part words, part hysteria.

'How dare you come here toting your high and mighty words, shoving your rights in my face, talking about roots! You tell me whose brother was an alcoholic? Whose brother couldn't face up to his responsibilities? Whose brother couldn't look after a wife? Whose family was nowhere to be seen nine years ago? And now you have the nerve to come here and shell out idle threats, you *Shaitaan*, you *haraami*. Get out of here, get out, go away, *get out of my sight!*'

Amjad, who had spent the past week rehearsing this tricky encounter and working on a dialogue parcelled in sensitivity, recoiled from the verbal bomb-blast. He stepped backwards fearing the reaction as much as the needle, shaking in Amina's hand. Her outburst had shocked him beyond all expectation. One of the behavioural protocols between in-laws was a mutual respect that would remain sacrosanct no matter how straitened relations ever became. But the effrontery he was now faced with verged on madness, especially when Amina resorted to the barrage of profanities. After seeing off the initial shock, Amjad stepped forward with his own parting shot.

'You have no right to speak to me like this. You may have succeeded in deceiving those around you, who may not speak of those bygone days, or who may have conveniently forgotten. But remember, you have denied a grandparent the pleasure of seeing her grandchild. You have done so by lying to him. Everything may be forgotten, except the lies. They go on and they grow. Your lie will live through the very boy you've lied to. You will suffer. Mark my words.'

He then turned and jumped back on his motorbike, kicking away the metal stand with a furious backheeler. The machine broke into angry life as he gunned the acceleration bar. He then rode off with a wheel-spin, leaving an ugly skidmark on the ground. Within seconds his presence receded to a mosquito whine in the distance. Amina stood rigid like a brittle rock face, watching fiercely, making sure the man didn't turn his motorbike back round. When Shilpi came out of scullery and asked what had happened and why the man left so abruptly, Amina calmly instructed her to take the kettle off the stove.

When the rest of the family returned from the hospital, Shilpi didn't waste a moment in pulling Amina's mother aside and telling her about the man who had earlier turned up and announced himself as Samir's uncle. Shilpi relayed the entire altercation almost verbatim, theatrically describing how Amina gave the poor man a tongue-lashing and drove him away without even offering him a glass of water.

Appaled by what she'd heard, *Nannijee* sought her daughter out. She found Amina at the back of the house, sitting alone on the *ghat* of the pond.

'I hear Samir's uncle came to see him.

Amina crossed her arms and ignored her mother.

'There was no reason to treat him so badly.'

The older woman came and sat down beside her daughter. She stroked her arm.

'Listen, Amina, what you did wasn't right. Whether you like it or not, they are a part of Samir's family. And, more importantly, you can't deny the boy the truth. Can't you see how much it's affecting you? What are you so frightened of? No one's going to take him away from you.

'*Amma*, you don't understand. You'll never understand!'

'How can I understand if you don't tell me?'

Amina looked away. Tears threatened her eyes.

'Tell me what you're so scared of?' her mother asked.

Amina uncrossed her arms and rested her head on her mother's shoulder.

'*Amma*, you weren't there when I found out I could never have children. You weren't there to see the look on his face. The disgust and hatred he felt for me. In the blink of an eye he suddenly thought nothing of me. He told me I was useless to him. It might have been different if it hadn't been for that mother of his who filled his ears with bile. She kept writing letters, horrible letters and made him stop loving me.'

'Oh, I'm so sorry,' her mother said squeezing her daughter closer to her.

'*Amma*, I yearned for the role of motherhood to come and save me. I prayed and prayed and prayed and prayed. But it never came. You know, I was dead inside when I returned to Bangladesh just before Samir's birth. And, as much as it pains me to say this, my sister's death brought me back to life. She left me the gift of motherhood and gave me a reason to live. *Appa* lives inside me because I carry her hopes inside me. We have a connection that only Allah understands. Samir is *our* child and I won't let anyone take him away from me. I won't let anyone fill his ears with bile and turn him against me. No. Never!'

Tears of resolve ran down Amina's cheek. *Nannijee* sat with her in silence.

That night, Amina lay beside her son and ran her hand through his jet-black hair. Under the light of a hurricane lamp, she tried to find some part of him that belonged to her. She looked for something in the nose, the eyes, the hands, the length of his fingers, even the arc of his nails – anything that could discredit the morning's allegations and keep the truth locked away.

Amina watched a small moth flutter around the flame on the verge of a pointless suicide. Love ached inside her every time she gazed at her son. His innocence fuelled the guilt she harboured for keeping him swaddled inside a lie.

In the gravity of the silence the morning's episode rang loud inside her head. Amjad's words went round in circles, his accusation sounding so loud that she feared the night outside to be listening to her thoughts. She drew comfort from the fact that Allah had kept Samir from witnessing the confrontation and, the more she thought about it, the more it seemed that some kind of divine intervention had taken place. It bolstered her belief that Samir was Allah's gift to her and he had ordained that their lives and futures, joys and sorrows would be forever intertwined.

Amina nestled up to her son. She pulled him close to her and held him tightly as if she couldn't possess him enough. Wracked by insecurity, she felt a compulsion to interrogate the future:

'Tell me, my darling, how much do you love me, your mother? If I die, how much will you cry?'

'*Amma*, what are you talking about?'

'Nothing, my *beta*. You go to sleep.'

She gave him a final hug before she snuck out of the mosquito net. At the doorway she heard him call her back in a faint whisper.

'*Amma?*'

'What is it, *beta?*'

'Whose picture is up on the wall?'

'Which wall?'

'The wall in the study room. Who are those two people you're in the photo with?'

Amina's mind had already been made up. She had decided to restore stability and deal with the threat posed to her world.

'It's my sister and her husband. Your aunt and uncle. They died many years ago.'

Her voice was galvanised; there was not even a hint of doubt.

'Now get some sleep, we have to confirm our return flights back to England first thing tomorrow morning.'

A sleepy smile appeared on Samir's face as he closed his eyes. The smile stayed with him for a while because he was returning to England, to his homeland.

Saving face

Upon awaking the next morning, Amina repeated to herself the promise Samir had made to her last night:

'I'll be back in a few days. I'll even stay over.'

She had slept a thin sleep, constantly flipping the pillow and wrestling with the blanket for much of the night. She found herself wide awake at five in the morning. When she did eventually manage to drop off, she was plunged into a fairground filled with lurid colour and lots of noise. She saw her son sitting on a giant Ferris wheel and being hauled up into the pearl-grey sky. His face was impassive under the hooded top, his eyes not so much looking at her but looking straight through her. With a crack of thunder and a rumble that made the dust on the earth shiver, the ground beneath her feet opened up and the scenery changed to a vast frothy, angry sea. Amina was flailing, clinging to pieces of floating timber and gasping from the brine lapping in her throat. She found herself sinking into the murky depths, the water ringing as it pressed against her ear. Eventually she kicked out, her body lurched from the effort and the fear frothing in her mouth was replaced by the sound of the clock ticking in her ear.

Amina sat up. The pillow was damp from her perspiration. She could not help interpreting her son's ascension in that steel contraption as some kind of bad omen. She stretched her eyes in an ocular yawn and massaged her temples with the heel of her hands. She was convinced that the air smelt of the seawater from her dream. She got up and made her bed; a faint tremor still lingered in her fingers. She opened the window to let the feeling out.

However, her fear changed to hope when she came downstairs and saw the money lying on the table. Her face lit up. In the light of a new day, those stacked notes with a fold in the middle were suddenly of utmost value to her.

Amina fingered the money affectionately. She picked up the sheaf like a bouquet and held it to her chest. She berated herself for having shouted at her son. In her crinkled copy of the *Hadith* she had read the sentence *'calm and patience is from Allah and haste is from Satan'* and she had marked it with a pen and had been repeating it on the prayer mat each night for the last six weeks.

She rolled the money neatly into her fist and went upstairs to her room. She tied the wad with an elastic band and tucked it away inside the top drawer of her dresser where it lay amongst other such bundles that Samir had delivered to her on a weekly basis.

Just after nine, shoes scraped the *coir* mat out on the porch. The doorbell then rang, followed by several sharp raps on the door. Amina didn't hear the sound over the loud drone of the vacuum cleaner. The phone started ringing. Amina turned off the machine and rushed to answer it.

'Samir, is that you?'

'Assalumu alaikum. Appa. It's Reena. We're standing outside your door.'

Amina let out a disappointed breath.

'Please give me a minute,' she replied. She put the phone down, wound in the power cord and wheeled the cleaner back into the cupboard under the staircase. She went to the door and peered into the eyehole. Reena and Rukhsana were leaning in, their bright faces stretched conical in the lens. Amina pulled the sari *achal* over her head. She opened the door, suddenly conscious of how heavy it felt, as if she were rolling a rock away from the mouth of a cave.

Reena immediately stepped forward. She was full of animation, like a travelling salesperson bursting into a rehearsed routine.

'Appa, we were just passing through after the school run. Thought we'd pop by to see how you are.'

'Do come inside,' Amina said, holding the door open.

The pair bustled into the hallway, fresh as flowers. Their buoyant smiles shook the house by its gloomy shoulders.

'Hope we're not intruding,' Reena said.

'No, of course not.'

Amina watched the yale lock slip into the catch with a soft thud. She turned round and addressed them with a forced air of perkiness.

'What a lovely surprise!'

Weeks had passed since she last bumped into Reena at the local Asda, where the woman had been pushing a loaded trolley through the cereal aisle with her kids at her side. On that day Reena managed to natter for over twenty minutes while her bored kids kept running around the aisle playing tag and irritating the other shoppers.

'Please, go through into the living room,' Amina said.

As they let themselves in, Amina slipped into the kitchen to put the kettle on. She quickly smelt the milk in the fridge. She glanced inside the biscuit jar which she pulled out of the back of the cupboard. She rubbed the betel leaves between her thumb and forefinger to assess their freshness. She made sure everything was presentable because failing to play the part of a perfect hostess was guaranteed to see ugly criticisms bubbling beneath the bustling bonhomie: *You know that Amina, she is such a konjuus. Yes, so tight. She doesn't know how to treat guests properly. Hai Allah, when she served tea it was served in a chipped cup, how thoughtless! Doesn't she know that drinking from a chipped cup shortens one's life?* Amina was convinced that these were the kind of cynical judgments that would travel around the locality as bubble-gum gossip, stuck to the roofs of their mouths.

Amina walked back into the room and dusted down the settee for her guests, who were being overly polite, waiting to be seated.

'Please,' Amina said.

Reena climbed out of her big coat. Underneath, she wore a claret *shelwar kameez* brocaded in a gold floral pattern. Thick twists of gold shackled her wrists. Her fingers were ringed with yet more gold.

'*Bala ni?*' Reena asked.

'How are you?' Rukhsana echoed.

'I'm fine. It's nice of you both to drop by,' Amina replied.

'We haven't seen you in a while,' Reena said.

'You'll have to stay for tea and biscuits.'

'Oh no, please, please, it won't be necessary,' Reena pleaded, customarily declining the first-time offer.

'None for me either,' Rukhsana said.

'I won't take no for an answer,' Amina insisted.

'We had a cup of tea before we left the house,' Reena persisted.

'In that case you shall have another.'

'We don't want to put you through all that trouble.'

'No trouble at all.'

'We haven't come here to drink your tea, but to see how you are,' Reena said, affectionately.

'Guests come to my house and I *don't* offer tea at the very least? What kind of person do you take me for?'

'Just a small cup, then,' Reena conceded.

'Yes, a small cup,' Rukhsana echoed, and made a *small* gesture, pinching the air as if she wanted hers served in a thimble.

'Please sit down, *Bahu-ma*,' Amina said to Rukhsana. 'Don't be so shy.' She took Rukhsana by the hand and guided her to the settee.

Wed eight months ago to one of Reena's British nephews, and only into her third month living in England, Rukhsana was a young woman who since arriving in Britain had reverted to behaving in the coy manner of a new bride. *'Keep your station, especially in the company of your Auntie Reena as she can be a bit of a stickler who doesn't take too kindly to a loose tongue,'* had been her mother-in-law's parting words at the airport as she heaped her blessing on Rukhsana. This meant exercising humility when offered tea and biscuits, or even a seat for that matter. And in keeping with these pretensions, she'd put on bridal airs with a renewed obsession, wearing the reddest saris, threading fresh flowers in her hair, decorating her hands in henna stencils. Each morning she even rubbed *Tibet Snow* cream in her face to give it that blanched, chalky look preferred by those accursed with a darker complexion.

'*Khala-amma*, we haven't seen you about for a while,' Rukhsana asked.

'Yes, we thought you'd gone back to Bangladesh for the winter,' Reena added.

'Oh no, no such luck,' Amina replied. 'I caught a slight cough as soon as the weather turned cold and have been staying indoors a lot.'

Reena indicated to Rukhsana to keep her coat on, a little worried what a cold snap could do to new arrivals. She was a little peeved too by the damp air in the room.

'It has turned a little colder lately,' she said, rubbing her hands.

'Yes, the season is changing,' Amina said.

'A bit of a shock for our *Bahu-ma*, this British weather,' Reena added.

'Yes, it's very important to acclimatise,' Amina said. 'We've all been through it. It can be really uncomfortable at first.'

'Oh my!' Reena said. 'When I arrived back in January '87, it was oh so, cold. They called it the big freeze. For the first two weeks I was too scared to step out of the house. Just the thought of going outside made my flesh shudder. I used to wear two pairs of tights under my sari.'

'The winters are getting milder, though,' Amina said.

'Yes, I suppose they are.'

For a while the trio traded small talk. Reena's gestures were grand, her words packed with flattery and punctuated with frequent blasts of laughter. Amina, who was still trying to shake off the woozy effects of the sleeping pills, had to concentrate hard to keep up with the conversation and respond as best she could. To her relief the kettle whistle went off in the kitchen.

'I think the water's boiling,' she said and excused herself.

The door slowly whined shut behind her. Reena sucked in her smile. She folded her arms and fixed Rukhsana with a serious face.

'Doesn't the woman look unwell?'

'I think so.'

'Her face looks withered. What do you think it could be?'

'What?'

'Her illness?'

Rukhsana shrugged.

'You don't suppose it's something, well, something… serious?'

'Like what?'

'I don't know. It could be anything.'

Reena steered her eyes across the room, narrowing her eyes on every piece of furniture and reading them like clues to the crisis. The pendulum of the clock on the mantelpiece swung from side to side. An electric heater warmed the room with its two bars of orange heat, although, clearly wasn't doing a good enough job. There was the old Singer sewing machine sitting nobly in the corner, its veneer cracked and the colour beneath gleaming like gunmetal. The patio door leading to a backyard looked out on to the garden where the lawn had grown wild from inattention and weeds had pushed through the cracks in the path. In the vegetable patch at the back, clods of earth lay in frosted hibernation, tilled like a shallow grave. Reena turned her nose up at the sight of this neglect. She drew her eyes back and smoothed out a crease in her shelwar.

'You know, Mohan Das's mother saw her at the doctor's only yesterday,' Reena said. 'She's always being spotted in the surgery.'

'*Acha!*' Rukhsana exclaimed, her eyes agape.

'It's completely understandable if you ask me.'

Teacups clinked in the kitchen. Reena turned and cocked her head back. She leant forward and spoke in a conspiratorial whisper.

'With no husband to speak of and a son who's not around much, things can't be too good. Living alone like this is unnatural. No one does it by choice. It certainly doesn't happen in the Bengali community.'

'Where is her son?' Rukhsana asked.

'He works away from home I've heard.'

'How old is he?'

Reena counted the years in her head.

'Twenty, twenty-two, twenty-three, maybe?'

'A grown man, then.'

'It's heartless though…' Reena said.

'What?'

'To leave a mother alone in a house. It's cold-blooded, if you ask me. It would never happen in Bangladesh. Well, certainly not from the parts we come from. Sons revere their mothers over there.'

Rukhsana's head bobbed up and down in agreement.

'What else can be expected from a fatherless boy?' Reena quipped.

'Surely he's old enough to be married?' Rukhsana asked, intrigue coaxing her out of her shy demeanour like a curious mouse. 'A lone mother can only benefit with a daughter-in-law about the house. A few grandchildren would bring a ray of sunshine back into the home. It would make all the difference.'

A knowing glint shone in Reena's eyes: a mute acknowledgment that Rukhsana's point had not gone overlooked. Reena, a renowned matchmaker in the community with a Midas touch for bringing families together, surely she could whirl her magic into this household.

'She's never mentioned anything to me,' Reena said.

It was Rukhsana's turn to cast her eyes about the room.

'You have to admit, she's very tidy,' she said.

'There's only so much mess a single person can make,' Reena fired back. She spotted a folded copy of the weekly *Potrika* newspaper on the shelf under the coffee table.

'That looks like Anwar Bhai?' she said, pointing at the mug shot on the cover.

'Who's Anwar Bhai?'

'*Hai Allah*, did I never tell you?'

'No.'

'You didn't hear?'

'No, what?'

'He comes from my husband's village. He's a middle-aged man who lived in Aldgate East.'

'What happened to him?'

'He went back to Bangladesh on holiday, leaving his wife and grown-up kids here and secretly married a woman half his age. A Bihari too.'

Rukhsana mouthed the word 'Bihari' as though it referred to an alien breed. She'd never seen one with her own eyes, and always thought of them as a race East Bengal should have sent across the border during the 1947 partition.

'That's not all,' Reena added. 'When he died last month, people said that his filthy corpse was spat out repeatedly by the earth, no matter how deep they buried it the next day. The rumour is that his first wife had cast a spell on him. She had used black magic to shorten his life.'

'It must be Allah's wrath as well,' Rukhsana added.

'Yes, that too.'

'What if Amina *Appa* is suffering because someone has done black magic on her?'

'Very possible, yes, very possible indeed,' Reena said. 'There are a lot of jealous people around. They cast their jealous spells in Bangladesh and sometimes post them as presents. The spells can be woven into the clothes they send. You can't be too careful these days. *Hai Allah*, even I have felt such evil! My entire body burned for months after I wore a sari my brother-in-law sent as an Eid present! He is very jealous of his brother, you see, and everything he has achieved in this country.'

'Oh Auntie, that's horrible.'

'Yes, *Bahu-ma*, you have to be careful. It wouldn't surprise me if someone's doing this to the poor woman just to get their hands on the golden ticket!'

'Golden ticket?'

'The red passport.'

'Red passport?'

'Her son.'

The tea tray knocked against the door as Amina returned with refreshments. Reena batted her palm in Rukhsana's face as if to fan away the gossip fug. They watched Amina place the tray on the coffee table, smiling at her in gratitude. Amina picked up the plate of biscuits and handed it round.

'Really, you shouldn't have.'

'Please take one.'

Reena picked up a custard cream and popped it into her mouth. She chewed open-mouthed.

'We're troubling you,' she said, through a spray of biscuit dust.

'No, not at all,' Amina replied. 'How are your children by the way?'

'They're very well.'

'Kukon's excelling at school, isn't he?' Rukhsana said.

'Kukon's my eldest,' Reena clarified.

'Is he a good student, then?' Amina asked.

'Yes, he has a sharp brain,' Reena replied, unable to contain the coo of pride, the roof of her mouth now plastered in the beige of biscuit mulch.

'He's a genius!' Reena added. 'On parents' evening we asked the teacher if she thought he was a good student and she said he was a pleasure to teach. His father asked if he was good enough for Ox-food, and the teacher said that he may well be good enough for Ox-food.'

'*Mash'allah*,' Amina said.

'It's important our children do well. Of course, we never had the opportunity,' Reena said. 'I am trying to make amends by having evening tuition twice a week, but it's difficult to learn a new language once you reach a certain age, the brain just isn't the same. How about you, *Appa*? You've been in this country longer than any of us?'

'Me?' Amina said.

'Yes, *Appa*.'

'Oh, I never had a chance to go to college, or anything like that. Once Samir started school he learnt English very quickly so there was no need for me to struggle on.'

'How is Samsur?' Reena asked.

'Good,' Amina replied. She did not bother to correct the mistake.

'Is he at work?' Reena asked.

'Yes.'

'Do remind me what he does?'

'Something in media,' Amina said, uncertainly.

Reena's ears pricked up in admiration.

'Is he earning good money?'

'I'm not sure.'

'Why, doesn't he tell you?'

'No, nothing like that.'

'What then?'

Amina tried to hide her ignorance with a white lie.

'It's a new job.'

Reena interpreted Amina's reluctance as an expression of modesty rather than a genuine ignorance. She sat back and sipped her tea, the cogs in her mind turning over the information. Media rang with the melody of success. She ran her tongue over the front of her teeth and looked thoughtfully at the sewing machine.

'Now that your son's earning good money, I guess you no longer have to do the sewing work?'

Amina remembered her dresser drawer stocked with the growing wads of valuable notes tied in elastic bands. In financial terms, she didn't need to work full-time; it wasn't hard for a lone middle-aged woman to eke out a living in Britain. Food bills were low, outgoings small. She hadn't been to Bangladesh in years. And while she might have been injured by the withdrawal of her son's presence, he did, as a point of duty, provide the money for her day-to-day needs.

'I only work to pass the time now,' she said, loyal to her son.

'He must be a very obedient boy,' Reena continued. 'What I mean is that it's hard enough for a normal Bengali family to keep children protected from English influences these days, but for you it must be harder.'

'Why harder?'

'Because you're living alone.'

'*Insha'Allah*, everything's fine.'

Between them grew a silence ringing with doubt.

'Still, it's not good for the soul, living alone like this,' Reena finally said.

The lips of Amina's smile tightened because the words 'living alone' had cut right through the façade. She wanted to put her hands over her mouth, hide the flush that had set fire to her cheeks, do anything to save face.

'Did you go to Saira's wedding?' she asked.

'Yes,' Reena said. 'I didn't see you there.'

'I couldn't make it,' Amina replied.

'Did you know Saira's already showing,' Reena said. 'Married only two months ago and a bump already pushing through the *shelwar*. Is it any wonder they rushed all the arrangements?'

'Really!' gasped Rukhsana.

'*Allah-tobah*, it's disgusting how our kids are falling prey to this wild culture,'

Reena shuddered at the thought of Anglo-Bengali youngsters engaging in pre-marital sex.

'It could be that the bump was something else?' Amina proposed. 'She never was all that thin, even as a young girl.'

'My eyes never deceive me.'

Saira's ignominy was all it took for Reena to begin picking at the Bengali community. Her claws dug into the parents whose children were becoming wayward and too westernised. She mentioned Mr Hamed, the kitchen porter working at her husband's restaurant, whose daughter ran off with a Jamaican man; Sonara's son who was spotted drunk leaning against the wall of the Elephant Inn pub; Mr Choudhury's nephew who was squandering all his wages on the horses and had no financial means to apply for a spousal visa to bring his wife over. In fact, her own life was the exemplar that underscored the failings of others; Reena herself was the sole repository of all that was upright and worthy in the Bengali community.

'It does seem that children born here don't have the same respect for family, or for the family name. All they care about is their independence.'

'There's not much one can do,' Amina conceded.

'Wrong, wrong. Absolutely wrong!' Reena snapped in outrage. 'There's everything one can do. It's all in the upbringing.'

'I know, but sometimes – '

'There is no sometimes!'

'It's never that straightforward, especially with all the influences around them. Mr Hamed couldn't do much about his daughter,' Amina said.

'*Ek jhate tin jhat, tare bole khom jhat!*' Reena hissed, resorting to an old adage: split one race into a mixed race, that's what they call a lesser race.

'But you can't keep them locked away for ever,' Amina said.

'That is just so defeatist, sister.'

Reena put her cup down and spoke about the way she was raising her children, keeping them in touch with their ancestral land. She mentioned the huge house that her husband had built in the *Uposhohar* area in Sylhet, where she took her children every summer so that they could spend quality time with the extended family, as well as the private tuition in the Bengali language that they were receiving. It sounded like a long-term military operation.

Meanwhile, Rukhsana studied Amina over the teacup tilted to her lips and wondered through the scrolling steam why the woman wore no jewellery apart from a couple of bangles on her wrists – even one of those was a copper band to relieve arthritic pain. She tried to imagine what fatal horror could have visited Amina's husband to warrant no gold stud in her nostril: a stroke, a heart attack, perhaps an aggressive cancer ate him from the inside. The woman did look incredibly bland wearing a sari the colour of a dishcloth – a sari barely fit for a maidservant. A spot of rouge on those cheeks would make a world of difference, she thought. There was no reason for the woman to look like this in Britain. When their eyes met, Rukhsana offered a sympathetic smile.

Amina started fidgeting in her seat because she had spotted a jagged tear in the upholstery and was desperately trying to conceal it from their view. She felt the prick of shame, realising the pair had probably seen it and made a disparaging remark while she was in the kitchen. She only had herself to blame, having clawed it open on the night Samir left. For a whole hour she had sat on it, digging her nails into the soft plastic until she found herself yanking out tufts of yellow foam like a demented surgeon. It was too late by the time she realised what she had done.

'Amina *Appa?*' Reena said, realising her rant had lost its audience. 'Can I ask you something?'

'Yes.'

'Forgive me for prying but how do you cope with your son living away?'

'It's hard, but you slowly adjust to these things.'

'Is that really possible?' Reena challenged.

'Well... I think so. It takes a lot of getting used to, but eventually it becomes easier.'

Amina didn't want to divulge too much in case all she did was whet their appetites with a juicy bit of tittle-tattle. She feared that Amina's tearaway son would then be relegated to the ranks of Mr Hamed's daughter, Sonara's son and Mr Choudhury's nephew. But Reena had tweaked a raw nerve too. Amina wanted to unload. She wanted to admit how she couldn't stop crying the night Samir left, and the fact that she was barely coping these days.

'It is hard, but jobs are difficult for young people to find these days,' Amina said.

Unconvinced eyes looked straight back at her, beams that shone a light through her chiffon-like subterfuge.

'The arrangement is only for a little while,' Amina added, softly, weakly, her voice clinging on to Samir's promise. Reena offered a condescending smile that acknowledged Amina's lack of confidence.

'Come on, *Appa*, surely you can't hide the truth from us. We can see that things aren't right. You look different, as if you're carrying a mountain of worry on your back. Tell me what's happening. There's no reason to be coy. Not with us.'

In her mind, Reena was clearing a space and waiting for the right moment to steer a proposition into the conversation.

Although Amina's son may be a bit wayward, he did have a job in media, a house to inherit and a British passport. Most relevant, he was a bachelor eligible for marriage. And Reena had a girl who sought all those technical requirements.

Her cousin's niece Shirin had been granted entry into the country for six months on a visitor's visa to see her ailing gran. Now five months on, the only way to secure indefinite residency was through a spousal visa, through playing the love-marriage card. The cousin came to Reena for help: *You must know someone suitable for our niece!* Reena immediately said yes and, unable to stop bragging, went on to elevate their hopes with gallant tales of her previous matchmaking successes.

Reena had been eyeing Amina's boy as a potential *damaad* for Shirin for some time now. She had even done some research and, through hearsay, found out that he was the son of a martyr: a *Shahid*. She didn't know which branch of caste he belonged to – equally important to Bengalis from Sylhet despite being incongruent with Islamic attitudes – but the wartime distinction certainly carried kudos points. She was keen for the girl to marry into the family. A family comprising only two people, with no relatives nearby to stick their noses in, dole out advice, express petty jealousies or, heaven forbid, suggest an unreasonable dowry. In fact, all things considered, a family of two could be easily absorbed into the bride's lot. Effectively, the bride's family would be gaining a son who they could then knock into shape. On all fronts it heralded a great acquisition for her cousin, clearly her best bet since in these situations it was usually the dark and the ugly or the dumb and disabled who shuffled forward. It was time for Reena to shift gears.

'*Appa*, don't misunderstand me but without a strong family presence in a boy's life it's inevitable that he will soon stray. Everyone knows how it's the respect for family that binds us Bengalis together. We look out for each other.'

'I know,' Amina said.

'We're like sisters,' Reena continued.

There was a pause.

'I can see what's going on here.'

Amina looked down and picked the arc of her fingernails. A peculiar change had come over her face. Reena's kindness had finally torn through the flimsy façade and she was forced to drop her gaze, sensing that if she maintained eye contact she would begin to cry.

'Are you all right?' Rukhsana asked.

'Yes,' Amina said quietly.

'Everything will be fine,' Reena said, leaning in to smooth back the stray lock of hair above Amina's temple.

'He won't listen to me,' Amina finally conceded. 'What am I supposed to do?' Reena edged closer. She hooked her arm around Amina, and kneaded the tension from her shoulders. Amina felt the rings digging into her back.

'Have you thought about getting him married off?' Reena asked.

Amina looked up.

'Marriage, how is that possible?'

'Easy. Very easy.'

Amina said nothing. She felt drawn in, gathered into Reena's confidence, into the comforting warmth of another human being. Reena's shawl draped Amina as if it were the cape of the cultural crusader.

'Even the wildest boys find maturity once they have a wife to take care of. It's a responsibility they subliminally crave,' Reena said.

'Do they?'

'Oh, of course!'

'Where am I supposed to find a bride?'

Reena tapped her cheek and pretended to think.

'I know a family who's looking for a bridegroom.'

'*Acha.*'

'Yes. The bride is my cousin's niece; she's a lovely girl. Beautiful, from a good stock, well-mannered, *doodher moto dola,*' Reena added to emphasise her fair skin. 'I think she will be perfect for your boy.'

Amina looked at Rukhsana whose protuberant eyes were in emphatic agreement with Reena. Still, a weak voice inside her head called for caution.

'But I'm not sure whether Samir would be prepared to listen.'

'Have faith in Allah,' Reena said. 'I've seen so many young boys come to their senses after marriage. It gives them a new focus.'

'Perhaps you are right.'

'Trust me. And anyway it can't hurt to try, can it?'

'No, I suppose not.'

'And you will have a *bahu* to look after you,' Rukhsana chimed in a sing-song.

'None of us are getting any younger,' Reena added. 'We all need to make provisions to be looked after when our skin starts to sag, the flesh starts to soften and the bones become weary. Is it OK if I quickly use your telephone?'

Amina nodded as she passed the handset to Reena. She sat back and listened to the conversation. She felt out of her depth listening to the woman with the high status, who was wiser and more assured of life, talking on the phone. She no longer saw the pair as adversaries, but as angels despatched by Allah in answer to her nightly prayers. Her heart filled with hope as her new allies unscrolled the future before her like a roadmap, showing her the route to guide Samir back from his straying path.

By the time the teacups were empty and the betel salver did the rounds, Reena had already set a date for the families to meet. The women smeared lime-paste on their betel leafs, sprinkled the sliced nut, added a slither of to-bacco leaf, rolled them up and popped them into their mouths in jubilant mood. Reena beamed at the prospect of playing matchmaker again. Rukhsana had found an occasion to try on a new sari. And Amina counselled herself silently against that timid voice in the back of her mind warning her that she was on a fool's gold rush. She rallied herself against it. Of course her son would listen. Of course he would. With Allah's guidance, he would finally come to his senses.

Piquancy of pain

S amir was sitting alone in his bedroom. Two days had passed since he had visited his mother and given her the housekeeping money as an act of duty, but somehow still managed to leave her angry and disappointed.

Samir adjusted his body in the pine chair so the armrest stopped digging into his ribs. His tailbone ached against its awkward geometry. His hair lay plastered down on one side and his eyes were weary with boredom. He rubbed his eyelids and tried once more to read the passage from the book his mother had given him:

> …there is, perhaps, no better illustration of the close links between Islam and science than the Prophet Muhammad's often-quoted statements:
>
> *"Seeking knowledge is compulsory on every Muslim."*
>
> *"wisdom is the lost property of the believer."*
>
> *"whoever follows a path seeking knowledge, Allah will make his path to paradise easy."*
>
> These statements and many others are veritable…

He stopped reading and looked at the room's bare walls. He let the book slip out of his hand; it fell onto his lap. As much as he wanted to understand its message, not a single word in the book spoke to him. For a start it was too hard to read and constantly reminded him of his difficulty with reading. He swatted the book away and watched it flutter through the air and end up face down on the floor. It lay on the carpet with its cover splayed open, like a dead bird.

Rain was falling lightly outside, tapping the windowpane like the pads of one's fingers. The guttering on the roof had developed a small crack and a slow drip spattered the windowsill at regular intervals.

Although past two in the morning, sleep was out of the question because of the noises that kept sneaking out of his landlord's bedroom – the clinking of champagne flutes and glassy giggles. His landlord was entertaining a girl who he had befriended at some corporate event: a fresh-faced starlet with slate-blue eyes, high cheekbones and a small upturned nose that gave her beauty an endearing aspect. They were flying to New York City the next morning. When Samir had returned to the flat after work, he had found the pair sprawled out on the leather couch, champagne happy. Samir was forced to engage in a minute of quick-fire small talk, enduring his landlord's silly one-liners, the subtext of which demanded that he made himself scarce. So he had slipped off into his room to read the book – the gift from Uncle Kamal that had travelled five thousand miles to find its reader – in a mission to force-feed him the truth.

Samir leant over to the bedside cabinet and yanked the bottom drawer open. He slid his hand inside to grab the vodka bottle. He held it up to his hungry eyes. It only contained a few drops. Samir threw the bottle into the wastebasket under the table. Seconds later, he lifted himself off the chair, bent down and picked up the book. He dusted it down with an apologetic deference and nestled it into the shelf amongst the others. Samir reached for his hooded fleece, but noticed that it had begun to drizzle heavily. Raindrops were slamming the windowpane and bursting into a fine spray, dispersing the streetlamps outside into minute globules of light on the glass. Samir slumped back in his chair.

With no booze or weed to provide the portal for disengagement, he could only look about him curiously, with the tense expression of a wild animal over which a trap had just fallen. His eyes fell on the bookshelf, to the book where he had once hidden the application form, the repository of his stupid ambition.

Being stuck in his room was like being forced to inhale his own spent breath carrying the stench of his deficiencies. Samir reached into the wastebasket and retrieved the bottle of vodka. He twisted the cap off and emptied the few drops inside him. He chucked the bottle back into the bin. He smoothed his cheeks down with both hands, kneading the anxiety beating beneath the skin, desperate to find the serenity to fall asleep.

Unable to do so, he got up and opened the window as wide as the mechanism allowed. The night sky spat on his arms and face. He lit a cigarette. The scratch of the matchstick sounded louder in the night, the sulphur smelt stronger, the flame appeared brighter. The match light wavered from side to side in his shaky hand as he flicked it out of the window, watching the tiny torch go out in mid-air. He leant out and took a lungful of smoke, and then another, his eyes homing in on the amber end that was becoming fiercer with each draw. And while the raindrops studded his forehead, the familiar duo of dread and desire appeared in the incendiary orbs of his eyes.

The little muscle in his jaw twitched when he took the cigarette from his mouth and pressed it into the underside of his forearm. The anxiety evaporated immediately and his eyes rolled back, emptied, like buoys that sprang from the deep after being snagged under a rock or ledge. He pressed harder until the butt twisted and the white shaft ruptured, spilling shreds of tobacco onto his arm. There was the smell of burning hair and skin. The ember went out with a corkscrew of smoke.

The act turned him into another person – a person who drew comfort in the singed flesh and who could no longer be hurt. It was the delicious piquancy of pain.

Samir flicked the cigarette from his fingers and closed the window. He sat on the bed, anaesthetised, having scolded his anxiety into temporary submission. And in the mesmerising beauty of its silence, he experienced a fleeting sensation of absolute contentment, an inner peace. With nothing else to feel aside from an even sting comparable to the sweetest flatline, a deep and delicious sleep came over him.

The strongest prevail

The bleat of his phone roused Samir with a start. The caller was his mother. She sounded unusually upbeat; it was a little disconcerting.

'Some relatives are visiting the house tomorrow evening. I'd like you to be here.'

Samir scrunched his eyes and wiped the sleep off them. His forearm brushed his cheek and he grimaced at the searing sensation. He cupped the site where he had stubbed out his delirium, but refused to look at the damaged skin. It was the doing of a person he felt remote from by day.

'What time is it?' he groaned, frog-throated.

'Quarter-to-nine,' his mother replied.

'I'm late for work!'

'Will you be here?'

'What for, and who are these relatives?'

'They're distant. You won't know them. They'd like to see you. Will you be here?'

'*Acha,*' he said, reluctantly.

'You promise?'

'What?'

'Please, just promise me you'll be here.'

'Yes, I promise.'

'Wear something nice, something smart for a change.'

'I'll speak to you later,' he said and ended the call.

Samir flung himself out of bed and rushed into the bathroom. He took out a medical kit tucked away at the back of the cabinet. After fumbling to prise open the plastic lid, he rubbed ointment on his forearm blowing gentle breaths on the wound before applying a dressing. He filled the basin, dunked his face into the cold water and felt the pores tighten and his eyelashes bunch up in this baptism into a new day.

An hour later Samir emerged out of the subway. The sky was an unflinching glare. He glowered at the heavens to rouse himself and ran the two-minute stretch from the tube station to the office building. At the entrance his reflection appeared severe in the coffee tint of its glass doors. While he searched for his pass, a pigeon touched down on to the pavement, flapping its wheezy wings before tilting its head and fixing him menacingly with a single eye.

Samir swiped the electronic key and pushed through, cursing the slow heavy hinges which, while lending a corporate gravitas to the doors, made them impossible to rush through. The receptionist in the lobby looked disapprovingly at his unkempt and grizzled appearance – her scarlet-coloured lips curled in a rebuff. The clock on the wall behind her had its hands splayed at ten minutes past ten. Samir grimaced at the sight; he hared up the stairs and into the office. Once safely at his desk, his worried eyes met Gannon's watchful ones.

'Where's Jill?' Samir asked.

'In the boardroom'

'In a meeting?'

'Sorting stuff.'

Samir continued to look questioningly at Gannon, thinking there was a snide air about him. Anything the man said sounded like a threat to Samir, couched in polite words. He was the sort of guy who Samir imagined had suffered a whole heap of bullying in the playground for being born with a lazy eye and, as consequence, had developed a bitter streak that he carried into adulthood. His position in the company provided a suitable environment in which to enact sublimated revenge on those bright-eyed, beautiful college graduates working as lowly researchers. Samir looked away and turned to Neville instead.

'What's going on?' he whispered.

'Don't know, Sam. Jill's been in the boardroom since I got in this morning.'

'You haven't heard anything?'

'No.'

Gannon's phone began to ring. He answered it. The conversation was brief and between responses he flicked a glance in Samir's direction. He put the phone down and looked at Samir:

'Jill would like to see you in the boardroom.'

The lid of Gannon's lazy eye sagged in a fixed half-wink, giving the odd impression that he wasn't being totally serious.

'Now?' Samir asked.

'Yes.'

In the boardroom Jill asked Samir to shut the door. The perspiration on his palm turned icy when he gripped the metal handle and pushed the tinted glass door into its frame. The door closed with a sharp clack. Samir sat down.

'How are you?' Jill asked. She was wearing a suit jacket with a silver butterfly brooch fastened to the lapel.

'Fine,' Samir said.

A rap on the door interrupted Jill. The HR secretary opened the door, popped her head inside and looked about curiously, peering over thick-rimmed spectacles that rode low on the narrow saddle of her nose.

'Hi, Jill.'

'Come in.'

Dressed in her customary trouser suit, and standing barely five foot on her five-inch heels, she clip-clopped in holding a clipboard in the crook of her arm. She handed Jill the sheaf of loose papers on top, nodded, smiled and clip-clopped out of the room, closing the door quietly behind her. Jill took her time. She slid the papers into her ring binder. She sipped tea from her mug and wiped the bottom before setting it down carefully on the glass table to avoid leaving a liquid ring. Beneath her pale skin, the delicate blue vein running through her temple pulsed when she clamped her teeth together to stifle a yawn.

'I'll get straight to the point' she began. 'The company is going through some large-scale streamlining. This means that the research department is being restructured.' She paused, drew another breath. She picked up her mug and then put it down again.

'I'm afraid the company cannot afford to renew your contract.'

There was a brief silence. Jill waited for a reaction from Samir, but nothing came.

'We've had to address individual performances,' Jill continued. She opened up her binder to a spreadsheet filled with figures. She spun it round to show Samir the evidence of his performance. His eyes were forced to trace the spreadsheet data. He only saw letters, columns and numbers, and his name languishing at the bottom. He noticed that she had written something at the foot of the tabulated figures. Her handwriting was like print, as precise as everything else about her.

'There's also been the issue of application,' Jill added, watching him scratch his brow with his chewed fingernail. 'I don't know what's going on in your life, but in the last couple of months your timekeeping's been poor. Your mind doesn't seem to be on the job. To be honest, you seem to me to be very much out of sorts.'

There followed another lull.

'Is there anything you'd like to ask?'

Samir looked over her shoulder at the open window and listened to the morning traffic thundering outside. He could make out a shopkeeper letting down the canvas awnings with a ruffle and slam. A gruff man's voice was hurling abuse at a delivery van for parking across a throughway, and the deliveryman was batting back the abuse with some choice words of his own. It all sounded like sweet bedlam, the incongruity as random and ordinary as life should be – un-cadenced, chaotic and yet perfectly balanced. It was an auditory maze he was suddenly keen to get lost inside. He revelled in the small consolation of never having to make another cold call again. Soon he would be evicted from this finely tuned corporate machine where his worth as a cogwheel had been ground into apathy. When he looked back at Jill, he saw in her face order and structure, focus and reason. There was nothing to ask but to accept the inevitable with a quiet dignity.

'No questions then?'

Samir kneaded his forehead in a thoughtful gesture, the sweat and oils coming off onto the swirls of his fingerprints. He opened his mouth, but merely held still in a foolish state of inarticulacy. What was there to ask? If the truth be told, he should have been sent packing weeks ago. Ever since he left his mother's house, he had come away with guilt strapped to him like a bomb. Small detonations were taking place all the time, dislodging chips of his resolve. The larger cracks had now begun to appear. His job had long fallen down the list of priorities. In the last few weeks he'd been sitting at his desk, going through the motions, waiting to be shown the door.

Samir directed his attention to the framed print in the room, a picture of a lone figure atop a mountain peak with his arms aloft. He'd been needled by the soulless, supercilious print ever since he had first stepped foot inside the room. He'd been exposed to it for so long that even the slogan underneath gave him no reading problems: *Only the strongest prevail.* Cheap boardroom bromide. The kind of thing the ones with power tell young men before packing them off to war. The sentiment acted like an earthing rod on Samir, safely conducted the embarrassing propulsion of tears pushing against his eyeballs.

'Did you hear what I said?' asked Jill.

Samir looked at Jill once more. His lips barely moved when he said:

'I have no questions.'

Jill pulled out a clean, freshly printed missive with the header: *Private and confidential.* Samir could smell the toner ink as she slid it across the table. Jill finally parted her slender lips and said, 'I'm sorry,' in a voice that for the first time broke with sympathy.

Broken Path

There is a Bengali proverb alluding to a nocturnal demon and repeated to children who are misbehaving at night that goes: *Dhiner hashi kushi-bashi, ratker hashi golaai pasha!* Roughly translated, this means: *Daytime laughter brings lots of fun, night-time laughter gets the neck wrung!* The fit of giggles Amina suffered when Reena had offered some cooking advice down the phone could have been censured with that proverb. Certainly, if her mother were about she would have rebuked Amina for being so frivolous. Nevertheless, even hours later, whenever Amina remembered Reena's words, she couldn't stop chuckling to herself.

After two hours of chopping, mixing, stuffing and stirring, she was standing over the cooker, wearing a pinafore now stained with streaks of turmeric and paprika. Her hair was tied back in a bun. Her face glazed in sweat. The dishes were almost cooked. She squeezed the basmati grain of the mutton pulao. It flattened like dough between her fingers. Satisfied, she put the dish in the oven to bake out the residual moisture. The vegetable *koftas* were already in a Tupperware container, as were the *Sondesh* and *Pitha*. The big pot of *magur* fish curry cooled on the side. Now all she waited for was the *korma* chicken to cook, which was bubbling on the stove, sending up the mingled aroma of onions, cardamom, bay leaves, cloves and peppercorn. The extractor fan was on full suction mode. It rattled and hummed as it did its job, seemingly as buoyant as the cook.

Amina wiped the mist off the window above the sink. She leant forward and her nose grazed the cold, wet glass. The stray cat had tripped the neighbour's security light. The light spilled over into her garden, leaving everything recessed in a slanting Gothic shadow. The apple tree cast the shadow of a claw over the fence. The rotary washing-line stamped a giant cobweb pattern on the paving. The chair with the torn upholstery had been abandoned in the vegetable patch, tilting slightly heavenwards, with its hind legs sinking into the mud, as if an invisible person were sitting on it and reflecting on spiritual matters. Amina had dumped it earlier to ensure that nothing would scupper her chances tomorrow of making the best possible impression.

Amina pulled away from the window. She returned to the cooker and stirred the chicken thighs with a wooden spoon. The meat was tenderising in the buttery marinade. She dabbed the spoon on the tip of her tongue to check the flavour of the sauce. She prodded the thighs and the skin stretched off readily to unveil the tenderest white meat underneath. Perfect for the aunt whose teeth – how Amina still laughed! – had perished under a lifetime of betel chewing and who was now resigned to wearing dentures and carrying a bamboo grinder wherever she went to keep feeding her betel addiction. Amina added some water, placed the lid over the saucepan, reduced the flame and left the food to simmer.

Remembering something quite important, she wiped her hands on the pinafore, tore it off and hurried upstairs to her bedroom. She searched inside her dresser drawer, her hand moving quickly over the contents, blindly patting the sheaves of rolled bank notes held tightly in elastic bands. Eventually she found the small box at the back. She drew it out carefully and sat down with it on the seat's edge. Amina switched on the desk lamp and put her glasses on. She flipped the lid open, picked the ring out of the spongy alcove, polished it on her palm and held it up to her face. The gemstone reflected on each lens.

She blew on the stone and wiped it with her thumb. She brought it closer to her eyes and threaded her finger through it. It was still a perfect fit. She had to admit that under the glare of modern taste the ring would be considered a little gaudy. The design was passé and the colour arguably garish in an era where white gold seemed all the rage. Still, the timeworn appearance gave it the weight of an heirloom. In fact, it was much more. For Amina, the moment took on the significance of a reunion with an old friend. In its antiquated cut lived a piece of her history.

It was thirty-two years ago when Amina had seen the ring for the first time from under the heavy bridal sari which was hooding her face completely. The engagement ceremony took place on an unbearably hot afternoon. She would never forget how her whole body trembled from stage fright, causing the chain mail of jewellery on her body to jangle incessantly. It forced her mother to step up on the dais and squeeze her arm hard trying to strangle the nerves while keeping up a smile for the guests in the room. Her mother feared what the in-laws might wonder seeing their new *bahu* shake uncontrollably, as if a mild form of epilepsy had taken possession of her. Allah-forbid, they might notice the strange behaviour and decide to call the whole thing off.

Naturally Amina hadn't seen her husband's face or any of the in-laws who, on the first viewing, had poked and prodded her like she was a marrow in a ba-zaar. The matriarchs had conducted a thorough inspection, their fingertips sticky from the generous helpings of *rasgullahs* and *jilebbis,* leaving oily smears on her skin. Their cloying voices were voluble in praising her beauty, lauding their own good fortune for having found a *bahu* with an angelic face. Oh, how their anger would swell a few years later at the realisation that, despite their meticulous examination, they'd taken away with them a fruit that bore no seed. But on that day, Amina was perfect. Fair skin. Long, silky locks. Prominent chin. Good figure. No sign of an extra finger, a clubfoot or webbed feet.

'The rice she cooks is always dry and fluffy, never stodgy,' her father blithe-ly said, proclaiming that the proper boiling of rice was the acid test of any young girl's culinary skills. Meanwhile, the groom had to make every effort not to leer at his bride during the exchanging of the rings. It was clear in his dilated eyes how much the choice was determined by his infatuation with her beauty. Amina tried to keep her eyes closed throughout. She maintained a firm clamp on them and sat through the whole ceremony with a slightly fur-rowed expression under the purdah. She almost toppled over when Saufina asked her to stand up and guided her to crouch down and touch her in-laws' feet. 'It was because of those dreaded heels!' she would later say, kicking them off with a tomboy spirit and getting into her comfy flip-flops.

After the ceremony was over and the party left, Kamal thrust a photo under Amina's nose trying to suppress a smirk that soon burst into a younger brother's irritating bray.

'Look *Appa*, look. Your Raj Kumar looks more like a monkey. Never mind…'

Amina tried to take a look but he snatched the picture back and pranced around the room jumping from furniture to furniture, teasing her betrothed for his dark complexion and the way he had kept leering at her each time he thought the elders weren't looking. It was only when Kamal ran into the scullery that their mother intervened and gave Kamal a clip round the ear.

'Stop saying these *oshuub* things, you thoughtless boy. Apologise to your sister at once, and give her the photograph!'

Her husband-to-be wasn't particularly handsome, but he did have an affable face. His forehead seemed a tad high, with a fringe that resembled a bird's nest on the peak of his skull. The brittle thatch of hair looked unlikely to see him through another decade. His expression was serious, but underlying it was something mischievous: a glimmer of tomfoolery characterised by a stubby nose and a dimple on his left cheek. The family celebrated Amina's good fortune, overwhelmed to find that a *Vilhayetti* man had knocked on their lowly door and asked for their daughter's hand. Even the dowry was manageable, considering the eminence of the groom's family compared to their own. During the evening their father sat out on the verandah smoking his hookah pipe and said to a visiting Azad: 'We're a family clearly blessed by Allah's grace.'

As for Amina's feelings, her idea of happiness was dictated by her father's wishes. She agreed to all his decisions with the obeisance expected from a good Bengali daughter, certain he would pave her future with the best intentions.

But had she entertained an opinion, or even harboured the smallest reservation, she couldn't have been expected to make much sense of it, for she was little more than a child fast-tracked into adulthood. A typical village girl with just four years of formal education, who had been removed from school as soon as she reached puberty and who now helped her mother with the housework while the family waited for marriage proposals to arrive. So when such a glorious opportunity presented itself, there wasn't much to think about but to follow the cultural footprints left by previous generations and delight in being the subject of the same rituals her sister had gone through only five months earlier.

Now, with thirty-two years of hindsight, while squeezing the metal band between her thumb and forefinger, Amina realised how precious that moment had been. The moment she sneaked a peek at her ringed finger from under her wedding veil and saw a future with a teenage romance, like a seafarer on his maiden voyage who watches the sun rise as his vessel pulls away from the dock. Beauty was the promise of happiness; the perfect portrait painted by an imagination yet to be sullied by the act of living. During the days after the engagement, her good fortune was the talk of the village. All the people envisaged Amina being whisked off by some rich Ala-ud-din who'd ridden into their humble world flashing his foreign threads. They could only imagine the clothes she would be wearing, the house she would be living in, the soft bed she would be sleeping on, the bouncing babies she would be bringing into her rosy world. All the other teenage girls envied her position. Jealous mothers poured their syrupy blessings when they dropped by, only to tear open their green souls behind the privacy of their own closed doors, deriding their own luckless daughters: *oh, if only he had knocked on our door first, it could have been you that he married!*

The weeks leading up to the wedding went at a frenetic pace. Amina's memory now retained only a stroboscopic flash of feelings and faces, and the ritual of being shepherded through a string of pre-nuptial ceremonies. Before she knew it, she was sitting inside a palanquin on her way to married life opposite a man she had yet to exchange words with. She remembered looking out from the curtain of marigolds draping the box and noticing how green the trees appeared, how azure the sky looked, how iridescent the hovering dragonflies were. The tweet of birds when they pulled up to her marital home made the world seem as lyrical as an Urdu Ghazal.

Staring at the ring now, she was surprised by how lucid that heady mix of curiosity, sensuality, fear and excitement still was. The memory of that day, even now, after all these years, she could summon like a genie from her forgotten jewel.

Amina slipped the ring back into the spongy glove and closed the box, deciding to gift it to her prospective daughter-in-law. She sat forwards in her chair and stared meditatively at her feet, her chin cupped in both hands. She contemplated what might have been had kismet not dropped that biological bombshell eighteen months after her wedding. But she quickly shook the errant thought away.

Instead her heart only had room for Samir. Samir was Allah's greatest blessing conferred upon her. His arrival had braced her life with a new strength and steered it away from that path broken by fate, into a much better direction. Briefly, the vanity of her independence washed over her. Then, all of a sudden, she thought about her son living away and the furrows in her forehead deepened.

Was she to lose it all now through estrangement, through the sudden diminution of her relationship with her son? Letting Samir go would be a gutless abandonment of all her hard work.

The more she thought about it, the more it bolstered her determination to make things better. Come what may, she would get him back. Her son's future lay in her hands; that much she knew. An arranged marriage was a sure way to put him back on track. A wife, kids, family, responsibilities – what better solution to breathe the Bengali identity back into his soul, to give him direction and make him realise the folly of youth?

She was grateful to Reena, whose involvement made things possible. Her authority in the matter, with its drill sergeant obduracy, forced Amina to visualise the outcome with a clearcut certainty. In the last few days, every time they spoke, the outcome of the plan seemed not so much a possibility as a forgone conclusion. Reena was good at drowning all of Amina's doubts in the surfeit of her enthusiasm: *how can your son refuse to marry such a lovely girl? Of course he will listen to his mother. It's up to you to be strong. Come on, sister, he is your blood. Have faith.*

Amina removed her glasses and put them back in the case. She was never more clear-sighted as she went downstairs to the livingroom and picked up the phone. She dialled Samir's number. Waiting, she heard her pulse beat against the receiver. It made her press the plastic cup tighter against her ear. Her warm breath bounced back from the mouthpiece. Silently, she implored her son to pick up. *Breeep-breep... breeep-breeep... breeep-breeep... breeep-breeep... breep-breep... breep-breep... breeep-breep...* A pause. A click. The call went directly to his voicemail: *The person you have dialled is currently unavailable. Please leave a message after the tone...* Amina took a deep breath as if steadying her mind:

'*Beta*, where are you? Have you eaten? I've spent the whole afternoon cooking your favourite foods. Can you come as early as you can tomorrow? Please dress smartly: wear a shirt and a pair of shoes. And, please, don't be late...'

She spoke fast, almost stumbling over her words, as if optimism was a thing on skates that threatened to rush from under her feet if she hesitated or stopped to think for too long. Deep down, some part of her knew the gamble she was taking and the potential for it all to go wrong. But she protected herself as best she could with the help of Reena's pep talk, some naivety, a bit of deliberate denial and a lot of wishful thinking. She clacked the handset back onto the cradle and returned to the kitchen to turn the gas off under the korma. She lifted the lid. Under the swirl of smoke the meat looked tender enough for a teething toddler, or even a toothless matriarch.

Coward in the cubicle

It was late in the evening when Samir alighted the tube train, came outside and stood at a crossroads. He leant against a lamppost and lit a cigarette. Lifting his head he exhaled the smoke and watched the white curlicue rise up and disappear into the night sky. He cupped his cold hands to his mouth and blew them like a conch-shell. From afar he looked like a Muslim praying to Allah. Without thinking he set off in the direction of his mother's house, but cognisance returned a few paces on and he stopped in his tracks. He blew on his hands again.

'What am I doing?' he muttered to himself.

He backtracked to the lamppost and studied the flickering light above him as if expecting from it some divine instruction. He looked at it, looked through it and looked at it again. All of a sudden it came to him. Divinity spoke to him in Morse. Samir flicked the half-smoked cigarette into a puddle and started down in the opposite direction at a brisk clip. He headed to the nearest off-licence and pushed hard on a door marked 'Pull'. The clatter startled the elderly man behind the counter.

Samir strode up to the counter and pointed to one of the spirit bottles ranked along the shelves. The short, stout shopkeeper sized up the shady figure. He turned to his neat collection, all the while maintaining a peripheral glare on Samir.

'This one?' he asked, trying to follow the point of Samir's finger.

'Yeah.'

Samir took the bottle and slammed a crumpled five-pound note into the shopkeeper's hand which the man un-crumpled and held up to the ultraviolet light beside the cash register. By the time he was satisfied the tender was legal, had placed it in the tray and scooped up the change, the shop bell had rung once more. Samir was gone.

He headed to the local park, just a few hundred yards away from a mother who was stirring chicken thighs in a korma sauce, picturing a happy ending to her son's waywardness. The gate was locked. He scaled the iron bars, using the fist-sized padlock as a foothold. The whole section juddered beneath his weight. He pulled himself to the top, jumped over, made a perfect landing and disappeared from the lights as fast as a fox fleeing from civilisation.

He moved silently along the path. Under the cover of night the path looked like a black ribbon strewn with wet leaves, which dissolved into a more cloying darkness. The trees were standing deathly still, silhouetted against the night gnarled and bare, the life in them consigned to a secret in winter. The wind that blew through the skein of branches extracted not the faintest rustle, effecting only the most stubborn sway. As Samir ventured deeper, his eyes turned more alive, more agile, more liquid.

He passed the children's play area where the swings lurched to the occasional breeze. He veered off and cut across the small stretch of lawn. He moved surefooted through the night, feeling the slick, wet grass cushion each tread, the squelch of mud, the odd snap of twig, the crunch of a snail shell. Some parts of the lawn felt like plaster beneath his feet, hardened by the threat of frost, while other parts were softer and kinder to the heel. Samir knew where he was heading. The old abandoned hut. It rose like a purple silhouette in the silver of moonshine.

Years ago the hut used to be the park's showpiece. It was the aviary his mother would bring him to when he was young. In those days it teemed with a squawking, psychedelic life. The colour and clamour of conures, cockatoos and parakeets. There was the beautiful zebra finch which spent hours in front of the hanging mirror, chirping away at its own vanity. He remembered how the squealing kids would dare each other to poke a finger inside the cage and then scarper at the slightest flap of a wing or pointed threat of a beak. There was Terence Stanton's Alsatian, which barked excitedly at the sight of the exotic birds and each time sent a chill through his mother, who used to pull Samir away although the dog was always on a leash. Oh, how his mother fears dogs!

'Why do some white people prefer to forge a relationship with an animal rather than a fellow human? To keep it in his house, allow it on his bed, clean up after its defecations. It's disgusting!'

Then there was the ice-cream van that stopped outside the play area and used its magical jingle to weave a spell upon infants like the Pied Piper of Hamlin. There was the spurt to join the queue, the asphalt showered by the patter of small, excited feet. Tiny hands tightly clutching pound coins and passing the heat of their palm onto the metal. Coins that promised the delight of a sweet icy cone just like the one pictured on the flank of the van. Then finally the first lick of a Flake 99. Cold tongue. Clenched mouth. Brain freeze. Some memories never fade, just crystallise with age.

But eighteen years on, the aviary stood as a carcass of its former glory. The aged masonry was now a petrie dish for mossy cancers and angry graffiti, while the roof, with its holes and missing slates, carried stains of the many passing seasons. The front was boarded up with two chipboard panels and looked like cataracts suffered by poor, lowly buildings. The door was blistered and warped at the edges and could be forced open with any makeshift crowbar. It could be a vagrant's winter palace.

Samir leapt over a portion of the surrounding fence that lay collapsed, uprooted after a losing battle against vandals. Inside, the 'No Trespassing' sign, despite maintaining its upright poise, struggled to salvage what remained of its authority. A warped white football sat impaled on top with a picture of a face scrawled on it.

Samir sat down with a dead thump and threw his head back against the boarding. The damp chill of concrete slid through the thick denim of his jeans and tautened the curl of his spine. He drew his knees to his chest and slipped the rucksack underneath the seat of his trousers. He reached inside his top and took out the bottle. He touched it to his forehead as if laying a *sajdah* to its powers, like a true believer. He snapped the top open and drew the bottle to his lips. A mad joy surged through him; his eyes became glassy with greed as he drank the first searing mouthful. It was followed by a second. And a third. And finally a fourth before he drew breath.

The day's disappointments dissolved in the familiar dip in vodka. It was a noiseless convalescence. That was its overwhelming beauty. Alcohol offered a deep-sea diver's peace, removed him from the cacophony of the human world. It was a moment of a simple and devastating charm, to submit once again to the elixir of escape. After the fifth swig Samir's head flopped forwards. His body wilted. If only he had a joint to light. A few puffs and he would scatter to the winds like a dandelion clock in springtime.

Samir soon finished the bottle. He held the empty vessel between his knees while gazing up into the middle distance. The alcohol gave everything around him a bright and beautiful nimbus. The sky was endlessly deep and teeming with secrets. When the wind struck and the same chord rang through the branches, he contemplated the cruel irony of nature rendering them leafless when what they needed most was a leafy duvet to get through the winter months. The football eyeing him seemed now to be wearing a droll expression. The aviary prompted a sardonic laugh as he swivelled round to stroke the boarding. To think that an edifice which had once attracted kids was now reduced to an ugly shack, but even in its derelict state probably attracted a few of the same kids back as teenagers and lent itself to their spray can assaults. How disappointed their mothers must be! Oh, how disappointed! *How did they mess up when their intentions were so true?* Of course, it was his own mother's disappointment that plagued him more than anything else.

What was he doing living away in some vain pursuit? He was a Bengali son, obligated to live by his mother's side. She had no one else in the world. She had raised him alone. In every way her happiness counted for more because she had earned it. He might have been handcuffed to a lunatic love, but it was a loyal love too. Alcohol brought the truth to the surface. The source of his anxieties, his rebellion, his anger and brittle hate also happened to be the only constant in his life. The one thing that would never change – his pillar of faith. She had never abandoned him, so what right did he have to leave her? She had every reason to be disappointed in him. For what a chip off the old block he had turned out to be! His father. The war hero. The martyr. The soldier who fought gallantly. Died gloriously. And what was he? His father's negative image. Spineless. Irresponsible. A heathen. A deserter. A deviate wholly preoccupied by personal demons, who couldn't even keep down a job and who found solace in drink. The contrast between them was untenable. He was a changeling, nature's sick joke.

Samir laughed at its absurdity. How genetics had betrayed him. How he'd fallen prey to the cliché of a generation lost. How he had fucked things up!

He chucked the bottle and closed his eyes briefly. He reached for his phone and punched the buttons ready to tell his mother that he would move back home, but the bleating engaged tone stopped him. He pressed his ear against the handset in deep affection until the tone timed itself out. By then the impulse to speak with her had faded too. Instead, he removed the dressing from his forearm and traced the crimson scar with a note of tender possessiveness. He liked its dark colour, the crater-like dip in the skin, still raw to touch. In fact, if he gave it a little tweak with the tip of his fingernail it would bleed a beautiful dot of blood.

Moments later Samir got up, picked up the empty vodka bottle and slipped it into the inside pocket of his fleece. He staggered back onto the path. He climbed over the fence unsteadily, resembling a spider on a wind-rattled web as he threw his leg over and came down back into the light.

It was past eleven. The back streets were muted by the late hour, occupied by the orderly lifelessness of the parked cars, brick houses and leafless hedgerows.

Samir walked along the pavement trying to maintain a straight course against the drunken inclination to weave into the hedgerows. He approached the main road, his hood pulled up like a tent, sheltering him from the intrusion of all the street neon that polluted the black sky with a lemony tinge. The ankles of his trousers were damp, fringed with muddy streaks. Blades of wet grass curtained the toes of his trainers.

He passed The Old Oak pub. Its lights were still on, but the interior was empty of people and the doors shut for the night. The four unsavoury characters from the previous week were loitering outside. The balding ringleader and his three stooges. Samir noticed them straight away. Their hatchet faces, their hoots and whistles. Their catcalls to each other brought back the memory of last week. There was no toilet attendant to harass tonight. Instinctively Samir dropped his head, retreated into his fleece. He looked away and walked on. A howl of derision pursued him. Or so he imagined. He began to see a hostility emanating from them that wasn't there and heard insults that weren't being flung in his direction. Like a mad ventriloquist he threw his own voice into their mouths, wanting to satiate that sudden craving for conflict so he could exorcise his inner demons.

He was the coward in the cubicle. Scared, spineless, pathetic, holding the door shut as if his life had depended on it. Keep walking, he told himself. Just look down and keep walking. But with each step the voice in his head rose up against him. It goaded him for being a coward. He felt it tweaking his ear and tugging at his legs.

Samir stopped. He turned back, tore his hood down and sought them with a fierce gaze. The adrenalin in him began to surge when they met his stare. His heart pounded in the manner of a war drum. And then the voice took control. Samir flung himself towards the group of men. But before he could get within touching distance, his foot caught the edge of a paving stone. He stumbled and his body felt the shock of a dull thud. The next time he opened his eyes he was lying in the gutter. The men were staring down at him, a little stupefied by his stupidity. And then all at once they burst into laughter. They looked monstrous flinging back their heads, pointing at him, and then doubling over in another fit of hysterics.

'Fucking clown!' one of them said, and spat out of the side of his mouth.

Samir lay doubled up on his side, arms splayed, his rucksack hanging off him at an ungainly angle. He wondered whether he had run into an army of fists. He lifted his head a little, and a low, guttural croak came from the back of his throat. Almost immediately his mobile phone bleated and its vibration made it fall out of his pockets. It skittered onto the paving. One of the men stepped forward. He looked around while rubbing the back of his neck. He bent down, picked up the flashing device, silenced it and slipped it into his pocket. Another man consulted his watch:

'Let's go, guys,' he said.

When Samir opened his eyes again they were gone. For a while he just lay there. He could hear the sandwich board outside the pub murmuring softly to the wind. His vision was still unfocused. The world lay tilted on its side, a crazy swirl of lights and glare riding over concrete. Coherence returned to him in fragments. The grit of the cold tarmac pressed against his face. There was the metallic taste of blood in his mouth when he rolled his tongue along his gums. He caught the smell of vinegar from a greasy chip bag that blew past his face. He slowly untangled his body and lifted his hand to the graze on his cheekbone, and the soft lump of a bloody lip. His chest still heaved from the effort of the sprint. Any physical pain was still numbed by the alcohol, but as things fell into place Samir remembered what he wanted most – not to exact any kind of revenge, nor to find some heady enlightenment, nor even to aspire to a Hollywood cliché. All he wanted was to have the guilt beaten out of him for being a bad son. But, predictably, he had even failed to orchestrate his own self-destruction. To add insult to injury, he sensed a warm dampness in his crotch spreading quickly to his thighs and seeping into the fabric of his trousers. He rocked up onto his elbows and spat the blood out of his mouth, annoyed by his stupid pretension to become his heroic father's equally heroic son. With blood on his cheek and piss in his pants, he stiffened his upper lip and rummaged in his pockets for his cigarettes.

Waterlily in a sea of darkness

Night had fallen by the time Amber reached the entrance to the flats after finishing her shift at the restaurant. She was carrying a bag of groceries. Someone somewhere was burning shrubbery and the air smelled faintly of woodsmoke. A clear sky suggested that it would be another cold night, just nippy enough for frost flowers to start appearing in the corner of window-panes and a film of ice to form over the puddles in the street. She wondered what the weather was like in Barcelona. A little warmer than this, she hoped, for that's where she planned to take Amy during half-term week. She was keen for her daughter to sample the creativity and culture of the city – a place where Amber had spent a year bandaging up her life after breaking up with Amy's father.

As she turned into the forecourt, she noticed activity by the cylindrical metal bins which were kept under the overhang attached to the main block. A dim but steady light lit up the dark figure of a man who was trying to dispose something into one of the tall bins, standing high up on tiptoes to drop the item over the lip. The bins were already filled to the brim so it was difficult to throw anything else in without it falling back down. His struggle was apparent in the manner he kept dropping back onto his heels, then staggering a little as if his legs were about to give way under him. As she drew closer she recognised the fleece that hung heavy over the wiry body. A streak of chalky dirt ran down the left shoulder of the woollen garment. She noticed a blue plastic crate by Samir's feet, stacked with half a dozen books. She stopped and watched him lumbering in frustration, grunting and cursing each time he failed to tip over the book in his hand.

'Would a step ladder help?' she asked.

Samir glanced over his shoulder.

'I'll be fine, thanks,' he replied and carried on.

Amber stepped closer until she was almost standing beside him. Samir turned away sharply as if trying to shield his face from her.

'Are you OK?' she asked.

'Yes.'

Amber looked at the crate of books. As far as she could tell they were books about art and artists. The soft plastic covering around each jacket gave away the fact that they had been loaned from a library.

'What are you doing?' she asked.

Samir ignored her. Amber put her grocery bag down. She reached into the crate and took out a book on Dali. She flicked through it and saw the library stamp on the opening page.

'They're perfectly good books. Why are you doing this?'

'I don't need them,' Samir snapped.

'Why don't you take them back?'

'What?'

'To the library, where they belong?'

'I'm not going back to that place.'

'Why?'

Samir turned towards her aggressively, grimacing as he swung his body round.

'Do you want them?' he snapped.

Amber's eyes widened in shock. She saw a purple bump on his forehead and a fresh scab marking the top of his cheek.

'What happened to you?' Amber asked.

'Nothing.'

'Nothing?'

Samir pulled his hood up.

'I walked into a door.'

'Was it made of iron?'

Samir touched his face lightly as if to re-assess the extent of the bruising, suddenly self-conscious, worried that it was worse than he had thought.

'Concrete, I think.'

'What?'

'Don't worry about it.'

'Your eyes are a little red. Are you sure you're OK?'

Samir turned back to the task at hand and tried once more to tip the book over, but this time he couldn't catch it when it failed to fall into the bin and landed on his foot instead.

'Fuck!'

'Calm down.'

Samir took a deep breath and picked up the book.

'I'm really sorry,' he said. 'There's this throbbing between my temples that won't stop, and the skin around my skull is tugging so tightly that it might just tear.'

'You're limping as well.'

Amber stepped forward and touched the bruise on his forehead. Samir flinched.

'Does it hurt that much?'

'It'll go down.'

Amber took the liberty of wresting the book from Samir's hand and placed it back in the crate with the others.

'I'll return these for you if you like.'

Samir face softened for the first time.

'Thanks.'

'Have you taken anything for the pain?' she asked.

'No,'

Samir had been lying in bed until late afternoon, curled up like an earwig beneath a rock. He awoke at midday to find the left side of his body stiff and sore, but remained in bed with his head under the duvet. He hadn't a clue at what time he had staggered back to his room, or how he managed to find his way back considering the disorientated state he was in.

'I think I might have some paracetamol,' Amber said.

'I'll be fine.'

Amber tilted her head and crossed her arms.

'Are you always this stubborn?'

Samir shrugged.

'Look, I don't know why you took off like that the other night. I still owe you for... you know, and I don't like to be indebted to anyone. So let me give you some painkillers and then we can call it even.'

Samir shrugged in concession.

'Good. Come on then, clumsy bones.'

Samir picked up the crate and shuffled behind Amber.

Samir stood waiting in the living room as Amber went into her bedroom in search of the box of painkillers. He gingerly lowered himself and put the blue crate down by his feet. He took in the worn furnishings around him: the battered sofa, an armchair with fraying seats, an old mahogany *teapoy* with its varnish cracked and its surface branded with tens of tea rings. An old television set was positioned opposite the sofa and bore a spiky antenna on top. Strangest of all, there was a gaudy simean mask hanging on the wall demanding all the attention in an otherwise drab room. Amber returned holding a silver blister strip in her hand. She popped a couple of caplets out of the strip and dropped them into Samir's outstretched palm. He swallowed the pills without water.

'Where's your daughter?' he asked.

'She's gone to the circus.'

'At this time of night?'

'Amy's staying with a friend tonight. We're going on holiday on Monday.'

'Where are you going?'

'Barcelona.'

'Lucky you.'

'Have you been?'

Samir shook his head. He looked around the room. There was a bouquet of flowers sitting on a shelf in a milk bottle filled with water.

'Where's her father?' he asked.

'We're no longer together,' Amber replied. She went back to the kitchen to empty out the grocery bag. She returned moments later holding a fruitbowl filled with a cluster of plums, tangerines, and a bunch of green grapes. She placed it carefully on the centre of the *teapoy*.

'We separated a long time ago.'

Amber rearranged the fruit so that the colours were equally apportioned, and the pattern looked more pleasing to her eye.

'So why were you throwing those books away? You're not a fascist, are you?'

Samir smiled.

'It's a long story.'

Amber looked at him.

'Are you an art student?'

Samir laughed.

'No.'

'It's just that all those books – '

'Don't belong to me,' Samir cut in. 'I moved in recently too, and was clearing out some space.'

Amber eyed the crate. She went to it and picked up the sketchbook which was at the bottom of the stack.

'What's this?'

'It's rubbish,' Samir replied as he lunged to snatch it off her, but was prevented by the pain that shot through his leg.

Amber began flicking through it. The pages were filled with pencil sketches of people mainly, all roughly hewn with a particular emphasis on the set of their body, as if therein lay the thrust of the narrative. The last drawing was unfinished. Amber could make out a wooden bench, but it was occupied by an outline of something quite shapeless.

'Did you draw these?'

'Yes.'

'So you are an artist!'

'No.'

'These are really good. You have talent.'

'They're OK.'

Amber flicked back a few pages, stopping at a picture of a woman in a sari sitting on a prayer mat, cupping her hands in front of her face. It was clear by the level of detail that Samir had spent more time on drawing this picture than the others. Underneath the drawing Samir had written: *Waterlili in a see of daknes.*

'And who's this?'

'It's a picture of my mother. I was just messing around.'

'You needn't be so defensive.'

'I draw pictures whenever I'm bored, that's all.'

Amber handed the pad back to Samir who dropped it into the crate. She was saddened by the fact that he showed no confidence in something he had an obvious talent for.

'Where does your family live?'

'Locally.'

'Your mother and father, brothers and sisters?'

'No, just my mother. There are only the two of us.'

'Just like me and Amy.'

'I suppose.'

'Your mother lives alone?'

'Yes.'

'It must be hard for her.'

'I'm going to move back.'

Samir had said this abruptly, as though Amber had accused him of neglect.

'I miss her cooking,' he added, softening his tone. When he looked back at her, he saw that her eyes were warm, a beautiful grey green and completely non-judgmental.

Amber found in him a tenderness that she had begun to warm to. The mere mention of his mother had pierced the carapace of anger under which he seemed so intent on keeping himself hidden.

'A cup of tea?' she asked.

'What time is it?'

'It's about seven.'

Samir immediately palmed his pockets. The search became more hurried when he couldn't find what he was looking for.

'What's the matter?' Amber asked.

'I think I lost my phone last night. It must have dropped out of my pocket.'

'Do you need to call someone?

'It's just that my mother usually calls me by now.'

'You can borrow my phone.'

'No, it's fine. I'll be going round later.'

'Was it an expensive phone?'

'No, no, it's just an inconvenience.'

'Well, first things first: let's clean that graze on your cheek. I've got some TCP somewhere. You sit down and make yourself comfortable.'

Amber left Samir standing in the room, still palming his pocket. As he stood there wracking his brain, trying to think as to where he might have misplaced the phone, he remained completely oblivious to the promise he had made his mother, who was waiting for him to show up, her house filled with guests and her honour poised on a knife edge.

Flailing in ignominy

The time on the mantelpiece clock had ceased to matter when Amina collected the empty teacups from the coffee table, including the one that was lying face down on the carpet.

She'd been sitting for a long while, long after the guests had fled, alone and in silence, entrenched in the blackest of moods. And as the clock ticked on, she was conscious of nothing except her failure as a mother. By the alchemy of rotten luck, yesterday's levity had turned to lead.

In the kitchen she chucked the crockery into the sink and turned on the tap with a brutal twist of her fingers. One of the cups cracked and a small chip skittered down the plughole. Undeterred, she stabbed the rubber plug down and began squeezing far too much detergent under the running tap, giving rise to a mountain of soapsuds. It was uncharacteristic of a person who was dead set against seeing anything going to waste. But this time Amina didn't care. Her fingers quaked as she continued to strangle the bottle with a corset grip. The liquid fell in a continuous stream. She thrashed the water with her hand. More bubbles formed.

Whatever had happened in the last six weeks, she never thought Samir would bring such shame upon her. She never thought he would break his promise and fail to turn up. But now she saw that her son was really capable of hurt, of tainting her *izzet* and turning her into a laughing stock. She was able to see all this because her judgment wasn't clouded by love, but clarified by its betrayal.

Earlier in the evening, Amina was all smiles when she had answered the door and stepped aside to allow Reena to usher in the prospective in-laws. They were a sunny lot who arrived bearing choice gifts and high hopes. They ceremoniously escorted their niece, who was dressed in a maroon-coloured *lehenga choli* with a matching *dupatta* which served as *purdah* for the occasion. Her dress was embroidered with pearls and beads and naqshis and sequins, which bedazzled Amina when the girl knelt down to pay her respects by touching Amina's feet.

'Oh *beti*, all this formality isn't necessary,' Amina had said as she picked her up by the shoulders and cupped her beautiful face.

The bride's uncle was the first to speak.

'Thank you for inviting us to your lovely home. I'm Jainul Haque; this is my wife; and this is my lovely niece, Shirin,' he said, pointing his hand to each member of his family.

'It's lovely to meet you all,' Amina replied.

'And doesn't Amina *Appa* have a lovely home?' Reena said, pleased that first impressions were positive.

'Please come into the sitting room,' Amina said

'So, where is our *damaad*?' Mrs Haque asked.

'He's on his way. Please go through and make yourselves at home.'

'Our *damaad* isn't here?' the uncle asked, raising a confused brow.

'Not yet. He must be held up,' Amina replied. She took their coats off them and hung them on the banister post in the hallway.

'So who else is here?' Mr Haque asked.

'It's just me.'

The aunt and uncle exchanged a questioning look, which was hardly surprising, considering they had decided – on Amina's insistence – to waive tradition and allow the bride-showing ceremony to be staged at the groom's house, so were expecting more of a fanfare on arrival. Mr Haque tried to make light of the situation.

'What have we here then, something of a sticky wicket? Are you sure our *damaad* isn't hiding upstairs? Is he too shy to come out into the middle?'

There was a ripple of laughter as Mr Haque waggled his thick eyebrows in the manner of a mini Mexican wave. The party then headed into the sitting room. Reena used the opportunity to drop step. She grabbed Amina's arm and took her to one side.

'Where is the boy, *Appa*?' she whispered.

'He said be would be here,' Amina replied.

'When?'

'He should he here any moment.'

'Have you tried calling him?'

'I will, but I should serve the tea first.'

'*Acha*, but don't be too long.'

After Amina had brought in the tray of refreshments, she picked up the cordless phone from the sewing table. She hid it behind her back and backed out of the room.

'Will you not take tea with us?' Mrs Haque asked a retreating Amina.

'Yes, in a moment, sister. Please help yourselves to the refreshments.'

She dashed upstairs leaving Reena to entertain the family. The family heard a door close behind Amina's hurried footsteps. Mrs Haque put her tea-cup down on the glass coffee table and nudged Reena's arm.

'Is everything all right, sister?'

Reena smiled awkwardly.

'You know what young men are like these days. He's probably gone to *Ambala* for some *jilebbis*, told the staff what occasion they're for and the staff are ribbing him and refusing to let him go.'

'I've never seen an *Ambala* near here.'

Fortunately, Amina was back within a couple of minutes. She didn't report anything on her return, but her behaviour had become more manic.

'Are you all warm enough? I hope so. I've had the heating on all day,' she said. She turned to the young girl. '*Beti*, are you comfortable? You're more than welcome to come out of your *purdah*. We're very informal here.'

Shirin merely shook her head and her bridal accoutrements jangled.

'Isn't the girl so demure?' Amina remarked to Mrs Haque.

'She takes after her mother – my sister. Shirin's been staying with us for the last five months. She arrived here on a student visa. She's so intelligent, but her family are poor so she's never had the opportunities. Fortunately, we had the means to sponsor her to come over to Britain. If only we can secure permanent residency for her it would set her up for life.'

'You are so lucky to have her,' Amina said. 'And I'm even luckier that you've brought her here to my humble home.'

'It's difficult to find families that are compatible these days. I'm just grateful to Reena for setting up this meeting.'

Reena smiled cloyingly at Mrs Haque.

'Oh, it's only my duty,' she said batting her eyelids.

The polite chitchat continued and things jollied along nicely. However, an hour passed and the *damaad* was yet to make an appearance; his absence was beginning to knock a dent into the proceedings. Mr Haque's wit had begun to wane. Mrs Haque's smile took on a forced quality, now seeming as artificial as her teeth.

All of a sudden the doorbell rang and its resonance inspired optimism back into the faces of the guests. However, when Amina answered the door it was only Rukhsana standing under the porch light.

'*Assalumu alaikum Appa*, I hope I'm not too late?'

'No, do come in.'

Rukhsana flounced into the house radiating a *sheherjahdi* chic, draped in a *Zardozi* sari and with a *ruli* of bangles on each wrist. A soft lamb leather purse dangled from her shoulder. The get-up caught Reena's eyes.

'Oh my goodness, the purse you borrowed from me really does complete the outfit,' she chimed.

Mr Haque felt an unexpected stirring of desire when he clapped eyes on the woman with the resplendent carriage of youth.

'Our sister Reena has spoken highly of you. How are you finding the country?' he asked as he sat up straight, sucked in the paunch, puffed out the chest and smoothed down his Zapata moustache.

'I'm slowly getting used to it,' Rukhsana replied, politely.

'Very good. Very good.'

Her arrival even tempted their niece to peak from under the purdah of the bridal regalia. It was little wonder Rukhsana had mistaken Amina's cold reception at the door to be a discreet affront to the effort she had made. So absorbed was she in her vanity that she hardly noticed the crisis of the missing bridegroom. She approached the bride with the unbridled excitement of an adolescent.

'And what does our lucky *damaad* think of our beautiful *kannya?*' she said, lifting Shirin's purdah high enough to get a good look.

'*Subhan Allah,* she's an angel!'

There was a stiff silence.

'We're still waiting for him to turn up,' Mrs Haque said, coldly.

'Oh?' Rukhsana said, dropping the veil at once, suddenly aware of the tense atmosphere in the room.

'It must be the traffic,' she said.

Amina sped to the kitchen and returned with a cup of tea for Rukhsana.

'Please help yourself to the snacks, *beti.*'

'Thank you, *khala-amma.* Don't worry. I'm sure your son will be here shortly.'

However, minutes later, Mr Haque coughed into his fist. He chewed his bottom lip in thought and scratched the bridge of his nose. He wasn't sure how to broach this delicate predicament. He turned to his niece first.

'Are you OK, Shirin *beti?*'

Amina picked up the platter of *nimki* and offered it to Mr Haque.

'Please take one.'

'No, thank you,' he said.

'Shirin *beti?*' Amina asked.

Shirin shook her head.

'How about you, sister?' she asked Mrs Haque.

The matriarch turned up her nose.

'You do realise we have much to discuss, and it is getting late.'

Reena intervened, doing her utmost to keep the atmosphere light.

'Oh, patience is a virtue in matters of matrimony.'

Mrs Haque gave her a carping look.

'Patience also happens to be futile in matters that show no signs of changing!'

Rukhsana tried to help by resorting to a diversionary tactic:

'Oh, Auntie Reena, is it true what you said about Shehab Uddin's eldest daughter.'

Reena turned to Mrs Haque.

'Have you not heard the story?'

'No,' Mrs Haque said, completely uninterested.

'Oh, the story's all over town.'

Reena launched into the tale of Shehab Uddin's eldest daughter – a young, unmarried girl who'd suffered major organ failure and was now on a donor waiting list. The gossip currently doing the rounds was that the girl had since met and moved in with a man from 'Africa'. Apparently, someone had spotted the pair driving through the high street in the same car.

'Oh my goodness, he's as black as soot and has a nose that looks like it's been stamped on by an elephant!' she said, incredulously.

'Can you believe that, he's an… African!' Rukhsana added, as if the poor girl had allowed herself to become the victim of an alien abduction.

'I know, it's completely vile!' Reena said.

'*Hai Allah!*' Rukhsana exclaimed, throwing a hand over her mouth.

'But she is damaged goods,' Reena quickly added, 'Let's face it, who's going to want her hand in marriage in our community?'

Amina, anxious to create a more pious impression, sat quietly at the edge of this conversation. Her face maintained its host-like glow; she put one platter down, picked up another and handed it around again, insisting they take one more *sondesh* or *kofta* telling them that the food would otherwise go to waste. She spoke on autopilot, not registering much at all, straining all the while to hear her son's footsteps stride up to the front door and rescue the evening.

'My Samir is a good boy at heart,' she reiterated to Mr and Mrs Haque.

'That is a splendid thing,' Mr Haque said. 'If only we can see that quality for ourselves.'

'You will, I promise. I cannot get through to his phone so he must be stuck in the underground. You know, he's offered to buy me a mobile phone. He can afford it now that he has a good job.'

Amina stretched out the little she knew about his job, talked up his six months living in Bangladesh where he was schooled in Islam, even lauded the fact that he never forgot the rent payments:

'The Council's never had a problem with us, and it's all because my son gives me the money,' she said. 'He doesn't have any extravagances.'

Mr Haque's interest flared up once again.

'Wasn't the *damaad*'s father a *shaheed*?' he asked.

'Yes, he died in the war before Samir was born.'

'And where was he from?'

'Bhatipara in Mymensingh.'

There was a pause. Mr and Mrs Haque exchanged another suspicious glance.

'He died during the war,' Amina said as if to bring the line of enquiry to a close.

'*Hai Allah*, the atrocities the Pakistani army committed in those days,' Mr Haque said. 'This generation growing up in Britain simply have no idea. And look at our country now, going to the dogs. The power baton is constantly passing between two unqualified matriarchs who merely symbolise the past, and then there's the discredited and corrupt former military dictator, of course. What does Samir think of his father's involvement in the war?'

'As I've said, he died before Samir was born – '

Out of the corner of her eye, Amina suddenly caught Mrs Haque looking at her wristwatch. It hijacked her attention and made her garrulous again.

'Have I told you that we've put in an application to buy this house? Now with my son's help the financies shouldn't be a problem. He really is quite responsible with his money. I'm someone who believes that it's not the amount of money you earn but what you do with it that defines your prosperity. My son is always giving me his money to look after. He will make a wonderful family man.'

Mr Haque began drumming his fingers on the arm rest. He tilted his head up at the clock and then turned back to meet his wife's face, whose dark eyes appeared as threatening as the muzzle of a double-barrelled gun. They were mutely demanding that he say something before she did. In response he un-crossed his ankles and ran his hand down the fold of his trouser leg. His hair was dyed jet black and gleaming with brilliantine. It stayed rigid even as he bent down to pull up a sock sagging at the ankles. He reached for his packet of Dunhills. He tore off the cellophane wrapper and pulled out a cigarette. He tapped it a few times on his yellow palm before lighting it. He sucked fiercely on the cushiony butt and then exhaled with a contemptuous sigh. Smoke bil-lowed from his nostrils and blew across his face.

'Someone please explain to me what's going on?' he demanded to know.

His raised voice shook Amina's nerves. She tried to say something but nothing came to her lips and she sat open-mouthed. Mr Haque, enlivened now by the nicotine rush, bristled behind his bulky moustache.

'Come on, sister, please say something!'

Unable to answer him, Amina kept slicing the betel nuts that she'd softened in a bowl of water for Mrs Haque during the previous night.

Mrs Haque, the prim old lady who had been keeping her real temper in check behind those flashy upper dentures, sucked her mouth into a horseshoe shape and then unleashed her most excoriating self.

'This is a goddamn bloody fiasco. You've insulted us by inviting us to this sham. For starters, there's no one here besides you. Have you ever heard of a wedding talk without a single elder in sight? I can't believe we've already wasted all this time. Where is your son? You don't expect us to sit here all night waiting for him?'

'No,' Amina replied.

'Have you no shame inviting us to this joke!'

'Joke?'

'What else can you call it?'

Mrs Haque no longer felt the need to accord the occasion any respect. With each question her tone turned more hostile. An angry stammer crept into her voice.

'Don't just sit there in s-s-silence. Give us a proper answer, for Allah's s-s-sake!'

Before Amina could reply, Mrs Haque swivelled her head round to Cousin Reena and demanded an explanation, jabbing her finger at the wedding broker while shielding her niece with the other hand, who appeared unfazed under the purdah, still playing her passive part to perfection.

'Don't you worry, *beti*. No harm will come to your honour while your uncle and I are still alive!'

Contrary to her outburst, it wasn't the waiting that had sapped Mrs Haque's enthusiasm, but the information the family had gleaned from Amina's looping monologues about her son. The former was a ruse to cover more serious concerns.

Of course they all knew Samir had no father, but in all this time there had been a clear reluctance to speak about his ancestry. Nothing clear had been said about the family lineage. Not a single anecdote to mark the generational progress. All they'd manage to tease out in the last two hours was that Samir's father had been an undecorated war hero who had lost his life during the War of Independence and, more crucially, that he came from Bhatipara – a popular fishing village with a low caste Hindu community. He could quite conceivably have been a fisherman who had been caught in the crossfire. Even if he had been killed in action, it was no secret that the Pakistani army took great pleasure in gunning down Hindus during that time.

Questions about the boy's legitimacy circled their thoughts. Then there was the minor disappointment over property ownership. A house owned by the council, inhabited by a lone mother whose empty neckline and wrists bore silent testament to a cultural dearth. In fact, what kind of Bengalis were they? So bloody disconnected! Were they refugees who had managed to kick and flap their way to British shores? The son's decision to stay away more or less vindicated their judgment. It raised an obvious doubt about his upbringing – now perfectly conceivable considering there was a clear absence of a family institution. He was probably the type of boy who would have his marital fun then disappear without a trace.

'What's going on, Reena? Mrs Haque said, staring harshly at the space around her.

'Where have you brought us? We placed our trust in you; we spent all this money on gifts for the *damaad* and his mother. Most of all, we were so hopeful...'

Looking into Mrs Haque's eyes, Reena recognised the fragility of her position, for she too had heard the gross appellation of a place name that connoted questionable ancestry. Suddenly she found herself in the firing line. The day she promised to help Amina get her son back, she had made a second promise to her cousin, claiming to have found a suitable groom for their niece: a young man who had landed a job in media, with no familial responsibilities to feed on his salary – aside from a lone mother – and, finally, the only heir to a house in the suburbs. Her cousin, seduced by the list of positives, had committed all marital arrangements into Reena's safe hands.

But now that pride was under threat. In fact, the moment she looked into her cousin's unblinking eyes she saw the subtext glowering at her: *Do you think this disobedient, low-caste bastard (in the truest sense of the word) is fit to marry my niece, Red passport or not?*

Reena accepted it was her fault for assuming the family owned the house. Admittedly she had paid insufficient attention to the boy's background – in particular the issue of caste, which she had thoughtlessly glossed over. But she couldn't bear responsibility for his failure to show up and what that revealed about his character. Even though she was aware of the fractious relationship between mother and son, how was she to know that the boy would leave his mother in the lurch like this? It wasn't the action of a loving son, but of a heartless heathen.

As Mrs Haque's finger jabbed at her like a bayonet, all Reena could see were people pointing at her at future weddings, nudging one another and talking in whispers. To make matters worse, she and her cousin came from the same village in Bangladesh. The details of her involvement in a shambles like this were sure to travel back home via the telephone lines and into the bemused ears of family and friends, spreading to random villagers and dragging her impeccable name through the hard-to-rid Bengali mud.

Reena did not panic, but allowed her cousin to finish her rant. She turned to the hostess and addressed her calmly:

'*Appa*, please tell us the meaning of this.'

Amina stared at her lap. She tried to say something but her voice trailed off. This gave Reena the perfect opportunity to hit back:

'I went to such an effort to bring the families together. I gave them the assurance by putting my word on the line. I trusted you to honour this meeting. Ensuring the boy's presence is your responsibility, isn't it? You are his mother after all!'

Amina's face flushed. She was thrown by the thinly veiled accusation. The last thing she expected was her ally to turn adversary. She sought Rukhsana for help.

'Please say something. You were here the other day, too.'

Rukhsana hid behind the grip of her empty teacup. All she could offer was a shrug, mindful of her station in this delicate crisis. All eyes fell back on Amina once more.

'I've done everything in my powers to make sure Samir would be here. He must be held up somewhere.'

She then extended her hand to Reena seeking support. But Reena got up from her seat, sidestepped Amina and anchored herself between aunt and niece.

'Her niece is my niece. Her *izzet* is my *izzet!*' she said to Amina.

'But I told you that things between Samir and me have been difficult recently.'

212

'Yes, we know all that, but it's hardly a reason for him to become an *awara* with no respect for his elders. How could he not turn up?'

'He does respect his elders,' Amina stressed. 'He's a good boy. He's just young, confused and impressionable.'

'That's just splendid!' Mr Haque said, crushing his cigarette butt into the china saucer in the absence of an ashtray. 'We're here to give our niece away to a *confused* and *impressionable* boy.'

'Why didn't you tell us any of this before, Reena?' Mrs Haque asked.

Reena threw her hands up in the air.

'I was told he is smart, which I'm sure he is, and has a good job, which he does. *Appa* gave me no reason to believe that he could do something like this. I really had no idea that he could cause us this embarrassment and leave our noses cut.'

'The boy's not fit to marry my niece, visa or no visa!' Mrs Haque declared. 'My Shirin deserves someone ten times better! She'll be a lot happier returning to Bangladesh and marrying a good farm boy. Oh Reena, you really raised our hopes.'

'It's the first time something like this has ever happened to me,' Reena replied. 'I've arranged so many marriages in the past, but believe me, I've never been party to something as embarrassing as this. I was as excited as you about the possibility of this union. Of course I want our Shirin to find a groom in this country and not have to go back to Bangladesh or become an overstayer. I really didn't know that this boy would turn out to be so wayward.'

Mrs Haque's gaze was now fixed like a target on Amina, her lips shrivelled in disapproval. Reena took the opportunity to clasp a hand to her breast in operatic style.

'*Hai Allah, hai Allah!*' she gasped. 'I had the best intentions all along, but I have been stupid. It is my fault. Yes, all of it. After all, it was my idea to bring the two families together. Yes, I accept it. All of this is down to me.'

She then hugged her niece with an excess of emotion, as if she were acting a part in a Bollywood melodrama.

'Oh, please forgive me *beti*, you are like my own daughter. How could I have brought you here, to this shameless house?'

The performance was utterly convincing. With half her face buried in the bride's shoulder and the other half alert to its dramatic effect, she appeared genuinely hurt, if not downright distraught.

'I think we should be leaving now,' Mr Haque said, pocketing his cigarettes and looking around for his coat.

'Don't cry,' Mrs Haque said, rubbing Reena's arm tenderly and smoothing the hair back behind her ears. 'You arranged all this with the whitest of hearts. How were you to know that things would turn out this way?'

She turned back to Amina. Her mouth twisted into the ugly horseshoe shape.

'We don't want to lose our niece's future to a son you've already lost,' she said.

Amina pulled the sari achal tight over her head.

'Please don't leave just yet,' she implored.

'There's no reason to stay,' Mrs Haque retorted. 'With a son like that, what guarantee can you give that he will turn up to the wedding when invitations have been sent, when the venue is full, when the gifts have been bought, when the caterers have been paid for?'

'He'll turn up. I'm sure of it,' Amina appealed.

'Hmmm, not very likely,' came Reena's aside.

'I'm his mother. I'll make sure he does what I ask him.'

'It's pointless, I tell you, pointless!' Reena started. 'He's gone. A rotten apple in the Bengali cart.'

She then looked at Amina fiercely.

'In this God forsaken country a lot of these youngsters are growing wild. A few are unmanageable, fallen victim to its temptations.'

Amina remembered the food in the oven: the *mutton pullao*, the *aiyrre* fish curry, the *bhaingan bhaji*, the chicken korma that she had left simmering under the hob until the skin came willingly off the meat.

'Please don't leave on an empty stomach. I've prepared so much food,' she said, looking to the young bride for encouragement. '*Beti*, you've all made such an effort to come here. Please try to make your aunt and uncle understand.'

'Enough!' Mrs Haque barked in English. In addressing her niece and inviting her into an altercation meant strictly for elders, Amina had delivered the final insult. Mrs Haque bucked from the effort, causing her false teeth to come loose and jolt forwards. Embarrassed, she clamped her mouth shut, turned away and sucked her dentures back into position. She saw no advantage in sticking around and was now grateful to the bridegroom for playing truant, for handing the family a get-out clause without the need for her to spell out the ancestral issue. So far, she had remained button-lipped on that particular issue.

Reena was eager to leave too. She looked at Rukhsana, indicating with a subtle tilt of the head that it was time to go. Rukhsana acknowledged the signal, but wishing to pay lip service to community relations she took Amina aside and spoke to her in a confiding whisper.

'Let it go, *Appa*,' she said. 'Your son may not be bad at all. But these people don't know him. They are naturally shocked and confused by his absence. They've come a long way. They are irritable. Maybe once the dust has settled...'

Amina stared right through Rukhsana, not quite sure how things had come to this. Rukhsana held Amina's hand and rubbed it soothingly.

'You see, *Khala-amma*, from a cultural standpoint, a son's obedience is important to the unity of any family. These issues run deep, especially for those of us living here, trying to protect who we are.'

'But you don't understand,' Amina blurted. 'He's young, easily influenced, buying into a culture that's not meant for him. All he needs is some guidance. I thought you were here to help.'

Rukhsana stared back, doubtfully.

'Yes, of course, but it's not as simple as that. How do I put it? This is a very traditional family with age-old values. Values that you and I know have changed, but they don't want to be seen to be going against those attitudes. For one, their nearest and dearest will ask questions, lots of questions; even the most liberal will look on suspiciously. You know what our people are like.'

Mrs Haque interrupted the private conference with such spite that she knocked a teacup off the table. Tea spilled everywhere. She didn't bother picking it up.

'Look, we're not stupid enough to allow any man to father future generations with our niece when, let's face it, he knows nothing of his own father,' she ranted. 'What's his caste? He could come from a line of *Maimols* for all we know. *Chi, chi, chi, chi!*'

The woman was now buttoned into her coat, which she had collected from the banister post in the hallway. She held the gifts tight in her hands, looking to her husband and wondering if the receipts had been kept. By now she was so incensed that she no longer addressed Amina directly but used Rukhsana as an intermediary to deliver her final words.

'Tell the woman there is nothing more to say on the matter.'

Amina made towards Reena and clasped her wrists in desperation.

'You promised me you'd help.'

Reena was a little taken aback by the pathetic display, but was more worried about the 'promises' that could be quoted with the tide of emotion rising in Amina's voice. In another situation she would have been inclined to shoo Amina away like a street beggar, but this situation required a little tact, a little diplomacy. She allowed Amina the comfort of holding on to her wrists.

'We live in a small community here,' she started, 'held together by *maan*, *shomman* and *morjada*. What sets us apart from the white people is our honour, our dignity, our values. We must do everything we can to preserve that.'

Nothing was reminiscent of the Reena from two days ago. This new voice she spoke with was foreign to Amina: vain, uncaring, dripping with duplicity. All Amina could see was Reena's ugly insincerity. And that arm-around-the-shoulder was the con she had fallen prey to. Seeing Reena's mouth jabbering on and on made something go off inside her head. Her grip on Reena turned fierce. She dug her nails into the woman's skin. She then lunged forward and shoved Reena with all her might.

'Get out of my house!' she yelled.

Reena staggered backwards, losing her footing and tripping on the high heel that had buckled under her foot. She was stunned that a passive woman's temper, when ignited, could be so explosive.

'It's all your fault!' Amina screamed. 'All this has happened because of you and your ideas. You're a two-faced liar!'

Reena regained her footing and gasped at the sudden lowering of tone.

'What did you say?' Reena spluttered

'You're a lying, meddling – '

Reena put her hand out as if to say *that's enough*. The gesture was so grand that the audience fell silent. All eyes were now on the diminutive lady who was suddenly unrestrained, and raging.

'If it wasn't for you, for you being an incompetent mother and only Allah knows what kind of wife, if ever you were respectful enough to hold that station, none of this would have ever happened. I wouldn't be here with my nose cut and my reputation in tatters.'

'How is your reputation in tatters?'

'What would you know about *izzet?*' Reena fired back.

'I know about telling people the truth.'

'That's rich, coming from you!'

'You were the one who offered to help.'

'Yes, before certain things came to light.'

The family slowly rose from the settee. Shirin made a small gesture to Mrs Haque, agreeing that it was time to leave. The family deliberately stayed outside the altercation and sidled past the pair, using the room's widest dimensions, dismayed at how common courtesy could be reduced to chaos. This time Shirin took the lead, her dupatta now dangling carelessly around her neck like a scarf, bemused that she had not been the central character in what was supposed to be a fluently stage-managed ceremony, but the audience around which a pantomime had unfolded. Once they left, Reena gave Amina one final glare.

'*Stop!* No longer do I want to continue this conversation. What did I do to deserve this humiliation? You just stay away from me.'

She turned away sharply and headed out the door. Rukhsana was the last to leave, saddened; the effervescence she had arrived with now a distant memory. She turned to wave goodbye to Amina who was sitting on the sofa with her face buried in her hands.

'*Khala-amma*, I'll see you soon,' she said.

Amina didn't even look up. Rukhsana blinked blankly and her lips curled into a sorry smile. She walked out of the room and shut the door behind her.

All that had happened over an hour ago. Amina was now standing in the kitchen; the crockery was on the sink rack drying off, including the chipped cup. On the stove the foods were cold and congealed. Amina's head was hot and heavy. Thirst scratched her throat. She grabbed the cup with the chip, filled it several times under the tap and drank until her thirst was quenched. She lifted one of the saucepan lids. The sight of the korma and its spicy smell made her feel sick.

Amina looked out of the kitchen window. Watermarks mottled the black background. Tonight there was no cat to trip the light so no garden features. No shadowy displays. Night's black curtain was heavily drawn. She turned away and began emptying the contents of each saucepan into the bin, working mechanically to put her house in order. She grabbed dish after dish and poured them out, leaving a mountain of different curries on intimate terms with each other. She walked back into the living room and sat down in her rocking chair, reconciled to the truth that Samir wasn't her son and she wasn't his mother. Something she had been told but had refused to believe many years ago. But now that cataract of fact refused to budge from her wild, open stare. She sat there, miserable with rage.

Like father, like son

Samir made his way to his mother's house stepping gingerly on his left leg which was still sore despite the painkillers. After returning from Amber's place he'd helped himself to his landlord's decanter of brandy before swapping it for a vintage Absinthe – a measure of which he had mixed in iced water and sugar, hopeful of its anaesthetising effect. He had remembered to brush his teeth before setting off and, erring on the side of caution, had popped a stick of chewing gum into his mouth before reaching for his keys. He was met with a deep and peculiar lull the moment he went inside and shut the door behind him. The light in the hallway was switched off and the soundless black pressed heavily against his eyes.

'*Amma?*' he called out.

There was no reply. His immediate guess was that she had gone to bed. With a blind hand, he groped along the wall and flicked on the light switch, squinting in the sudden assault of light. The doors of all the rooms were shut, not ajar as was usually the state, creating a tight capsule of space wherein the wall clad with the framed Qur'anic verses, embroidered in *Naskh* calligraphy, glared at him.

'*Amma?*' he called again, this time louder. Still there was no reply. He crouched with his hand to the banister and, squinting against the glare, scanned the curve of the stairway. He started up the stairs but stopped upon hearing a faint, rhythmic croon coming from behind the door of the living room. He limped back down the steps and opened the door. Sitting there, swaying back and forth in her rocking chair, he saw his mother. The motion accentuated her profile which moved in and out of the pool of light carved by the table lamp. She had released her hair from its bun and an oily lock had fallen over her face with a silver hairpin clinging to it, glinting like a reflector on the spoke of a wheel. Her gaze was deadly ceramic, fixed to a spot on the carpet. The plastic prayer beads of her *tasbie* dangled low from her fist, swaying also.

'*Amma?*' Samir repeated. 'Didn't you hear me calling you?'

Amina's eyes did not move.

'Why are you sitting in the dark like this?' he asked.

He looked at the television screen. It was turned off.

'Has the television stopped working?'

No response.

'Isn't it a little hot and stuffy in here?'

His questions were like stones hurled at an apparition. He stepped further into the room and closed the door to keep in the heat. He remembered that she'd been suffering from a cold. In fact, he had passed a pharmacy on the way and bought a cough tincture, making sure it was alcohol free. He fished it out of his hooded top.

'Are you OK?' he asked.

The light of the lamp flickered.

'What's happened?'

The bow of the rocking chair creaked. Amina tilted her head fractionally to look at him. She saw the bump on his forehead and the graze on his cheek.

'Look at the state of you! Why are you here?' she finally asked.

'What do you mean… you always wait up?'

'I'm always waiting, I've always been waiting.'

'I've brought something for your cough. It's a tincture. It'll get rid of the irritation.'

Samir tried to give her the box, but her hand did not reach out to accept it. He placed it awkwardly on her lap. As soon as she rocked forward it toppled and fell on the carpet.

'What's going on?' he asked.

The room appeared strange and unfamiliar. The removal of a single chair had upset the whole balance to which he had been accustomed since childhood. There was a dark stain on the carpet and a cluster of liquid tea-rings on the glass coffee table. It was a jarring sight, considering what a house-proud woman he knew his mother to be. There was a purse lying in the other armchair, partially wedged between the cushions. The stone-studded catch on it gleamed like a doll's tiara, and looked horribly intrusive in a room alien to such flourishes of opulence. There also lingered a residual odour of tobacco and a mix of perfumes that had mingled into a sweet and sickly smell.

'Whose purse is that?' he asked.

Amina twisted her neck to look balefully at the object.

'I suppose Reena will now accuse me of being a thief as well!'

'Was she here?' Samir asked.

Samir bent down and pawed the wet stain, grimacing from the pain that shot through his haunches. He rubbed his fingers and smelled them.

'Is this tea?'

He used the tissue in his pocket to mop it up, dabbing at the damp pile, aware all the while of his mother lurching to and fro in her chair, her shadow skimming over his cold hand at regular intervals.

'I think it's about time we replaced the carpet,' he said, making his voice sound as blithe as possible. As he worked to the edge of the stain, out of the corner of his eye he saw how hard her feet were pressing down on the footrest, like boulders of immovable flesh. His mother's rocking became the only living thing about her. Samir held out the tissue in his hand. It flowered like an offering.

'Look how much dirt has come off the carpet. Have we ever had it professionally cleaned?'

'Leave my carpet alone,' Amina snapped.

Samir put the damp tissue in the waste bin.

'Is there any food?' he asked.

'Food!' Amina exclaimed in mockery, remembering how she had dumped all those carefully cooked dishes: the slices of fish, each hunk of tender chicken, the purple strips of *brinjal* and every grain of *pullao*. She pictured the congealed sauces falling from the saucepans and into the bin in waxen lumps. She let out a snigger, dropped her head back and shut her eyes. Samir noticed that the creases around her eyes were lightly clogged in face powder.

'Why are you wearing make up?' he asked.

Samir edged closer to his mother.

'*Amma*, I haven't eaten all day. Well, I did have a slice of stale bread but it didn't even touch the bottom of my stomach. You know what you said about the Bengali appetite only being satisfied by the rice and curry diet. Well, I think you might be right. My stomach's making strange noises.'

Amina's eyes remained closed throughout. It started to frustrate Samir. In times gone by he could always gain access to his mother's affections by making the slightest allusion to his hunger. But, tonight, she refused to be sentient to her maternal role. In fact, she seemed resentful of it.

'I'm sorry I'm late,' he said. And, this time, he was truly sorry – not only for being late but also for behaving the way he had in the last six weeks. He stepped forward and thought about touching her delicately boned hand which was curled over the armrest, but resisted, fearing she might snatch it away. So, instead, he placed his fingers on her shoulder.

'*Amma?*' he said, softly.

Amina continued rocking without the slightest break in rhythm.

'Why are you being like this?'

Amina's eyes snapped open.

'There's no more food,' she replied, quietly.

It was the truth. Samir was confused. Where was all that furious rage that characterised her angriest moments? Samir was not able to read the expression on her face, though he sensed the coldest thoughts germinating beneath the rocking shell of her skull, something beyond anger, a lucidity that was bereft of emotion. This could never have taken place if he hadn't left home, he thought. Disfavour needs its invitation, hatred its reasons, rejection that fatal stab of betrayal.

'Have you eaten?' Samir asked.

'Just leave me alone.'

'No,' he replied and gave the carpet a fretful kick.

'Go.'

'I will not go,' he reiterated. And now a desperate urgency was beginning to thin out his voice. Amina began chanting Allah's ninety-nine names out loud, flicking the plastic counters of her *tasbie* through her fingers one at a time:

'*...Ar-Rahman', Ar-Rahim, Al-Malik, Al-Quddoos, As-Salam, Al-Mu'min, Al-Muhaymin...*'

And while she entered that familiar trance of worship, Samir cut a pathetic figure standing over his mother, feeling queasy as he watched her torso roll back and forth. What he wanted most was to be held by her. The desire to crouch down and lay his head on her lap was intensified by the physical ache that afflicted him. He hankered to give over to the theatrics of the gesture, as corny as it was, and have her hand tenderly brush the back of his neck. Had they built up a more tactile relationship over the years, he would have collapsed over her knees and poured out his anguish. But even in his inebriated state he could see that the opportunity wasn't available to him.

'I'm staying over,' he announced.

Amina continued her incantation, intense and unflinching.

'...*Al-Mutakabbir, Al-Khaliq, Al-Bari...*'

'Say something!' he appealed, and the child tumbled out of his voice.

'...*Al-Fattah, Al-Aleem, Al-Qabid, Al-Basit...*'

The cold brush off began to infuriate Samir. He wanted his old mother back. He wanted to do something to rouse her anger, her erstwhile complaints, her strictures, her loyal love – anything just to break that fucking obstinacy of hers so that they could start over again and put his stupidity and hubris behind them.

'Stop it!' he snapped.

'...*Al-Musawwir, Al-Ghaffar...*'

'Why are you acting this way?'

Amina stopped.

'You've ruined my *izzet*,' she finally admitted.

'What, how?'

'I told you to arrive at seven and you promised me you would.'

'I'm here.'

'Take a look at the time.'

Samir looked at the clock. It was past nine.

'But I didn't know – '

'I left all those messages.'

Samir took a jagged breath, and jabbed his forehead with the heel of his palm.

'I lost my phone,' he replied and pressed his pockets as if to verify his claim.

'It doesn't matter,' Amina said. 'They've gone now...'

'Who?'

'It doesn't matter.'

Samir vaguely remembered an arrangement. The details were still hazy in his mind. All he could recall was that it involved meeting 'relatives'. He rapped his head with his fist. Lately, he couldn't be sure of much.

'I don't have my phone,' he claimed again.

'It doesn't matter.'

Samir realised that this time he was being beaten down without confrontation or quarrel. Her apathy was all it took to shift the balance of power.

'Who were they?' he asked. 'What did they say to you? Who spilt the tea?'

With each question Samir's voice became more desperate. By taking on his mother's characteristics, unconsciously at least, he hoped to resuscitate that part of her that he was so used to battling against.

'I called and you didn't pick up,' Amina said

'I lost my phone. It was stolen!'

'I left so many messages.'

'*Amma*, it was stolen by some thugs. It happened last night, otherwise I would have called and I would have answered your calls – '

'It no longer matters.'

Samir wanted to grab his mother by the shoulders and rattle her like a moneybox. He wanted to shake out that maternal tenderness that belonged solely to him.

'I'm sorry. Please forgive me.'

'Sorry won't return my *izzet*. You've cut off my nose. Reena was right. You're a foreigner, you're wild, unmanageable.'

'I didn't get a single message,' he pleaded.

Amina continued rocking in the chair, staring fiercely at her own shadow skimming the carpet.

'Did you hear me?' Samir said, raking back his hair. And as he waited, desperate, apologetic and guilt-ridden, he realised just how vengeful his mother could be.

'I don't have a phone,' he said, pausing between each word.

But still his mother refused to yield. The woman just sat there reciting the names of Allah, her eyes feverish and fanatical.

Overwhelmed by her mute strength and the uselessness of his own words, Samir swung forward and swiped her prayer beads away, as if he held the inanimate object responsible for her mulish behaviour. The *tasbie* fell from her fist, ricocheted off her swaying knees and lay like a dead serpent by her feet. The symbol embodying Allah's ninety-nine names was suddenly dirtied and denounced by an act of childish impetuosity. Amina's eyes flinched in horror.

'Ishstaghfirullah!' she exclaimed.

Samir immediately crouched down in panic, scooped the *tasbie* up into his palm and placed it on his mother's lap, deferential as a chastened servant. He hadn't meant to disrespect her faith. All he wanted was her attention.

But as he sprang back up, the empty vodka bottle he'd drunk our of the previous night toppled out from the pocket of his hooded top. Time slowed as he watched it somersault through the air. He tried to make a grab for it, but only caught a fistful of air. The bottle cracked the bow of the chair and lay on the carpet. They both locked eyes on it at the same time.

Amina needed no second guess to realise what foul, iniquitous poison lay by her feet. The sight was like a sledgehammer to her lifetime effort to raise the child she had rescued from the home destroyed by alcohol. Her eyes widened into embers of rage, behind which rolled pictures of an irresponsible brother-in-law, and for a few seconds she lived through the horrors of his death and the hurt it had caused. The bed-ridden Azad with the yellow skin, the sallow face, the bony limbs. And then she remembered her sister who had developed shadows under the eyes and steep hollows around her collarbones from sitting forever at the back of her husband's bed, pinning her hopes on the baby growing inside her belly.

'Like father, like son,' Amina uttered.

Samir's brow creased.

'What did you say?'

She glowered at him.

'You're a drunkard, just like your father.'

Samir's face hardened in confusion.

'You make me sick!' his mother said, snarling in disgust.

Samir wiped his face. The touch of his fingertips left cold streaks across both cheeks.

'What are you saying?'

'You're a *modwa*, just like your father.'

'What are you talking about?' Samir demanded. 'Tell me!'

Against no perceivable future, Amina had no reason to keep guarding the past.

'Yes, your father thought he was a hero. How stupid and how juvenile he turned out to be. He was nothing but a flaming drunkard!' She laughed.

'Why are you laughing?'

'He was ready to shed his own blood to free his country. The books had taught him that. Oh, and how he listened to those words and marched into the battlefield. But the Pakistani army did a number on him. The man returned a cripple. And then he became a slave to self-pity. He neglected his young family. He didn't care about anything but himself. And then there was the drink, bottles and bottles and bottles and bottles of it. And how did he pay for it? Why, by gradually pawning everything in the house. And then there was the debt, and then finally Allah had seen enough and struck him down with the illness. Oh, how conveniently he checked out of life on the eve of your birth. And, tonight I've realised that his evil didn't die with him, but was passed on to you!'

With each revelation, the mythical hero's picture Samir had kept like a gallery piece inside his head fell face down and shattered. And in its place hung a picture of the hideous truth: the face of the ugly alcoholic – the image that gave Samir his reflection. In that moment he realised that the ancestral lineage was faithful and genetics had not betrayed him, but had obeyed precisely to the letter. He was history's shameful reincarnation standing before its long-term victim.

'Forgive me, *Amma*,' he said.

'Go away!'

Amina began to cough and smothered her mouth with her forearm. Samir rushed to the kitchen. Amina heard him banging the cupboard doors, twisting the tap, and then shoving the glass under the rush of water. When he returned to the room and offered it to her she pushed it away. Water spilled over his wrist and left his sleeve sodden.

'Take it,' he persisted.

'I told you to leave the house.'

'I won't!'

226

Samir clung not only to the glass, but also to the only truth that now mattered. He still had his mother. She was there in front of him. A real person – not a phantom, a simulacrum, or the cipher that his father had always been. Half of her blood coursed through him and it was this good blood that had compelled him to return to the house to make amends.

'Go!'

'No!' he said.

'You're making my house impure. You're a stranger to me, you're a *kaffir* destined for hellfire.'

'*Amma?*'

'Go away.'

'You can't do this.'

'Yes, I can.'

'*Amma*, I'm your son.'

'I am not your mother!!' Amina declared fiercely, ripping out the lie that formed the very bedrock of their relationship. She continued to glare at him even after the truth had spilled out into the silence.

Samir stood slack-jawed and a glassy idiocy came over him. Instinct told him this wasn't just a mother's outburst but the truth revealed in cold contempt.

'Now you've heard it. Get out of my house. You belong with the infidels. You are no different from them,' Amina ranted.

'Who is my mother?'

Amina offered no answer. In the stillness, only the clock on the mantelpiece ticked on, its pendulum kept swinging, time kept moving.

'Who is she?' he yelled. He grabbed her by the shoulders and shook her with the force of all his frustration.

She looked coldly into his eyes.

'My older sister died giving birth to you. She bled to death to bring sin into the world. If only I'd read the signs. If only I'd left you in that bassinet you'd probably have lived your life on the streets, polishing shoes, begging or thieving. Instead I took you into my arms. I brought you to this country, gave you a future. And look at you now – a heathen drowned in the devil's piss!'

Samir let go of her shoulders and stepped back. His eyes flickered at her in dismay. He was incensed by Amina's self-righteousness; even now she had to haul herself up onto the moral platform.

'I didn't ask you to,' he replied through gritted teeth.

'It's easy for you to say that now.'

'What do you want, a medal?'

'You've grown up in this country. How can I possibly expect you to know anything about gratitude?'

'Stop being so high and mighty,' Samir screamed.

'What did you say?'

'You always think yourself to be so right.'

'I raised you.'

'And to what end. What selfish end?'

'How dare you!'

'You lied to me,' Samir cried. 'I didn't ask you to bring me to this country. I didn't ask you to invent a glorious father for me. I didn't ask you to pretend to be my mother. You made those decisions. You created the rules of this game; you've directed this façade. You raised me for your sake, your pension scheme, that's all I am to you. You're just a bitter woman hiding behind your sanctimonious ideas. You keep praying to a God waiting for the payoff. You're the impostor, the real hypocrite.'

Amina abandoned her chair and charged at Samir throwing her fists like a person deranged. Samir – who was once the recipient of all her maternal affections – now became the focus of her deepest hate.

'*Harami, modwaar bachcha!*' she screamed, beating his chest.

Samir stood his ground and allowed Amina to spill her fury upon him. In attacking her faith he had chosen a false target. And he knew it too, feeling the thud of her wild blows, and the rage in her voice drumming against his ears.

'Go to hell!' she yelled. 'All that money I squandered getting the *Maulana* to teach you who we are. And now you have the nerve to question my beliefs and speak so obscenely about my religion. You even have the gall to challenge Allah!'

Samir clasped Amina's wrists so she could no longer hit him. He squeezed the delicate bones as hard as he could in the hope she would absorb some of his pain and for once feel the living, breathing sickness inside him which she hadn't the capacity to sense, so blinkered was she by her commitment to build an orderly world where she could display him like her framed certificate to tell the world that she had conquered life.

'You have no idea,' he said.

'Let go of me!'

Amina contorted her arms to free herself until Samir released her wrists and she rocked back.

'That man was dirt!' he said.

'What are you talking about?'

'The fucking *Maulana!*'

'Don't you dare!'

'A filthy rat, that's what he was,'

Amina clapped her hands over her ears. Samir stepped forward and pulled them away.

'Listen to me,' he shouted. 'That man did things to me. And you weren't there to save me. You kept putting me back in there, forcing me back into that same room.'

'What?'

'You revered the ground he walked on. *A pillar of the community*, those were your words, don't you remember? You left me in that room alone with him, day in, day out. I tried to tell you but you didn't listen, you didn't want to know. All you cared about was shovelling as much religion into me as possible. There was no one else I could go to. I was so scared. And after he used me, he said that it was my fault. He said that no one would listen to me and even if they did that no one would believe me. He was right. You let him do that to me! He — '

'What are you talking about? You're not making any sense,' Amina said.

Samir stuttered. He swore out loud:

'*Fuck, fuck, fuck, fuck, fuck…*'

The Bengali words weren't available to him because he didn't know what they were. Try as he might, he could not articulate the horror of those memories now fractured by time. He briefly closed his eyes and relived those episodes when his neck would turn goosebumpy, his toes curl up, the hot

breath of the *Maulana* fill his ear and his body clench up. When he opened
his eyes they were glazed over.

'The man touched me. He made me touch him. And he touched me,
breathed on me, held me, touched me, and he threatened me. He, he, he, he...'

Claustrophobia came upon him. Samir felt like he was an animal writhing
through a burrow, but the exit was tapering. He felt his breath becoming
shallower. But he had come too far to stop. He had to make himself understood.
So he resorted to simple description, suddenly inured to the vulgarity, as if the
innocent child in him stepped out of the past to complete his most painful
revelation.

'The man used to force me to sit on his lap. He used to pull my *lungi* up
and pull his *lungi* down. And all I could do was scrunch my eyes closed and
wait for it to stop. He raped me.'

'What?' Amina queried in disgust, repelled both by what she heard and the
implication that she was the one who had done wrong. Her eyes darted wildly
as she tried to make sense of what he'd said. But it sounded wrong to her.

'You're a drunkard! You have no idea what you're saying, just get out of my
house, you drunken dog, you *kaffir*, just go!' she barked.

In the moment she was convinced that the alcohol was to blame.

'You come into my house and utter such filth! Have you no shame?'

Samir screwed up his face in disbelief. He clenched every filament of his
body and then swung his bruised leg at the coffee table. It toppled over, the
vessel of water sailed across the room and the glass-top shattered sending
shards across the carpet. Unsatisfied, he swiped up the table lamp from the
carpet, smashed the light bulb against the wall and threw the metal carcass at
the clock on the mantelpiece. Its white cable trailed, now torn from its plug
which remained partially lodged in the socket.

Samir picked up the vodka bottle from the floor and stormed out of the
room. He slammed the front door so brutally that the windows juddered from
the force. Amina heard the gate crash against the latch and then snap back
with a quieter echo.

In the ensuing lull Amina stepped over the entrails of her son's anger
strewn all over the room. She picked up the cough syrup by her feet, the box
still in its cellophane seal. She tried to read the ingredients. She was con-

vinced it contained alcohol. The words on the box confused her. She sneered at the fact that even after all these years she couldn't read English with much fluency or confidence. Thirty years in the same country and she couldn't read the bloody language. She took a few steps and dropped the box in the wastebasket by her sewing machine.

Amina returned to her rocking chair and sat back down. There she rocked and rocked and rocked. The prayer beads had fallen from her lap a long time ago. The string had come apart beneath her feet and a few beads had rolled underneath the bow spindles where the sway of the wood crushed them into the carpet. Her faith turned to dust.

Removing the mask

Samir limped through the dark, empty street. He spat out the gum he'd been chewing savagely since leaving the house. His tongue was so parched from the fight that the cold air tasted faintly of brine. Each breath he took scratched the back of his throat.

He glared straight ahead, with flat, stony composure. Unlike Amina he had no faith to lean upon. No prayer to utter. No *tasbee* beads to slide through his fingers. Worst of all, he had no weed to roll up. Only a couple of uppers were buried in one of his pockets, but these were not a good idea in his current state. He had no phone, hence no number to call Ali, from whom he could buy an eighth of hash and see the night away toking on a park bench.

Walking, he remained heedless of everything around him, even as he passed a horde of teenagers loitering on a half-demolished wall, one of whom slid off and approached him hunched like a pugilist to ask for a cigarette, then *tsked* aggressively when Samir ignored the request and walked on. Only the full moon pursued Samir intimately, its silvery reflection sliding from window to window in the upper storeys of the terraced tenements.

Samir hailed a passing bus, jumped on board, flashed his travelcard and crashed down on the nearest seat. The elderly woman who he sat next to shifted to the seat's corner, pressing her ageing bulk nervously against the side of the bus. But Samir didn't notice her either. Presently nothing reached his senses.

When he reached the door of his flat he patted his trousers but couldn't find his keys. He rummaged through every pocket, but all he fished out was his wallet and the empty bottle. He guessed that he must have dropped the keys back at the house.

'For fucksakes!' he growled.

He hurled the bottle on the steps. It shattered against the asphalt with a glassy crash. Several lights came on, each window snapping open at the indiscretion like a sleeping dog's eye. He shot a look at each lit window and saw the curtain twitch behind one of them. The lights then went out one by one. Again he searched his pockets, emptying them of all the rubbish they had accumulated over time: receipts, sweet wrappers, coins and an empty Rizzla packet. Then forgetting about the keys altogether, he hunted instead for a joint, hoping that one might have got lodged somewhere, but the search ended again in disappointment.

He sat on the cold steps raking back his hair. Instinctively, he reached for his cigarettes. He put one between his lips and struck a match, only to decide that he didn't want it. He watched the matchstick as the flame burned through it, slowly annihilating its lean architecture. He spat the cigarette out and cast his attention on the wooden sign nailed on the trunk which instructed the residents to 'Keep off the grass'. Samir expelled a bark of laughter.

A thought suddenly came into Samir's head. He got up, stepped forward a few paces and turned to gaze up at Amber's balcony. Lo and behold, there she was watching him from behind the patio window, her presence attesting to the growing intimacy of their fortuitous encounter. He rubbed his eyes to make sure that it wasn't his state of high emotion playing a cruel trick on him.

As if reading his doubt, Amber moved closer to the window and touched the pane of glass with her fingertips. He almost felt the tender tap of her fingers on his face. Samir yanked out the lining of his trouser pockets to mime his keyless predicament. He looked as eager as a doe-eyed dog gazing at its owner, wanting to be let back into the house.

Amber raised a palm in a *wait there* gesture and went back inside. Squinting, he could just about make out the ghostly breath she had left on the windowpane and the skeletal imprint of her hand.

A moment later the buzzer on the entryphone sounded and the door jerked loose from its frame. Samir propelled himself towards it. He limped up the steps as quickly as he could, sending an echo up the stairwell. He went up to the second floor landing.

He found her door already ajar. He pushed through, but on the threshold he stopped. He experienced a bolt of panic realising that there was nothing to suggest the invitation had been extended to her flat. But, no, the door was open. It was the seductive profile of Amber's silhouette in the candle-lit hallway that fazed him. Something in the curvature of her body beneath the dressing gown stoked a feeling he tried to suppress by standing as still as he could. He was physically drained too, his lips chapped from the wind-chill, his leg still hurting, the back of his neck prickled by a cold sweat. Suddenly everything about this meeting appeared impregnated with unspoken intention. He was hit by a pang of embarrassment, realising that he, the lodger from upstairs, was intruding on her at this late hour.

'Hi,' she said.

'Hi,' Samir replied, between gasps of air, his heart banging like a drum.

'What is it?' Amber asked.

'I'm sorry. I shouldn't have come up.'

'What were you doing outside?'

'I'm locked out of the flat.'

Amber read the anxiety on his face, the full, almost girlish lips quivering in fright. The ghost-like resident she had got to know in the last few days looked in a sorry state. He had about him the vulnerability of a lost child with no claimant in sight.

Besides, his appearance offered up a delightful diversion from the alternative, which was to spend the evening alone while her daughter was away, subsumed by the room's depressing décor. Tonight fate had served her someone to clink glasses with.

'Why don't you stay here, then?' she asked.

Samir didn't reply, but stood still.

'You can't just stand there, though.'

Samir stepped inside and Amber brushed past him. She drove away the ills of the outside world with a light push of the door. The silver bracelets around her slender wrists jangled.

'I'm sorry,' he said again.

'What for?'

'For troubling you.'

Samir began chewing his fingernails.

'What's the matter?' she asked. 'I thought you were going to spend the evening with your mother?'

Samir was convinced she could see the same ugliness his mother had seen in him tonight. He tugged on his hooded top as if trying to bring down a curtain, willing his eyes not to peel away from her face in case she read it as a sign of admission.

'We had a fight,' he said.

'What?'

'She told me to leave the house.'

Amber touched his arm.

'Don't worry. Things will be better in the morning. I promise.'

'I'm locked out,' he said. 'And there's no one to let me in.'

'Where's your key?'

'I lost it.'

Amber laughed.

'It's not been a lucky few days for you.'

Amber took him by the elbow. She steered him into the lounge and ushered him to one of the easy chairs.

'I think you need a drink.' She left him perched on the edge of the old fraying seat, disappeared to the kitchen and returned with a bottle of wine and a couple of mugs hooked on her fingers. She glared at the label myopically; the bottle was uncorked and sweaty from fridge mist.

'What have we here?' she said, scanning the label. 'It's from the Rhone Valley.'

She poured him half a mug.

'There,' she said, extending it to him.

Samir reached out and fumbled for the drink. Once gripping it, he took rapid gulps, his diffidence now overcome by thirst. Amber watched, mesmerised by his Adam's apple bobbing like a buoy under the taut young skin.

'Why did you have a fight?' she asked, pouring some wine for herself.

Samir finished the wine, wincing as the last drop went down. It tasted cheap with a tart, vinegary kick.

'It no longer matters,' Samir said.

Amber shook her head.

'You're angry at the moment. We all say things in the heat of the moment, but then we regret them, say sorry and things go back to normal.'

Samir turned to the shelf behind the television where the bouquet of fresh roses blossomed out of an old milk bottle, the clutch of stalks submerged in clear tap water.

'Are those from your boyfriend?' he asked.

Amber smiled, a little taken aback by the question.

'I'm trying to get rid of the smell in the flat.'

'What's wrong with air-freshener?'

'Nothing.'

'It would probably be more fragrant,' Samir said.

'I prefer flowers.'

Samir glided his forefinger over the rim of the mug in thought.

'There's something crazy about shoving flowers into a vase.'

'What are you talking about?'

'Think about it. You pull 'em out of the ground because they look alive and colourful and beautiful. But by doing that you've already killed them and you're just watching them wither and rot away. Don't you think it's a crazy thing to do?'

'More wine, Herr Philosopher?'

Samir offered his mug and Amber poured the wine with a hand behind her arched back, imitating the elegance with which she refilled glasses at work. Her manager, who claimed to have learned his trade in London's swankiest eateries, insisted on the importance of an upright posture and kept drilling it into every member of his team, claiming that it was all part of the service.

'*Voilà!*' she said, once she'd finished filling his mug.

Samir could already sense his head becoming pleasantly liquid, all of his mother's vitriol being gradually hosed down by the alcohol. The anger had ebbed too, replaced by a feverish renaissance – a rebirth as the person he now knew he really was – armed with the crazy new knowledge that drink was his birthright. He raised his mug to toast this new truth.

'Cheers.'

'What happened to you tonight, then?' Amber asked.

'What?'

'You're acting strangely?'

'I'm celebrating a new beginning.'

Amber put her mug down on the carpet and plonked herself beside him. She placed the bottle between them. She mimed a cylindrical telescope with both hands and eyed Samir through it.

'Hmmm, this sure don't look like a celebration to me.'

Samir continued to drink quickly, appreciating how each swallow was loosening the flesh from his bones, the thoughts from his brain.

'Relax,' she said, leaning back and propping herself up on one arm. 'You can take your time. I don't think there's a leak in the cup.'

Samir put the mug down.

'I'm sorry I caused all that commotion outside,' he said.

'No apologies, please.'

'Well, for what it's worth.'

'Everyone has their cross to bear.'

'I –'

Amber raised her hand, intimating that no explanation was necessary. She put her finger to her lips and rolled her eyes up to the Andean mask that was hanging on the wall behind Samir.

'You do realise that these walls have eyes and ears,' she whispered, leaning forward, her body rocking unsteadily from the waist up, threatening to topple over at the slightest touch.

Samir craned his neck to look up over his shoulder.

'What is it?'

'Can you see how it stares? I think it carries a curse.'

'Don't be silly,' Samir said.

'It's scary. It glares at me all day.'

Samir studied the crudely crafted artefact. The tombstone teeth set in a snarl did its best to appear scary. The touch of rouge on its cheeks hinted at the grotesque. Samir bared his teeth and snarled back at it.

'It's not scary at all,' he said. 'It's kind of pathetic.'

'How so?'

'Well consider this. Whoever wears it is trying to be something they're not. They're hiding behind it.'

'Oh really, wise guy.'

Samir kept staring. The more he stared at it, the more he saw his own story unravel from it and the less he liked it. It symbolised the ugly deception unmasked only an hour ago. The shock of it returned to him, a pinprick of pain. To be duped by a mother who wasn't his mother for all these years was so outrageous that it verged on the ridiculous. A silent rage sprang from a lucidity that lay further than any hurt he could quell by shouting or throwing a tantrum. He kept it at bay by drinking more alcohol.

'It's hideous!' he said.

A memory from earlier returned to him. His mother chanting all those Arabic names, names she had learnt by rote. He stared hard at the floor.

'How poetically marvellous,' he muttered. 'The masked woman duped by the mask of God!'

'What?'

Samir looked up, his large eyes gleaming, vindication swimming within them.

'Is it yours?' he asked.

'Yes,' Amber replied.

'Well if you hate it that much, why don't we get rid of it?'

'OK,' Amber said, beaming in drunken glee.

Samir finished the drink. He slammed the mug down on the carpet and rose to his feet. He went to the mask and, rocking on tiptoes, unhooked it and brought it down. It was insubstantial in weight, carved from a lightwood. He felt he could snap it with his hands if he wanted.

'Easy!'

Amber let out a yelp of delight. Samir looked about the room, holding the mask by hooking his fingers into the hollows of its eyes. He strode to the balcony door, put the mask down against his shin. He slid the door open.

'What are you going to do?' Amber asked.

Samir picked up the mask and stepped outside into the cold. Amber staggered to her feet and followed him. Samir held the mask out over the railing with a religious flourish, as if he were about to perform a sacrificial offering. He turned to face Amber. She stood wide-eyed, hugging herself, braced against the cold. Samir lowered his voice to a whisper:

'How about it, yes?'

'Erm, yes.'

'You sure?'

'Can't argue,' Amber said in sheer admiration.

Samir let go of the wooden face and shouted 'Timber!' at the top of his voice to an empty forecourt, his arms spread out theatrically in front of him, making it sound like a holy appellation. The two then leant their elbows on the cold railing, craned their neck over the guard and watched it hurtle through the air and hit the concrete ground with a feeble clonk that didn't live up to the operatic preamble. It split into two, each half toppling on its side like a cracked walnut. The pair looked at each other, at the remains below and then again at each other. They both let out a laugh. Amber planted an enthusiastic kiss on his cheek; the kiss of an enthralled schoolgirl.

They went back indoors, sat on the carpet, clinked mugs merrily. They drank once again. Amber lay on her side, with one hand propping up her head in a classical chaise longue pose. Samir sat cross-legged beside her. He drained his mug of its last drop and refilled from the bottle. He was indifferent now to the wine's rancid taste. And as he drank, he caught her looking at the pale, maskless outline left on the wall.

'What's wrong?'

Amber rolled onto her stomach, rested her chin on both fists and lifted her heels off the ground. She looked squarely at Samir.

'Gail will throw a fit when she finds out,' she said.

'Who's Gail? I thought you said – '

'I lied.'

They fell about in a fit of giggles.

'So it belongs to Gail?'

'Technically. I think it might actually belong to her mother.'

'Oh you're in big trouble then.'

'I'll just have to face the consequence,' Amber said, and the two rolled about with laughter once again.

'You're a little crazy,' Amber said.

'A total headcase.'

Amber rocked forward and touched Samir's brow. She moved closer to him. Samir bit his lip in silent protest and his body knotted tight. He caught the lavender fragrance on her neck.

'What's wrong?' she asked.

'Nothing,' Samir replied, looking down to deflect the gaze. 'Nothing at all.'

'You're still wound up,' Amber said. 'I might just have the magic to mellow things.'

Amber reached for her cigarette packet and took out the joints that Samir had given her. She looked around for her lighter but couldn't see it.

'Do you have a light?'

Samir threw a matchbox into her lap. He watched her take out a stick, strike it several times before the flame spurted, then she held it up to the joint while cupping her beautiful hands, her head bent low, the tumble of curly hair spilling over her face. She took a draw and blew a perfect smoke ring.

'That's better,' she said.

She passed it to him. They smoked. They drank. They talked about frivolous things that didn't matter to either of them. When Amber asked him about why he had left his mother in the first place, Samir laughed. His lids were beginning to feel heavy.

'I longed for solitude so that I could find myself and, when I found it, I longed to go back home,' he said.

'Why?' she said, trying to suppress a laugh.

'Because I'm afraid of the dark,' he said, pulling up his hood and flailing his arms.

They fell about laughing like school kids, until there was no more laughter left inside them. Samir finished the joint and stubbed it out on the heel of his trainers.

'I've caused a terrible mess,' he said.

He then looked deep into Amber's eyes.

'All I wanted was a chance to go to college.'

Amber sensed his sadness. Her smile tightened.

'What's stopping you?' she asked.

'I'm a waster. I left school without any qualifications. I can't spell.'

Amber furrowed her brow.

'I think it might be your lack of confidence that's stopping you. You should do an art course. Clearly you're talented, but you can't see it.'

Samir thought to himself. Of course now that there was no mother to please, he could draw to his heart's content.

'Maybe I will.'

'I've got the munchies,' Amber suddenly declared. 'You hungry?'

Samir shook his head.

'You wait here,' Amber said, as she rolled onto her bottom then swayed to her feet, briefly grabbing Samir's shoulder to steady herself. She went to the kitchen. Samir heard her knocking about the room. He pictured her clumsy hands opening drawers, bashing plates, grabbing cutlery. It sounded like the fumblings of a blind person in an unfamiliar room. Amber walked back holding a cherry cheesecake on a plate. A bread knife sat precariously on top. She used it to saw the cake messily into three segments. The jam from the cherries stuck to the knife and cream oozed richly from the flanks.

'A slice for me, a slice for you and the rest for Amy.'

'Amy likes cake?' Samir asked.

'It's her favourite treat.'

'She's got a sweet tooth?'

'She takes after her mother,' Amber said.

'Do you know the secret to good parenting?' Samir asked.

'What?'

'Always end the name of your child with a vowel, so that when you yell the name your voice will carry,' he said.

'Where did you get that from, a Christmas cracker?'

'The Cosby Show,' Samir replied.

'Any other pearls of wisdom you'd like to share?'

'Not at the moment.'

As she laughed, she looked at him with a remote expression in her eyes, as if in that instant she saw through him, at the bruises he carried beneath the muscle and sinew of his body.

'Hey, you're not a waster! Believe me, I know. You just need to believe in yourself a bit. That's one of the biggest hurdles any of us ever faces when we're young.'

'Well, what do you know, I've got my first fan.'

Amber smiled.

'Underneath all the clobber, and reckless behaviour, you're a good person. I know it. And I'm sure your mother knows it too.'

Samir's face tingled and the feeling spread through his arms to his hands. As much as he sensed the night segueing into narcosis, he equally wanted to preserve it, to be in possession of it. He sought to do whatever he could to prolong this alliance. In that instant he thought he had fallen in love with Amber because she accepted him without judgment or expectation.

'I'm afraid I might fall asleep,' he said.

'In that case, let's get up and dance,' she said.

'Are you being serious?'

'Go on, get up,' she said.

'But there's no music.'

'Ye of little faith.'

Amber searched the floor and reached for her portable CD player. She put the earphones clumsily over Samir's head so that the cans weren't in line with the ears and one side was playing to his cheekbone. She turned it on, put the player into his fleece pocket and pulled him to his feet. Samir obliged even though the music wasn't conducive to dancing. He doffed his imaginary top hat. She took Samir's hand and arranged their bodies into a ballroom stance. They pranced about, spinning in the small space, Samir giving into the bizarre performance and moueing like a matinee idol. His body was too anesthetised to feel any pain. After several twirls she stopped and leant backwards over his arm until her leg lifted into the air and the tumble of hair cascaded down to the carpet. When he pulled her up, they lost their balance and fell about on the sofa in a heap, heads touching and legs tangled up. Accidentally, she butted his cheekbone with her forehead.

'Oops, sorry,' she said. 'Are you OK?'

'Yes.'

They were both gasping for breath. She touched the graze on his cheek and traced a finger down the ridge of his nose. She removed the earphones.

'You're beautiful,' she said.

The caress made Samir flinch, but he relaxed and let her draw closer to him. He closed his eyes. He allowed himself to smell her hair, pressed his nose against her temple and glided the hunger in his nostrils down the length of her neck to the lavender smell on the vale of her throat. He caught the intimacy of her warm breath.

'You're beautiful too,' he said.

He ran his fingertips over her mouth and moved his closer to hers. They finally kissed, lightly at first but then pressing their lips harder against each other's, wallowing in their drug-filled pleasure, the night's alcohol oozing from their pores as they clung to one another. The thrill of arousal went off like tiny flares against the darkening skies of their cognisance. Samir's eyes struggled to stay open and she threatened to disappear into a blur. He had to do something. With his remaining strength he pulled away from her.

'Can I use the bathroom?'

Amber smiled at him sleepily and lifted a heavy arm in the direction of the bathroom. Samir stood up and wove his way to where the arrow of her arm had pointed. The instant he found himself in the bathroom he clicked the lock shut. He groped the air and snatched the light cord, pulled it, giving life to the crudest florescent tube. Its sides were furred in dust.

'What a mess!' he muttered, leaning over the basin, trying to get a steady focus on his gaunt reflection in the mirror. 'Where are they, where are they?' he repeated to himself, searching inside his back pocket from which he eventually took out the two yellow dexies. He popped one in his mouth and swallowed it. Samir turned the taps and splashed cold water in his face, flicking it into his pupils. He leaned into the mirror and examined the dark circles under his eyes. He stuck his tongue out to make sure it was clean, scraped it with his fingernails and washed them under the tap. He slammed the toilet seat down, sat on it and waited several minutes. Impatience caused him to swallow the other pill as well. He waited. He counted to a hundred. He waited a bit longer, counted to another hundred. Gradually he sensed every cord of his body find strength and pull tight as the dexies provided the necessary scaffolding for him to go back to the living room and into Amber's arms. He unlocked the bolt and emerged.

But when he came out he found Amber sprawled on the sofa, fast asleep. The wine bottle was also on its side beside the sofa, and the cheesecake, half eaten, looked an amputated mess, the bloody jam smeared all over the plate and the knife sticking out of it like a murder weapon left in its victim. Samir leant over Amber's face. She looked happier asleep, somehow, more content. He draped the bath towel from the radiator over her. He touched the curve of her forehead. It was warm, emphatically human. He planted a soft kiss on her brow.

Samir cleaned the plate with his thumb and took it to the kitchen. His forehead began to perspire a little. He put his head against the refrigerator door then opened it to meet the blast of cool air. Several minutes later he put the cheesecake back in the fridge. He chucked the bottle in the bin, collected the mugs to rinse, but abandoned them in the sink. He came back to the living room and tried to sit down on the chair, put his feet up and curl up like a cat, but felt increasingly fidgety. His teeth chattered and his limbs refused to sit still. Worst of all, it caused the memory of the fight with his mother, previously quelled by alcohol, to come rushing together and find form, like scattered metal shavings drawn by a magnet of lucidity.

Samir got up and hurried to the door, knowing he had to get outside. He needed to walk this off in the absolute stillness of night, melt into the inkblot where nothing could invade his senses. So he set off down the stairwell, holding on to the banister and taking care to be as quiet as possible. Back outside, he headed straight for his hideaway hut in the park where no one could find him; not that he expected anyone to come looking.

Samir beta, kuay tuuy?

With prayer beads crushed and her faith turned to dust, Amina sat in the dark, rocking in her chair. The room was bisected by a single bone of streetlight that had crept in through the gap in the curtain. She stared blindly at the clock face, now a web of shattered glass behind which the hand quivered with a violent impotence, like a trapped insect. The pendulum below hung motionless, its ticking quelled, leaving a dearth in the room that Amina wasn't used to. In this unfamiliar silence, guilt towered over Amina demanding an explanation.

What had she done?

Crazed by her own pain, she had ripped open Samir's past and performed the most brutal autopsy to expose the lie on which she had raised him. She had revealed his father's true identity merely to exact her revenge. Possessed by anger, she had reduced Samir to the demon child that murdered her sister the moment he slid out of her bleeding birth canal.

But, perhaps worst of all, she had refused to listen to Samir's awful secret all those years ago, and even tonight when he forced her to hear the truth she had rejected it outright. Now the reality weighed down on her: the fact that she had meant none of the things she had said. It was just fury blasting its hot air. And now that it had blown itself out, she felt nothing but the most altruistic affection for her son. She knew that the hatred she had felt towards Samir tonight amounted to nothing more than a fingermark upon the smooth glass of a mother's soul. And her love had wiped it clean. She wanted to tell him all this now – draw him to her, calm him, care for him, comfort him. But it was all too late. Where on earth could he be at this time of night?

Lurching between dread and disbelief, wherever Amina turned, every shard of glass she looked at, all she could see was the extent to which her boy had suffered in his childhood. The violation brutally pulled on her conscience, forcing her to live through her child's darkest past. She envisioned every snatch of detail: the *Maulana* calling Samir in for his daily lesson, closing the door of the annex, pulling Samir onto his lap, laying his filthy hands on her boy's trembling skin, kneading his young flesh for his own gratification. She imagined the strength with which he must have held on to the child's wafer thin hips. She remembered her child's pleas not to be sent to those lessons, how he used to climb the roof and hide himself away. And how she used to force him to come down and order him back in there, time and again. Amina buried her head into her hands. She didn't know what else to do.

How easily had the man gnawed rodent-like through her child's innocence – what's more, under her own roof, in her homeland! The revelation debased her maternal role to a single act of irresponsibility. Now things began to make sense. Her son had always been a shy and reticent boy, but now her mind fixed itself on the episodes when he had inexplicably retreated into himself. The nights after returning from their trip to Bangladesh when she would hear him wake from some nightmare and rush into his room, switch the light on, and sit helplessly by his side, sweeping back his sweaty fringe, laying her cool hand on his burning brow.

Amina had no idea what her son had suffered during those six months. Other than witnessing tonight's fit of rage, she had no way of knowing how damaged he really was. The only thing she could be certain of was that the man he had grown into bore little resemblance to the man he was supposed to be. She had failed as a mother.

Plagued by these thoughts, she recited verses of the Qur'an, staring blindly into space. But after a short while her throat became tight and rough, and the melody of her voice distorted. Eventually, the words crumbled into incomprehensible noise and the noise changed into a desperate sob.

It took a while for her wretched cries to stop, the sound of each gasp of breath travelling to the farthest corners of the empty house, but there was no one to come running and offer the comfort she needed. Abruptly, Amina roused herself. She slipped her feet into her sandals and left the room. Glass crunched beneath her feet. She took the creaking stairs to the bathroom and headed straight for her medicine cabinet. She opened it and riffled through the contents. She threw out packs of aspirin, a bottle of antibiotics, shampoos, creams and other toiletries, hungering only for the pills that mattered.

Eventually she found them. Doctor Godwin's pills. The melded yellow-and-red capsules. The ones to take before bedtime. She dropped a couple into her mouth, and then another two for good measure. For a while she stood still, then came downstairs, turned on the taps in the kitchen and thrust her hands under the rapid stream. She cupped her palms and drank palm after palm of cold water. Her feverish mind bolted from one thought to another as if her memory was a corridor filled with cupboards, and behind each door lived the testimony of another failing.

She suffered a spell of dizziness, and her heart began beating so hard it felt as though someone had taken a sledgehammer inside her. The pictures of her son being molested behind the closed doors of the annex returned to haunt her. She spoke out loud to herself. She ordered her body to calm down: *stop shaking, you stupid woman, just stop it,* but anxiety was like an evil man groping her with rough hands and deaf ears, hungry, and showing no compunction.

In the moments that followed the only thing Amina could do was pace up and down the hallway. But with silence clotting the air like something thick and viscous, each step felt long and laboured, and an effort against everything and nothing. So she went back into the kitchen, up to the sink, reached for the stream of water and rinsed her mouth again. The water dripped down her nose and chin. Her wet fringe clung to her sweaty forehead, creating the illusion that her face was rimed with fractures, and about to crumble. She made herself sit down on the kitchen chair. With her feet she pushed down on the wooden stretch, drew her knees up and buried her head in them. She swayed madly. She began to cry again and the tears rolled down her face.

'Why, why, why, why, why, why?' she asked.

An old warning returned to haunt her. A voice she recognised immediately: '*...and remember, too, that everything may be forgotten, except the lies. They go on and they grow. They live through those that suffer. You will suffer.*'

Hounded by the quiet and the unspoken sense that her condition was a judgment, and her life a long, redemptive haul for that one lie, Amina was suddenly determined to make amends. She wanted her Samir back. He was hurt, hungry and cast out into the cold. She wasn't bound by any duty, but simply driven by the purest love. She dropped her feet back onto the floor.

'He's my son no matter what,' she muttered. She rose from the seat, made her way out of the house and slammed the door shut behind her. She walked down the street, calling out his name, '*Samir beta, kuay tuuy?*' She was convinced that he was just round the corner, or hiding behind a bramble bush, or crouched behind a parked car, or squatting in someone's front garden, sulking, waiting for her to call him home and serve him the food he had asked for.

'Samir, where are you?' she repeated, in her warm motherly way. The way she used to call out to him after setting the dinner table.

Her voice gradually grew louder and more desperate. Her legs became increasingly uncertain as she wandered down the cold, hard pavement. She passed the rows of houses, looking at the white sign with the street name, distracted at one point by the silver wind-chime under the architrave of a house which tinkled with an eerie musical tone in the draught. Soon she arrived at the street's mouth. The vagrant with the cleft lip was sitting on a low garden wall trying to pull his boots off to examine the black blisters on his toes.

'You all right, love?' he asked as she passed him.

She wasn't right at all. The space she stood in grew out like a dark desert and subdued her with its lifelessness, its complete apathy towards her search, its unwillingness to comply and give back her son. Inside the all-encompassing night her calls lifted into the black skies, drifted aimlessly and died. Two cars went by. Their headlamps jerked in the dip of the road and offered a passing flood of light. But Samir was nowhere to be seen in the momentary glare.

'Can you spare fifty pence, love?' she heard the vagrant call out behind her.

Amina was overcome by fatigue. When she breathed, the phlegm whirred in her throat. *He always returns*, she told herself as she turned back, ignoring the vagrant whose polite plea had turned to scorn: *to hell with you, fucking tight, Paki bitch.*

When she returned, it occurred to her that she didn't have her keys. She was locked out. She used the side entrance to get into her garden, fumbling along the brick and mortar of her house. Her face was pale and bloodless. Her eyes struggled to make sense of anything in the unlit yard. Before long, the silhouette of the discarded chair rose before her. The moment felt numinous. She was being pilloried, cast out into the cold and instructed to go to the chair to receive her punishment for being the murderess of her child's innocence.

Sensing the thick drip of Doctor Godwin's antidote working its way into her veins, plying her with the sleep she sought, Amina was lured into the chair where she sat down to rest. She drew into herself. Mist came out in small breaths from her shivering mouth. Her fingertips grew numb. They were no longer a part of her.

She gazed at the back of her house, its paintwork peeling, its body angular in repose. She could make out the dark moss between the paving, the weeds and ferns breaking through the stepping-stones that led to the back of the garden. She realised it was stupidity that had stopped her from telling Samir the truth. She couldn't excuse herself, or even see how it was possible that the secret she kept from him had any worth, because, to her, Samir had always been her son. From his birth onwards she had been his mother. Come what may she would always be his mother.

A flush from the pills spread colour in her face. Her lungs stopped clamouring for air and her breath came and went in tiny batches. A sleepy tingle that began in her toes spread through her legs and crawled to her chest. She could no longer feel the cold. She felt as warm as liquid wax beneath a serene candle flame. In the sweet helplessness she saw fiery colours, tints of green, blue, and an iridescent corona rise over the house. The sky changed colour: the moon emerged from behind a passing cloud and looked like a bulb lit just for her.

She curled up in the chair, like a pale question mark with her hands pressed between her knees. The apple tree seemed to lean over until she was taken into its shadow. She looked up to see the moon appear like a hole in the sky. The light up there was an immense round blazing thing with a magnificence that diminished the darkness and enveloped her. She felt like a tide being pulled up. A warm tranquillity spread through her body, from her toes to her brow, to the very roots of her hair.

Amina lay back, sensing the whole of her being rise up into another world, warm and white and filled with wellbeing. She luxuriated in the vision of faith and, feeling an enormous sense of gratitude, she recited the *Shahadah*. Her lips barely moved:

lā 'ilāha 'illā l-Lāh, Muḥammad rasūlu l-Lāh

There is no god but God, Muhammad is the messenger of God.

A minute later the moon disappeared behind another cloud. Darkness fell over the garden and in that instant Amina was barely visible wrapped in her white sari. A waterlily in a pool of darkness. Inside the house there was only stillness except for a tap left running in the kitchen, its silver stream gleaming wonderfully in the night.

Buried treasure

In the dead of night Samir gripped the wrought iron bars of the park gates. His fingers were curled tight around the cold metal, holding on to his composure as much as the bars themselves. He hauled himself up and over, grimacing at the bruised leg, the tendons tensing in pain as he groped to reach the other side. He jumped down, bending his knees to cushion the fall. One of his feet landed in a puddle, the splash soaking him to his ankle. He scurried through the clearing, taking the familiar route, and hunkered down on the steps of the derelict hut, his back curled against the door.

A gust of wind cuffed the side of his face. He drew his knees to his chin and braced his arms around his ankles. Another gust blew and he shrivelled against the wind-chill that flayed his skin. He rested until his breathing returned to normal. In the dark his teeth chattered between each misty breath. He unzipped his hooded fleece and took out the blanket that he'd stolen from someone's washing line and draped it over him like a shawl. But his sodden foot was sucking up the cold, freezing the blood in the toes. He stood up, grabbed a stick lying on the grass and used it to lever the door open. It yielded without a fight. Inside, he pawed the dank and dirty floor, caking his nails with crud as he rounded up dry twigs, bits of paper, discarded cartons, empty sacking, anything that came within reach of his blind search. He swept the debris outside and created a small pyre. He struck a match, set light to a scrap of paper and used it as kindling. He stoked the tiny flame and saw it grow.

Paper burned, twigs snapped, and coarse hessian crackled as the fire roared, casting his shadow that shimmied across the grass. He held his palms out over the fire, sat back and splayed his feet, allowing those numb toes to find life again in the proximity of its heat. He flicked his hood back and felt the warmth caress his face. For as long as the fire burned, he sat perfectly still, glaring at the flame and waiting for the chatter in his teeth to wear off.

A part of him knew that, somewhere within, the love for his mother was buried deep in his heart, like treasure, padlocked by fury and, presently, beyond his reach. Even if she were to suddenly appear before him and open her arms like the beautiful wings of an angel, he would not be able to offer that love to her.

The default state

It was Rukhsana who found Amina's body the next morning when she returned to collect her purse, which she had accidentally left behind at the house during last night's embarrassing debacle.

Her polite knocking went unanswered and, even when she rapped harder, no one came to the door. Intuition perhaps, but she found Amina's absence a little strange, particularly on a Sunday; she was quite certain, too, that when she'd passed Shiny Seams en route, its lights were off and there was no member of staff standing behind the counter. All morning she had been feeling guilty. Yesterday's events were still not completely real to her; it was like a scene from a *jatra*, a Bengali burlesque in which stories, initially sound and believable, descend to the ridiculous. But there was nothing funny about last night. As party guests they had behaved obnoxiously, cruelly even, and her conscience demanded that she make an apology. Being new to the country, she was also determined to build healthy ties with the few people she knew. After all, as a new citizen it was vital to be surrounded by as many Bengali friends as possible to stave off those pangs of homesickness. Added to which, she genuinely liked Amina, and wanted to do all she could to express her regret and offer support. She knocked again, but no one came to the door.

As a last ditch effort, she crouched down, pushed the letter flap back and her mouth through the letterbox. She called Amina at the top of her voice:

'Khala-amma.'

Silence.

'It's Rukhsana... are you in?'

Not a breath. Giving up, she set off down the terracotta steps, her heels clacking on the tiles. She passed the front gate before a scratching noise

253

from the side entrance stopped her in her tracks. She turned to see a cat's paw clawing the underside of the gateway. The thin blade of light widened and the rest of the feline's body emerged out of the gap, clutching a bird's speckled egg in its jaws. The black cat brushed past her sari as it bolted to take shelter under a parked car. Rukhsana waited for Amina to come to the gate, but it remained ajar. It was strange that the access was unlocked and no one around. Rukhsana turned back to investigate.

She pushed the gate open and stepped into the garden. Her eyes darted quickly over the unruly lawn, tracing the dozen stepping-stones to the gnarled apple tree outlined against the anaemic English sky. Her gaze eventually worked its way to the vegetable patch where a figure lay slumped in a chair. She blinked and craned her neck, at first refusing to believe what her eyes saw. But there was no denying what the broad daylight had revealed. The crown of Amina's head was wrapped in a shawl. Her white sari achal had fallen off her shoulder and flapped wildly in the wind.

'*Khala-amma,*' she called out, uncertainly.

A burst of wind ruffled the white sari into a rippling frenzy. It made a wave of the lawn and caused the rotary clothesline to swivel in a half-pirouette.

Rukhsana inched forward, confused by the sight, but not suspecting the severity of what she was about to stumble upon. Then, on the ninth step, a terrible suspicion crawled up her skin. And on the next, it sunk its teeth into her flesh. In proximity, she registered Amina's irises lost in the awkward tilt of her head, as if they'd rolled back inside in surrender to death. Her face was an almost grey colour, drained of every corpuscle of blood. The faint circles under her eyes were blue. Amina's sandals were lying on the soil, face down. On the ground a small sparrow pecked at her toe trying to wring out the earthworm wriggling beneath. Death's transformation had something decisive about it.

Rukhsana scampered out of the garden, barging past the gate and sending it crashing against the sidewall. At the front of the house she fumbled through her handbag for her mobile phone. Her gold bangles clinked fiercely as she punched the buttons, now jumping before her eyes. She kept making mistakes and was forced to start again. On hearing Reena's voice she gasped for breath as if she'd emerged from underwater.

'*Chachi, Chachi*, please, please, please, come quickly, *jaldi, jaldi, jaldi…*'

'Is that you Rukhsana?'

'I think she's – she's…'

'What's happened?'

'She's, she's, I think she's – '

'Where are you?'

'*Hai Allah*, I think she's… she's on the chair!'

'What are you talking about?'

'I'm in her garden. In Amina-*Khala*'s garden. I think she's dead.'

'Stay there. We're on our way.'

When Reena arrived with her husband and the two stepped into the garden, they recognised the face of death instantly. They saw the body bracketed against the seat, the neck wilting with all the ungainliness of a marionette left abandoned by its puppeteer. Reena's husband called the police immediately. Reena began circling the lawn, covering her face with both hands, whipping herself into a terrible frenzy.

'How in Allah's name did I land in this terrible mess? *Hai Allah*, how can it be? *Hai Allah* help me please, *hai Allah* have mercy on me…'

It wasn't until her husband intervened by shaking her by the arm that she stopped.

'What will happen now?'

'The police are on their way.'

'How could this have happened?'

'Don't worry about that now.'

Afterwards, they waited silently at the front of the house, perched on the doorstep under the overhang of the porch, huddled like chickens during a monsoon downpour. Time seemed to stretch like elastic. It was as if they were cramped into a lifeboat, trapped in the eerie lull, waiting for the rescue vessel to appear on the horizon. Rukhsana could not rid herself of the image of Amina's dead face. It was worse whenever she closed her eyes. Reena threaded her fragile fingers into her husband's hand and sought comfort in his touch.

Neither women mentioned the previous night, both terrorised by the unspoken fear that details of their bullying behaviour might otherwise spool out and disclose something incriminating. They didn't even make eye contact.

A police vehicle eventually turned into the street and pulled up outside the house. Reena's husband led the two officers through the side gate. The first officer bent over and touched Amina's neck pulse; he slid a finger under her nose. He immediately called the control room demanding medical assistance. Minutes later an ambulance pulled up behind the police car. Two paramedics in green overalls jumped out and trooped in, lugging their green bag bearing a white cross symbol. They fell to work immediately. They checked the pulse. Nothing. They shone a torch in the eyes. No response. They performed CPR. No life. They laid the body out on the grass.

PC Durkin ushered the trio away to the front of the garden. From his black utility belt he drew out his notebook and pen. His voice was official, the words practiced and deliberate.

'May I ask who discovered the lady?'

Two reflex glances pinned the responsibility on Rukhsana. Rukhsana was still visibly shaking. PC Durkin removed his hat. He lowered the volume on his radio. He spoke gently to her, like a concerned father.

'Please tell me your name?'

'*Ami mora faisi!*' Rukhsana spluttered.

The officer raised his palm in a kindly gesture.

'Don't worry, madam,' he said. 'You are in shock. It's perfectly natural.'

At the front of the house, PC Ambrose used his bulky frame to force the door open. He pounded in through the hallway, leaving muddy bootprints on the beige carpet. He opened the door to the lounge to find it in a wrecked state. He reached for his notebook and scribbled down 'aggravated burglary', but after a second look slammed a large question mark beside it. There were no telltale signs of drawers left yawning or contents strewing the floor to suggest larceny of any kind. There was only the mess and, as far as he could tell, it was confined to a single room. He noted down the shattered table turned over on its back, the stalk of a lamp lying in a corner and bits of glass everywhere. He noticed the smashed clock face on the mantelpiece with the hands flinching at a quarter-past-nine. He made a note of the time as well. The faint sound of a trickling tap then drew him to the kitchen.

Outside, Reena saw the ambulance crew slide the corpse into a blue plastic bag and pull the zipper over the face with an unequivocal rip. When they hoisted the bag on to a stretcher and carried it away past her, she fumbled at her neckline for the clutch of *tabeezes* and kissed them fervently, harried by some nameless fear. PC Durkin finished writing up his notes.

'I understand that the two of you were here last night?' he said, scanning back over his notes, trying to make sense of the night's chronology.

Reena's husband played the spokesman. He watched the officer underline something on his pad. Whatever he had said no longer seemed retractable.

'This isn't going to appear in the papers, is it?' he asked, tentatively. 'You see I run a restaurant on the high street and the local people know me. I don't see the point of being involved in all this.'

When PC Ambrose joined his colleague, the officers stepped away from the group and engaged in a brief conversation. They swapped their findings, cross-referenced times, searched for discrepancies. After some preliminary investigation PC Ambrose reported that the woman living next door claimed to have heard a disturbance – some screaming and shouting, and definitely a man's voice, which she assumed was the woman's son, although she was also of the understanding that the son no longer lived with his mother and added how this change of circumstance had left the woman lonely and desperate. The time of the witness' account coincided roughly with the recording he had taken from the broken clock, which officer Durkin surmised would have been about an hour after Reena's party had left.

Once satisfied, the men disbanded. PC Ambrose went to cordon off the room for the forensics team. PC Durkin returned to the group. He cleared his throat and put his notebook away.

'I understand the deceased has a son who may have been present last night. Do you know whether he lives at this address?'

Reena registered the word 'son' and her eyes became alert.

'Mother and son, no good, always arguing, no respect, he's selfish boy,' she said, desperate to cash in the chip of knowledge while she had the chance. She turned to her husband and bombarded him instead:

'The woman's been devastated ever since her son moved away. She was spotted at the doctor's surgery by Mohan Das's mother – you know, the Bengali Hindu woman. The truth is that the boy indirectly killed his mother.'

'Was she ill?' her husband asked, surprised all of a sudden by how much his wife appeared to know about Amina.

'Yes, yes, yes. His *awaragiri* had affected her health a lot. She was begging me to find a bride for him. She was desperate… I had to do something to help. Ask Rukhsana if you don't believe me.'

Reena cast her stare like a floodlight on her niece.

'You were only trying to help,' Rukhsana said in a small voice.

'Where is this son?' Reena's husband asked.

'That good-for-nothing!' Reena hissed. 'Only Allah knows where he is or what he's doing. What I do know for sure is that he's the one to blame for this tragedy.'

'Why?'

'Because he's an *awara,* totally gone off the rails!'

'It's imperative I'm made aware of anything that might be relevant,' the officer reminded the party.

'My wife believes the son may have some part in this,' Reena's husband said.

'In what way?'

'By abandoning her.'

With the help of local knowledge, the officer began to pull all the strands together. He learned about the 'unruly' son and the loneliness the woman had been suffering from – a convoluted story of a failed marriage talk and of compromised honours. Every so often Reena butted in and held the son culpable (although that part he found a little more difficult to digest bearing in mind that they also cited him as absent). What he could deduce from the testimony was that the deceased had been in an extremely vulnerable state of mind. The prescribed pills that officer Ambrose had found strewn across the bathroom floor hinted at the possibility of an overdose. And the tap left running in the kitchen added further to the speculation. Although the post mortem would confirm this, it was imperative he spoke to the son and ascertained his involvement, if any, to test the veracity of the claims made against him.

Much to Rukhsana's annoyance, until fingerprints were taken the officers refused to let anyone into the room so she was unable to recover Auntie Reena's precious purse. She didn't mention anything for the time being.

A quarter of a mile away, the winter sun inched up the sky and its rays fell on the back of Samir's neck as he lit the last of his cigarettes to rid the vile, morning taste from his mouth. His eyes were bloodshot from the night's wanderings. It was unusually bright for a November day. Buildings bore a sharper outline; birdsong serenaded the air; the door knockers of houses gleamed an unnatural bronze colour. Samir squinted each time the sunlight flashed like a blade off the windscreens of the vehicles that drove past.

Samir ambled down a side street and towards the Oasis Café. He stood by its window smoking. Once finished, he flicked the butt and crushed it underneath his toe. He stepped inside and brushed his feet on the threshold with a decency and thoughtfulness that was at odds with his shabby appearance.

The café was virtually empty. A wispy song came out of the tinny speakers stationed in each corner. A man with tousled hair, which fell at the nape in a shy homage to the mullet, occupied the table nearest to the counter. His forearms were hefty and clad in tattoos – the largest of which depicted a rose garlanding the words *'Mi Amore Louisa'*. He regarded Samir with a friendly nod.

The waitress behind the counter was rubbing a stubborn stain on the Formica top with her stubby, work-hardened fingers. The backlit menu behind her kept flickering from a bad bulb or faulty wiring; at first glance it seemed like a deliberate publicity gimmick to draw the eye. The waitress rose from her stoop and greeted Samir with a start of surprise and easy familiarity.

'God, you look like something the cat dragged in.'

Samir didn't speak. He jangled the coins in his pockets.

'You're fine. We don't operate a dress code here,' the woman said.

Samir managed a beleaguered smile, the smell of filter coffee and fresh toast tantalising his cold-pinched nose.

'Did you sleep in a hedge?' she asked, noticing the grassy streaks on his trousers.

His cuffs were mud-stained. His face needed a wash.

'...or just pass out in one!'

The woman chuckled at her own wit, but got carried away and it crumpled into a strangled gasp for breath, her lungs labouring from the ravages of the twenty-a-day habit. She pointed Samir to a table by the window. To his relief she didn't say anything more.

Samir sat down. The back of the plastic chair lurched from his body weight. Furry-tongued and dehydrated, his brain was suffering the hangover of the dexies. Involuntary jolts came in waves and sent spasms through his body. He rubbed the back of his neck for a long while. He watched the old waitress fling open the hatch and waddle out. She was carrying a platter filled with rashers of bacon, fried bread, mushrooms, hash browns, and sausages, with two glistening egg yolks shivering on top. She set it down in front of the tattooed customer. The man was poised with the cutlery, knife and fork upright in his thick hands, arms so fleshy that the elbows were soft curvatures rather than pronounced joints. Samir shut his eyes and buried his face in the crook of his arm. The blackout boomed from ear to ear. The weight of the new day pressed down on the base of his skull. Everything seemed gorged with a dull ache. He wished only to huddle into himself in the manner of a sick bird nestling into the pillow of its own feathers.

'You gonna just sit there and warm the seat?'

Samir lifted his head, using up a couple of seconds to focus on the source of the jovial voice. The waitress looked back at him. Now that she was closer she saw the extent of his self-neglect. He looked pallid. The skin under the stubble was shedding scurf. His eyes bore testimony to a night without sleep.

'How about I fix you a nice English breakfast?' she asked.

Samir bared his side-teeth in a pained grin.

'Just a black coffee please.'

The waitress went and returned with a tray holding a large cup atop a saucer, and a pot of Demerara sugar. The cup rattled precariously as she set it down on the table. She held the glass coffee pot in her other hand which lolled with hot, tarry liquid. She poured and its enticing smell wafted with the twist of steam.

Samir had a flashback to the previous night: Amber, erect as a seahorse (and in complete contrast to this woman virtually bent double), pouring wine into his tumbler with a maitre d' flourish. It never ceased to amaze him how alcohol coupled with weed made intimacy the most natural thing in the world. He remembered them dancing to music. He also remembered the kiss. He fingered his chapped mouth for some sort of validation, as if his fingers would pick up a smidgeon of her lipstick. Memory then recalled the awful taste of the wine and he clenched his tongue in disgust. The cords of his neck stiffened. They felt brittle, like rusted filigree of wires about to snap and send his head rolling across the café floor.

'That'll make you feel better,' the waitress said and smiled, her mouth pinched by age but suddenly appearing wholesome, as sweet as a sultana. She tore the chit from the order book, placed it on the side of the table and dropped the pad back in the pouch of her apron before waddling off. Samir gazed out of the window. The sunlight was no longer slanting in. Clouds had scrolled in from the west in hefty clumps and had turned the sky grimy. The weather looked set to change.

Samir's mind had begun to calm sometime after four in the morning. He managed a couple of hours of fitful sleep by wrapping himself in the stolen blanket. But then, discomfited by its concrete floor, which was maculated in dirt, he left the park's derelict hut and used up the languid, empty hours by criss-crossing the streets, prowling under smelly railway bridges, passing through errant alleyways, taking a u-turn at each dead-end and hiding in the shadows of urban crevices every time a patrolling police car drove past. All the while, he was bitterly aware that although drink and drugs could warp the worst state of mind into an agreeable sensation, there was something he'd always have to return to – reality in the default state of sobriety – and this he had no power to change unless he just remained intoxicated. There was one tiny consolation. He had managed to walk off the pain in his leg.

Until yesterday he had only been a half-boiled orphan but now he had reached hard-boiled status. He was the real deal, de facto. When he recalled the events of the previous night, the needle of his memory kept getting stuck on the flat tone of his mother's voice, the dissonance of her cold-blooded revelation. Even now, he couldn't quite accept the vicious manner in which she had pressed the detonation button on their relationship: *Get out, you dog, you kaffir, go to hell!*

Samir's face turned grave and he put the hot teaspoon to his temple, pressed hard, almost bending the metal handle on the paper-thin skin. The angry thought lifted off with the steam.

Out of sight, an emergency vehicle wailed past. Samir clapped his hands over his ears. When he removed them the sound had receded to a faint whine. A minute later he saw an ambulance scream by. A gust of wind caused the windows to rattle.

'What is it with the emergency services today?' the waitress said. 'Anyone would think a bomb's gone off, Police first and then an ambulance; somebody must be in a right old fix.'

Samir felt a cramp of fear in his belly and stood up. He emptied all the change in his pockets on the table and rushed out of the café, leaving the glass on the door ringing, the Open/Closed sign dancing on its bit of string.

Samir broke into a sprint the instant he turned into the street and saw the strobe of lights on the vehicles parked outside his mother's house. When he got closer the ambulance passed him. Its siren was turned off. It appeared to be in no immediate rush. Samir ran up to the door. It was wide open, the lock kicked in. The mouth of the latch was hanging from a loose screw, which had broken away with a splinter of pale wood belonging to the door frame. Flecks of paint littered the doormat. A muddy boot print had stamped its incursion into the house. He ran inside. In the hallway the two uniformed men stopped him by laying their hands on his shoulders.

'Calm down, son. Who are you?'

'It's my... my mother's house.'

The officers looked at each other.

'Where's my mother?'

The two officers ranged themselves around him. They studied him for what felt like an inordinate length of time, as if trying to gauge something from the rise and fall of his chest. The unslept eyes tinged in red were a cause for suspicion. They sensed the distress. Officer Durkin took off his hat and tucked it under his arm. His hair was combed flat across his head. Officer Ambrose followed the lead.

'I'm afraid, sir, that –'

Samir felt a hand of heavy gold rings on his arm. He turned sharply over his shoulder to see Reena, her face clenched in sorrow.

'What's going on?' he asked.

Reena took his hand. She rubbed it in a soothing gesture. Samir pulled it away.

'What are you doing here?'

'It's your mother,' she began.

'Where is she?'

'The ambulance – '

'What's happened to her?'

Her husband and Rukhsana joined Reena, and the three of them banded together and broke the news like the chorus from a Greek tragedy.

'Your mother is in Allah's house.'

'What?'

'She's passed on.'

Burden to feel

Following the coroner's report, which established the primary cause as 'death by hypothermia' (though subject to revision pending the toxicologist's findings), Amina's body had been transferred to the mortuary. The next morning it was laid out in the viewing suite where it waited for its custodian to arrive.

Samir strode through the hospital, convinced that the blue signposts were sending him on a wild goose chase. His rubber soles squeaked on the clean linoleum floor, which gave off the faint odour of disinfectant. He passed ward after ward, weaving through the corridors – arteries teeming with activity. There were surgeons responding to their slick-black bleepers and holding conferences by the lifts. Nurses were pushing patients who were in paper-white gowns and sitting despondently on foldaway wheelchairs. When a swing door lurched open and a porter came out with a trolley of medicine bottles, Samir almost ran into her. The porter balked and yanked her trolley back. The bottles made a sonorous clink.

'This is a hospital corridor, not a racetrack!' she said.

Samir apologised and asked for directions. She told him that he'd taken the wrong entrance. She regarded him with suspicion when his eyes fell for the second time on the contents of her trolley. His hair was plastered down in a sort of lank Beatles moptop. His face was covered with dark and patchy stubble. She thought the light rain on his face could feasibly be a drug-induced sweat or, conversely, a symptom of cold turkey. All too quickly she read the clues, put two and two together to make five, and concocted a character not only mired in the abyss of some sort of addiction, but who had also wandered into the hospital building to inveigle her strips of methadone.

The rucksack on his shoulder added further to her speculation. She casually stepped in front of her trolley in case he attempted a desperate smash-and-grab.

'I can't imagine how you ended up here. All the departments are clearly signposted on each level,' she said.

'What's clear to me is that the signs are not clear enough,' Samir replied.

'You'll find there's also a map on each level.'

'I haven't seen any.'

'You better go back downstairs,' the porter said, hands on hips, wondering whether to inform a superior. 'This is the haematology department.'

Samir turned back towards the direction he'd come from. He exited the hospital via an overpass. He took the stairs back to the ground level, came outside and walked several hundred yards along a flagstone footpath towards a much smaller building separated by a tall hedgerow. He approached the large, oak door. It was an Edwardian building in a quiet setting, which had about it a regality, with its round arch and mansard roof, and was in complete contrast to the utilitarian rock of the main building. He walked inside and found himself plunged into a solemn silence. The crossing marked the point beyond which the enterprise to save life reached complete cessation. No nurses came here. No bleepers went off. No doctors held conference. No mobile dispensaries did the rounds. There was no smell of disinfectant either. The claret-coloured carpet – itself harking to a spiritual motif – even muted the squeak of his footsteps. Under this roof, silence was heavy and absolute. It was as if every component inside the building was contributing towards giving death its sacred dignity.

The message on the noticeboard in the lobby asked visitors to keep their voices down and show courtesy to the bereaved. The phone numbers of bereavement counsellors were listed on the board, a few written in looping handwriting to appear more personable, more sympathetic. Samir followed signs to reception.

Reception was an anteroom at one end of the freshly painted white lobby. Inside, an elderly man in a tweed jacket was sitting in a worn leather chair, his elbow patches propped on its armrests. He was flicking through a Sunday magazine, with his chin tilted upwards so that specs and eyes were in line with the text. He saw Samir, put the magazine down and eased himself off the seat. Everything about him had an arthritic slowness, a reserve that needled Samir. He leant over the edge of the desk and picked up the pen. It was tied to a string.

'Yes?'

'I've come to see… my mother.'

The man craned his neck to scope the space around Samir. Concern etched his pinstriped brow.

'Have you come alone?'

'Do you see anyone else?' Samir snapped back.

The man smiled tightly at the hostility.

'You are…?'

'Samir.'

'Mr…?'

Samir gave the surname that belonged neither to his mother nor his father.

'Ah yes, we spoke earlier.'

The man adjusted his reading glasses.

'Can you confirm the name of the deceased?'

Samir glared back at the man in defiance as if it was an obscene request.

'It's a strict code of practice,' the man clarified, his voice flattened by the echo of a thousand repetitions. 'Understandably', he said, opening up the appointment book and running his index finger down its spine, 'the last thing anyone wants is any kind of confusion. You know, any misunderstanding on our part. Names and times can get mixed up. It has been known to happen. It can be very unsettling for families to find themselves looking at the body of someone else's relative.'

'What a fuck up that would be,' Samir said, listlessly.

The man acted as if he hadn't heard the comment. He carried on with his duty, unruffled, intent on maintaining the eager-to-please air. He'd seen it umpteen times before. Call it what you will: shock misfiring as anger, the brain lost at sea, perspective swimming out of focus. He knew all about the hurt that throws common civility aside and gives the tongue a profane and despairing edge. After years of standing behind the same desk, he could sense a senseless mind when he saw one. One thing he knew for certain: bereaved and grieving people could be notoriously unpredictable in the way they reacted to loss. Especially in sudden death cases when the deceased happens to pass on well before their time.

Since there was only the single female body among the four corpses currently being held in the morgue, he chose to exercise common sense and overlook protocol. He simply ticked off the slot in the appointment book. He flipped the leather-bound register round and asked for a signature. Samir took the pen tied to the string and scrawled across it with disdain, the final stroke so wild that it encroached on the line below that awaited the signature of a Mr Ezra Marshall's next of kin. The elderly man took the register back and closed it in a dignified manner. He opened the hatch and motioned Samir to follow him.

'It's this way,' he said, grabbing a clipboard for no apparent reason other than to look officious.

Samir shuffled along at the worn heels of the man's slip-on shoes, his eyes glued to the floor. They walked through a corridor and into a vestibule with a single window and a low ceiling that bore down like a lid. There the man stood aside, leaving Samir facing two doors: Viewing Suite 1 and Viewing Suite 2.

'It's room number one. It's a thirty-minute viewing. If you want to leave any time before that, just press the bell by the door and I will come to meet you outside.'

The elderly man nodded a butler's nod and excused himself, delicately closing the door behind him. His movements were measured, imbued with an air of theatre.

Samir stepped into the room. The air inside was cold and a little damp, like dungeon air. The light fittings were styled into ornate candelabrums that jutted from two of the walls. The thick curtains were drawn, incarcerating the artificial light. In the middle a body was lying on a stately bed, tucked under a heavy velvet cover which was trimmed with a gilt edging. Curiously, there was no headboard to complete the hollow resplendence, but instead a steel hatch through which the body had presumably been slipped in, like post through a letterbox. Samir imagined the morgue on the other side. Brightly lit and breath-mist cold, with a battery of metal drawers filled with frozen corpses – each accounted for by the serial number knotted around the ankle or big toe.

He dragged the chair towards the bed, slid the bag off his shoulder. It dropped to the floor. He lowered himself into the chair. He adjusted his body and sat stock still, with a flat expression on his face. He sought an excuse not to look at the body. With none found, he eventually committed himself to the task of viewing.

And there she was. His mother. His aunt. His guardian. Fast asleep. The pouches under her eyes were a delicate purple, like creased satin. The rest of her face gave off a matt sheen as if it had been burnished by a morgue-keeper who took an obvious pride in presentation. Her hair was brushed back, smoothed down with wax. Frost studded the hairline at the nape of the neck. She possessed the most serene expression, such as almost only a lifeless state can evoke. Her face was the most exquisite thing he had ever seen. She looked like a work of art created by a sculptor from an age where a beautiful face was imaginable only in its immobile, captured form. He kept staring at her, his eyes becoming increasingly wide and curious. He was completely still. There wasn't a single crease on his face.

He then reached over and touched her brow. The cold from her skin slid inside him like an electrical charge. It was the shock of touching flesh that felt like porcelain. He rocked back a little. Until then, the emoting part of him hadn't really considered the news of her death as anything more than a temporary state. A death that would resolve itself back to life if he waited long enough.

After providing the detectives with a statement yesterday, he had been driven to the hospital by officer Durkin. Samir had sat in a waiting room, still disconnected from it all. Her death seemed so immeasurably nonsensical that he refused to believe it altogether, and waited for news to the contrary, marking out the long vigil with cups of weak tea and out-of-date confectionary from a vending machine. An underling eventually popped out of an office to inform him that the coroner would not release the body until the following day, so he left and, after a convoluted detour about town, trudged back to his mother's house, almost believing, as he rounded the corner into the street, that he would step into the house and find his mother heating some food in the kitchen or quietly reciting her Qur'an in the living room.

The reality could not have been more different. Stepping through the mess in the living room was like returning to a shipwreck when the sea had calmed and the clouds had cleared only to witness the remnants of the destruction lapping calmly against the shore. For a while he looked around gravely, meditating his own capacity for aggression. Then an overwhelming fatigue took hold of him and he sat down on her rocking chair and fell asleep.

When he woke up it was six the following morning. If it hadn't been for the state of the room he would have assumed that he'd woken up from a particularly vivid nightmare. As it was the mess still surrounded him, lightly smattered by the dust left by the forensics team. But still he didn't truly believe that Amina had died, not even as he journeyed to the mortuary.

But now, in Viewing suite 1, with the cold of her skin knifing through his finger, Samir realised that she had fled the scene for good. Death pronounced itself with a valedictory silence. He left the grip of a grotesque delusion and was forced to glare at this truth. He tried to feel something that would signify that he had entered the phase of mourning. The person dearest to him had departed. *Feel, feel, feel, for fucksakes feel something*, he commanded his being. But this shock was like the zap of a stun-gun, which paralysed his ability to summon up a single tear of sadness.

Samir so desperately wanted to cry, but his heart just rolled through the realisation as impermeable as a stone. As he kept wringing and wringing this pitied heart of his, the only drop of emotion he could draw out was anger – an ugly, gnawing aversion to the woman lying before him.

For logic also told him that in death she hadn't stepped out of his life, but had committed herself to stay put – to force the guilt of his irresponsibility eternally upon him so that no matter where he went his wrongdoing would be there, twisted around his ankle, weighing down his heel like the iron teeth of a beartrap. Her death: what an act of cowardly vengeance it seemed to him.

'Do you think I'm upset? Do you think I honestly give a damn about you or my boozing excuse for a father?' he hissed.

Samir unzipped his bag and took out a book. An old, dog-eared book with a loose cover held together crudely with staples. He held it over her and began tearing the pages out – two, three at a time. Tagore's collection of poems, stories and paintings became a blizzard of paper falling over the stately bed. When he couldn't rip the pages any more, he hurled the stubby remains across the room.

Samir collapsed into the seat. There he sat for a long time. In the darkness, in the horrible quietness, he sensed his tantrum to be too contrived, a little overplayed, kitsch even. Slowly, the lids of his eyes closed. It became a kind of armour, that familiar piquancy of pain performing a necessary shutdown.

Samir gave into the lethargy, which caused him to nod off and seek comfort in the short and wonderfully remote stretch of sleep.

A knock at the door was followed by the intrusion of doorway light. Samir flinched in his seat. He shook his head in bewilderment. He saw the figure at the door pointing at his watch. He must have been asleep for fifteen minutes at least.

'I'm sorry but we have to prepare for another appointment,' the elderly man whispered, trying to ignore all the pages scattered over the bed. He turned and left, closing the door with the same butler's deference as before. After a minute or so, Samir got up. He was incapable of leaning over to kiss his mother on the forehead. He simply picked up his rucksack and walked out of the room. Eyes sore from the tears they had refused to shed. Back outside, he was instructed to go to another office to recover the patient's valuables. He signed a receipt for them. Two gold bangles. Earrings. A gold ring in its box. And a *tabeez* cut from the arm. Samir's hand turned clammy as it gripped the plastic wallet containing the residue of his mother's life.

As he trudged out of the building, stooped and brittle, he really wished his gaze had fallen on someone else's dead relative. The elderly man couldn't have been more wrong. It is much more unsettling to see your own dead relative than someone else's.

Heroic tears

Once the hospital released Amina's body, Samir took advice and appointed the services of a mosque in East London to deal with the funeral arrangements. When the time came to make the dreaded phone call to Bangladesh, he clutched the phone in a strangulating grip. It was Uncle Kamal who answered. Having not heard Samir's voice in the last seventeen years, it took him a moment to make sense of the long-distant hiss and the slightly clunky Bengali accent on the line.

'Samir *beta*, it's you after all these years.'

Samir relayed the news like a bulletin. A series of crackles bridged the silence born of shock. When Uncle Kamal's voice returned, it weakly recited the Arabic phrase: *Innaa Lillaahi Wa Innaa Ilayhi Raaji'oon.* To Allah we belong and to Him is our return. The grave words drew other family members to the phone. Samir could hear their concerned voices tearing at him: *what's happened, what's happened, who is it?* As if to ramp up the difficulty quotient, Samir then heard a woman begin to cry in the background and a chorus of other voices rallying around her. The obvious question followed, and for which he resorted to a mentally rehearsed script. He explained to his uncle that Amina had died suddenly in her sleep and insisted that there was no illness as such, aside from a slight cold, but which had no bearing on her death. He didn't mention their fight on the fated evening, his stormy departure, how death's icy hand came to strangle her in the garden in the middle of the night, or even the elevated levels of diazepam found in her bloodstream (and for which the authorities retained the body for an extra week). In fact, his flat tone betrayed no sign of how guilt-stricken he was, knowing in his heart that her death symbolised his gross failure as a son. He felt like a Sophocles character in a ghastly tale of

271

retribution, ensnared by fate, condemned by the gods to commit a dreadful wrong but far too gutless in its aftermath to poke out his eyes and cast himself out into the wilderness. He was Oedipus-*lite*.

For the *Janazzah* ceremony the mosque's community members had cleansed and wrapped Amina's body in a white *kafan*, bought and blessed from Mecca, before laying it inside the coffin. The coffin was made from teak and finished with a gloss varnish. Under the lights the wood gleamed like honey. The inside was left untreated and gave off a fresh wood smell. Samir paid the organisers with money he found in Amina's dresser drawer. All the money he had left on the table or posted through the door was tied into little bundles.

The mosque's main prayer hall thronged with Friday worshippers. The smell of rosewater, attar and sweaty feet was cloying. The clerics opened the windows a little and the curtains billowed gently, bringing in a welcome batch of fresh air. People used the tessallation pattern of prayer mats on the carpet to stand neatly in file. Genders were divided in separate rooms, brought together in prayer by the *imam*, aided by a sound system that took his mellifluous voice to the women's quarters. Samir was sitting at the front wearing a prayer *topi* that he had borrowed from an elderly mosque official. There wasn't a familiar face in sight.

After the *Janazzah* prayer the assembly disbanded. Samir got up, removed his prayer cap and collected his shoes from the rack stationed at the back of the room. A young man training to become a *hafeez* ushered him into one of the rooms where Amina's coffin waited to be taken to the airport for the burial in Bangladesh. There was another family in the next room also paying final respects to their loved one; as the mosque tended to band together several *Janazzahs* on a Friday to capture a collective spirit of mourning. Samir could hear members of the deceased's family sobbing, while others offered words of comfort.

Samir stood in silence amidst the cloud of incense. His face was as hard as stone, his eyes tracking the dust motes tumbling in the shaft of window light that fell behind the casket and lit up the handles and brass hinges.

He was cold sober. Since the day he returned from the mortuary, he had developed an aversion to alcohol. But that wasn't before he'd taken one final dip into that drunken netherworld in an attempt to wash away the pain. That same night, stuck in an empty house and with no one to tell him otherwise, he had tried to drink himself into an alternative consciousness in a last ditch effort to find a lightless space inside his head to crawl within, like a bug under a stone, but found himself turning a full circle back to sobriety. His mother's death was like a stake driven through his conscience that fixed him to a singular reality: to the truth of how his father had perished. The thought made him unable to put the bottle to his lips. The next day he tried to warp reality with a binge on tranquilisers instead, wrapping his senses in a deafening hum, but some rational part refused to embrace this untruth and he simply felt like a wayfarer lost on another plane of existence, just wasting time before the ground cracked open and he was regurgitated back into the lonesome, cold and horrible world. Then there was the dreaded insomnia that had been haunting him for the past week. All too frequently he had found himself lying in bed, his eyes staring into space during a graveyard hour in the middle of the night, reliving the fight with his mother, wondering what he should have said, and contemplating the things he should have done differently.

The attendant sidled up behind Samir and placed a hand on his shoulder. The man was young, not much older than Samir, lean-faced. He was wearing a goatee beard as well as thin, sickle-shaped sideburns which suggested an allegiance to both fashion and faith.

'Brother, shall I secure the lid?' he asked. 'Or would you like – '

His question was interrupted by a high-pitched cry that came from the next room. It was an unashamed howl, hideously contorted, but in this context it sounded heroic to Samir. The sheer abandon of it was probably the greatest affirmation of a life lived, an eloquent emotional summation of a loved one lost forever, better than a poetic epitaph in a newspaper or a message an *imam* got paid to say.

'Brother, shall I secure the lid or would you like some more time?' the attendant repeated.

Samir felt a slow burning flush of shame for being so miserly with his tears, for not being able to give Amina the emotional send off that she so richly deserved.

'You should pray for your mother's soul on its journey into *Allah's darbar*,' the attendant advised.

'You can put the lid on,' Samir said and walked out.

Outside, the taxi driver who had tried to be friendly when he drove Samir to the mosque earlier was waiting by his car. He watched Samir push through the crowd and up to the car.

'You OK, my friend?'

Samir nodded.

'What happens now?'

'They're going to drive the coffin to the airport and I'll meet them there.'

'That's very good of them.'

'It's included in the price.'

The road was swamped with people streaming out of the gates of the mosque, getting into their cars, starting up their engines, flashing their indicator lights as they struggled to escape the clamorous knot of traffic. A group of Bengali hip-hopsters in their Friday fineries was gathered around a friend's black Golf GTI, wowed by the growl of its 16-valve engine. It was incredibly loud, giving the impression that it had been taken from a small jet plane.

'There will be a lot of traffic,' the taxi driver said. 'We should head off now if we want to miss the rush hour.'

Samir walked round to the passenger side of the car, but just as he was about to climb in, he heard his name being called from the other side of the road. Reena rushed through the melée, trying not to trip up on the white burqua that cloaked her from head to toe. She had come to pay her last respects, but from afar, refusing to enter the back room to view the coffin. After the service she had been standing outside with her husband, insisting she see the boy before he left because *it was the right thing to do.*

'If there's anything you need after you get back please feel free to drop by.'

Samir nodded. What could he possibly want from her?

'How long will you be staying in Bangladesh?' she asked.

'It's an open return ticket.'

'Oh, that's good. It will give you some time to learn about your own country. It's very important. You'll be with your family too.'

Samir still couldn't think of anything to say to the woman.

'If you find the time, be sure to visit our house in Bangladesh. It's in the town centre – a double-storey building. We've even installed an air-conditioner for when we take our children. I'll give you the phone number.'

Samir raised his palm to stop her.

'I'll only lose it.'

The hard tone of his voice was enough to stop Reena rummaging her bag for a pen. Instead, she looked around her.

'No other family here today?' she asked.

'No.'

'No next of kin?'

'No.'

'All in Bangladesh, I suppose.'

'Mostly dead,' Samir replied.

Overhead an aeroplane crossed the sky, obscured by the clouds, leaving a faint, lingering boom. Samir looked up. His mind sang the old rhyme but his lips didn't move.

> *Mr Aeroplane high in the sky*
> *flying to countries far and wide.*
> *Over the green and over the blue.*
> *Mr Aeroplane, I am going with you.*

The taxi driver rolled down the car window and propped his elbow on the glass.

'I really think we should leave now.'

Samir nodded to him and then turned back to Reena whose beady eyes were looking awkwardly out of the letterbox slit in the veil.

'My flight leaves this evening. I have to go.'

Reena placed her palm on Samir's arm.

'If only we'd known what state your mother was in we would have been there to help.'

She tilted her head up to the sky. 'But it is God's will. We can only pray that our sister's soul is granted a place in *Jannaat*.'

'I almost forgot,' Samir interrupted.

He tore his rucksack open. He pulled out Reena's purse and pushed it into her hands.

'What's this?' Reena said, instinctively.

'It's yours.'

She turned the purse over in her hands.

'Oh yes, so it is.'

Samir's eyes shone with intensity, trying to fix Reena with the exact knowledge of her evasions and chicanery. The line of questioning the police had taken was a fair indication of the type of statement she must have made to them.

Sensing this sudden fall from grace, Reena's face turned wan behind the veil. Reflexively she patted her chest, feeling for the shiny new *tabeez* dangling beneath the fleshy folds of her neck.

'*Assalamu-alaikum,*' Samir said.

'*Wailaikum-assalum.* I'll pray for you, *beta.*'

Samir slipped inside the car and slammed the door shut. The tyres rolled and the vehicle edged away from the kerb to join the queue of traffic.

Message from beyond

Samir stepped up to the arrivals terminal at Sylhet Osmani Airport and stared up at its modest control tower and the radar spinning on top, like a toy propeller on a child's baseball cap. The walls of the building were weather-stained, a section of which was being rendered by a band of labourers who were up on bamboo scaffolding – men *free-styling*, wearing neither a harness nor helmet. A crowd standing on the peak of a hill were shielding their eyes from the mid-morning sun, watching the planes take off and land. It was a popular pastime amongst the locals.

Inside the building, a bright yellow placard said 'Welcome' in both English and Bengali. The official in the booth at passport control didn't appear to extend the same courtesy. Stern-eyed, his attention flicked from face to photo as he rubber-stamped each passport page with all the authority of a judge with a gavel. Samir followed the queue of mostly returning migrants, tightly clasping his rucksack. He was a tense creature camouflaged amongst the throng of sunny faces, many of whom were inhaling the fecund *deshi* air and feeling its tight claim on their hearts.

He stood with a trolley at the carousel poised to pick up his luggage. For what reason he wasn't sure, since the mouth of the carousel wasn't designed for the cargo the mosque officials had checked in on his behalf. The luggage soon arrived and people began plucking away, piling up their trolleys before making their way towards the exit door. Samir waited, twiddling the green button of his shirt, unsure of what to do or where else to go. The crowd soon thinned. A lonely suitcase began its tenth lap with no claimant in sight. Nothing else emerged from the black aperture of its mouth and the hatch closed. The carousel stopped turning altogether. Samir was forced to stop a passing official.

'Excuse me.'

'*Ki saar?*'

'I was on the flight that has just landed. I'm waiting for my mother's…' Samir stopped and scratched his forehead trying to think of the word.

'*Coffin?*' he said in English.

The official narrowed his eyes.

'*Ji?*'

Samir handed him a special check-in note. The official cast his eyes over it and turned the scrap of paper over in his hands.

'Oh, *acha*,' he mouthed, sympathetically. 'No, no. It won't arrive through this channel. Such things never arrive in this manner. No, no, no, no, never.'

It was stupid for Samir to think otherwise. He suffered an adolescent twinge of embarrassment. Urns were much more suitable for travel, he thought. Why couldn't he have been born into a religion that had a more practical means of dealing with its dead, or at least offered a dispensation when it involved a five thousand mile transit?

'Where do I have to go?' he asked the man.

'*One mint, saar.*'

The official looked this way and that, impatient, hands on hips. He eventually spotted an idle airport hand and beckoned him over with a shout and an authoritative flick of the finger.

'*Ey, Lal Babu, ey dike aai!*'

A small man with yellow eyes scurried over, genuflected, eager-to-please, stinking of stale beedi smoke and the sweat of hard labour.

'*Ji saar?*'

'Take this to the cargo bay and give it to the baggage handler,' he said, foisting the note into the man's hand. 'Tell him to get one of the boys to bring it to the front, *jaldi!*'

The man scurried off armed with the scrap of paper. The official called the man back.

'*Shuno!*'

'*Ji Saar?*'

'What are you doing, have you nothing between the ears? Take a trolley!'

'*Ji Saar,*' the hand replied again, as if those were the only words he was permitted to use. The official turned back to Samir.

'Please go ahead and wait in the arrivals lounge. Someone will bring it to you. I'll meet you there in a *mint.*'

Samir went through the glass doors. On the other side, discrete reunions were taking place all around him. Passengers were carting their trolleys towards the exit doors purposefully. A few drivers were holding up signs with names written on them. One man was holding a sign as well as a bouquet of flowers as though he was playing the driver as well as the lover. Samir searched for his pick-up, Uncle Kamal. It was then that the obvious dawned on him: other than a hazy childhood memory to draw upon, he had no way of recognising Uncle Kamal. And how was Uncle Kamal to recognise him after nearly two decades, in which time he had shed the boy fat and turned into a gangly pothead? Any suggestions offered during their phone conversation would have sounded silly: *I'll be the one with the coffin. There can't be many.* Even if he'd suggested something so crude, for the time being he was *sans* coffin.

Samir shuffled his weight from foot to foot waiting to be noticed, the ruck-sack pressing down on his shirt and the shirt clinging to his sweat-drenched back. He was desperate for a cigarette to busy his hands and deflect attention from his sense of isolation in a country foreign to him.

But he needn't have worried. For a trio whose eyes were clumped into a single organ took no more than a few seconds to recognise their kin once he had stepped into their view. It was *Nannijee* who spotted Samir first, recognising his face because he looked so much like her eldest daughter. Her eyes lit up and the skin around them folded into a hundred relieved wrinkles. She prodded the young man who was standing beside her:

'That's him! Go and help him with his bags.'

The young man sprang into action at his elder's request. He exchanged a few words with the gatekeeper and slipped some *tea money* into his palm. With permission purchased for a small fee, he leapt over the barrier and cantered up to Samir gazelle-like. He instantly made a grab for Samir's papery hand and pumped it with a bumptious handshake.

'How do you do?' he asked, in English. 'I'm Rashid, do you remember me?'

Rashid wrested the bag from his cousin's hand and laid a hand on his shoulder. 'Come this way, *Bhai.*'

Samir allowed his cousin to lead the way and sloped towards the small party, using Rashid's back to shield the family's eyes, which he imagined were fixed on him like crosshairs. As they neared the group, Rashid stepped aside. His movement was so unexpected that it left Samir exposed to the full glare of the family's combined gaze as though it were the brutal beam of a searchlight. Samir put his hand to his cheek in a vain attempt to shield his face.

'*Kita re nati?*' *Nannijee* asked, quietly. Samir's head lifted in surprise. There was an echo of Amina in her voice.

'*Assalumu alaikum,*' he said.

'*Walaikum-assalam.*'

'I've been waiting to see you since you last visited us,' she said.

'How are you?' Uncle Kamal asked, his smile frail and almond eyes shining in the wake of recent grief.

'I'm fine,' Samir replied. He looked back over his shoulder. 'Someone should be wheeling it over here shortly.'

He stood back from the party. It was *Nannijee* who drew nearer to him. He felt her touch his arm, the pressure of her tender fingers hinting at affection. She slipped her hand into his and laid her head gently on his chest. Samir sensed his grandmother's frailty and wrapped his fingers around the warmth, unable to freeze his heart enough to deny her. For the time being it was the only concession he was prepared to make. In this manner and without exchanging another word they engaged in the horrible wait, staring in the same direction in empty anticipation.

The wheels of a cart with the casket upon it rolled through the arrivals door, carving a parting through the crowd. People played down their happiness and deferred to the tragic sight. Behind it, a coolie boy in a frayed shirt pushed from the balls of his bare feet. He was all bone and sinew. Behind him the official barked the orders; he was a round and lardy figure, his belly softened by his status.

'*Darrao!*'

The coolie boy set the trolley down. Sweat beads broke down his temples and he wiped them with the back of his hand. The official overseeing the delivery marched to the front to take over proceedings. He doffed his cap.

'Here you go, sir,' he politely said to Samir.

'Thank you.'

Thank you was not nearly enough. He stared at Samir.

'For the boy's troubles?' the man hinted, kneading his cap.

Samir reached for his wallet, but Rashid quickly stepped in and pressed some money into the man's open palm.

'Now get out of here!'

The man reluctantly accepted the gratuity and trudged off muttering his dissatisfaction. The coolie boy tagged along still trying to catch his breath, his blistered hands a truer testament to the harsh treatment suffered by the poor.

It was *Nannijee* who removed the velour cloth attached to the window of the casket. And then her eyes fell on the corpse. Seeing her daughter's bloodless face behind the glass sent something seismic through her heart. Amina's death brought back the memory of Saufina's death. Her mouth instantly tightened into a mesh of hurt and her buttery eyes filled up with tears, agonised by the awful realisation that she had outlived both her daughters. Uncle Kamal and Rashid were quick to wrap their arms around her, using their hands to wipe away her tears.

'Please don't cry, *Nannijee*.'

'You have to be strong, *Ammu*.'

Samir stood on the edge of this display while the men cosseted *Nannijee*. The trio remained like this for what seemed an eternity, bound in an impregnable bubble of affection, giving Samir a crash course in how familial love worked. Eventually Rashid broke away and came to him, his head lowered in sadness.

'*Bhai*, I have a minibus waiting outside to take the *shobadar* to the burial ground. Fareed is with the driver. We'll carry it into the minibus. You can travel with *Nannijee* and the others,' he said and wrested the responsibility off Samir.

'Why are we burying her on a hilltop?' Samir asked Uncle Kamal, tugging at his arm like a child. The peak, though small, was large enough to accommodate the hole they had dug, but the descent was steep on all sides. Samir pushed his heels into the earth, worried about losing his footing and ending up sliding down the scree slope. No one else had any qualms about standing on the edge. Even *Nannijee* managed without a problem. Uncle Kamal didn't answer but raised a brow, making Samir feel stupid for asking what was obviously a silly question.

The soil was soft and Samir's heels were beginning to sink a little. He couldn't actually lean forward to view the casket being lowered into the grave. Rashid put his arms around Uncle Kamal and *Nannijee*, and the three of them stepped closer to the grave, leaving Samir on his own. The party closed into a huddle. The distance between them seemed to stretch telescopically, like a camera pulling out. Their backs were turned to Samir. He could hear their sobs as they watched the coffin being lowered further and further into the grave. He realised that he was the black sheep, reviled and rejected for abandoning Amina in the first place. His presence was merely tolerated on the fringes.

Samir was desperate to be part of the huddle because otherwise he would fail to fulfil a son's final rites. He attempted to step forward, but the weight on his feet was getting heavier. The soil turned into clods of mud, then into thick, sucking clay. He pulled his feet so hard that they came out of his shoes. He lost his balance and began to roll down the slope. He stopped halfway down and began clambering back up, digging his nails into the damp earth. Hot nettles scratched his soles; they got caught between his toes and tore his skin. In the distance he heard the imam recite a final prayer before Rashid began shovelling soil over the casket. The imam's voice was deep and sonorous, the same imam who had led the janazzah in London. Listening, Samir seemed to hear within each sentence the summation of his own history, the hatred lodged in his heart, his weaknesses and sins. The people from which he sprang and among whom he was now sentenced to live would decide what punishment to levy upon him. A book appeared in Samir's left hand. It was Tagore's collection of stories and art, the pages crudely patched back together with staples and Sellotape. Therein he would find the answer. Everything was about to be reversed with the utterance of a beautiful line, or the power of resolution drawn from the message in a picture. After the madness and the cruelty of fate, all the wickedness would vanish in a puff of smoke. The spell would be lifted. The darkness would dissipate. A new day would dawn. He no longer felt the urge to reach the site of the grave. Instead, he looked up at the sky. It was blue and peaceful at first, but then a huge Boeing flew low overhead and turned it a steely grey colour. The noise spun inside his ears and he suffered a dreadful sense of vertigo. He fell over backwards, and rolled back down the hill. He sprang awake with a jerk. Samir hated such overt dreams.

The rooster outside shrieked the dawn call. Moments later it delivered another robust crow. Samir looked out through bleary eyes, but strained to see anything of the room because the window shutters had sealed off the first light of dawn. It took him a moment to make sense of his whereabouts, for his mind to recall yesterday's events: the flight into Sylhet's airport, the burial, the journey back to the village, the awkward conversations, the twinge of anger he felt when he overheard the family apportion his physical form to a gene pool that excluded Amina altogether.

He sat up on the bed, reached out and glided his fingertips along the silky lace of the mosquito net. He pulled the material up and reached for a window shutter. He gave it a gentle push. It whined open and the light spilled in and washed the room in a clean, sleep-cleansing white. It was accompanied by the lambent, dawn air.

How odd it seemed to be back in the annex; the room that for years had been the setting of his childhood nightmares with its inescapable walls and floor-tilting delirium, the feel of muscular hands and the harsh stubble pressing down on his soft neck. All the signature props were there too. The old books with their creased spines lining the shelves, the table on which he used to set his Qur'an – now shunted to the corner to accommodate the bed. The black and white picture of his parents hanging on the wall, a little faded and which he had scanned yesterday for a long while, searching for clues that would reveal something about his lineage.

He rubbed his eyes and refocused. Surely, fewer things should be as piercingly evocative as returning to inhabit the room in which one's childhood was murdered? But the evocation never came. Not with any degree of force. Because it was also the place where he had learned to forget. There was only the irritating knowledge that this was the dreaded room where it had happened. All of it now seemed so passive, so prosaic, and so ordinary. So fucking ordinary.

Samir got out of bed. He slipped on his trousers and pulled a loose t-shirt over his head. He stretched his limbs, scratched his arms, driving his fingernails along the underside pitted with scars where it tended to itch the most. He unzipped his travel bag and dug out his hooded fleece. He covered himself up. He stepped outside in a pair of sandals which belonged to Rashid. They were a little too narrow for his feet and chafed at the sides.

The predawn mist was thick, the air dewy, the ground a little slippery. The sun was yet to break through and the sky looked as white as a new page. The main house stood regally still against the sky, surrounded by the verdant bamboo culms, the tall date palms and the squat banana plants, seemingly ensconced in nature's greenest fabric. The main door was closed, its inhabitants, he presumed, were still sleeping.

Samir wedged a cigarette between his lips. He walked round the back of the main house, passing the door of the scullery. He looked back at the building and glanced at the flat roof where he used to sit as a child. He let his gaze stride across paddyfields and the corrugated roofs of the houses dotted all the way to the gorgeous hills of the tea gardens. He remembered the 'bad' word he had once etched on the wall – the child's panicked plea which had been washed away by the passing monsoon seasons. He headed towards the pond, following the stone steps that led to the *ghat*. He sat down on the steps and watched the water gently lapping the banks.

In the silence he was receptive to every earthly sound, the slightest breath of wind, the smallest rustle in the undergrowth, the tweet of the morning birds. When he tilted his eyes skywards he saw a kingfisher perched on the branch of the neem tree playing the early bird, waiting for breakfast to rise to the water's surface. Meanwhile, a bug with splayed legs walked on the water, assiduously searching for bugs smaller than itself to feed on. Watching, Samir understood the deep nostalgia that must have afflicted his mother during all those bleak, lugubrious and lonely English winters.

He fished in his pockets for matches and felt a hard edge pressing against the inside pouch. He pulled out the offending envelope. It was the last thing he had picked up from the flat after cleaning out his room and telling his landlord to keep the deposit as a settlement for the damage he had caused his car. At the time, faced with everything else, he hadn't paid the envelope much attention and had left it in his pocket.

Samir tore it open. Inside, there was a postcard from Amber gracing a picture of the Sagrada Família church. Her phone number was written on the other side, followed by a solitary kiss. Samir blinked at the memory of that night, and the gift of friendship it promised. He put the card away. Deep in thought, he tore strips off the envelope, rolled them into small pellets and flicked them into the water, one after another.

'What are you doing here?'

Samir glanced over his shoulder to see Rashid standing at the top of the steps. He acknowledged his cousin with a slight nod of the head. Rashid was draped in a *chador* with his arms folded over his chest.

'*Bhai*, aren't you cold?' he asked.

'No.'

'I suppose it's a lot colder where you're from.'

'Do you have a match?'

Rashid shook his head.

'Didn't you sleep well?' Rashid asked.

Samir shrugged.

'You're up so early. Was it the bed?'

Samir turned his attention back to the water. The odd fish was beginning to peck. Rashid came down a few steps. He studied the back of Samir's head, waiting for an answer.

'How are you feeling?' Rashid asked.

'What?'

'Are you OK?'

Samir remained silent, certain only of one thing: he could not communicate the incommunicable. He thought about it. He wasn't sure whether the appropriate word existed. He could list a few adjectives. Dreadful? Tired? Relieved? Confused? His silence pretty much summed it up.

'How long will you stay for?' Rashid asked.

Samir watched a caterpillar slide off the leaf of the tree and fall into the pond, which set off a whole chain of events. A minnow instantly popped up to the surface and swallowed the bug. The kingfisher took the ripple as its cue, swooped down and flew back up again with breakfast flapping a silver tail in its beak. It tilted its neck and the minnow disappeared down its gullet, after which it sat fatly on the branch. Samir looked at Rashid.

'I don't know,'

Rashid wasn't sure what to say.

'I can go to the shop and get you some matches if you want,' he offered.

'Is it nearby?'

'There's a little store on the main road just outside the village boundary. It will only take me five minutes.'

'It's fine,' Samir said, 'I'll go later.' He slipped the cigarette behind his ear.

Rashid came down to the *ghat* and perched on the step next to him. He looked sidelong at Samir and his eyes flicked a little critically over the gaunt profile he saw.

'I expected you to look healthier.'

Samir bit his lip.

'When Karim *cha-cha's* son visited, he looked wonderful, like a movie star. He was handsome and was always so fashionably dressed. He had a body like Sanjay Dutt. For the three months he stayed here all the aunts were parading their made-up daughters, hoping he would choose to marry one of them.'

The anecdote evoked a stiff silence.

'I hope to go to London one day to earn lots of money for the family,' Rashid said. 'This taxi business just isn't earning me enough. Majid's in Bahrain, working in a hotel, but the low income doesn't allow him to send money home regularly. England's different, though. Even *Fufu-amma* used to send us money from time to time,' he added, referring to Amina.

'Where is *Nannijee*?' Samir asked.

'She's praying,' Rashid replied. '*Amma* sent me to ask you what you'd like for breakfast.'

'Whatever's easy to make,' Samir said.

'Tea and *roti* is good,' Rashid said. 'Mum makes great rotis. She bakes them over the old *chulah*. It's never the same over the gas stove.'

'Yes, that sounds great.' Samir said.

Rashid got up and turned to leave. He'd taken a few paces when Samir called him back.

'Yes?'

The two young men looked searchingly at each other, re-living between them in that split second the horrors of their childhood experience.

'What?' Rashid asked.

Samir broke eye contact.

'Thanks for lending me your *chappals*,' he said.

There was a pause.

'If you need anything at all, just give me a shout.'

Samir smiled, nodded and watched his cousin walk off. He turned back to stare at the ripples in the pond water. He continued to manufacture more paper pellets and flick them into the pond, watching the minnows surface and peck at them, and then disappear with a disappointed flick of the tail. A waterlily caught his attention. It was bound like a secret waiting to bloom in the heat of the rising sun. The tip was wonderfully white, as if it were a clot of cloud that had fallen from the sky. Samir had a sudden urge to capture the image by drawing it, but realised that his sketchbook was back in London. He hadn't felt this desire to draw in a while, but the fact that it had sprung up inside him so urgently made him realise that, for all the failings he might have inherited from his father, the man had also bequeathed him an artist's sensibility, the same sensibility with which the man had collected and read all those books in the study, the spines of which Samir had studied intently after returning from yesterday's burial. Drawing had always been the one thing that brought Samir joy and succour – the eye in which he could seek sanctuary while the storms raged on around his life. What's more, Amber thought his drawings were good. Try as he might, he couldn't deny how much the core of his being had lit up when she had complimented his artwork a few days ago.

Now, as he looked around him, he found his eyes feeding on the weaves of light glistening on the water, the flowers surrounding the pond, pulsating with colour, while his ears were attuned to the verdant habitat teeming with the orchestral score of fauna. It was all serenading his senses. He suddenly felt inspired and wanted to draw all of it and, in doing so, get closer to the land of his birth and embrace it. Forgetting about the need for matches to serve his nicotine need, he wondered instead whether the shop sold pencils and a pad.

Samir heard his name being called from indoors. It was Rashid asking him to come inside for breakfast. He didn't respond, but sat in silence, meditating on the energy that had shot through him, the epiphany that there existed something in his life that brought him fulfilment, and it was wholly up to him to nurture it. He heard his name being called again. Again he remained rooted to the *ghat* and as the seconds passed he became more and more averse to the idea of heading back indoors where any interaction was bound to be stilted, with everyone couching their dialogue in diplomacy, all desperate to know the details surrounding Amina's death. The speculation from Uncle Kamal's family had begun after yesterday's burial and echoed through the night. His aunt played the sceptic: a *woman, barely fifty, dead! How could this be?* The rest added fuel to the conjecture with their pointed silences. Samir felt he would tear off his ears if he had to endure another round of questions pitched as platitudes because this time it wasn't a pair of arbitrary officers he had to satisfy but his grandmother – a woman heartbroken at having lost both her daughters. Every time he looked at his *Nannijee*'s face, the guilt pressed against his conscience like a jagged cut of glass. Regardless of the circumstances, he couldn't say that he hadn't played a part in both deaths.

Samir picked himself up and decided to find the shops. He wanted to avoid going past the house so skirted around the pond, threading his body through the banana palms and sliding down a grassy verge spangled with hovering dragonflies.

He strolled through the village, watching its people limber up to a new day. Small houses had shot up everywhere in the village. The paddyfields that he used to stare at from the roof of the house were now real estate, the huddle of huts reflecting the high premium placed on space by such a densely populated country. The bamboo fences that drew up the boundaries between the homes were draped by a patchwork of sacking and made the village appear horribly sequestered. In the frontyard of a house he passed, ducks released from their coop were gabbing wildly as they waddled to their feed. A woman was sweeping the front verandah, bandaging her mouth against the rearing dust with the loose strip of sari. She stopped and looked up.

'*Baba*, where are you going?' she asked.

'For a walk,' Samir replied, and continued walking.

Samir came onto the main road. Traffic was still sparse. A produce seller was heading to the morning bazaar carrying two baskets stacked with ripe tomatoes on either end of a bamboo stick which was balanced on his shoulders like giant measuring scales. A SUV Pajero reared up behind the man, wove impatiently and overtook him with such a reckless swerve that the wing of the vehicle knocked one of the baskets, sending a dozen tomatoes crashing over the bonnet. The driver sounded his horn – not an apologetic toot but a furious honk. Unsatisfied, he slammed on the brakes, pulled up, stormed out of the vehicle and gave the poor produce seller a clip around the ear for taking up too much of the road. Samir rushed to the scene.

'Oi, why did you hit him?'

The man sneered at Samir. He was short and stocky with his hair slicked back. He clenched his hands into little fists but kept them by his side. Samir responded with a quiet stare, self-assured, without anger or malice.

'You should be ashamed of yourself.'

The man could tell by Samir's accent that he was a foreigner.

'Who are you?' he asked, suddenly finding his bullying power drained.

'My family lives in this village. This is my village. If I call loud enough I can gather a crowd who'll beat you black and blue for your thuggish behaviour.'

The man moistened his lips with a flick of his tongue and muttered a few words under his breath, but then relented. He got back into the vehicle and sped off. The produce seller thanked Samir. A film of sweat had gathered on the coarse hairs on his top lip. Samir helped him pick up the fruits and place them back in the basket. He watched the man trundle off with the twin baskets. The man looked back twice to wave at Samir and Samir waved back each time. Samir crossed the road and walked along the edge of the tarmac trying to work out which of the stores on the strip looked most likely to sell drawing materials.

'*Arre beta,*' a voice called out to him. The man stuck his head out from the small shop. The awning above it bore a green cross symbol.

'Where are you going, *beta?*' he asked. 'Come here.' Samir couldn't find a reason to say no. 'Where are you off to so early in the morning?'

'Nowhere,' Samir replied.

The man studied him briefly. Behind him, a 1999 calendar was still pinned to the wall, picturing a Bollywood starlet in a Kathakali dance pose.

'You don't remember me, do you?'

Samir shook his head.

'I was at your mother's burial yesterday,' the man said. 'I'm an uncle of yours too.

I'm your aunt's brother,' the man clarified. 'Your Uncle Kamal is my *Dula Bhai.*'

The mobile phone in his *kurta* pocket began to ring. He raised his index finger to excuse himself and took the call. The conversation was swift and businesslike. He hung up without saying goodbye and then slipped the handset back into the pocket of his *kurta*. It stuck out in a bulge.

'It's a tragedy!' the man said fixing his attention squarely back on Samir. His bottom teeth were large, like tombstones held in a clenched square jaw, giving him a severe underbite. 'It was Allah's will. We must remember everything is Allah's will.' The man then leant forward to add: 'Though it is very unfortunate, so young, so very young to die.' He shook his head exaggeratedly from side to side. 'How about some tea?'

'No,' Samir said.

'The tea stall is only on the other side.'

'It's OK.'

'How about a glass of tamarind juice then?'

'No, thanks.'

There was a pause.

'Do you know where I can buy a pencil and a sketchpad?' Samir asked.

The man narrowed his eyes in thought.

'You'd have to walk to the school. There's a shop outside it. It's about two miles from here.'

'In which direction?'

The man looked at Samir, a little bemused that the young man was willing to walk such a distance for what were inessential items. He then opened the drawer by his feet, fished around for a while and took out a couple of pencils and an old A4 notepad, coverless, with the top sheet scribbled with doodles and stained in tea rings.

'Here you go, *beta*.'

'How much do I owe you?'

The man laughed, belching like a bullfrog. He shook his head and waved both hands as if he'd heard a particularly funny joke. Once he calmed down, he sat back and twiddled his eyebrows in ruminant fashion.

'So, *beta*, the doctor's didn't tell you anything?'

The man looked stealthy, tight-lipped, perhaps a little annoyed by Samir's reticence to spill the inside story in exchange for the freebie items.

'Cause of your mother's death?' he suddenly asked in English and a manner that made him sound like a prosecuting lawyer. He could no longer contain his curiosity.

'It's not clear yet,' Samir lied. He put the pencils in his pocket and rolled up the pad and slipped it into the inside pocket of his hooded top.

'They don't know,' Samir reiterated, his voice solemn, dispirited. 'It just happened.'

'*Chi, chi, chi*,' the man said and tutted in dismay. 'In a medically advanced country like England, it's very disappointing!'

Samir wanted to change the conversation. He looked around him. A few hundred yards away the minaret of the mosque stood tall and imposing.

'Does that *Maulana* still teach in the village?'

'Which one?'

Samir uttered the name. The man thought about it for a moment. He then jutted his bottom lip out. He didn't have a clue.

'I think he's probably in his fifties now,' Samir added, deliberately sounding vague.

'Why do you want to know?' the man asked.

The sound of shuffling feet saved Samir from having to give an answer. A customer was dragging herself towards the counter. She was so old and bony that her walking stick seemed like an extension of her limb.

'*Chachi, assalumu-alaikum.* How are you?' the pharmacist asked.

The woman's voice was thin and reedy, barely rising above a whisper.

'What can I say... *batija*? The pain is getting worse in my stomach. The doctor has given me this.'

The woman inched forwards, barely lifting her feet off the ground, and placed the prescription on the counter. Samir caught a glimpse of the scrawny hand, the skin looking like a dried tobacco leaf, and the web of bones almost visible underneath. Her fingers trembled severely.

'Let me see,' the pharmacist said, picking up the chit and adjusting his glasses to read the doctor's scrawl.

'*Chachi*?' the pharmacist asked. 'This is Kamal Bhai's nephew. He's from London. He wants to know about a *Maulana* who used to teach in the village. If anyone knows then that person would be you.'

The woman peered at Samir, turning her neck with a turtle's slowness. She studied Samir's face for a while.

'You're Kamal's nephew?'

Samir nodded.

'Saufina's son. I knew your mother. She used to come to see me to have her palm read. You were in her belly at the time.'

His biological mother had played no part in his life and he saw no point in dragging her into the conversation. He ignored the woman's oblique offer of a story.

'But do you know the *Maulana*?' he asked.

'The *Maulana*?'

Samir repeated the name. The woman took her time to sift through the dusty library of her years. She had seen so many Islamic teachers come and go in her time.

'He died two years ago,' she finally said.

There was a pause.

'How do you know him?'

'It doesn't matter,' Samir replied.

Samir returned from his walk and sat down on the steps of the verandah, his head humming like a hive. He felt stifled by his hooded fleece and wanted to tear it off him. He pulled at the garment so hard that the stitching split. He yanked it off his back and left it by his side. He lifted his head and watched the leaves on the bamboo culms rustle and felt the breeze blowing on his face. There was a cavernous feeling inside him and right at the bottom sat a hard lump of pain. It had been sitting there ever since the night of the argument, growing heavier and more difficult to ignore. The galvanising inner voice instructed him to pick up the pencils and pad, but he continued to sit still. Eventually he closed his eyes and covered his face with his hands. The weight of the pain had left him completely drained.

Nannijee was indoors reading her Qur'an after the *Fajr* prayers. He listened to the recitation – her voice swelling in song and sounding so familiar, like a message from beyond. As a young boy when he lay in bed at night unable to fall asleep, he didn't count sheep but preferred to hear Amina's voice reciting *suras* in the next room. It was a comforting sound that would often lull him to sleep. And now, hearing the same intonation, Samir remembered the light of faith in his mother's eyes and felt that weight begin to lift from inside him. A ripple of emotion stirred and grew into a swell, rising higher and higher, and suddenly it overwhelmed him. It was as if something locked out for years had finally found the strength to burst and flood through all the bitterness, washing it away. He clenched his fist and held his jaw tight against this attack of emotion. He tried to blink back the tears shining in his eyes. He fought for his only possession: the wall of hatred fencing off his heart from the love it felt for the woman who had raised him, as if it might be something worth fighting to keep. But it crumbled against the realisation that the painful tenderness he felt was carved from loss – the loss of his mother. Yes, she was his mother. The loss of her was as palpable as the sunlight on his skin. His entire body shook as he let out an unashamed howl. His eyes filled with tears. Then he began to cry, whimpering childlike, each sharp draw of breath making a jagged noise that travelled through the filigree grille of the open window and into the very corners of the house. At last those tears rolled down his face.

Nannijee finished the passage and closed the book. Then she rushed out, her bare feet slapping worriedly against the verandah floor. She gathered her grandson into her arms. Her hand, with its age spots and knotted veins, rubbed the back of his neck and patted him gently. She didn't ask any questions but held him tightly to her chest. And whatever the rest of the world cared to think, deep down she knew that her grandson's heart was bleeding for a simple reason. Like any child he loved his mother dearly and mourned her loss with the whole of his being.

Acknowledgements

Thanks to: Dimitris Kioussis for his comments on the early drafts when I was still finding my feet as a novelist; Charles Beckett at the ACE for helping me secure a grant to complete the novel; Aamer Hussein, Jacob Ross and Robin Yassin-Kassab for all their wisdom and kind words of support; everyone at the Muslim Writers Awards; Saskia Janssen for her brilliant and creative contribution to the cover design; Adam Williams for keeping me sane by dragging me to the gym during the five years it took to write the book; Rob Walker and Matthew Barger for their unerring support when times were tough and the writing energy seemed spent; my mother and father, and my siblings Rezaul, Parvez, Shuaib and Shireena for putting up with the bad moods, especially Shireena for being the first to offer to read a complete draft; Ryan Raymond for understanding the frustrations of the creative process; Peggy Vance for trying her damnedest to open doors for me; Emma Maule for believing in my work and frequently telling me so; and, finally, all those writers who have inspired me and who continue to do so, forever convincing me that it's worth it in the end.

About the author

Suhel Ahmed spent many of his childhood years growing up in the verdant countryside of Bangladesh. *Broken Paths* is his first novel; it won the best unpublished novel award at Muslim Writers Awards in 2009. The novel was also awarded a grant from the Arts Council England. Suhel has written several short stories. *Faith in Love* was published by Hurst in its journal "The Critical Muslim" in 2012.

Suhel is currently working on his second novel, *Disinherited*, a dark tale about twin sisters living in an unnamed Bangladeshi village, whose lives are torn apart when one falls victim to an acid attack.

More about Suhel Ahmed on www.suhelahmed.com